The gateway to modern art is impressionism, that late phase of realism that sought, during the closing decades of the nineteenth century, to represent with increasing refinement the more elusive aspects of light, mood, atmosphere, and character. As a result of this more refined analysis of reality, the established forms in painting, music, and literature all broke down, and art became peculiarly formless. It was this vacuum of form created by impressionism that prepared the way for the magnificently inventive free forms of modern art.

All in all, the stories in this collection are of an astonishing variety and range. But this is only to be expected since they cover a unique phase of cultural evolution in which Europe passes through not one but two devastating modern technological wars, as well as the emancipation of the laboring classes and of women, the violent reversion to barbarism of fascism, and an unprecedented revolution in social manners, scientific knowledge, and peacetime technology.

SYLVIA ANGUS and DOUGLAS ANGUS
From the *Introduction*

Other Fawcett Premier Short Story Anthologies:

**THE BEST SHORT STORIES OF
  THE MODERN AGE**
  selected by Douglas Angus
CONTEMPORARY AMERICAN SHORT STORIES
  selected by Douglas and Sylvia Angus
**CONTEMPORARY LATIN AMERICAN
  SHORT STORIES**
  edited by Pat McNees Mancin

GREAT MODERN EUROPEAN SHORT STORIES

Selected and Introduced by
Douglas and Sylvia Angus

FAWCETT PREMIER • NEW YORK

A Fawcett Premier Book
Published by Ballantine Books.

ISBN 0-449-30052-8

The editors and publishers wish to thank all those who have contributed to this volume. Acknowledgments for individual short stories will be found on the first page of each selection.

Printed in Canada

First Fawcett Premier Edition: August 1967
First Ballantine Books Edition: December 1983
Twentieth Printing: December 1992

Contents

Introduction

The gateway to modern art is impressionism, that late phase of realism that sought, during the closing decades of the nineteenth century, to represent with increasing refinement the more elusive aspects of light, mood, atmosphere, and character. As a result of this more refined analysis of reality, the established forms in painting, music, and literature all broke down, and art became peculiarly formless. It was this vacuum of form created by impressionism that prepared the way for the magnificently inventive free forms of modern art.

In fiction Chekhov is the pioneer impressionist, so this collection begins appropriately with a story by this Russian master. With Chekhov the short story ceased to be a "tale" and became a "slice of life," sometimes rather formless, but always delicate and accurate, full of interesting nuances of character and setting, and united by theme and mood rather than by careful plot structure.

Katherine Mansfield's special contribution to the new impressionism was, of course, her feminine warmth and sensitivity. Her stories are so full of delicate perceptions that they seem to shimmer with intensity. "Her First Ball" explores a theme especially important in her work—youthful innocence and hope confronting adult disillusionment. But the ending is unexpected. It is youth and hope that triumph.

The new impressionism is also brilliantly demonstrated in Joyce's early story "Araby" by the delicacy with which the boy's first love is delineated, by the swift, accurate strokes that catch the essential qualities of character, and above all by the remarkable analysis of mood and atmosphere in the closing scenes at the fair. In his later stories, Joyce, like Conrad, moves beyond impressionism to profoundly symbolic and psychological explorations of character and theme.

Conrad's remarkable evocations of the sea are probably the most luminous in the language, but Conrad's interest in certain moral imperatives focuses his work on an almost metaphysical probing into man's capacity for courage and self-knowledge. In such a story as "The Secret Sharer" he plumbs psychic and moral depths far more complex than those of early impressionism.

When we arrive at Thomas Mann, we are leaving impressionism behind. Mann is, above all, the interpreter of the outcast, fascinated by the morbid, the malformed and the diseased, exploring the tormented world of substitute dreams and other compensations that fill the unhappy soul of the outsider. His early story "The Infant Prodigy" already illustrates his concern with the artist as an outsider, a theme that recurs in many of his longer works. Symphonic in form and highly expressionistic, Mann's fiction is rich in symbol and motif. His preoccupation with physical and mental decay goes beyond analysis of the individual to present the whole of Western civilization as a society in a state of decay. In his works the Spenglerian hypothesis of the decline of the West finds its most convincing artistic form.

It is significant that there did not appear in Europe after World War I a group of writers equivalent to the brilliant young disillusioned romantics of the twenties in America. This situation may have been due to the terrible psychic drain of the war upon Europe, or simply to the death toll of the war upon the young men. There was also the fact that the disillusionment with Victorian romanticism and sentimentalism, having been delayed in the United States, came with a double force following the disillusionments of the First World War. At any rate, the most distinguished writers of short fiction in Europe during the decade following the war were older writers like Lawrence, Maugham, Joyce, Mann, and Kafka, whose genius had been mainly shaped before the war. It was not until well into the thirties that a new generation of European writers, too young to have served in World War I, reached maturity and began to write fiction as original and powerful as that of Hemingway, Faulkner, and Fitzgerald.

Among the older writers who continued to write outstanding short stories during the twenties, none possessed a more intensely personal vision of life than D. H. Lawrence. If Mann's central preoccupation was disease, Lawrence's was sex, and he must be placed in that small group of literary geniuses who have fundamentally altered the attitudes of Western man with regard to sexual love. Lawrence arrived at his new insights into the nature of love partly as a result of his own neurotic sexual frustrations, probably originating in a mother fixation, and partly as a result of his rebellion against Victorian sentimentalism and prudery. However, his new ideas on love were part of the wave of anti-civilization feeling that intensified after World War I until it culminated in the atavistic doctrines and attitudes of fascism. All these aspects of Lawrence's genius are magnificently illustrated in his story "The Horse Dealer's Daughter." Here the young doctor represents overcivilized, overrational, overcautious, and therefore sexually weak modern man, while the girl, strong with the primitive urging of the blood, sweeps the man's resistance away in the violent flood of her simple, mindless passion. Striking details of Lawrence's special artistry in the story are the symbolism of the two lovers sinking together under the murky waters of the pond, as if purified by a kind of passing through death and resurrection, and the sudden loss of the girl's mystical power over the man when she puts on a conventional dress.

Lawrence died at the age of forty-five. Somerset Maugham, the other great master of the English short story throughout the twenties (Katherine Mansfield having died in 1923), lived on into the sixties. Yet in spite of his long and productive career, Maugham's basic style and attitudes changed little. He remained to the end cool, sardonic, cosmopolitan, ruthlessly anti-Victorian, neat, crisp, subtle, and witty. His orderly mind revolted very early in his career against the formlessness of impressionism just as surely as Cezanne's blunt and honest peasant's need for certainty and solidity led him to revolt against the fuzziness of impressionistic painting. Maugham's historical importance in this respect has not been fully appreciated. His triumph was that he retained the subtlety (although not the warmth) of Chekhov, while controlling it with a fine feeling for structure. Maugham, like Seurat or the musician Pierre Boulez, represents modern classicism, a new level of order and subtlety, and he is protected from sentimentalism or extravagance at all times by his magnificent irony.

The great advantage of European fiction over American fiction in the thirties was the influence upon the former of existentialism, which gave to it a metaphysical scope and depth as well as an emotional tension that was lacking in American fiction during this decade. It was as if the writer had to be close to that enormous frustration concentrated in central Europe after the fateful Treaty of Versailles to respond to this philosophical formulation of disillusionment that had been steadily accumulating in the West for half a century. For the existentialist, modern science had produced an utterly paradoxical universe, a universe of magnificent order, the function of which appeared to be to produce pain rather than pleasure, like the intricate, logical, systematic torture machine in Kafka's story "In the Penal Colony."

There are really only two ways of rising above such a fearful universe: one is to laugh bitterly at its absurdity, as Kafka does; the other is to be sadly but philosophically stoical about it, as are the characters in Camus' works. Kafka was a surrealist, whose typical stories deal with a nightmarish, continually frustrated quest for love, enlightenment, and justice. Camus found his inspiration in the landscape of North Africa, with its overwhelming suggestion of the endless tide of death and defeat down through the ages. Both Camus and the other great existentialist short story writer of the thirties, Jean-Paul Sartre, are engaged in a search for identity and self-realization, and both come to recognize that what gives identity to people in the ordinary course of their lives is the outer purposes of daily existence. Sartre made it quite clear in his philosophical writing that the introspective search for identity ends with the discovery that apart from such outer goals the self is nothing, a "NOT." This is the central theme of his famous story "The Wall." The wall in this story is the death that awaits three condemned prisoners in the morning. These men have no tomorrow with all the external goals and purposes that tomorrow holds under normal conditions, and as a result they begin to disintegrate physically and psychologically. The irrational and inhuman acts of men in time of war, together with a random, ironic twist of events at the end, make this story a simulacrum of the absurd universe as it appeared to the existentialist living under the spreading shadow of fascism.

Similarly the heroine of Camus' story "The Adulterous Woman," enveloped by the strangeness, indifference, emptiness, and death in the alien environment of North Africa, is forced to the realization of her own tenuous grip on her identity. For without children, having married only to achieve identity in her husband's need for her, which she now realizes is no more than periodic lust, she has never known the one purpose and joy that a woman needs to give her life meaning and her psyche identity—total love. In the climax of the story she rushes out into the desert night, where under the vast empty universe of stars she has a very strange experience, one of the most remarkable ever conceived by a writer, in which she achieves a kind of psychic victory over the indifference of the universe. In this scene Camus has projected in fantasy a solution to the dilemma of the existentialist that he would have liked to believe possible.

Camus is able to reach this resolution of the existentialist dilemma by clearing his mind of the formulas of Christian theology. Kafka, on the other hand, failed to reach even the satisfaction of such a sublimated psychic resolution, partly because his neurotic problems were more serious and partly because he continued to apply old religious formulas resolutely contradicted by modern science. He could not discard the Christian Father-God figure because of his desperate personal need for the loving, understanding father he never had in real life. Indeed, much of his writing is a quest for that Father-God, lost somewhere in the bureaucracy of his society and the mechanical system of the universe. In his story "Arabs and Jackals" Kafka is once again depicting the fate of the "deprived." In a strange, ritualistic sequence of action, the jackals, who represent the weak, even when given the instruments of destruction, cannot compete with the strong, and are endlessly betrayed by being tossed a bone. This is one of Kafka's most powerful and significant stories, which has, unfortunately, been generally overlooked by anthologists.

Four of the writers in the anthology fit no easy category: Isak Dinesen, Isaac Babel, Alberto Moravia, and Karel Čapek. Isak Dinesen's stories portray a strange, faraway world unlike any other in fiction, but they are not simply romances. The characters are eccentric, stoic, and inhabit a landscape of moral imperatives almost mythic in quality. They are sophisticated, disillusioned idealists, but their disillusionment stems not from externals like war or the failures of technology, but from the complex texture of existence itself, the death of youth, the difficulty of choosing a moral position. In "Sorrow-Acre," for example, one starts initially by abhorring the cruel inflexibility of the old lord of the manor. One concludes, however, as does the young nephew, by understanding that the old lord is merely the symbolic instrument of an implacable world in which sacrifice and suffering are inevitable elements. In this way Dinesen escapes our particular modern form of sentimentalism. The only analogy for this attitude is Greek tragedy, where wisdom consists in seeking to understand the fundamentally incomprehensible will of a God or a universe that sets its own rules. The style is almost baroque, lavish, but also charged and strange, like a city seen under the sea.

Isaac Babel's isolation is of quite a different order. A Russian-Jewish writer caught up in the storm of anti-Semitism that eventually killed him, his stories are filled with the humor and pathos of a tough but gentle people attacked by the mindless cruelties of racial prejudice. "In the Basement" is a moving reminiscence of a familiar pretension of childhood, the desire to impress. It is one of Babel's least politically oriented stories, but the background of a vanishing ghetto world gives body and focus to a universal impulse, and carries its own echoes of disaster to a world that has since known Hitler.

Moravia is best known in the United States as a novelist, but he is also a fine and prolific short story writer. His recurrent motif-like theme is the conflict of sexual love, many of his stories dealing with a balked and somehow menacing sensuality. The relationship between the characters is nonintellectual, based on a desire that never develops into true intimacy and which is filled with fear of its own power. Moravia is preeminently the psychological explorer of the sensual relationship between the sexes.

Karel Čapek, the versatile Czech poet, storyteller, and playwright, has an antic wit and a satirical thrust that make even his early works seem remarkably contemporary. He does not, however, merely play games with his imaginative flights. "The Last Judgment" is a fantasy, but it presents a definite moral position and suggests the humane quality of Chekhov's stories. The protagonist in "The Last Judgment" is judged in heaven not by God but by other men. God, we are shown, is truly *Love* and can condemn no one because he sees all. He is the ultimate humanitarian. Only man himself is so flawed, so partial in his vision, that he can judge his fellows. It is his ability to condemn that shows man's spiritual distance from God.

Isaac Bashevis Singer's "Gimpel the Fool" shares with Babel's story the background of middle-European ghetto life, but Singer's story is more philosophical; he asks the significant question: Are human values so debased that only the simpleton is wise? If only the unsuccessful fool is kind, forgiving, and gentle, what is wrong with the clever and successful people of the world? It is a question that takes us back directly to the long line of "holy fools" so important in nineteenth-century Russian literature.

The question of dislocated human values is also an important theme in Pirandello's story "War." Here the supposedly noble value of patriotism is shown up as rationalization. Patriotism is the cloak under which the intolerable is made to appear not only tolerable but good, until a simple question pushes aside the cloak and shows the bitter truth. What matters, Pirandello is saying, is personal relationships.

Pirandello, and Sartre in "The Wall," are reacting to moral dilemmas growing out of war. Interesting enough, following World War II, there is very little powerful fiction dealing with war. It is as if the theme had been exhausted following World War I. After the Second World War there emerges a quite new kind of fiction, the symbolic, surrealistic and archetypal fiction of Wolfgang Hildesheimer, Jakov Lind, Heinz Huber, Tomasso Landolfi, and Heinrich Böll, which concentrates on the fragmentation of the human psyche caused by the breakdown of traditional values. Often the treatment is humorous, analogous to that of the theater-of-the-absurd. Life is seen as ridiculous, sterile, increasingly invaded by a technology which seems to be mechanizing and depersonalizing people. The connection with earlier, existential modes of thought is evident, but both the focus and the method of attack have changed. Life is meaningless not because the universe is meaningless, but more specifically because man is allowing himself to be gobbled up by commercialism and mechanization. The tone is not anguish but a barbed, savage humor, and the technique is most frequently symbolistic.

Hildesheimer's "A World Ends" is a masterpiece of elegance and controlled irony. The story is a fitting starting point for a discussion of the new wave in European fiction because it succeeds so well in destroying an older world of manners, wealth, and leisured cultivation. What Hildesheimer does is to refine this mannered world into such an extreme of preciosity that it becomes absurd and destroys itself. There is probably no funnier, nor more scathing description in modern fiction of the decline of an era than the one in which the sole modern man, the contemporary realist, rows about a Venetian lagoon watching the sinking of an island of outdated values. One can imagine the story set to the music of Debussy's "La Cathédrale Engloutie." An added poignance attaches to the story because one realizes, in the midst of one's laughter, that these doomed people, no matter how absurd, superficial, and precious, nevertheless belong to a kind of life not without its own attractions of taste and integrity.

Jakov Lind, however, in his savagely satirical "Journey through the Night," declares that man has left himself so little of value in his life that he might as well finish off the job of destroying himself by pure cannibalism. Lind's story is realistic in detail in much the same way that Ionesco's *Rhinoceros* is. In each case, built up on a base of realistic, if absurd, detail, what emerges is a monstrous indictment of modern man. Heinz Huber, in a somewhat gentler vein, is also dealing with the sterility of contemporary life. The actors in his story "The New Apartment" represent the elite of the new technological society. The preoccupation of the characters with externals—not only the superficialities of taste in objects, but also of ideas and feelings—is set against the hinted strangeness of an earlier life in which people actually *felt* emotions and dared to be individuals. The new residents of Huber's story are modern robots, performing empty rituals whose utter sterility horrifies the reader.

Heinrich Böll's marvelous story "Murke's Collected Silences" symbolically disintegrates the same world of commercial values. Here we are shown the deletion of God from the mechanical universe man has made for himself by the brilliant plot device of cutting the word "God" off a radio tape made by a venal commentator. The central character is a technician repelled by the action of the "important radio personality," but his only solution is to collect "silences" off scissored tape. It is, of course, no solution at all; it is just a small, pathetic, bitterly ironic rebellion.

This sterility of the modern technological society is one of the most recurrent themes of the new fiction of the sixties. Landolfi's "Gogol's Wife" carries this tendency to its logical conclusion. All pretense is here abandoned. Gogol's wife is a totally mechanical apparatus . . . a balloon. Gogol is attempting a human relationship with a robot. The story is funny, but the humor is the monstrous absurdity of Albee's *An American Dream*. The individual has become totally isolated. All deeply felt emotion has been swallowed up in sterile, mechanical responses.

Russian and English short story writers have tended to be less expressionistic than other European writers. Obviously in Russia the government position limited experimentalism. Yuri Kazakov, for example, has been considered a controversial writer, although by comparison with the work of other European contemporaries, his stories seem realistic and technically traditional. Nevertheless, his writing throws a powerful searchlight on some of the harsh realities of Soviet life, and so rises above its polemic limitations. Such stories as "Autumn in the Oak Woods" demonstrate not only his fine capacity for psychological realism, but also a poetic, lyrical love of nature that relates him to the great Russian writers of the nineteenth century.

The "angry young men" writing in England since World

War II have developed a realism with a new bite and satiric thrust. The writers of this group have zoomed in on the emotional center of England following the war—the bitterly awakened new generation of working class youth, fiercely aware of their exclusion from the "establishment," which still branded them as inferior. Alan Sillitoe is probably the most successful short story writer of this group. His stories are skillful but not highly polished. They are appropriately rough in style and violent in subject matter, but they are powerful and full of insight into the frustration and impotence of the young working class.

In Ireland, Frank O'Connor and Mary Lavin are outside the "angry young men" group and the new symbolistic, expressionistic trend. O'Connor's stories are sensitive, humorous evocations of Irish life. Rooted though they often are in the Irish folk tale, they are made fresh and contemporary by O'Connor's awareness of current psychological and social problems of twentieth-century Ireland. Mary Lavin, American by birth but Irish by adoption, deals in her fiction with the lives of ordinary people. Her range, however, is wide, enabling her to move with ease from the satirical to the gothic or the tragic power of "The Great Wave."

All in all, the stories in this collection are of an astonishing variety and range. But this is only to be expected since they cover a unique phase of cultural evolution in which Europe passes through not one but two devastating modern technological wars, as well as the emancipation of the laboring classes and of women, the violent reversion to barbarism of fascism, and an unprecedented revolution in social manners, scientific knowledge, and peacetime technology. These stories are a kind of spiritual record of this remarkable breakthrough in cultural evolution.

—SYLVIA ANGUS *and* DOUGLAS ANGUS

New York
April, 1967

DOUGLAS ANGUS was born in Nova Scotia, the son of a fur trader. He received his B.A. from Acadia University (Canada), his M.A. from the University of Maine, and his Ph.D. from Ohio State University. He has taught at several universities in the United States, was Fulbright Lecturer at the University of Istanbul, 1963-1964, and is presently connected with the English Department at St. Lawrence University. He has contributed articles to *Esquire, American Scholar, Texas Quarterly*, and other publications. Under a Lilly Foundation grant he is now finishing a philosophical study, *Universal Evolution.*

SYLVIA ANGUS was born in Brooklyn, attended Cornell and George Washington Universities until marriage and children interrupted her studies, and then received her B.A. and M.A. at St. Lawrence University. In 1947 she won the *Mademoiselle* college fiction contest. She has contributed articles to numerous periodicals, including *Mademoiselle, The Antioch Review,* and *Southern Review,* and she is now working on a novel. Like her husband, she has taught at several universities, including the University of Istanbul, and she is presently on the staff of the English Department at the State University of New York at Potsdam. The Anguses have two children and live in Canton, New York.

ANTON CHEKHOV

The Kiss

Anton Chekhov (1860–1904) was born in Taganrog, Russia, the grandson of a serf. Through herculean effort he achieved a medical degree, but he practiced medicine only a short while before the urge to write took over his life. Chekhov brought impressionism into modern literature. The distinguishing features of his work are subtle exploration of character and mood, a penetrating sympathy, and a minimum interest in formal plot—all qualities that have come to dominate the modern short story. His contributions to the short story and to the drama have had a profound influence all over the world.

A T EIGHT O'CLOCK on the evening of the twentieth of May all the six batteries of the N—— Reserve Artillery Brigade halted for the night in the village of Mestechki on their way to camp. At the height of the general commotion, while some officers were busily occupied around the guns, and others, gathered together in the square near the church enclosure, were receiving the reports of the quartermasters, a man in civilian dress, riding a queer horse, came into sight round the church. The little dun-colored horse with a fine neck and a short tail came, moving not straight forward, but as it were sideways, with a sort of dance step, as though it were being lashed about the legs. When he reached the officers, the man on the horse took off his hat and said:

"His Excellency Lieutenant-General von Rabbeck, a local landowner, invites the officers to have tea with him this minute. . . ."

The horse bowed, danced, and retired sideways; the rider raised his hat once more and in an instant disappeared with his strange horse behind the church.

"What the devil does it mean?" grumbled some of the officers, dispersing to their quarters. "One is sleepy, and here this von Rabbeck with his tea! We know what tea means."

The officers of all the six batteries remembered vividly an incident of the previous year, when during maneuvers they, together with the officers of a Cossack regiment, were in the same way invited to tea by a count who had an estate in the neighborhood and was a retired army officer; the hospitable and genial count made much of them, dined and wined them, refused to let them go to their quarters in the village, and made them stay the night. All that, of course, was very nice—nothing better could be desired, but the worst of it was, the old army officer was so carried away by the pleasure of the young men's company that till sunrise he was telling the officers anecdotes of his glorious past, taking them over the house, showing them expensive pictures, old engravings, rare guns, reading them autograph letters from great people, while the weary and exhausted officers looked and listened, longing for their beds and yawning in their sleeves; when at last their host let them go, it was too late for sleep.

Might not this von Rabbeck be just such another? Whether he were or not, there was no help for it. The officers changed their uniforms, brushed themselves, and went all together in search of the gentleman's house. In the square by the church they were told they could get to his Excellency's by the lower road—going down behind the church to the river, walking along the bank to the garden, and there the alleys would take them to the house; or by the upper way—straight from the church by the road which, half a mile from the village, led right up to his Excellency's barns. The officers decided to go by the upper road.

"Which von Rabbeck is it?" they wondered on the way. "Surely not the one who was in command of the N—— cavalry division at Plevna?"

"No, that was not von Rabbeck, but simply Rabbe and no 'von.' "

"What lovely weather!"

At the first of the barns the road divided in two: one

branch went straight on and vanished in the evening darkness, the other led to the owner's house on the right. The officers turned to the right and began to speak more softly. . . . On both sides of the road stretched stone barns with red roofs, heavy and sullen-looking, very much like barracks in a district town. Ahead of them gleamed the windows of the manor house.

"A good omen, gentlemen," said one of the officers. "Our setter leads the way; no doubt he scents game ahead of us! . . ."

Lieutenant Lobytko, who was walking in front, a tall and stalwart fellow, though entirely without mustache (he was over twenty-five, yet for some reason there was no sign of hair on his round, well-fed face), renowned in the brigade for his peculiar ability to divine the presence of women at a distance, turned round and said:

"Yes, there must be women here; I feel that by instinct."

On the threshold the officers were met by von Rabbeck himself, a comely looking man of sixty in civilian dress. Shaking hands with his guests, he said that he was very glad and happy to see them, but begged them earnestly for God's sake to excuse him for not asking them to stay the night; two sisters with their children, his brothers, and some neighbors, had come on a visit to him, so that he had not one spare room left.

The General shook hands with everyone, made his apologies, and smiled, but it was evident by his face that he was by no means so delighted as last year's count, and that he had invited the officers simply because, in his opinion, it was a social obligation. And the officers themselves, as they walked up the softly carpeted stairs, as they listened to him, felt that they had been invited to this house simply because it would have been awkward not to invite them; and at the sight of the footmen, who hastened to light the lamps at the entrance below and in the anteroom above, they began to feel as though they had brought uneasiness and discomfort into the house with them. In a house in which two sisters and their children, brothers, and neighbors were gathered together, probably on account of some family festivity or event, how could the presence of nineteen unknown officers possibly be welcome?

Upstairs at the entrance to the drawing-room the officers were met by a tall, graceful old lady with black eyebrows and a long face, very much like the Empress Eugénie. Smiling graciously and majestically, she said she was glad and happy to see her guests, and apologized that her husband and she were

on this occasion unable to invite *messieurs les officers* to stay
the night. From her beautiful majestic smile, which instantly
vanished from her face every time she turned away from her
guests, it was evident that she had seen numbers of officers
in her day, that she was in no humor for them now, and if
she invited them to her house and apologized for not doing
more, it was only because her breeding and position in society
required it of her.

When the officers went into the big dining-room, there were
about a dozen people, men and ladies, young and old, sitting
at tea at the end of a long table. A group of men wrapped in
a haze of cigar smoke was dimly visible behind their chairs;
in the midst of them stood a lanky young man with red
whiskers, talking loudly in English, with a burr. Through a
door beyond the group could be seen a light room with pale
blue furniture.

"Gentlemen, there are so many of you that it is impossible
to introduce you all!" said the General in a loud voice,
trying to sound very gay. "Make each other's acquaintance,
gentlemen, without any ceremony!"

The officers—some with very serious and even stern faces,
others with forced smiles, and all feeling extremely awkward
—somehow made their bows and sat down to tea.

The most ill at ease of them all was Ryabovich—a short,
somewhat stooped officer in spectacles, with whiskers like a
lynx's. While some of his comrades assumed a serious expression, while others wore forced smiles, his face, his lynx-like
whiskers, and spectacles seemed to say, "I am the shyest,
most modest, and most undistinguished officer in the whole
brigade!" At first, on going into the room and later, sitting
down at table, he could not fix his attention on any one face
or object. The faces, the dresses, the cut-glass decanters
of brandy, the steam from the glasses, the molded cornices
—all blended in one general impression that inspired in Ryabovich alarm and a desire to hide his head. Like a lecturer
making his first appearance before the public, he saw everything that was before his eyes, but apparently only had a dim
understanding of it (among physiologists this condition, when
the subject sees but does not understand, is called "mental
blindness"). After a little while, growing accustomed to his
surroundings, Ryabovich regained his sight and began to observe. As a shy man, unused to society, what struck him first
was that in which he had always been deficient—namely, the
extraordinary boldness of his new acquaintants. Von Rab-

beck, his wife, two elderly ladies, a young lady in a lilac dress, and the young man with the red whiskers, who was, it appeared, a younger son of von Rabbeck, very cleverly, as though they had rehearsed it beforehand, took seats among the officers, and at once got up a heated discussion in which the visitors could not help taking part. The lilac young lady hotly asserted that the artillery had a much better time than the cavalry and the infantry, while von Rabbeck and the elderly ladies maintained the opposite. A brisk interchange followed. Ryabovich looked at the lilac young lady who argued so hotly about what was unfamiliar and utterly uninteresting to her, and watched artificial smiles come and go on her face.

Von Rabbeck and his family skillfully drew the officers into the discussion, and meanwhile kept a sharp eye on their glasses and mouths, to see whether all of them were drinking, whether all had enough sugar, why someone was not eating cakes or not drinking brandy. And the longer Ryabovich watched and listened, the more he was attracted by this insincere but splendidly disciplined family.

After tea the officers went into the drawing-room. Lieutenant Lobytko's instinct had not deceived him. There were a great many girls and young married ladies. The "setter" lieutenant was soon standing by a very young blonde in a black dress, and, bending over her jauntily, as though leaning on an unseen sword, smiled and twitched his shoulders coquettishly. He probably talked very interesting nonsense, for the blonde looked at his well-fed face condescendingly and asked indifferently, "Really?" And from that indifferent "Really?" the "setter," had he been intelligent, might have concluded that she would never call him to heel.

The piano struck up; the melancholy strains of a waltz floated out of the wide open windows, and everyone, for some reason, remembered that it was spring, a May evening. Everyone was conscious of the fragrance of roses, of lilac, and of the young leaves of the poplar. Ryabovich, who felt the brandy he had drunk, under the influence of the music stole a glance towards the window, smiled, and began watching the movements of the women, and it seemed to him that the smell of roses, of poplars, and lilac came not from the garden, but from the ladies' faces and dresses.

Von Rabbeck's son invited a scraggy-looking young lady to dance and waltzed round the room twice with her. Lobytko, gliding over the parquet floor, flew up to the lilac young lady and whirled her away. Dancing began. . . . Ryabovich stood near the door among those who were not dancing and looked on. He had never once danced in his whole life, and he had never once in his life put his arm round the waist of a respectable woman. He was highly delighted that a man should in the sight of all take a girl he did not know round the waist and offer her his shoulder to put her hand on, but he could not imagine himself in the position of such a man. There were times when he envied the boldness and swagger of his companions and was inwardly wretched; the knowledge that he was timid, round-shouldered, and uninteresting, that he had a long waist and lynx-like whiskers deeply mortified him, but with years he had grown used to this feeling, and now, looking at his comrades dancing or loudly talking, he no longer envied them, but only felt touched and mournful.

When the quadrille began, young von Rabbeck came up to those who were not dancing and invited two officers to have a game of billiards. The officers accepted and went with him out of the drawing-room. Ryabovich, having nothing to do and wishing to take at least some part in the general movement, slouched after them. From the big drawing-room they went into the little drawing-room, then into a narrow corridor with a glass roof, and thence into a room in which on their entrance three sleepy-looking footmen jumped up quickly from couches. At last, after passing through a long succession of rooms, young von Rabbeck and the officers came into a small room where there was a billiard table. They began to play. Ryabovich, who had never played any game but cards, stood near the billiard table and looked indifferently at the players, while they, in unbuttoned coats, with cues in their hands, stepped about, made puns, and kept shouting out unintelligible words.

The players took no notice of him, and only now and then one of them, shoving him with his elbow or accidentally touching him with his cue, would turn round and say *"Pardon!"* Before the first game was over he was weary of it, and began to feel that he was not wanted and in the way. . . . He felt disposed to return to the drawing-room and he went out.

On his way back he met with a little adventure. When he had gone half-way he noticed that he had taken a wrong turning. He distinctly remembered that he ought to meet three sleepy footmen on his way, but he had passed five or six rooms, and those sleepy figures seemed to have been swallowed up by the earth. Noticing his mistake, he walked back a little way and turned to the right; he found himself in a little room which was in semidarkness and which he had not seen on his way to the billiard room. After standing there a little while, he resolutely opened the first door that met his eyes and walked into an absolutely dark room. Straight ahead could be seen the crack in the doorway through which came a gleam of vivid light; from the other side of the door came the muffled sound of a melancholy mazurka. Here, too, as in the drawing-room, the windows were wide open and there was a smell of poplars, lilac, and roses. . . .

Ryabovich stood still in hesitation. . . . At that moment, to his surprise, he heard hurried footsteps and the rustling of a dress, a breathless feminine voice whispered "At last!" and two soft, fragrant, unmistakably feminine arms were clasped about his neck; a warm cheek was pressed against his, and simultaneously there was the sound of a kiss. But at once the bestower of the kiss uttered a faint shriek and sprang away from him, as it seemed to Ryabovich, with disgust. He, too, almost shrieked and rushed towards the gleam of light at the door. . . .

When he returned to the drawing-room his heart was palpitating and his hands were trembling so noticeably that he made haste to hide them behind his back. At first he was tormented by shame and dread that the whole drawing-room knew that he had just been kissed and embraced by a woman. He shrank into himself and looked uneasily about him, but as he became convinced that people were dancing and talking as calmly as ever, he gave himself up entirely to the new sensation which he had never experienced before in his life. Something strange was happening to him. . . . His neck, round which soft, fragrant arms had so lately been clasped, seemed to him to be anointed with oil; on his left cheek near his mustache where the unknown had kissed him there was a faint chilly tingling sensation as from peppermint drops, and the more he rubbed the place the more distinct was the chilly sensation; all of him, from head to foot, was full of a strange new feeling which grew stronger and stronger. . . . He wanted to dance, to talk, to run into the garden, to laugh aloud. . . . He quite forgot that he was round-shouldered and uninteresting, that he had lynx-like whiskers and an "undistinguished appearance" (that was how his appearance had been described by some ladies whose conversation he had accidentally overheard). When von Rabbeck's wife happened to pass by

him, he gave her such a broad and friendly smile that she
stood still and looked at him inquiringly.

"I like your house immensely!" he said, setting his spectacles straight.

The General's wife smiled and said that the house had belonged to her father; then she asked whether his parents were
living, whether he had long been in the army, why he was so
thin, and so on. . . . After receiving answers to her questions,
she went on, and after his conversation with her his smiles
were more friendly than ever, and he thought he was surrounded by splendid people. . . .

At supper Ryabovich ate mechanically everything offered
him, drank, and without listening to anything, tried to understand what had just happened to him. . . . The adventure
was of a mysterious and romantic character, but it was not
difficult to explain it. No doubt some girl or young married
lady had arranged a tryst with some man in the dark room;
had waited a long time, and being nervous and excited had
taken Ryabovich for her hero; this was the more probable as
Ryabovich had stood still hesitating in the dark room, so that
he, too, had looked like a person waiting for something. . . .
This was how Ryabovich explained to himself the kiss he had
received.

"And who is she?" he wondered, looking round at the
women's faces. "She must be young, for elderly ladies don't
arrange rendezvous. That she was a lady, one could tell by the
rustle of her dress, her perfume, her voice. . . ."

His eyes rested on the lilac young lady, and he thought her
very attractive; she had beautiful shoulders and arms, a clever
face, and a delightful voice. Ryabovich, looking at her, hoped
that she and no one else was his unknown. . . . But she
laughed somehow artificially and wrinkled up her long nose,
which seemed to him to make her look old. Then he turned
his eyes upon the blonde in a black dress. She was younger,
simpler, and more genuine, had a charming brow, and drank
very daintily out of her wineglass. Ryabovich now hoped that
it was she. But soon he began to think her face flat, and
fixed his eyes upon the one next her.

"It's difficult to guess," he thought, musing. "If one were to
take only the shoulders and arms of the lilac girl, add the
brow of the blonde and the eyes of the one on the left of
Lobytko, then . . ."

He made a combination of these things in his mind and so

formed the image of the girl who had kissed him, the image that he desired but could not find at the table. . . .

After supper, replete and exhilarated, the officers began to take leave and say thank you. Von Rabbeck and his wife began again apologizing that they could not ask them to stay the night.

"Very, very glad to have met you, gentlemen," said von Rabbeck, and this time sincerely (probably because people are far more sincere and good-humored at speeding their parting guests than on meeting them). "Delighted. Come again on your way back! Don't stand on ceremony! Where are you going? Do you want to go by the upper way? No, go across the garden; it's nearer by the lower road."

The officers went out into the garden. After the bright light and the noise the garden seemed very dark and quiet. They walked in silence all the way to the gate. They were a little drunk, in good spirits, and contented, but the darkness and silence made them thoughtful for a minute. Probably the same idea occurred to each one of them as to Ryabovich: would there ever come a time for them when, like von Rabbeck, they would have a large house, a family, a garden—when they, too, would be able to welcome people, even though insincerely, feed them, make them drunk and contented?

Going out of the garden gate, they all began talking at once and laughing loudly about nothing. They were walking now along the little path that led down to the river and then ran along the water's edge, winding round the bushes on the bank, the gulleys, and the willows that overhung the water. The bank and the path were scarcely visible, and the other bank was entirely plunged in darkness. Stars were reflected here and there in the dark water; they quivered and were broken up—and from that alone it could be seen that the river was flowing rapidly. It was still. Drowsy sandpipers cried plaintively on the farther bank, and in one of the bushes on the hither side a nightingale was trilling loudly, taking no notice of the crowd of officers. The officers stood round the bush, touched it, but the nightingale went on singing.

"What a fellow!" they exclaimed approvingly. "We stand beside him and he takes not a bit of notice! What a rascal!"

At the end of the way the path went uphill, and, skirting the church enclosure, led into the road. Here the officers, tired with walking uphill, sat down and lighted their cigarettes. On the farther bank of the river a murky red fire came into sight, and having nothing better to do, they spent a long time in discussing whether it was a camp fire or a light in a window, or something else. . . . Ryabovich, too, looked at the light, and he fancied that the light looked and winked at him, as though it knew about the kiss.

On reaching his quarters, Ryabovich undressed as quickly as possible and got into bed. Lobytko and Lieutenant Merzlyakov—a peaceable, silent fellow, who was considered in his own circle a highly educated officer, and was always, whenever it was possible, reading *The Messenger of Europe*, which he carried about with him everywhere—were quartered in the same cottage with Ryabovich. Lobytko undressed, walked up and down the room for a long while with the air of a man who has not been satisfied, and sent his orderly for beer. Merzlyakov got into bed, put a candle by his pillow and plunged into *The Messenger of Europe*.

"Who was she?" Ryabovich wondered, looking at the sooty ceiling.

His neck still felt as though he had been anointed with oil, and there was still the chilly sensation near his mouth as though from peppermint drops. The shoulders and arms of the young lady in lilac, the brow and the candid eyes of the blonde in black, waists, dresses, and brooches, floated through his imagination. He tried to fix his attention on these images, but they danced about, broke up and flickered. When these images vanished altogether from the broad dark background which everyone sees when he closes his eyes, he began to hear hurried footsteps, the rustle of skirts, the sound of a kiss—and an intense baseless joy took possession of him. . . . Abandoning himself to this joy, he heard the orderly return and announce that there was no beer. Lobytko was terribly indignant, and began pacing up and down the room again.

"Well, isn't he an idiot?" he kept saying, stopping first before Ryabovich and then before Merzlyakov. "What a fool and a blockhead a man must be not to get hold of any beer! Eh? Isn't he a blackguard?"

"Of course you can't get beer here," said Merzlyakov, not removing his eyes from *The Messenger of Europe*.

"Oh! Is that your opinion?" Lobytko persisted. "Lord have mercy upon us, if you dropped me on the moon I'd find you beer and women directly! I'll go and find some at once. . . . You may call me a rascal if I don't!"

He spent a long time in dressing and pulling on his high boots, then finished smoking his cigarette in silence and went out.

"Rabbeck, Grabbeck, Labbeck," he muttered, stopping in the outer room. "I don't care to go alone, damn it all! Ryabovich, wouldn't you like to go for a walk? Eh?"

Receiving no answer, he returned, slowly undressed, and got into bed. Merzlyakov sighed, put *The Messenger of Europe* away, and extinguished the light.

"H'm! . . ." muttered Lobytko, lighting a cigarette in the dark.

Ryabovich pulled the bedclothes over his head, curled himself up in bed, and tried to gather together the flashing images in his mind and to combine them into a whole. But nothing came of it. He soon fell asleep, and his last thought was that someone had caressed him and made him happy—that something extraordinary, foolish, but joyful and delightful, had come into his life. The thought did not leave him even in his sleep.

When he woke up the sensations of oil on his neck and the chill of peppermint about his lips had gone, but joy flooded his heart just as the day before. He looked enthusiastically at the window-frames, gilded by the light of the rising sun, and listened to the movement of the passersby in the street. People were talking loudly close to the window. Lebedetzky, the commander of Ryabovich's battery, who had only just overtaken the brigade, was talking to his sergeant at the top of his voice, having lost the habit of speaking in ordinary tones.

"What else?" shouted the commander.

"When they were shoeing the horses yesterday, your Honor, they injured Pigeon's hoof with a nail. The vet put on clay and vinegar; they are leading him apart now. Also, your Honor, Artemyev got drunk yesterday, and the lieutenant ordered him to be put in the limber of a spare gun-carriage."

The sergeant reported that Karpov had forgotten the new cords for the trumpets and the pegs for the tents, and that their Honors the officers had spent the previous evening visiting General von Rabbeck. In the middle of this conversation the red-bearded face of Lebedetzky appeared in the window. He screwed up his short-sighted eyes, looking at the sleepy faces of the officers, and greeted them.

"Is everything all right?" he asked.

"One of the horses has a sore neck from the new collar," answered Lobytko, yawning.

The commander sighed, thought a moment, and said in a loud voice:

"I am thinking of going to see Alexandra Yevgrafovna. I must call on her. Well, good-bye. I shall catch up with you in the evening."

A quarter of an hour later the brigade set off on its way. When it was moving along the road past the barns, Ryabovich looked at the house on the right. The blinds were down in all the windows. Evidently the household was still asleep. The one who had kissed Ryabovich the day before was asleep too. He tried to imagine her asleep. The wide-open window of the bedroom, the green branches peeping in, the morning freshness, the scent of the poplars, lilac, and roses, the bed, a chair, and on it the skirts that had rustled the day before, the little slippers, the little watch on the table—all this he pictured to himself clearly and distinctly, but the features of the face, the sweet sleepy smile, just what was characteristic and important, slipped through his imagination like quicksilver through the fingers. When he had ridden a third of a mile, he looked back: the yellow church, the house, and the river, were all bathed in light; the river with its bright green banks, with the blue sky reflected in it and glints of silver in the sunshine here and there, was very beautiful. Ryabovich gazed for the last time at Mestechki, and he felt as sad as though he were parting with something very near and dear to him.

And before him on the road were none but long familiar, uninteresting scenes. . . . To right and to left, fields of young rye and buckwheat with rooks hopping about in them; if one looked ahead, one saw dust and the backs of men's heads; if one looked back, one saw the same dust and faces. . . . Foremost of all marched four men with sabers—this was the vanguard. Next came the singers, and behind them the trumpeters on horseback. The vanguard and the singers, like torchbearers in a funeral procession, often forgot to keep the regulation distance and pushed a long way ahead. . . . Ryabovich was with the first cannon of the fifth battery. He could see all the four batteries moving in front of him. To a civilian the long tedious procession which is a brigade on the move seems an intricate and unintelligible muddle; one cannot understand why there are so many people round one cannon, and why it is drawn by so many horses in such a strange network of harness, as though it really were so terrible and heavy. To Ryabovich it was all perfectly comprehensible and therefore uninteresting. He had known for ever so long why at the head of each battery beside the officer there rode a stalwart

noncom, called bombardier; immediately behind him could
be seen the horsemen of the first and then the middle units.
Ryabovich knew that of the horses on which they rode, those
on the left were called one name, while those on the right
were called another—it was all extremely uninteresting. Behind the horsemen came two shaft-horses. On one of them sat
a rider still covered with the dust of yesterday and with a
clumsy and funny-looking wooden guard on his right leg. Ryabovich knew the object of this guard, and did not think it
funny. All the riders waved their whips mechanically and
shouted from time to time. The cannon itself was not pre-
sentable. On the limber lay sacks of oats covered with a
tarpaulin, and the cannon itself was hung over with kettles,
soldiers' knapsacks, bags, and looked like some small harmless animal surrounded for some unknown reason by men and
horses. To the leeward of it marched six men, the gunners,
swinging their arms. After the cannon there came again more
bombardiers, riders, shaft-horses, and behind them another
cannon, as unpresentable and unimpressive as the first. After
the second came a third, a fourth; near the fourth there was
an officer, and so on. There were six batteries in all the
brigade, and four cannon in each battery. The procession
covered a third of a mile; it ended in a string of wagons near
which an extremely appealing creature—the ass, Magar,
brought by a battery commander from Turkey—paced pen-
sively, his long-eared head drooping.

Ryabovich looked indifferently ahead and behind him, at
the backs of heads and at faces; at any other time he would
have been half asleep, but now he was entirely absorbed in
his new agreeable thoughts. At first when the brigade was
setting off on the march he tried to persuade himself that
the incident of the kiss could only be interesting as a mysterious little adventure, that it was in reality trivial, and to think
of it seriously, to say the least, was stupid; but now he bade
farewell to logic and gave himself up to dreams. . . . At one
moment he imagined himself in von Rabbeck's drawing-room
beside a girl who was like the young lady in lilac and the
blonde in black; then he would close his eyes and see himself
with another, entirely unknown girl, whose features were very
vague. In his imagination he talked, caressed her, leaned over
her shoulder, pictured war, separation, then meeting again,
supper with his wife, children. . . .

"Brakes on!" The word of command rang out every time
they went downhill.

He, too, shouted "Brakes on!" and was afraid this shout would disturb his reverie and bring him back to reality. . . .

As they passed by some landowner's estate Ryabovich looked over the fence into the garden. A long avenue, straight as a ruler, strewn with yellow sand and bordered with young birch-trees, met his eyes. . . . With the eagerness of a man who indulges in daydreaming, he pictured to himself little feminine feet tripping along yellow sand, and quite unexpectedly had a clear vision in his imagination of her who had kissed him and whom he had succeeded in picturing to himself the evening before at supper. This image remained in his brain and did not desert him again.

At midday there was a shout in the rear near the string of wagons:

"Attention! Eyes to the left! Officers!"

The general of the brigade drove by in a carriage drawn by a pair of white horses. He stopped near the second battery, and shouted something which no one understood. Several officers, among them Ryabovich, galloped up to him.

"Well? How goes it?" asked the general, blinking his red eyes. "Are there any sick?"

Receiving an answer, the general, a little skinny man, chewed, thought for a moment and said, addressing one of the officers:

"One of your drivers of the third cannon has taken off his leg-guard and hung it on the fore part of the cannon, the rascal. Reprimand him."

He raised his eyes to Ryabovich and went on:

"It seems to me your breeching is too long."

Making a few other tedious remarks, the general looked at Lobytko and grinned.

"You look very melancholy today, Lieutenant Lobytko," he said. "Are you pining for Madame Lopuhova? Eh? Gentlemen, he is pining for Madame Lopuhova."

Madame Lopuhova was a very stout and very tall lady long past forty. The general, who had a predilection for large women, whatever their ages, suspected a similar taste in his officers. The officers smiled respectfully. The general, delighted at having said something very amusing and biting, laughed loudly, touched his coachman's back, and saluted. The carriage rolled on. . . .

"All I am dreaming about now which seems to me so impossible and unearthly is really quite an ordinary thing," thought Ryabovich, looking at the clouds of dust racing after the general's carriage. "It's all very ordinary, and everyone goes through it. . . . That general, for instance, was in love at one time; now he is married and has children. Captain Wachter, too, is married and loved, though the nape of his neck is very red and ugly and he has no waist. . . . Salmanov is coarse and too much of a Tartar, but he had a love affair that has ended in marriage. . . . I am the same as everyone else, and I, too, shall have the same experience as everyone else, sooner or later. . . ."

And the thought that he was an ordinary person and that his life was ordinary delighted him and gave him courage. He pictured *her* and his happiness boldly, just as he liked. . . .

When the brigade reached their halting-place in the evening, and the officers were resting in their tents, Ryabovich, Merzlyakov, and Lobytko were sitting round a chest having supper. Merzlyakov ate without haste and, as he munched deliberately, read *The Messenger of Europe,* which he held on his knees. Lobytko talked incessantly and kept filling up his glass with beer, and Ryabovich, whose head was confused from dreaming all day long, drank and said nothing. After three glasses he got a little drunk, felt weak, and had an irresistible desire to relate his new sensations to his comrades.

"A strange thing happened to me at those von Rabbecks'," he began, trying to impart an indifferent and ironical tone to his voice. "You know I went into the billiard-room. . . ."

He began describing very minutely the incident of the kiss, and a moment later relapsed into silence. . . . In the course of that moment he had told everything, and it surprised him dreadfully to find how short a time it took him to tell it. He had imagined that he could have been telling the story of the kiss till next morning. Listening to him, Lobytko, who was a great liar and consequently believed no one, looked at him skeptically and laughed. Merzlyakov twitched his eyebrows and, without removing his eyes from *The Messenger of Europe,* said:

"That's an odd thing! How strange! . . . throws herself on a man's neck, without addressing him by name. . . . She must have been some sort of lunatic."

"Yes, she must," Ryabovich agreed.

"A similar thing once happened to me," said Lobytko, assuming a scared expression. "I was going last year to Kovno. . . . I took a second-class ticket. The train was crammed, and it was impossible to sleep. I gave the guard half a rouble;

he took my luggage and led me to another compartment. . . .
I lay down and covered myself with a blanket. . . . It was
dark, you understand. Suddenly I felt someone touch me on
the shoulder and breathe in my face. I made a movement
with my hand and felt somebody's elbow. . . . I opened my
eyes and only imagine—a woman. Black eyes, lips red as a
prime salmon, nostrils breathing passionately—a bosom like
a buffer. . . ."

"Excuse me," Merzlyakov interrupted calmly, "I understand
about the bosom, but how could you see the lips if it was
dark?"

Lobytko began trying to put himself right and laughing
at Merzlyakov's being so dull-witted. It made Ryabovich
wince. He walked away from the chest, got into bed, and
vowed never to confide again.

Camp life began. . . . The days flowed by, one very much
like another. All those days Ryabovich felt, thought, and
behaved as though he were in love. Every morning when his
orderly handed him what he needed for washing, and he
sluiced his head with cold water, he recalled that there was
something warm and delightful in his life.

In the evenings when his comrades began talking of love
and women, he would listen, and draw up closer; and he
wore the expression of a soldier listening to the description
of a battle in which he has taken part. And on the evenings
when the officers, out on a spree with the setter Lobytko at
their head, made Don-Juanesque raids on the neighboring
"suburb," and Ryabovich took part in such excursions, he
always was sad, felt profoundly guilty, and inwardly begged
her forgiveness. . . . In hours of leisure or on sleepless
nights when he felt moved to recall his childhood, his father
and mother—everything near and dear, in fact, he invariably
thought of Mestechki, the queer horse, von Rabbeck, his
wife who resembled Empress Eugénie, the dark room, the
light in the crack of the door. . . .

On the thirty-first of August he was returning from the
camp, not with the whole brigade, but with only two batteries. He was dreamy and excited all the way, as though
he were going home. He had an intense longing to see again
the queer horse, the church, the insincere family of the von
Rabbecks, the dark room. The "inner voice," which so often
deceives lovers, whispered to him for some reason that he
would surely see her . . . And he was tortured by the
questions: How would he meet her? What would he talk to

her about? Had she forgotten the kiss? If the worst came
to the worst, he thought, even if he did not meet her, it
would be a pleasure to him merely to go through the dark
room and recall the past. . . .

Towards evening there appeared on the horizon the familiar church and white barns. Ryabovich's heart raced. . . .
He did not hear the officer who was riding beside him and
saying something to him, he forgot everything, and looked
eagerly at the river shining in the distance, at the roof of
the house, at the dovecote round which the pigeons were
circling in the light of the setting sun.

When they reached the church and were listening to the
quartermaster, he expected every second that a man on horseback would come round the church enclosure and invite the
officers to tea, but . . . the quartermaster ended his report,
the officers dismounted and strolled off to the village, and
the man on horseback did not appear.

"Von Rabbeck will hear at once from the peasants that
we have come and will send for us," thought Ryabovich, as
he went into the peasant cottage, unable to understand why
a comrade was lighting a candle and why the orderlies were
hastening to get the samovars going.

A crushing uneasiness took possession of him. He lay down,
then got up and looked out of the window to see whether
the messenger were coming. But there was no sign of him.

He lay down again, but half an hour later he got up and,
unable to restrain his uneasiness, went into the street and
strode towards the church. It was dark and deserted in the
square near the church enclosure. Three soldiers were standing silent in a row where the road began to go downhill.
Seeing Ryabovich, they roused themselves and saluted. He
returned the salute and began to go down the familiar path.

On the farther bank of the river the whole sky was flooded
with crimson: the moon was rising; two peasant women, talking loudly, were pulling cabbage leaves in the kitchen garden;
beyond the kitchen garden there were some cottages that
formed a dark mass. . . . Everything on the near side of the
river was just as it had been in May: the path, the bushes,
the willows overhanging the water . . . but there was no
sound of the brave nightingale and no scent of poplar and
young grass.

Reaching the garden, Ryabovich looked in at the gate. The
garden was dark and still. . . . He could see nothing but
the white stems of the nearest birch-trees and a little bit

of the avenue; all the rest melted together into a dark mass. Ryabovich looked and listened eagerly, but after waiting for a quarter of an hour without hearing a sound or catching a glimpse of a light, he trudged back. . . .

He went down to the river. The General's bathing cabin and the bath-sheets on the rail of the little bridge showed white before him. . . . He walked up on the bridge, stood a little, and quite unnecessarily touched a sheet. It felt rough and cold. He looked down at the water. . . . The river ran rapidly and with a faintly audible gurgle round the piles of the bathing cabin. The red moon was reflected near the left bank; little ripples ran over the reflection, stretching it out, breaking it into bits, and seemed trying to carry it away. . . .

"How stupid, how stupid!" thought Ryabovich, looking at the running water. "How unintelligent it all is!"

Now that he expected nothing, the incident of the kiss, his impatience, his vague hopes and disappointment, presented themselves to him in a clear light. It no longer seemed to him strange that the General's messenger never came and that he would never see the girl who had accidentally kissed him instead of someone else; on the contrary, it would have been strange if he had seen her. . . .

The water was running, he knew not where or why, just as it did in May. At that time it had flowed into a great river, from the great river into the sea; then it had risen in vapor, turned into rain, and perhaps the very same water was running now before Ryabovich's eyes again. . . . What for? Why?

And the whole world, the whole of life, seemed to Ryabovich an unintelligible, aimless jest. . . . And turning his eyes from the water and looking at the sky, he remembered again how Fate in the person of an unknown woman had by chance caressed him, he recalled his summer dreams and fancies, and his life struck him as extraordinarily meager, poverty-stricken, and drab. . . .

When he had returned to the cottage he did not find a single comrade. The orderly informed him that they had all gone to "General Fontryabkin, who had sent a messenger on horseback to invite them. . . ."

For an instant there was a flash of joy in Ryabovich's heart, but he quenched it at once, got into bed, and in his wrath with his fate, as though to spite it, did not go to the General's.

KATHERINE MANSFIELD

Her First Ball

Katherine Mansfield (1888–1923) was a native of New Zealand who settled in England in 1909 and later married the English critic John Middleton Murry. Before her early death she published more than seventy stories, a genre she made peculiarly her own. Reminiscent of Chekhov's stories in their impressionism, her stories are remarkable for the shimmering sensitivity with which they record fragile and elusive emotional states.

EXACTLY WHEN THE ball began Leila would have found it hard to say. Perhaps her first real partner was the cab. It did not matter that she shared the cab with the Sheridan girls and their brother. She sat back in her own little corner of it, and the bolster on which her hand rested felt like the sleeve of an unknown young man's dress suit; and away they bowled, past waltzing lamp-posts and houses and fences and trees.

"Have you really never been to a ball before, Leila? But, my child, how too weird——" cried the Sheridan girls.

"Our nearest neighbour was fifteen miles," said Leila softly, gently opening and shutting her fan.

Oh, dear, how hard it was to be indifferent like the others! She tried not to smile too much; she tried not to care. But every single thing was so new and exciting . . . Meg's tuberoses, Jose's long loop of amber, Laura's little dark head, pushing above her white fur like a flower through snow. She would remember for ever. It even gave her a pang to see her cousin Laurie throw away the wisps of tissue paper he pulled from the fastenings of his new gloves. She would like to have kept those wisps as a keepsake, as a remembrance. Laurie leaned forward and put his hand on Laura's knee.

"Look here, darling," he said. "The third and the ninth as usual. Twig?"

Oh, how marvellous to have a brother! In her excitement Leila felt that if there had been time, if it hadn't been impossible, she couldn't have helped crying because she was an only child, and no brother had ever said "Twig?" to her; no sister would ever say, as Meg said to Jose that moment, "I've never known your hair go up more successfully than it has to-night!"

But, of course, there was no time. They were at the drill hall already; there were cabs in front of them and cabs behind. The road was bright on either side with moving fan-like lights, and on the pavement gay couples seemed to float through the air; little satin shoes chased each other like birds.

"Hold on to me, Leila; you'll get lost," said Laurie.

"Come on, girls, let's make a dash for it," said Laurie.

Leila put two fingers on Laura's pink velvet cloak, and they were somehow lifted past the big golden lantern, carried along the passage, and pushed into the little room marked "Ladies." Here the crowd was so great there was hardly space to take off their things; the noise was deafening. Two benches on either side were stacked high with wraps. Two old women in white aprons ran up and down tossing fresh armfuls. And everybody was pressing forward trying to get at the little dressing-table and mirror at the far end.

A great quivering jet of gas lighted the ladies' room. It couldn't wait; it was dancing already. When the door opened again and there came a burst of tuning from the drill hall, it leaped almost to the ceiling.

Dark girls, fair girls were patting their hair, tying ribbons again, tucking handkerchiefs down the fronts of their bodices, smoothing marble-white gloves. And because they were all laughing it seemed to Leila that they were all lovely.

"Aren't there any invisible hair-pins?" cried a voice. "How most extraordinary! I can't see a single invisible hair-pin."

"Powder my back, there's a darling," cried some one else.

"But I must have a needle and cotton. I've torn simply miles and miles of the frill," wailed a third.

Then, "Pass them along, pass them along!" The straw bas-

ket of programmes was tossed from arm to arm. Darling
little pink-and-silver programmes, with pink pencils and fluffy
tassels. Leila's fingers shook as she took one out of the basket.
She wanted to ask some one, "Am I meant to have one too?"
but she had just time to read: "Waltz 3. *Two, Two in a
Canoe*. Polka 4. *Making the Feathers Fly*," when Meg cried,
"Ready, Leila?" and they pressed their way through the crush
in the passage towards the big double doors of the drill hall.

Dancing had not begun yet, but the band had stopped tuning, and the noise was so great it seemed that when it did
begin to play it would never be heard. Leila, pressing close
to Meg, looking over Meg's shoulder, felt that even the little
quivering coloured flags strung across the ceiling were talking.
She quite forgot to be shy; she forgot how in the middle
of dressing she had sat down on the bed with one shoe off
and one shoe on and begged her mother to ring up her
cousins and say she couldn't go after all. And the rush of
longing she had had to be sitting on the veranda of their
forsaken up-country home, listening to the baby owls crying
"More pork" in the moonlight, was changed to a rush of
joy so sweet that it was hard to bear alone. She clutched her
fan, and, gazing at the gleaming, golden floor, the azaleas,
the lanterns, the stage at one end with its red carpet and gilt
chairs and the band in a corner, she thought breathlessly,
"How heavenly; how simply heavenly!"

All the girls stood grouped together at one side of the
doors, the men at the other, and the chaperones in dark
dresses, smiling rather foolishly, walked with little careful
steps over the polished floor towards the stage.

"This is my little country cousin Leila. Be nice to her.
Find her partners; she's under my wing," said Meg, going up
to one girl after another.

Strange faces smiled at Leila—sweetly, vaguely. Strange
voices answered, "Of course, my dear." But Leila felt the
girls didn't really see her. They were looking towards the
men. Why didn't the men begin? What were they waiting for?
There they stood, smoothing their gloves, patting their glossy
hair and smiling among themselves. Then, quite suddenly,
as if they had only just made up their minds that that was
what they had to do, the men came gliding over the parquet.
There was a joyful flutter among the girls. A tall, fair man
flew up to Meg, seized her programme, scribbled something;
Meg passed him on to Leila. "May I have the pleasure?" He
ducked and smiled. There came a dark man wearing an eye-

glass, then cousin Laurie with a friend, and Laura with a little freckled fellow whose tie was crooked. Then quite an old man—fat, with a big bald patch on his head—took her programme and murmured, "Let me see, let me see!" And he was a long time comparing his programme, which looked black with names, with hers. It seemed to give him so much trouble that Leila was ashamed. "Oh, please don't bother," she said eagerly. But instead of replying the fat man wrote something, glanced at her again. "Do I remember this bright little face?" he said softly. "Is it known to me of yore?" At that moment the band began playing; the fat man disappeared. He was tossed away on a great wave of music that came flying over the gleaming floor, breaking the groups up into couples, scattering them, sending them spinning. . . .

Leila had learned to dance at boarding school. Every Saturday afternoon the boarders were hurried off to a little corrugated iron mission hall where Miss Eccles (of London) held her "select" classes. But the difference between that dusty-smelling hall—with calico texts on the walls, the poor terrified little woman in a brown velvet toque with rabbit's ears thumping the cold piano, Miss Eccles poking the girls' feet with her long white wand—and this was so tremendous that Leila was sure if her partner didn't come and she had to listen to that marvellous music and to watch the others sliding, gliding over the golden floor, she would die at least, or faint, or lift her arms and fly out of one of those dark windows that showed the stars.

"Ours, I think—" Some one bowed, smiled, and offered her his arm; she hadn't to die after all. Some one's hand pressed her waist, and she floated away like a flower that is tossed into a pool.

"Quite a good floor, isn't it?" drawled a faint voice close to her ear.

"I think it's most beautifully slippery," said Leila.

"Pardon!" The faint voice sounded surprised. Leila said it again. And there was a tiny pause before the voice echoed, "Oh, quite!" and she was swung round again.

He steered so beautifully. That was the great difference between dancing with girls and men, Leila decided. Girls banged into each other, and stamped on each other's feet; the girl who was gentleman always clutched you so.

The azaleas were separate flowers no longer; they were pink and white flags streaming by.

"Were you at the Bells' last week?" the voice came again.

It sounded tired. Leila wondered whether she ought to ask him if he would like to stop.

"No, this is my first dance," said she.

Her partner gave a little gasping laugh. "Oh, I say," he protested.

"Yes, it is really the first dance I've ever been to." Leila was most fervent. It was such a relief to be able to tell somebody. "You see, I've lived in the country all my life up until now. . . . "

At that moment the music stopped, and they went to sit on two chairs against the wall. Leila tucked her pink satin feet under and fanned herself, while she blissfully watched the other couples passing and disappearing through the swing doors.

"Enjoying yourself, Leila?" asked Jose, nodding her golden head.

Laura passed and gave her the faintest little wink; it made Leila wonder for a moment whether she was quite grown up after all. Certainly her partner did not say very much. He coughed, tucked his handkerchief away, pulled down his waistcoat, took a minute thread off his sleeve. But it didn't matter. Almost immediately the band started, and her second partner seemed to spring from the ceiling.

"Floor's not bad," said the new voice. Did one always begin with the floor? And then, "Were you at the Neaves' on Tuesday?" And again Leila explained. Perhaps it was a little strange that her partners were not more interested. For it was thrilling. Her first ball! She was only at the beginning of everything. It seemed to her that she had never known what the night was like before. Up till now it had been dark, silent, beautiful very often—oh, yes—but mournful somehow. Solemn. And now it would never be like that again—it had opened dazzling bright.

"Care for an ice?" said her partner. And they went through the swing doors, down the passage, to the supper room. Her cheeks burned, she was fearfully thirsty. How sweet the ices looked on little glass plates, and how cold the frosted spoon was, iced too! And when they came back to the hall there was the fat man waiting for her by the door. It gave her quite a shock again to see how old he was; he ought to have been on the stage with the fathers and mothers. And when Leila compared him with her other partners he looked shabby. His waistcoat was creased, there was a button off his glove, his coat looked as if it was dusty with French chalk.

"Come along, little lady," said the fat man. He scarcely troubled to clasp her, and they moved away so gently, it was more like walking than dancing. But he said not a word about the floor. "Your first dance, isn't it?" he murmured.

"How *did* you know?"

"Ah," said the fat man, "that's what it is to be old!" He wheezed faintly as he steered her past an awkward couple. "You see, I've been doing this kind of thing for the last thirty years."

"Thirty years?" cried Leila. Twelve years before she was born!

"It hardly bears thinking about, does it?" said the fat man gloomily. Leila looked at his bald head, and she felt quite sorry for him.

"I think it's marvellous to be still going on," she said kindly.

"Kind little lady," said the fat man, and he pressed her a little closer, and hummed a bar of the waltz. "Of course," he said, "you can't hope to last anything like as long as that. No-o," said the fat man, "long before that you'll be sitting up there on the stage, looking on, in your nice black velvet. And these pretty arms will have turned into little short fat ones, and you'll beat time with such a different kind of fan—a black bony one." The fat man seemed to shudder. "And you'll smile away like the poor old dears up there, and point to your daughter, and tell the elderly lady next to you how some dreadful man tried to kiss her at the club ball. And your heart will ache, ache"—the fat man squeezed her closer still, as if he really was sorry for that poor heart—"because no one wants to kiss you now. And you'll say how unpleasant these polished floors are to walk on, how dangerous they are. Eh, Mademoiselle Twinkletoes?" said the fat man softly.

Leila gave a light little laugh, but she did not feel like laughing. Was it—could it all be true? It sounded terribly true. Was this first ball only the beginning of her last ball after all? At that the music seemed to change; it sounded sad, sad; it rose upon a great sigh. Oh, how quickly things changed! Why didn't happiness last for ever? For ever wasn't a bit too long.

"I want to stop," she said in a breathless voice. The fat man led her to the door.

"No," she said, "I won't go outside. I won't sit down. I'll just stand here, thank you." She leaned against the wall, tapping with her foot, pulling up her gloves and trying to smile. But deep inside her a little girl threw her pinafore over her head and sobbed. Why had he spoiled it all?

"I say, you know," said the fat man, "you mustn't take me seriously, little lady."

"As if I should!" said Leila, tossing her small dark head and sucking her underlip. . . .

Again the couples paraded. The swing doors opened and shut. Now new music was given out by the bandmaster. But Leila didn't want to dance any more. She wanted to be home, or sitting on the veranda listening to those baby owls. When she looked through the dark windows at the stars, they had long beams like wings. . . .

But presently a soft, melting, ravishing tune began, and a young man with curly hair bowed before her. She would have to dance, out of politeness, until she could find Meg. Very stiffly she walked into the middle; very haughtily she put her hand on his sleeve. But in one minute, in one turn, her feet glided, glided. The lights, the azaleas, the dresses, the pink faces, the velvet chairs, all became one beautiful flying wheel. And when her next partner bumped her into the fat man and he said, "Par*don*," she smiled at him more radiantly than ever. She didn't even recognize him again.

JAMES JOYCE

Araby

James Joyce (1882–1941) was the first novelist of Ireland, and is probably the most significant and seminal writer of the twentieth century. Born and bred in Dublin, he won his first success with a collection of stories called Dubliners. *He lived for many years with his wife and children in Europe, often in great poverty, plagued by ill health and later by blindness. His celebrated novels* Ulysses *and* Finnegan's Wake *extended the stylistic brilliance and originality already visible in his earlier* Portrait of the Artist as a Young Man. *Joyce's enormously erudite mind moved through impressionism to expressionism and surrealism and explored the fictional possibilities of the stream of consciousness technique. The sensitivity and delicacy of his perceptions are well illustrated in the luminous story "Araby."*

NORTH RICHMOND STREET, being blind, was a quiet street except at the hour when the Christian Brothers' School set the boys free. An uninhabited house of two storeys stood at the blind end, detached from its neighbours in a square ground. The other houses of the street, conscious of decent lives within them, gazed at one another with brown imperturbable faces.

The former tenant of our house, a priest, had died in the back drawing-room. Air, musty from having been long enclosed, hung in all the rooms, and the waste room behind

From DUBLINERS by James Joyce. Originally published by B. W. Huebsch Inc., in 1916. All rights reserved. Reprinted by permission of The Viking Press, Inc.

the kitchen was littered with old useless papers. Among these I found a few paper-covered books, the pages of which were curled and damp: *The Abbot*, by Walter Scott, *The Devout Communicant* and *The Memoirs of Vidocq*. I liked the last best because its leaves were yellow. The wild garden behind the house contained a central apple-tree and a few straggling bushes under one of which I found the late tenant's rusty bicycle-pump. He had been a very charitable priest; in his will he had left all his money to institutions and the furniture of his house to his sister.

When the short days of winter came dusk fell before we had well eaten our dinners. When we met in the street the houses had grown sombre. The space of sky above us was the colour of everchanging violet and towards it the lamps of the street lifted their feeble lanterns. The cold air stung us and we played till our bodies glowed. Our shouts echoed in the silent street. The career of our play brought us through the dark muddy lanes behind the houses where we ran the gauntlet of the rough tribes from the cottages, to the back doors of the dark dripping gardens where odours arose from the ashpits, to the dark odorous stables where a coachman smoothed and combed the horse or shook music from the buckled harness. When we returned to the street light from the kitchen windows had filled the areas. If my uncle was seen turning the corner we hid in the shadow until we had seen him safely housed. Or if Mangan's sister came out on the doorstep to call her brother in to his tea we watched her from our shadow peer up and down the street. We waited to see whether she would remain or go in and, if she remained, we left our shadow and walked up to Mangan's steps resignedly. She was waiting for us, her figure defined by the light from the half-opened door. Her brother always teased her before he obeyed and I stood by the railings looking at her. Her dress swung as she moved her body and the soft rope of her hair tossed from side to side.

Every morning I lay on the floor in the front parlour watching her door. The blind was pulled down to within an inch of the sash so that I could not be seen. When she came out on the doorstep my heart leaped. I ran to the hall, seized my books and followed her. I kept her brown figure always in my eye and, when we came near the point at which our ways diverged, I quickened my pace and passed her. This happened morning after morning. I had never spoken to her, except for a few casual words, and yet her name was like a summons to all my foolish blood.

Her image accompanied me even in places the most hostile to romance. On Saturday evenings when my aunt went marketing I had to go to carry some of the parcels. We walked through the flaring streets, jostled by drunken men and bargaining women, amid the curses of labourers, the shrill litanies of shop-boys who stood on guard by the barrels of pigs' cheeks, the nasal chanting of streetsingers, who sang a *come-all-you* about O'Donovan Rossa, or a ballad about the troubles in our native land. These noises converged in a single sensation of life for me: I imagined that I bore my chalice safely through a throng of foes. Her name sprang to my lips at moments in strange prayers and praises which I myself did not understand. My eyes were often full of tears (I could not tell why) and at times a flood from my heart seemed to pour itself out into my bosom. I thought little of the future. I did not know whether I would ever speak to her or not or, if I spoke to her, how I could tell her of my confused adoration. But my body was like a harp and her words and gestures were like fingers running upon the wires.

One evening I went into the back drawing-room in which the priest had died. It was a dark rainy evening and there was no sound in the house. Through one of the broken panes I heard the rain impinge upon the earth, the fine incessant needles of water playing in the sodden beds. Some distant lamp or lighted window gleamed below me. I was thankful that I could see so little. All my senses seemed to desire to veil themselves and, feeling that I was about to slip from them, I pressed the palms of my hands together until they trembled, murmuring: *"O love! O love!"* many times.

At last she spoke to me. When she addressed the first words to me I was so confused that I did not know what to answer. She asked me was I going to *Araby*. I forgot whether I answered yes or no. It would be a splendid bazaar, she said she would love to go.

"And why can't you?" I asked.

While she spoke she turned a silver bracelet round and round her wrist. She could not go, she said, because there would be a retreat that week in her convent. Her brother and two other boys were fighting for their caps and I was alone at the railings. She held one of the spikes, bowing her head towards me. The light from the lamp opposite our door caught the white curve of her neck, lit up her hair

that rested there and, falling, lit up the hand upon the railing.
It fell over one side of her dress and caught the white border
of a petticoat, just visible as she stood at ease.

"It's well for you," she said.

"If I go," I said, "I will bring you something."

What innumerable follies laid waste my waking and sleeping thoughts after that evening! I wished to annihilate the
tedious intervening days. I chafed against the work of school.
At night in my bedroom and by day in the classroom her
image came between me and the page I strove to read. The
syllables of the word *Araby* were called to me through the
silence in which my soul luxuriated and cast an Eastern en-
chantment over me. I asked for leave to go to the bazaar
on Saturday night. My aunt was surprised and hoped it was
not some Freemason affair. I answered few questions in class.
I watched my master's face pass from amiability to stern-
ness; he hoped I was not beginning to idle. I could not call
my wandering thoughts together. I had hardly any patience
with the serious work of life which, now that it stood between me and my desire, seemed to me child's play, ugly
monotonous child's play.

On Saturday morning I reminded my uncle that I wished
to go to the bazaar in the evening. He was fussing at the
hallstand, looking for the hat-brush, and answered me curtly:

"Yes, boy, I know."

As he was in the hall I could not go into the front parlour
and lie at the window. I felt the house in bad humour and
walked slowly towards the school. The air was pitilessly raw
and already my heart misgave me.

When I came home to dinner my uncle had not yet been
home. Still it was early. I sat staring at the clock for some
time and, when its ticking began to irritate me, I left the
room. I mounted the staircase and gained the upper part
of the house. The high cold empty gloomy rooms liberated
me and I went from room to room singing. From the front
window I saw my companions playing below in the street.
Their cries reached me weakened and indistinct and, leaning
my forehead against the cool glass, I looked over at the
dark house where she lived. I may have stood there for an
hour, seeing nothing but the brown-clad figure cast by my
imagination, touched discreetly by the lamplight at the curved
neck, at the hand upon the railings and at the border below
the dress.

When I came downstairs again I found Mrs. Mercer sit-

ting at the fire. She was an old garrulous woman, a pawn-
broker's widow, who collected used stamps for some pious
purpose. I had to endure the gossip of the tea-table. The
meal was prolonged beyond an hour and still my uncle did
not come. Mrs. Mercer stood up to go: she was sorry she
couldn't wait any longer, but it was after eight o'clock and
she did not like to be out late, as the night air was bad for
her. When she had gone I began to walk up and down the
room, clenching my fists. My aunt said:

"I'm afraid you may put off your bazaar for this night of
Our Lord."

At nine o'clock I heard my uncle's latchkey in the halldoor.
I heard him talking to himself and heard the hallstand
rocking when it had received the weight of his overcoat.
I could interpret these signs. When he was midway through
his dinner I asked him to give me the money to go to the
bazaar. He had forgotten.

"The people are in bed and after their first sleep now," he
said.

I did not smile. My aunt said to him energetically:

"Can't you give him the money and let him go? You've kept
him late enough as it is."

My uncle said he was very sorry he had forgotten. He said
he believed in the old saying: "All work and no play makes
Jack a dull boy." He asked me where I was going and, when
I had told him a second time he asked me did I know
The Arab's Farewell to his Steed. When I left the kitchen
he was about to recite the opening lines of the piece to my
aunt.

I held a florin tightly in my hand as I strode down Buckingham Street towards the station. The sight of the streets
thronged with buyers and glaring with gas recalled to me
the purpose of my journey. I took my seat in a third-class
carriage of a deserted train. After an intolerable delay the
train moved out of the station slowly. It crept onward among
ruinous houses and over the twinkling river. At Westland
Row Station a crowd of people pressed to the carriage doors;
but the porters moved them back, saying that it was a special
train for the bazaar. I remained alone in the bare carriage.
In a few minutes the train drew up beside an improvised
wooden platform. I passed out on to the road and saw by
the lighted dial of a clock that it was ten minutes to ten.
In front of me was a large building which displayed the
magical name.

I could not find any sixpenny entrance and, fearing that the bazaar would be closed, I passed in quickly through a turnstile, handing a shilling to a weary-looking man. I found myself in a big hall girdled at half its height by a gallery. Nearly all the stalls were closed and the greater part of the hall was in darkness. I recognized a silence like that which pervades a church after a service. I walked into the centre of the bazaar timidly. A few people were gathered about the stalls which were still open. Before a curtain, over which the words *Café Chantant* were written in coloured lamps, two men were counting money on a salver. I listened to the fall of the coins.

Remembering with difficulty why I had come I went over to one of the stalls and examined porcelain vases and flowered tea-sets. At the door of the stall a young lady was talking and laughing with two young gentlemen. I remarked their English accents and listened vaguely to their conversation.

"O, I never said such a thing!"

"O, but you did!"

"O, but I didn't!"

"Didn't she say that?"

"Yes. I heard her."

"O, there's a . . . fib!"

Observing me the young lady came over and asked me did I wish to buy anything. The tone of her voice was not encouraging; she seemed to have spoken to me out of a sense of duty. I looked humbly at the great jars that stood like eastern guards at either side of the dark entrance to the stall and murmured:

"No, thank you."

The young lady changed the position of one of the vases and went back to the two young men. They began to talk of the same subject. Once or twice the young lady glanced at me over her shoulder.

I lingered before her stall, though I knew my stay was useless, to make my interest in her wares seem the more real. Then I turned away slowly and walked down the middle of the bazaar. I allowed the two pennies to fall against the sixpence in my pocket. I heard a voice call from one end of the gallery that the light was out. The upper part of the hall was now completely dark.

Gazing up into the darkness I saw myself as a creature driven and derided by vanity; and my eyes burned with anguish and anger.

JOSEPH CONRAD

The Secret Sharer

*Joseph Conrad (1857–1924) was born a Pole, but his
boyhood desire for adventure involved him first in
Carlist revolutionary activities and then in a long
career as a merchant seaman. He rose to the rank of
captain in the British merchant marine and retired
to devote himself to writing only in his middle years.
Writing in English, his second language, he became
a remarkable stylist. His stories and novels often
used the sea as setting, but his work always went
far beyond mere adventure to probe profound moral
and philosophic questions.*

ON MY RIGHT hand there were lines of fishing stakes re-
sembling a mysterious system of half-submerged bamboo
fences, incomprehensible in its division of the domain
of tropical fishes, and crazy of aspect as if abandoned forever by some nomad tribe of fishermen now gone to the other
end of the ocean; for there was no sign of human habitation
as far as the eye could reach. To the left a group of barren
islets, suggesting ruins of stone walls, towers, and blockhouses,
had its foundations set in a blue sea that itself looked solid,
so still and stable did it lie below my feet; even the track of
light from the westering sun shone smoothly, without that
animated glitter which tells of an imperceptible ripple. And
when I turned my head to take a parting glance at the tug
which had just left us anchored outside the bar, I saw the
straight line of the flat shore joined to the stable sea, edge
to edge, with a perfect and unmarked closeness, in one leveled

floor half brown, half blue under the enormous dome of the sky. Corresponding in their insignificance to the islets of the sea, two small clumps of trees, one on each side of the only fault in the impeccable joint, marked the mouth of the river Meinam we had just left on the first preparatory stage of our homeward journey; and, far back on the inland level, a larger and loftier mass, the grove surrounding the great Paknam pagoda, was the only thing on which the eye could rest from the vain task of exploring the monotonous sweep of the horizon. Here and there gleams as of a few scattered pieces of silver marked the windings of the great river; and on the nearest of them, just within the bar, the tug steaming right into the land became lost to my sight, hull and funnel and masts, as though the impassive earth had swallowed her up without an effort, without a tremor. My eye followed the light cloud of her smoke, now here, now there, above the plain, according to the devious curves of the stream, but always fainter and farther away, till I lost it at last behind the miter-shaped hill of the great pagoda. And then I was left alone with my ship, anchored at the head of the Gulf of Siam.

She floated at the starting point of a long journey, very still in an immense stillness, the shadows of her spars flung far to the eastward by the setting sun. At that moment I was alone on her decks. There was not a sound in her—and around us nothing moved, nothing lived, not a canoe on the water, not a bird in the air, not a cloud in the sky. In this breathless pause at the threshold of a long passage we seemed to be measuring our fitness for a long and arduous enterprise, the appointed task of both our existences to be carried out, far from all human eyes, with only sky and sea for spectators and for judges.

There must have been some glare in the air to interfere with one's sight, because it was only just before the sun left us that my roaming eyes made out beyond the highest ridges of the principal islet of the group something which did away with the solemnity of perfect solitude. The tide of darkness flowed on swiftly; and with tropical suddenness a swarm of stars came out above the shadowy earth, while I lingered yet, my hand resting lightly on my ship's rail as if on the shoulder of a trusted friend. But, with all that multitude of celestial bodies staring down at one, the comfort of quiet communion with her was gone for good. And there were also disturbing sounds by this time—voices, footsteps forward; the steward flitted along the main-deck, a busily ministering spirit; a hand bell tinkled urgently under the poop deck. . . .

I found my two officers waiting for me near the supper table, in the lighted cuddy. We sat down at once, and as I helped the chief mate, I said:

"Are you aware that there is a ship anchored inside the islands? I saw her mastheads above the ridge as the sun went down."

He raised sharply his simple face, overcharged by a terrible growth of whisker, and emitted his usual ejaculations: "Bless my soul, sir! You don't say so!"

My second mate was a round-cheeked, silent young man, grave beyond his years, I thought; but as our eyes happened to meet I detected a slight quiver on his lips. I looked down at once. It was not my part to encourage sneering on board my ship. It must be said, too, that I knew very little of my officers. In consequence of certain events of no particular significance except to myself, I had been appointed to the command only a fortnight before. Neither did I know much of the hands forward. All these people had been together for eighteen months or so, and my position was that of the only stranger on board. I mention this because it has some bearing on what is to follow. But what I felt most was my being a stranger to the ship; and if all the truth must be told, I was somewhat of a stranger to myself. The youngest man on board (barring the second mate), and untried as yet by a position of the fullest responsibility, I was willing to take the adequacy of the others for granted. They had simply to be equal to their tasks; but I wondered how far I should turn out faithful to that ideal conception of one's own personality every man sets up for himself secretly.

Meantime the chief mate, with an almost visible effect of collaboration on the part of his round eyes and frightful whiskers, was trying to evolve a theory of the anchored ship. His dominant trait was to take all things into earnest consideration. He was of a painstaking turn of mind. As he used to say, he "liked to account to himself" for practically everything that came in his way, down to a miserable scorpion he had found in his cabin a week before. The why and the wherefore of that scorpion—how it got on board and came to select his room rather than the pantry (which was a dark place and more what a scorpion would be partial to), and how on earth it managed to drown itself in the inkwell of his writing desk—had exercised him infinitely. The ship within the islands was much more easily accounted for; and just as we were about to rise from table he made his pronouncement. She was, he doubted not, a ship from home lately arrived. Probably she drew too much water to cross the bar except at the top of spring tides. Therefore she went into that natural harbor to wait for a few days in preference to remaining in an open roadstead.

"That's so," confirmed the second mate, suddenly, in his slightly hoarse voice. "She draws over twenty feet. She's the Liverpool ship *Sephora* with a cargo of coal. Hundred and twenty-three days from Cardiff."

We looked at him in surprise.

"The tugboat skipper told me when he came on board for your letters, sir," explained the young man. "He expects to take her up the river the day after tomorrow."

After thus overwhelming us with the extent of his information he slipped out of the cabin. The mate observed regretfully that he "could not account for that young fellow's whims." What prevented him telling us all about it at once, he wanted to know.

I detained him as he was making a move. For the last two days the crew had had plenty of hard work, and the night before they had very little sleep. I felt painfully that I—a stranger—was doing something unusual when I directed him to let all hands turn in without setting an anchor watch. I proposed to keep on deck myself till one o'clock or thereabouts. I would get the second mate to relieve me at that hour.

"He will turn out the cook and the steward at four," I concluded, "and then give you a call. Of course at the slightest sign of any sort of wind we'll have the hands up and make a start at once."

He concealed his astonishment. "Very well, sir." Outside the cuddy he put his head in the second mate's door to inform him of my unheard-of caprice to take a five hours' anchor watch on myself. I heard the other raise his voice incredulously —"What? The Captain himself?" Then a few more murmurs, a door closed, then another. A few moments later I went on deck.

My strangeness, which had made me sleepless, had prompted that unconventional arrangement, as if I had expected in those solitary hours of the night to get on terms with the ship of which I knew nothing, manned by men of

whom I knew very little more. Fast alongside a wharf, littered
like any ship in port with a tangle of unrelated things, invaded by unrelated shore people, I had hardly seen her yet
properly. Now, as she lay cleared for sea, the stretch of her
main-deck seemed to me very fine under the stars. Very
fine, very roomy for her size, and very inviting. I descended
the poop and paced the waist, my mind picturing to myself
the coming passage through the Malay Archipelago, down
the Indian Ocean, and up the Atlantic. All its phases were
familiar enough to me, every characteristic, all the alterna-
tives which were likely to face me on the high seas—everything! . . . except the novel responsibility of command. But
I took heart from the reasonable thought that the ship was
like other ships, the men like other men, and that the sea was
not likely to keep any special surprises expressly for my dis-
comfiture.

Arrived at that comforting conclusion, I bethought myself
of a cigar and went below to get it. All was still down there.
Everybody at the after end of the ship was sleeping profoundly. I came out again on the quarter-deck, agreeably at
ease in my sleeping suit on that warm breathless night, barefooted, a glowing cigar in my teeth, and, going forward, I
was met by the profound silence of the fore end of the ship.
Only as I passed the door of the forecastle I heard a deep,
quiet, trustful sigh of some sleeper inside. And suddenly I
rejoiced in the great security of the sea as compared with the
unrest of the land, in my choice of that untempted life presenting no disquieting problems, invested with an elementary
moral beauty by the absolute straightforwardness of its appeal
and by the singleness of its purpose.

The riding light in the forerigging burned with a clear, untroubled, as if symbolic, flame, confident and bright in the
mysterious shades of the night. Passing on my way aft along
the other side of the ship, I observed that the rope side ladder,
put over, no doubt, for the master of the tug when he came
to fetch away our letters, had not been hauled in as it should
have been. I became annoyed at this, for exactitude in some
small matters is the very soul of discipline. Then I reflected
that I had myself peremptorily dismissed my officers from
duty, and by my own act had prevented the anchor watch
being formally set and things properly attended to. I asked
myself whether it was wise ever to interfere with the established routine of duties even from the kindest of motives.
My action might have made me appear eccentric. Goodness

only knew how that absurdly whiskered mate would "account" for my conduct, and what the whole ship thought of that informality of their new captain. I was vexed with myself.

Not from compunction certainly, but, as it were mechanically, I proceeded to get the ladder in myself. Now a side ladder of that sort is a light affair and comes in easily, yet my vigorous tug, which should have brought it flying on board, merely recoiled upon my body in a totally unexpected jerk. What the devil! . . . I was so astounded by the immovableness of that ladder that I remained stockstill, trying to account for it to myself like that imbecile mate of mine. In the end, of course, I put my head over the rail.

The side of the ship made an opaque belt of shadow on the darkling glassy shimmer of the sea. But I saw at once something elongated and pale floating very close to the ladder. Before I could form a guess a faint flash of phosphorescent light, which seemed to issue suddenly from the naked body of a man, flickered in the sleeping water with the elusive, silent play of summer lightning in a night sky. With a gasp I saw revealed to my stare a pair of feet, the long legs, a broad livid back immersed right up to the neck in a greenish cadaverous glow. One hand, awash, clutched the bottom rung of the ladder. He was complete but for the head. A headless corpse! The cigar dropped out of my gaping mouth with a tiny plop and a short hiss quite audible in the absolute stillness of all things under heaven. At that I suppose he raised up his face, a dimly pale oval in the shadow of the ship's side. But even then I could only barely make out down there the shape of his black-haired head. However, it was enough for the horrid, frost-bound sensation which had gripped me about the chest to pass off. The moment of vain exclamations was past, too. I only climbed on the spare spar and leaned over the rail as far as I could, to bring my eyes nearer to that mystery floating alongside.

As he hung by the ladder, like a resting swimmer, the sea lightning played about his limbs at every stir; and he appeared in it ghastly, silvery, fishlike. He remained as mute as a fish, too. He made no motion to get out of the water, either. It was inconceivable that he should not attempt to come on board, and strangely troubling to suspect that perhaps he did not want to. And my first words were prompted by just that troubled incertitude.

"What's the matter?" I asked in my ordinary tone, speaking down to the face upturned exactly under mine.

"Cramp," it answered, no louder. Then slightly anxious, "I say, no need to call anyone."

"I was not going to," I said.

"Are you alone on deck?"

"Yes."

I had somehow the impression that he was on the point of letting go the ladder to swim away beyond my ken—mysterious as he came. But, for the moment, this being appearing as if he had risen from the bottom of the sea (it was certainly the nearest land to the ship) wanted only to know the time. I told him. And he, down there, tentatively:

"I suppose your captain's turned in?"

"I am sure he isn't," I said.

He seemed to struggle with himself, for I heard something like the low, bitter murmur of doubt. "What's the good?" His next words came out with a hesitating effort.

"Look here, my man. Could you call him out quietly?"

I thought the time had come to declare myself.

"*I* am the captain."

I heard a "By Jove!" whispered at the level of the water. The phosphorescence flashed in the swirl of the water all about his limbs, his other hand seized the ladder.

"My name's Leggatt."

The voice was calm and resolute. A good voice. The self-possession of that man had somehow induced a corresponding state in myself. It was very quietly that I remarked:

"You must be a good swimmer."

"Yes. I've been in the water practically since nine o'clock. The question for me now is whether I am to let go this ladder and go on swimming till I sink from exhaustion, or—to come on board here."

I felt this was no mere formula of desperate speech, but a real alternative in the view of a strong soul. I should have gathered from this that he was young; indeed, it is only the young who are ever confronted by such clear issues. But at the time it was pure intuition on my part. A mysterious communication was established already between us two—in the face of that silent, darkened tropical sea. I was young, too; young enough to make no comment. The man in the water began suddenly to climb up the ladder, and I hastened away from the rail to fetch some clothes.

Before entering the cabin I stood still, listening in the lobby at the foot of the stairs. A faint snore came through the closed door of the chief mate's room. The second mate's door was on the hook, but the darkness in there was absolutely soundless. He, too, was young and could sleep like a stone. Remained the steward, but he was not likely to wake up before he was called. I got a sleeping suit out of my room and, coming back on deck, saw the naked man from the sea sitting on the main hatch, glimmering white in the darkness, his elbows on his knees and his head in his hands. In a moment he had concealed his damp body in a sleeping suit of the same gray-stripe pattern as the one I was wearing and followed me like my double on the poop. Together we moved right aft, barefooted, silent.

"What is it?" I asked in a deadened voice, taking the lighted lamp out of the binnacle, and raising it to his face.

"An ugly business."

He had rather regular features; a good mouth; light eyes under somewhat heavy, dark eyebrows; a smooth, square forehead; no growth on his cheeks; a small, brown mustache, and a well-shaped, round chin. His expression was concentrated, meditative, under the inspecting light of the lamp I held up to his face; such as a man thinking hard in solitude might wear. My sleeping suit was just right for his size. A well-knit young fellow of twenty-five at most. He caught his lower lip with the edge of white, even teeth.

"Yes," I said, replacing the lamp in the binnacle. The warm, heavy tropical night closed upon his head again.

"There's a ship over there," he murmured.

"Yes, I know. The *Sephora*. Did you know of us?"

"Hadn't the slightest idea. I am the mate of her———" He paused and corrected himself. "I should say I *was*."

"Aha! Something wrong?"

"Yes. Very wrong indeed. I've killed a man."

"What do you mean? Just now?"

"No, on the passage. Weeks ago. Thirty-nine south. When I say a man———"

"Fit of temper," I suggested, confidently.

The shadowy, dark head, like mine, seemed to nod imperceptibly above the ghostly gray of my sleeping suit. It was, in the night, as though I had been faced by my own reflection in the depths of a somber and immense mirror.

"A pretty thing to have to own up to for a Conway boy," murmured my double, distinctly.

"You're a Conway boy?"

"I am," he said, as if startled. Then, slowly . . . "Perhaps you too———"

It was so; but being a couple of years older I had left before he joined. After a quick interchange of dates a silence
fell; and I thought suddenly of my absurd mate with his
terrific whiskers and the "Bless my soul—you don't say so"
type of intellect. My double gave me an inkling of his
thoughts by saying: "My father's a parson in Norfolk. Do
you see me before a judge and jury on that charge? For
myself I can't see the necessity. There are fellows that an
angel from heaven—— And I am not that. He was one of
those creatures that are just simmering all the time with a
silly sort of wickedness. Miserable devils that have no business
to live at all. He wouldn't do his duty and wouldn't let anybody else do theirs. But what's the good of talking! You know
well enough the sort of ill-conditioned snarling cur——"

He appealed to me as if our experiences had been as
identical as our clothes. And I knew well enough the
pestiferous danger of such a character where there are no
means of legal repression. And I knew well enough also that
my double there was no homicidal ruffian. I did not think
of asking him for details, and he told me the story roughly in
brusque, disconnected sentences. I needed no more. I saw it
all going on as though I were myself inside that other sleeping
suit.

"It happened while we were setting a reefed foresail, at
dusk. Reefed foresail! You understand the sort of weather.
The only sail we had left to keep the ship running; so you
may guess what it had been like for days. Anxious sort of
job, that. He gave me some of his cursed insolence at the
sheet. I tell you I was overdone with this terrific weather
that seemed to have no end to it. Terrific, I tell you—and a
deep ship. I believe the fellow himself was half crazed with
funk. It was no time for gentlemanly reproof, so I turned
round and felled him like an ox. He up and at me. We
closed just as an awful sea made for the ship. All hands saw
it coming and took to the rigging, but I had him by the
throat, and went on shaking him like a rat, the men above
us yelling, 'Look out! look out!' Then a crash as if the sky
had fallen on my head. They say that for over ten minutes
hardly anything was to be seen of the ship—just the three
masts and a bit of the forecastle head and of the poop all
awash driving along in a smother of foam. It was a miracle
that they found us, jammed together behind the forebitts.
It's clear that I meant business, because I was holding him
by the throat still when they picked us up. He was black

in the face. It was too much for them. It seems they rushed us aft together, gripped as we were, screaming 'Murder!' like a lot of lunatics, and broke into the cuddy. And the ship running for her life, touch and go all the time, any minute her last in a sea fit to turn your hair gray only a-looking at it. I understand that the skipper, too, started raving like the rest of them. The man had been deprived of sleep for more than a week, and to have this sprung on him at the height of a furious gale nearly drove him out of his mind. I wonder they didn't fling me overboard after getting the carcass of their precious shipmate out of my fingers. They had rather a job to separate us, I've been told. A sufficiently fierce story to make an old judge and a respectable jury sit up a bit. The first thing I heard when I came to myself was the maddening howling of that endless gale, and on that the voice of the old man. He was hanging on to my bunk, staring into my face out of his sou'wester.

" 'Mr. Leggatt, you have killed a man. You can act no longer as chief mate of this ship.' "

His care to subdue his voice made it sound monotonous. He rested a hand on the end of the skylight to steady himself with, and all that time did not stir a limb, so far as I could see. "Nice little tale for a quiet tea party," he concluded in the same tone.

One of my hands, too, rested on the end of the skylight; neither did I stir a limb, so far as I knew. We stood less than a foot from each other. It occurred to me that if old "Bless my soul—you don't say so" were to put his head up the companion and catch sight of us, he would think he was seeing double, or imagine himself come upon a scene of weird witchcraft; the strange captain having a quiet confabulation by the wheel with his own gray ghost. I became very much concerned to prevent anything of the sort. I heard the other's soothing undertone.

"My father's a parson in Norfolk," it said. Evidently he had forgotten he had told me this important fact before. Truly a nice little tale.

"You had better slip down into my stateroom now," I said, moving off stealthily. My double followed my movements; our bare feet made no sound; I let him in, closed the door with care, and, after giving a call to the second mate, returned on deck for my relief.

"Not much sign of any wind yet," I remarked when he approached.

"No, sir. Not much," he assented, sleepily, in his hoarse voice, with just enough deference, no more, and barely suppressing a yawn.

"Well, that's all you have to look out for. You have got your orders."

"Yes, sir."

I paced a turn or two on the poop and saw him take up his position face forward with his elbow in the ratlines of the mizzen rigging before I went below. The mate's faint snoring was still going on peacefully. The cuddy lamp was burning over the table on which stood a vase with flowers, a polite attention from the ship's provision merchant—the last flowers we should see for the next three months at the very least. Two bunches of bananas hung from the beam symmetrically, one on each side of the rudder casing. Everything was as before in the ship—except that two of her captain's sleeping suits were simultaneously in use, one motionless in the cuddy, the other keeping very still in the captain's stateroom.

It must be explained here that my cabin had the form of the capital letter L, the door being within the angle and opening into the short part of the letter. A couch was to the left, the bed placed to the right; my writing desk and the chronometers' table faced the door. But anyone opening it, unless he stepped right inside, had no view of what I call the long (or vertical) part of the letter. It contained some lockers surmounted by a bookcase; and a few clothes, a thick jacket or two, caps, oilskin coat, and such like, hung on hooks. There was at the bottom of that part a door opening into my bathroom, which could be entered also directly from the saloon. But that way was never used.

The mysterious arrival had discovered the advantage of this particular shape. Entering my room, lighted strongly by a big bulkhead lamp swung on gimbals above my writing desk, I did not see him anywhere till he stepped out quietly from behind the coats hung in the recessed part.

"I heard somebody moving about, and went in there at once," he whispered.

I, too, spoke under my breath.

"Nobody is likely to come in here without knocking and getting permission."

He nodded. His face was thin and the sunburn faded, as though he had been ill. And no wonder. He had been, I heard presently, kept under arrest in his cabin for nearly seven weeks. But there was nothing sickly in his eyes or in his expression. He was not a bit like me, really; yet, as we stood leaning over my bed place, whispering side by side, with our dark heads together and our backs to the door, anybody bold enough to open it stealthily would have been treated to the uncanny sight of a double captain busy talking in whispers with his other self.

"But all this doesn't tell me how you came to hang on to our side ladder," I inquired, in the hardly audible murmurs we used, after he had told me something more of the proceedings on board the *Sephora* once the bad weather was over.

"When we sighted Java Head I had had time to think all those matters out several times over. I had six weeks of doing nothing else, and with only an hour or so every evening for a tramp on the quarter-deck."

He whispered, his arms folded on the side of my bed place, staring through the open port. And I could imagine perfectly the manner of this thinking out—a stubborn if not a steadfast operation; something of which I should have been perfectly incapable.

"I reckoned it would be dark before we closed with the land," he continued, so low that I had to strain my hearing, near as we were to each other, shoulder touching shoulder almost. "So I asked to speak to the old man. He always seemed very sick when he came to see me—as if he could not look me in the face. You know, that foresail saved the ship. She was too deep to have run long under bare poles. And it was I that managed to set it for him. Anyway, he came. When I had him in my cabin—he stood by the door looking at me as if I had the halter round my neck already—I asked him right away to leave my cabin door unlocked at night while the ship was going through Sunda Straits. There would be the Java coast within two or three miles, off Angier Point. I wanted nothing more. I've had a prize for swimming my second year in the Conway."

"I can believe it," I breathed out.

"God only knows why they locked me in every night. To see some of their faces you'd have thought they were afraid I'd go about at night strangling people. Am I a murdering brute? Do I look it? By Jove! If I had been he wouldn't have trusted himself like that into my room. You'll say I might have chucked him aside and bolted out, there and then —it was dark already. Well, no. And for the same reason

I wouldn't think of trying to smash the door. There would
have been a rush to stop me at the noise, and I did not
mean to get into a confounded scrimmage. Somebody else
might have got killed—for I would not have broken out only
to get chucked back, and I did not want any more of that
work. He refused, looking more sick than ever. He was afraid
of the men, and also of that old second mate of his who had
been sailing with him for years—a gray-headed old humbug;
and his steward, too, had been with him devil knows how
long—seventeen years or more—a dogmatic sort of loafer
who hated me like poison, just because I was the chief mate.
No chief mate ever made more than one voyage in the
Sephora, you know. Those two old chaps ran the ship. Devil
only knows what the skipper wasn't afraid of (all his nerve
went to pieces altogether in that hellish spell of bad weather
we had)—of what the law would do to him—of his wife, perhaps. Oh, yes! she's on board. Though I don't think she would
have meddled. She would have been only too glad to have
me out of the ship in any way. The 'brand of Cain' business,
don't you see. That's all right. I was ready enough to go off
wandering on the face of the earth—and that was price enough
to pay for an Abel of that sort. Anyhow, he wouldn't listen
to me. 'This thing must take its course. I represent the law
here.' He was shaking like a leaf. 'So you won't?' 'No!' 'Then
I hope you will be able to sleep on that,' I said, and turned
my back on him. 'I wonder that *you* can,' cries he, and locks
the door.

"Well after that, I couldn't. Not very well. That was three
weeks ago. We have had a slow passage through the Java
Sea; drifted about Carimata for ten days. When we anchored
here they thought, I suppose, it was all right. The nearest
land (and that's five miles) is the ship's destination; the consul
would soon set about catching me; and there would have been
no object in bolting to these islets there. I don't suppose there's
a drop of water on them. I don't know how it was, but
tonight that steward, after bringing me my supper, went out to
let me eat it, and left the door unlocked. And I ate it—all
there was, too. After I had finished I strolled out on the
quarter-deck. I don't know that I meant to do anything. A
breath of fresh air was all I wanted, I believe. Then a sudden
temptation came over me. I kicked off my slippers and was
in the water before I had made up my mind fairly. Somebody
heard the splash and they raised an awful hullabaloo. 'He's
gone! Lower the boats! He's committed suicide! No, he's

swimming.' Certainly I was swimming. It's not so easy for a
swimmer like me to commit suicide by drowning. I landed
on the nearest islet before the boat left the ship's side. I
heard them pulling about in the dark, hailing, and so on,
but after a bit they gave up. Everything quieted down and the
anchorage became as still as death. I sat down on a stone
and began to think. I felt certain they would start searching
for me at daylight. There was no place to hide on those
stony things—and if there had been, what would have been
the good? But now I was clear of that ship, I was not
going back. So after a while I took off all my clothes, tied
them up in a bundle with a stone inside, and dropped them
in the deep water on the outer side of that islet. That was
suicide enough for me. Let them think what they liked, but
I didn't mean to drown myself. I meant to swim till I sank
—but that's not the same thing. I struck out for another of
these little islands, and it was from that one that I first saw
your riding light. Something to swim for. I went on easily,
and on the way I came upon a flat rock a foot or two
above water. In the daytime, I dare say, you might make
it out with a glass from your poop. I scrambled up on it
and rested myself for a bit. Then I made another start.
That last spell must have been over a mile."

His whisper was getting fainter and fainter, and all
the time he stared straight out through the porthole, in which
there was not even a star to be seen. I had not interrupted
him. There was something that made comment impossible
in his narrative, or perhaps in himself; a sort of feeling, a
quality, which I can't find a name for. And when he ceased,
all I found was a futile whisper: "So you swam for our light?"

"Yes—straight for it. It was something to swim for. I
couldn't see any stars low down because the coast was in
the way, and I couldn't see the land, either. The water was
like glass. One might have been swimming in a confounded
thousand-feet deep cistern with no place for scrambling out
anywhere; but what I didn't like was the notion of swimming
round and round like a crazed bullock before I gave out; and
as I didn't mean to go back . . . No. Do you see me being
hauled back, stark naked, off one of these little islands by
the scruff of the neck and fighting like a wild beast? Somebody would have got killed for certain, and I did not want
any of that. So I went on. Then your ladder——"

"Why didn't you hail the ship?" I asked, a little louder.
He touched my shoulder lightly. Lazy footsteps came right

over our heads and stopped. The second mate had crossed from the other side of the poop and might have been hanging over the rail for all we knew.

"He couldn't hear us talking—could he?" My double breathed into my very ear, anxiously.

His anxiety was in answer, a sufficient answer, to the question I had put to him. An answer containing all the difficulty of that situation. I closed the porthole quietly, to make sure. A louder word might have been overheard.

"Who's that?" he whispered then.

"My second mate. But I don't know much more of the fellow than you do."

And I told him a little about myself. I had been appointed to take charge while I least expected anything of the sort, not quite a fortnight ago. I didn't know either the ship or the people. Hadn't had the time in port to look about me or size anybody up. And as to the crew, all they knew was that I was appointed to take the ship home. For the rest, I was almost as much of a stranger on board as himself, I said. And at the moment I felt it most acutely. I felt that it would take very little to make me a suspect person in the eyes of the ship's company.

He had turned about meantime; and we, the two strangers in the ship, faced each other in identical attitudes.

"Your ladder——" he murmured, after a silence. "Who'd have thought of finding a ladder hanging over at night in a ship anchored out here! I felt just then a very unpleasant faintness. After the life I've been leading for nine weeks, anybody would have got out of condition. I wasn't capable of swimming round as far as your rudder chains. And, lo and behold! there was a ladder to get hold of. After I gripped it I said to myself, 'What's the good?' When I saw a man's head looking over I thought I would swim away presently and leave him shouting—in whatever language it was. I didn't mind being looked at. I—I liked it. And then you speaking to me so quietly—as if you had expected me—made me hold on a little longer. It had been a confounded lonely time—I don't mean while swimming. I was glad to talk a little to somebody that didn't belong to the *Sephora*. As to asking for the captain, that was a mere impulse. It could have been no use, with all the ship knowing about me and the other people pretty certain to be round here in the morning. I don't know—I wanted to be seen, to talk with somebody, before I went on. I don't know what I would have said. . . . 'Fine night, isn't it?' or something of the sort."

"Do you think they will be round here presently?" I asked with some incredulity.

"Quite likely," he said, faintly.

He looked extremely haggard all of a sudden. His head rolled on his shoulders.

"H'm. We shall see then. Meantime get into that bed," I whispered. "Want help? There."

It was a rather high bed place with a set of drawers underneath. This amazing swimmer really needed the lift I gave him by seizing his leg. He tumbled in, rolled over on his back, and flung one arm across his eyes. And then, with his face nearly hidden, he must have looked exactly as I used to look in that bed. I gazed upon my other self for a while before drawing across carefully the two green serge curtains which ran on a brass rod. I thought for a moment of pinning them together for greater safety, but I sat down on the couch, and once there I felt unwilling to rise and hunt for a pin. I would do it in a moment. I was extremely tired, in a peculiarly intimate way, by the strain of stealthiness, by the effort of whispering and the general secrecy of this excitement. It was three o'clock by now and I had been on my feet since nine, but I was not sleepy; I could not have gone to sleep. I sat there, fagged out, looking at the curtains, trying to clear my mind of the confused sensation of being in two places at once, and greatly bothered by an exasperating knocking in my head. It was a relief to discover suddenly that it was not in my head at all, but on the outside of the door. Before I could collect myself the words "Come in" were out of my mouth, and the steward entered with a tray, bringing in my morning coffee. I had slept, after all, and I was so frightened that I shouted, "This way! I am here, steward," as though he had been miles away. He put down the tray on the table next the couch and only then said, very quietly, "I can see you are here, sir." I felt him give me a keen look, but I dared not meet his eyes just then. He must have wondered why I had drawn the curtains of my bed before going to sleep on the couch. He went out, hooking the door open as usual.

I heard the crew washing decks above me. I knew I would have been told at once if there had been any wind. Calm, I thought, and I was doubly vexed. Indeed, I felt dual more than ever. The steward reappeared suddenly in the doorway, I jumped up from the couch so quickly that he gave a start.

"What do you want here?"

"Close your port, sir—they are washing decks."

"It is closed," I said, reddening.

"Very well, sir." But he did not move from the doorway and returned my stare in an extraordinary, equivocal manner for a time. Then his eyes wavered, all his expression changed, and in a voice unusually gentle, almost coaxingly:

"May I come in to take the empty cup away, sir?"

"Of course!" I turned my back on him while he popped in and out. Then I unhooked and closed the door and even pushed the bolt. This sort of thing could not go on very long. The cabin was as hot as an oven, too. I took a peep at my double, and discovered that he had not moved, his arm was still over his eyes; but his chest heaved; his hair was wet; his chin glistened with perspiration. I reached over him and opened the port.

"I must show myself on deck," I reflected.

Of course, theoretically, I could do what I liked, with no one to say nay to me within the whole circle of the horizon; but to lock my cabin door and take the key away I did not dare. Directly I put my head out of the companion I saw the group of my two officers, the second mate barefooted, the chief mate in long India-rubber boots, near the break of the poop, and the steward halfway down the poop ladder talking to them eagerly. He happened to catch sight of me and dived, the second ran down on the main-deck shouting some order or other, and the chief mate came to meet me, touching his cap.

There was a sort of curiosity in his eye that I did not like. I don't know whether the steward had told them that I was "queer" only, or downright drunk, but I know the man meant to have a good look at me. I watched him coming with a smile which, as he got into point-blank range, took effect and froze his very whiskers. I did not give him time to open his lips.

"Square the yards by lifts and braces before the hands go to breakfast."

It was the first particular order I had given on board that ship; and I stayed on deck to see it executed, too. I had felt the need of asserting myself without loss of time. That sneering young cub got taken down a peg or two on that occasion, and I also seized the opportunity of having a good look at the face of every foremast man as they filed past me to go to the after braces. At breakfast time, eating nothing myself,

I presided with such frigid dignity that the two mates were only too glad to escape from the cabin as soon as decency permitted; and all the time the dual working of my mind distracted me almost to the point of insanity. I was constantly watching myself, my secret self, as dependent on my actions as my own personality, sleeping in that bed, behind that door which faced me as I sat at the head of the table. It was very much like being mad, only it was worse because one was aware of it.

I had to shake him for a solid minute, but when at last he opened his eyes it was in the full possession of his senses, with an inquiring look.

"All's well so far," I whispered. "Now you must vanish into the bathroom."

He did so, as noiseless as a ghost, and then I rang for the steward, and facing him boldly, directed him to tidy up my stateroom while I was having my bath—"and be quick about it." As my tone admitted of no excuses, he said, "Yes, sir," and ran off to fetch his dustpan and brushes. I took a bath and did most of my dressing, splashing, and whistling softly for the steward's edification, while the secret sharer of my life stood drawn up bolt upright in that little space, his face looking very sunken in daylight, his eyelids lowered under the stern, dark line of his eyebrows drawn together by a slight frown.

When I left him there to go back to my room the steward was finishing dusting. I sent for the mate and engaged him in some insignificant conversation. It was, as it were, trifling with the terrific character of his whiskers; but my object was to give him an opportunity for a good look at my cabin. And then I could at last shut, with a clear conscience, the door of my stateroom and get my double back into the recessed part. There was nothing else for it. He had to sit still on a small folding stool, half smothered by the heavy coats hanging there. We listened to the steward going into the bathroom out of the saloon, filling the water bottles there, scrubbing the bath, setting things to rights, whisk, bang, clatter—out again into the saloon—turn the key—click. Such was my scheme for keeping my second self invisible. Nothing better could be contrived under the circumstances. And there we sat; I at my writing desk ready to appear busy with some papers, he behind me out of sight of the door. It would not have been prudent to talk in daytime; and I could not have stood the excitement of that queer sense of whispering to myself. Now and then, glancing over my shoulder, I saw him far back there, sitting rigidly on the low stool, his bare feet close together, his arms folded, his head hanging on his breast—and perfectly still. Anybody would have taken him for me.

I was fascinated by it myself. Every moment I had to glance over my shoulder. I was looking at him when a voice outside the door said:

"Beg pardon, sir."

"Well!" . . . I kept my eyes on him, and so when the voice outside the door announced, "There's a ship's boat coming our way, sir," I saw him give a start—the first movement he had made for hours. But he did not raise his bowed head.

"All right. Get the ladder over."

I hesitated. Should I whisper something to him? But what? His immobility seemed to have been never disturbed. What could I tell him he did not know already? . . . Finally I went on deck.

II

The skipper of the *Sephora* had a thin red whisker all round his face, and the sort of complexion that goes with hair of that color; also the particular, rather smeary shade of blue in the eyes. He was not exactly a showy figure; his shoulders were high, his stature but middling—one leg slightly more bandy than the other. He shook hands, looking vaguely around. A spiritless tenacity was his main characteristic, I judged. I behaved with a politeness which seemed to disconcert him. Perhaps he was shy. He mumbled to me as if he were ashamed of what he was saying; gave his name (it was something like Archbold—but at this distance of years I hardly am sure), his ship's name, and a few other particulars of that sort, in the manner of a criminal making a reluctant and doleful confession. He had had terrible weather on the passage out—terrible—terrible—wife aboard, too.

By this time we were seated in the cabin and the steward brought in a tray with a bottle and glasses. "Thanks! No." Never took liquor. Would have some water, though. He drank two tumblerfuls. Terrible thirsty work. Ever since daylight had been exploring the islands round his ship.

"What was that for—fun?" I asked, with an appearance of polite interest.

"No!" He sighed. "Painful duty."

As he persisted in his mumbling and I wanted my double to hear every word, I hit upon the notion of informing him that I regretted to say I was hard of hearing.

"Such a young man, too!" he nodded, keeping his smeary blue, unintelligent eyes fastened upon me. "What was the cause of it—some disease?" he inquired, without the least sympathy and as if he thought that, if so, I'd got no more than I deserved.

"Yes; disease," I admitted in a cheerful tone which seemed to shock him. But my point was gained, because he had to raise his voice to give me his tale. It is not worth while to record that version. It was just over two months since all this had happened, and he had thought so much about it that he seemed completely muddled as to its bearings, but still immensely impressed.

"What would you think of such a thing happening on board your own ship? I've had the *Sephora* for these fifteen years. I am a well-known shipmaster."

He was densely distressed—and perhaps I should have sympathized with him if I had been able to detach my mental vision from the unsuspected sharer of my cabin as though he were my second self. There he was on the other side of the bulkhead, four or five feet from us, no more, as we sat in the saloon. I looked politely at Captain Archbold (if that was his name), but it was the other I saw, in a gray sleeping suit, seated on a low stool, his bare feet close together, his arms folded, and every word said between us falling into the ears of his dark head bowed on his chest.

"I have been at sea now, man and boy, for seven-and-thirty years, and I've never heard of such a thing happening in an English ship. And that it should be my ship. Wife on board, too."

I was hardly listening to him.

"Don't you think," I said, "that the heavy sea which, you told me, came aboard just then might have killed the man? I have seen the sheer weight of a sea kill a man very neatly, by simply breaking his neck."

"Good God!" he uttered, impressively, fixing his smeary blue eyes on me. "The sea! No man killed by the sea ever looked like that." He seemed positively scandalized at my suggestion. And as I gazed at him certainly not prepared for anything original on his part, he advanced his head close to mine and thrust his tongue out at me so suddenly that I couldn't help starting back.

After scoring over my calmness in this graphic way he nodded wisely. If I had seen the sight, he assured me, I would never forget it as long as I lived. The weather was too bad to give the corpse a proper sea burial. So next day at dawn they took it up on the poop, covering its face with a bit of bunting; he read a short prayer, and then, just as it was, in its oilskins and long boots, they launched it amongst those mountainous seas that seemed ready every moment to swallow up the ship herself and the terrified lives on board of her.

"That reefed foresail saved you," I threw in.

"Under God—it did," he exclaimed fervently. "It was by a special mercy, I firmly believe, that it stood some of those hurricane squalls."

"It was the setting of that sail which——" I began.

"God's own hand in it," he interrupted me. "Nothing less could have done it. I don't mind telling you that I hardly dared give the order. It seemed impossible that we could touch anything without losing it, and then our last hope would have been gone."

The terror of that gale was on him yet. I let him go on for a bit, then said, casually—as if returning to a minor subject:

"You were very anxious to give up your mate to the shore people, I believe?"

He was. To the law. His obscure tenacity on that point had in it something incomprehensible and a little awful; something, as it were, mystical, quite apart from his anxiety that he should not be suspected of "countenancing any doings of that sort." Seven-and-thirty virtuous years at sea, of which over twenty of immaculate command, and the last fifteen in the *Sephora,* seemed to have laid him under some pitiless obligation.

"And you know," he went on, groping shame-facedly amongst his feelings, "I did not engage that young fellow. His people had some interest with my owners. I was in a way forced to take him on. He looked very smart, very gentlemanly, and all that. But do you know—I never liked him, somehow. I am a plain man. You see, he wasn't exactly the sort for the chief mate of a ship like the *Sephora.*"

I had become so connected in thoughts and impressions with the secret sharer of my cabin that I felt as if I, personally,

were being given to understand that I, too, was not the sort
that would have done for the chief mate of a ship like the
Sephora. I had no doubt of it in my mind.

"Not at all the style of man. You understand," he insisted,
superfluously, looking hard at me.

I smiled urbanely. He seemed at a loss for a while.

"I suppose I must report a suicide."

"Beg pardon?"

"Sui-cide! That's what I'll have to write to my owners
directly I get in."

"Unless you manage to recover him before tomorrow," I
assented, dispassionately. . . . "I mean, alive."

He mumbled something which I really did not catch, and
I turned my ear to him in a puzzled manner. He fairly
bawled:

"The land—I say, the mainland is at least seven miles off
my anchorage."

"About that."

My lack of excitement, of curiosity, of surprise, of any
sort of pronounced interest, began to arouse his distrust. But
except for the felicitous pretense of deafness I had not tried
to pretend anything. I had felt utterly incapable of playing
the part of ignorance properly, and therefore was afraid to
try. It is also certain that he had brought some ready-made
suspicions with him, and that he viewed my politeness as a
strange and unnatural phenomenon. And yet how else could
I have received him? Not heartily! That was impossible for
psychological reasons, which I need not state here. My only
object was to keep off his inquiries. Surlily? Yes, but surliness
might have provoked a point-blank question. From its novelty
to him and from its nature, punctilious courtesy was the
manner best calculated to restrain the man. But there was
the danger of his breaking through my defense bluntly. I
could not, I think, have met him by a direct lie, also for
psychological (not moral) reasons. If he had only known
how afraid I was of his putting my feeling of identity with
the other to the test! But, strangely enough—(I thought of
it only afterwards)—I believe that he was not a little dis-
concerted by the reverse side of that weird situation, by
something in me that reminded him of the man he was
seeking—suggested a mysterious similitude to the young fellow he had distrusted and disliked from the first.

However that might have been, the silence was not very
prolonged. He took another oblique step.

"I reckon I had no more than a two-mile pull to your ship. Not a bit more."

"And quite enough, too, in this awful heat," I said.

Another pause full of mistrust followed. Necessity, they say, is mother of invention, but fear, too, is not barren of ingenious suggestions. And I was afraid he would ask me point-blank for news of my other self.

"Nice little saloon, isn't it?" I remarked, as if noticing for the first time the way his eyes roamed from one closed door to the other. "And very well fitted out, too. Here, for instance," I continued, reaching over the back of my seat negligently and flinging the door open, "is my bathroom."

He made an eager movement, but hardly gave it a glance. I got up, shut the door of the bathroom, and invited him to have a look round, as if I were very proud of my accommodation. He had to rise and be shown round, but he went through the business without any raptures whatever.

"And now we'll have a look at my stateroom," I declared, in a voice as loud as I dared to make it, crossing the cabin to the starboard side with purposely heavy steps.

He followed me in and gazed around. My intelligent double had vanished. I played my part.

"Very convenient—isn't it?"

"Very nice. Very comf . . ." He didn't finish and went out brusquely as if to escape from some unrighteous wiles of mine. But it was not to be. I had been too frightened not to feel vengeful; I felt I had him on the run, and I meant to keep him on the run. My polite insistence must have had something menacing in it, because he gave in suddenly. And I did not let him off a single item; mate's room, pantry, storerooms, the very sail locker which was also under the poop—he had to look into them all. When at last I showed him out on the quarter-deck he drew a long, spiritless sigh, and mumbled dismally that he must really be going back to his ship now. I desired my mate, who had joined us, to see to the captain's boat.

The man of whiskers gave a blast on the whistle which he used to wear hanging round his neck, and yelled, "*Sephora*'s away!" My double down there in my cabin must have heard, and certainly could not feel more relieved than I. Four fellows came running out from somewhere forward and went over the side, while my own men, appearing on deck too, lined the rail. I escorted my visitor to the gangway ceremoniously, and nearly overdid it. He was a tenacious beast. On the very ladder he lingered, and in that unique, guiltily conscientious manner of sticking to the point:

"I say . . . you . . . you don't think that——"

I covered his voice loudly:

"Certainly not. . . . I am delighted. Good-by."

I had an idea of what he meant to say, and just saved myself by the privilege of defective hearing. He was too shaken generally to insist, but my mate, close witness of that parting, looked mystified and his face took on a thoughtful cast. As I did not want to appear as if I wished to avoid all communication with my officers, he had the opportunity to address me.

"Seems a very nice man. His boat's crew told our chaps a very extraordinary story, if what I am told by the steward is true. I suppose you had it from the captain, sir?"

"Yes. I had a story from the captain."

"A very horrible affair—isn't it, sir?"

"It is."

"Beats all these tales we hear about murders in Yankee ships."

"I don't think it beats them. I don't think it resembles them in the least."

"Bless my soul—you don't say so! But of course I've no acquaintance whatever with American ships, not I, so I couldn't go against your knowledge. It's horrible enough for me. . . . But the queerest part is that those fellows seemed to have some idea the man was hidden aboard here. They had really. Did you ever hear of such a thing?"

"Preposterous—isn't it?"

We were walking to and fro athwart the quarter-deck. No one of the crew forward could be seen (the day was Sunday), and the mate pursued:

"There was some little dispute about it. Our chaps took offense. 'As if we would harbor a thing like that,' they said. 'Wouldn't you like to look for him in our coalhole?' Quite a tiff. But they made it up in the end. I suppose he did drown himself. Don't you, sir?"

"I don't suppose anything."

"You have no doubt in the matter, sir?"

"None whatever."

I left him suddenly. I felt I was producing a bad impression, but with my double down there it was most trying to be on deck. And it was almost as trying to be below. Altogether a nerve-trying situation. But on the whole I felt less

torn in two when I was with him. There was no one in the
whole ship whom I dared take into my confidence. Since
the hands had got to know his story, it would have been impossible to pass him off for anyone else, and an accidental
discovery was to be dreaded now more than ever. . . .

The steward being engaged in laying the table for dinner,
we could talk only with our eyes when I first went down.
Later in the afternoon we had a cautious try at whispering.
The Sunday quietness of the ship was against us; the stillness
of air and water around her was against us; the elements,
the men were against us—everything was against us in our
secret partnership; time itself—for this could not go on forever. The very trust in Providence was, I suppose, denied to
his guilt. Shall I confess that this thought cast me down very
much? And as to the chapter of accidents which counts for
so much in the book of success, I could only hope that it
was closed. For what favorable accident could be expected?

"Did you hear everything?" were my first words as soon
as we took up our position side by side, leaning over my bed
place.

He had. And the proof of it was his earnest whisper, "The
man told you he hardly dared to give the order."

I understood the reference to be to that saving foresail.

"Yes. He was afraid of it being lost in the setting."

"I assure you he never gave the order. He may think he
did, but he never gave it. He stood there with me on the
break of the poop after the main topsail blew away, and
whimpered about our last hope—positively whimpered about
it and nothing else—and the night coming on! To hear one's
skipper go on like that in such weather was enough to drive
any fellow out of his mind. It worked me up into a sort of
desperation. I just took it into my own hands and went away
from him, boiling, and—— But what's the use telling you?
You know! . . . Do you think that if I had not been pretty
fierce with them I should have got the men to do anything?
Not I! The bo's'n perhaps? Perhaps! It wasn't a heavy sea
—it was a sea gone mad! I suppose the end of the world will
be something like that; and a man may have the heart to see
it coming once and be done with it—but to have to face it
day after day—— I don't blame anybody. I was precious little
better than the rest. Only—I was an officer of that old coal
wagon, anyhow——"

"I quite understand," I conveyed that sincere assurance into
his ear. He was out of breath with whispering; I could hear

him pant slightly. It was all very simple. The same strung-up force which had given twenty-four men a chance, at least, for their lives, had, in a sort of recoil, crushed an unworthy mutinous existence.

But I had no leisure to weigh the merits of the matter—footsteps in the saloon, a heavy knock. "There's enough wind to get under way with, sir." Here was the call of a new claim upon my thoughts and even upon my feelings.

"Turn the hands up," I cried through the door. "I'll be on deck directly."

I was going out to make the acquaintance of my ship. Before I left the cabin our eyes met—the eyes of the only two strangers on board. I pointed to the recessed part where the little campstool awaited him and laid my finger on my lips. He made a gesture—somewhat vague—a little mysterious, accompanied by a faint smile, as if of regret.

This is not the place to enlarge upon the sensations of a man who feels for the first time a ship move under his feet to his own independent word. In my case they were not unalloyed. I was not wholly alone with my command; for there was that stranger in my cabin. Or rather, I was not completely and wholly with her. Part of me was absent. That mental feeling of being in two places at once affected me physically as if the mood of secrecy had penetrated my very soul. Before an hour had elapsed since the ship had begun to move, having occasion to ask the mate (he stood by my side) to take a compass bearing of the pagoda, I caught myself reaching up to his ear in whispers. I say I caught myself, but enough had escaped to startle the man. I can't describe it otherwise than by saying that he shied. A grave, preoccupied manner, as though he were in possession of some perplexing intelligence, did not leave him henceforth. A little later I moved away from the rail to look at the compass with such a stealthy gait that the helmsman noticed it—and I could not help noticing the unusual roundness of his eyes. These are trifling instances, though it's to no commander's advantage to be suspected of ludicrous eccentricities. But I was also more seriously affected. There are to a seaman certain words, gestures, that should in given conditions come as naturally, as instinctively as the winking of a menaced eye. A certain order should spring on to his lips without thinking; a certain sign should get itself made, so to speak, without reflection. But all unconscious alertness had abandoned me. I had to make an effort of will to recall myself back (from the cabin) to the conditions of the moment. I felt that I was appearing an irresolute commander to those people who were watching me more or less critically.

And, besides, there were the scares. On the second day out, for instance, coming off the deck in the afternoon (I had straw slippers on my bare feet) I stopped at the open pantry door and spoke to the steward. He was doing something there with his back to me. At the sound of my voice he nearly jumped out of his skin, as the saying is, and incidentally broke a cup.

"What on earth's the matter with you?" I asked, astonished.

He was extremely confused. "Beg your pardon, sir. I made sure you were in your cabin."

"You see I wasn't."

"No, sir. I could have sworn I had heard you moving in there not a moment ago. It's most extraordinary . . . very sorry, sir."

I passed on with an inward shudder. I was so identified with my secret double that I did not even mention the fact in those scanty, fearful whispers we exchanged. I suppose he had made some slight noise of some kind or other. It would have been miraculous if he hadn't at one time or another. And yet, haggard as he appeared, he looked always perfectly self-controlled, more than calm—almost invulnerable. On my suggestion he remained almost entirely in the bathroom, which, upon the whole, was the safest place. There could be really no shadow of an excuse for anyone ever wanting to go in there, once the steward had done with it. It was a very tiny place. Sometimes he reclined on the floor, his legs bent, his head sustained on one elbow. At others I would find him on the campstool, sitting in his gray sleeping suit and with his cropped dark hair like a patient, unmoved convict. At night I would smuggle him into my bed place, and we would whisper together, with the regular footfalls of the officer of the watch passing and repassing over our heads. It was an infinitely miserable time. It was lucky that some tins of fine preserves were stowed in a locker in my stateroom; hard bread I could always get hold of; and so he lived on stewed chicken, *pâté de foie gras*, asparagus, cooked oysters, sardines—on all sorts of abominable sham delicacies out of tins. My early-morning coffee he always drank; and it was all I dared do for him in that respect.

Every day there was the horrible maneuvering to go through so that my room and then the bathroom should be done in the usual way. I came to hate the sight of the steward, to abhor the voice of that harmless man. I felt that it was he who would bring on the disaster of discovery. It hung like a sword over our heads.

The fourth day out, I think (we were then working down the east side of the Gulf of Siam, tack for tack, in light winds and smooth water)—the fourth day, I say, of this miserable juggling with the unavoidable, as we sat at our evening meal, that man, whose slightest movement I dreaded, after putting down the dishes ran up on deck busily. This could not be dangerous. Presently he came down again; and then it appeared that he had remembered a coat of mine which I had thrown over a rail to dry after having been wetted in a shower which had passed over the ship in the afternoon. Sitting stolidly at the head of the table I became terrified at the sight of the garment on his arm. Of course he made for my door. There was no time to lose.

"Steward," I thundered. My nerves were so shaken that I could not govern my voice and conceal my agitation. This was the sort of thing that made my terrifically whiskered mate tap his forehead with his forefinger. I had detected him using that gesture while talking on deck with a confidential air to the carpenter. It was too far to hear a word, but I had no doubt that this pantomime could only refer to the strange new captain.

"Yes, sir," the pale-faced steward turned resignedly to me. It was this maddening course of being shouted at, checked without rhyme or reason, arbitrarily chased out of my cabin, suddenly called into it, sent flying out of his pantry on incomprehensible errands, that accounted for the growing wretchedness of his expression.

"Where are you going with that coat?"

"To your room, sir."

"Is there another shower coming?"

"I'm sure I don't know, sir. Shall I go up again and see, sir?"

"No! never mind."

My object was attained, as of course my other self in there would have heard everything that passed. During this interlude my two officers never raised their eyes off their respective plates; but the lip of that confounded cub, the second mate, quivered visibly.

I expected the steward to hook my coat on and come out at once. He was very slow about it; but I dominated my nervousness sufficiently not to shout after him. Suddenly I became aware (it could be heard plainly enough) that the fellow for some reason or other was opening the door of the bathroom. It was the end. The place was literally not big enough to swing a cat in. My voice died in my throat and I went stony all over. I expected to hear a yell of surprise and terror, and made a movement, but had not the strength to get on my legs. Everything remained still. Had my second self taken the poor wretch by the throat? I don't know what I could have done next moment if I had not seen the steward come out of my room, close the door, and then stand quietly by the sideboard.

"Saved," I thought. "But, no! Lost! Gone! He was gone!"

I laid my knife and fork down and leaned back in my chair. My head swam. After a while, when sufficiently recovered to speak in a steady voice, I instructed my mate to put the ship round at eight o'clock himself.

"I won't come on deck," I went on. "I think I'll turn in, and unless the wind shifts I don't want to be disturbed before midnight. I feel a bit seedy."

"You did look middling bad a little while ago," the chief mate remarked without showing any great concern.

They both went out, and I stared at the steward clearing the table. There was nothing to be read on that wretched man's face. But why did he avoid my eyes, I asked myself. Then I thought I should like to hear the sound of his voice.

"Steward!"

"Sir!" Startled as usual.

"Where did you hang up that coat?"

"In the bathroom, sir." The usual anxious tone. "It's not quite dry yet, sir."

For some time longer I sat in the cuddy. Had my double vanished as he had come? But of his coming there was an explanation, whereas his disappearance would be inexplicable. . . . I went slowly into my dark room, shut the door, lighted the lamp, and for a time dared not turn round. When at last I did I saw him standing bolt-upright in the narrow recessed part. It would not be true to say I had a shock, but an irresistible doubt of his bodily existence flitted through my mind. Can it be, I asked myself, that he is not visible to other eyes than mine? It was like being haunted. Motionless, with a grave face, he raised his hands slightly at me in a gesture which meant clearly, "Heavens! what a narrow escape!" Narrow indeed. I think I had come creeping quietly as near insanity as any man who has not actually gone over the border. That gesture restrained me, so to speak.

The mate with the terrific whiskers was now putting the ship on the other tack. In the moment of profound silence which follows upon the hands going to their stations I heard on the poop his raised voice: "Hard alee!" and the distant shout of the order repeated on the main-deck. The sails, in that light breeze, made but a faint fluttering noise. It ceased. The ship was coming round slowly: I held my breath in the renewed stillness of expectation; one wouldn't have thought that there was a single living soul on her decks. A sudden brisk shout, "Mainsail haul!" broke the spell, and in the noisy cries and rush overhead of the men running away with the main brace we two, down in my cabin, came together in our usual position by the bed place.

He did not wait for my question. "I heard him fumbling here and just managed to squat myself down in the bath," he whispered to me. "The fellow only opened the door and put his arm in to hang the coat up. All the same——"

"I never thought of that," I whispered back, even more appalled than before at the closeness of the shave, and marveling at that something unyielding in his character which was carrying him through so finely. There was no agitation in his whisper. Whoever was being driven distracted, it was not he. He was sane. And the proof of his sanity was continued when he took up the whispering again.

"It would never do for me to come to life again."

It was something that a ghost might have said. But what he was alluding to was his old captain's reluctant admission of the theory of suicide. It would obviously serve his turn—if I had understood at all the view which seemed to govern the unalterable purpose of his action.

"You must maroon me as soon as ever you can get amongst these islands off the Cambodge shore," he went on.

"Maroon you! We are not living in a boy's adventure tale," I protested. His scornful whispering took me up.

"We aren't indeed! There's nothing of a boy's tale in this. But there's nothing else for it. I want no more. You don't suppose I am afraid of what can be done to me? Prison or gallows or whatever they may please. But you don't see me coming back to explain such things to an old fellow in a wig and twelve respectable tradesmen, do you? What can they know whether I am guilty or not—or of *what* I am guilty, either? That's my affair. What does the Bible say? 'Driven

off the face of the earth.' Very well, I am off the face of
the earth now. As I came at night so I shall go."

"Impossible!" I murmured. "You can't."

"Can't? . . . Not naked like a soul on the Day of Judgment.
I shall freeze on to this sleeping suit. The Last Day is not
yet—and . . . you have understood thoroughly. Didn't you?"

I felt suddenly ashamed of myself. I may say truly that
I understood—and my hesitation in letting that man swim
away from my ship's side had been a mere sham sentiment,
a sort of cowardice.

"It can't be done now till next night," I breathed out.
"The ship is on the off-shore tack and the wind may fail us."

"As long as I know that you understand," he whispered.
"But of course you do. It's a great satisfaction to have got
somebody to understand. You seem to have been there on
purpose." And in the same whisper, as if we two whenever
we talked had to say things to each other which were not fit
for the world to hear, he added, "It's very wonderful."

We remained side by side talking in our secret way—but
sometimes silent or just exchanging a whispered word or two
at long intervals. And as usual he stared through the port.
A breath of wind came now and again into our faces. The
ship might have been moored in dock, so gently and on an
even keel she slipped through the water, that did not murmur
even at our passage, shadowy and silent like a phantom sea.

At midnight I went on deck, and to my mate's great surprise put the ship round on the other tack. His terrible whiskers flitted round me in silent criticism. I certainly should
not have done it if it had been only a question of getting
out of that sleepy gulf as quickly as possible. I believe he told
the second mate, who relieved him, that it was a great want
of judgment. The other only yawned. That intolerable cub
shuffled about so sleepily and lolled against the rails in such
a slack, improper fashion that I came down on him sharply.

"Aren't you properly awake yet?"

"Yes, sir! I am awake."

"Well, then, be good enough to hold yourself as if you
were. And keep a lookout. If there's any current we'll be
closing with some islands before daylight."

The east side of the gulf is fringed with islands, some solitary, others in groups. On the blue background of the high
coast they seem to float on silvery patches of calm water,
arid and gray, or dark green and rounded like clumps of
evergreen bushes, with the larger ones, a mile or two long,

showing the outlines of ridges, ribs of gray rock under the dank mantle of matted leafage. Unknown to trade, to travel, almost to geography, the manner of life they harbor is an unsolved secret. There must be villages—settlements of fishermen at least—on the largest of them, and some communication with the world is probably kept up by native craft. But all that forenoon, as we headed for them, fanned along by the faintest of breezes, I saw no sign of man or canoe in the field of the telescope I kept on pointing at the scattered group.

At noon I gave no orders for a change of course, and the mate's whiskers became much concerned and seemed to be offering themselves unduly to my notice. At last I said:

"I am going to stand right in. Quite in—as far as I can take her."

The stare of extreme surprise imparted an air of ferocity also to his eyes, and he looked truly terrific for a moment.

"We're not doing well in the middle of the gulf," I continued, casually. "I am going to look for the land breezes tonight."

"Bless my soul! Do you mean, sir, in the dark amongst the lot of all them islands and reefs and shoals?"

"Well—if there are any regular land breezes at all on this coast one must get close inshore to find them, mustn't one?"

"Bless my soul!" he exclaimed again under his breath. All that afternoon he wore a dreamy, contemplative appearance which in him was a mark of perplexity. After dinner I went into my stateroom as if I meant to take some rest. There we two bent our dark heads over a half-unrolled chart lying on my bed.

"There," I said. "It's got to be Koh-ring. I've been looking at it ever since sunrise. It has got two hills and a low point. It must be inhabited. And on the coast opposite there is what looks like the mouth of a biggish river—with some towns, no doubt, not far up. It's the best chance for you that I can see."

"Anything. Koh-ring let it be."

He looked thoughtfully at the chart as if surveying chances and distances from a lofty height—and following with his eyes his own figure wandering on the blank land of Cochin-China, and then passing off that piece of paper clean out of sight into uncharted regions. And it was as if the ship had two captains to plan her course for her. I had been so worried and restless running up and down that I had not had the patience to dress that day. I had remained in my sleeping suit, with straw slippers and a soft floppy hat. The closeness of the heat in the gulf had been most oppressive, and the crew were used to seeing me wandering in that airy attire.

"She will clear the south point as she heads now," I whispered into his ear. "Goodness only knows when, though, but certainly after dark. I'll edge her in to half a mile, as far as I may be able to judge in the dark——"

"Be careful," he murmured, warningly—and I realized suddenly that all my future, the only future for which I was fit, would perhaps go irretrievably to pieces in any mishap to my first command.

I could not stop a moment longer in the room. I motioned him to get out of sight and made my way on the poop. That unplayful cub had the watch. I walked up and down for a while thinking things out, then beckoned him over.

"Send a couple of hands to open the two quarter-deck ports," I said, mildly.

He actually had the impudence, or else so forgot himself in his wonder at such an incomprehensible order, as to repeat:

"Open the quarter-deck ports! What for, sir?"

"The only reason you need concern yourself about is because I tell you to do so. Have them open wide and fastened properly."

He reddened and went off, but I believe made some jeering remark to the carpenter as to the sensible practice of ventilating a ship's quarter-deck. I know he popped into the mate's cabin to impart the fact to him because the whiskers came on deck, as it were by chance, and stole glances at me from below—for signs of lunacy or drunkenness, I suppose.

A little before supper, feeling more restless than ever, I rejoined, for a moment, my second self. And to find him sitting so quietly was surprising, like something against nature, inhuman.

I developed my plan in a hurried whisper.

"I shall stand in as close as I dare and then put her round. I will presently find means to smuggle you out of here into the sail locker, which communicates with the lobby. But there is an opening, a sort of square for hauling the sails out, which gives straight on the quarter-deck and which is never closed in fine weather, so as to give air to the sails. When the ship's way is deadened in stays and all the hands are aft at the main braces you will have a clear road to slip out and get overboard through the open quarter-deck port. I've had them both fastened up. Use a rope's end to lower your-self into the water so as to avoid a splash—you know. It could be heard and cause some beastly complication."

He kept silent for a while, then whispered, "I understand."

"I won't be there to see you go," I began with an effort. "The rest . . . I only hope I have understood, too."

"You have. From first to last"—and for the first time there seemed to be a faltering, something strained in his whisper. He caught hold of my arm, but the ringing of the supper bell made me start. He didn't though; he only released his grip.

After supper I didn't come below again till well past eight o'clock. The faint, steady breeze was loaded with dew; and the wet, darkened sails held all there was of propelling power in it. The night, clear and starry, sparkled darkly, and the opaque, lightless patches shifting slowly against the low stars were the drifting islets. On the port bow there was a big one more distant and shadowily imposing by the great space of sky it eclipsed.

On opening the door I had a back view of my very own self looking at a chart. He had come out of the recess and was standing near the table.

"Quite dark enough," I whispered.

He stepped back and leaned against my bed with a level, quiet glance. I sat on the couch. We had nothing to say to each other. Over our heads the officer of the watch moved here and there. Then I heard him move quickly. I knew what that meant. He was making for the companion; and presently his voice was outside my door.

"We are drawing in pretty fast, sir. Land looks rather close."

"Very well," I answered. "I am coming on deck directly."

I waited till he was gone out of the cuddy, then rose. My double moved too. The time had come to exchange our last whispers, for neither of us was ever to hear each other's natural voice.

"Look here!" I opened a drawer and took out three sover-eigns. "Take this anyhow. I've got six and I'd give you the lot, only I must keep a little money to buy some fruit and vegetables for the crew from native boats as we go through Sunda Straits."

He shook his head.

"Take it," I urged him, whispering desperately. "No one can tell what——"

He smiled and slapped meaningfully the only pocket of the

sleeping jacket. It was not safe, certainly. But I produced a large old silk handkerchief of mine, and tying the three pieces of gold in a corner, pressed it on him. He was touched, I supposed, because he took it at last and tied it quickly round his waist under the jacket, on his bare skin.

Our eyes met; several seconds elapsed, till, our glances still mingled, I extended my hand and turned the lamp out. Then I passed through the cuddy, leaving the door of my room wide open. . . . "Steward!"

He was still lingering in the pantry in the greatness of his zeal, giving a rub-up to a plated cruet stand the last thing before going to bed. Being careful not to wake up the mate, whose room was opposite, I spoke in an undertone.

He looked round anxiously. "Sir!"

"Can you get me a little hot water from the galley?"

"I am afraid, sir, the galley fire's been out for some time now."

"Go and see."

He flew up the stairs.

"Now," I whispered, loudly, into the saloon—too loudly, perhaps, but I was afraid I couldn't make a sound. He was by my side in an instant—the double captain slipped past the stairs—through a tiny dark passage . . . a sliding door. We were in the sail locker, scrambling on our knees over the sails. A sudden thought struck me. I saw myself wandering barefooted, bareheaded, the sun beating on my dark poll. I snatched off my floppy hat and tried hurriedly in the dark to ram it on my other self. He dodged and fended off silently. I wonder what he thought had come to me before he understood and suddenly desisted. Our hands met gropingly, lingered united in a steady, motionless clasp for a second. . . . No word was breathed by either of us when they separated.

I was standing quietly by the pantry door when the steward returned.

"Sorry, sir. Kettle barely warm. Shall I light the spirit lamp?"

"Never mind."

I came out on deck slowly. It was now a matter of conscience to shave the land as close as possible—for now he must go overboard whenever the ship was put in stays. Must! There could be no going back for him. After a moment I walked over to leeward and my heart flew into my mouth at the nearness of the land on the bow. Under any other circumstances I would not have held on a minute longer. The second mate had followed me anxiously.

I looked on till I felt I could command my voice.

"She will weather," I said then in a quiet tone.

"Are you going to try that, sir?" he stammered out incredulously.

I took no notice of him and raised my tone just enough to be heard by the helmsman.

"Keep her good full."

"Good full, sir."

The wind fanned my cheek, the sails slept, the world was silent. The strain of watching the dark loom of the land grow bigger and denser was too much for me. I had shut my eyes—because the ship must go closer. She must! The stillness was intolerable. Were we standing still?

When I opened my eyes the second view started my heart with a thump. The black southern hill of Koh-ring seemed to hang right over the ship like a towering fragment of the everlasting night. On that enormous mass of blackness there was not a gleam to be seen, not a sound to be heard. It was gliding irresistibly towards us and yet seemed already within reach of the hand. I saw the vague figures of the watch grouped in the waist, gazing in awed silence.

"Are you going on, sir?" inquired an unsteady voice at my elbow.

I ignored it. I had to go on.

"Keep her full. Don't check her way. That won't do now," I said, warningly.

"I can't see the sails very well," the helmsman answered me, in strange, quavering tones.

Was she close enough? Already she was, I won't say in the shadow of the land, but in the very blackness of it, already swallowed up as it were, gone too close to be recalled, gone from me altogether.

"Give the mate a call," I said to the young man who stood at my elbow as still as death. "And turn all hands up."

My tone had a borrowed loudness reverberated from the height of the land. Several voices cried out together: "We are all on deck, sir."

Then stillness again, with the great shadow gliding closer, towering higher, without a light, without a sound. Such a hush had fallen on the ship that she might have been a bark of the dead floating in slowly under the very gate of Erebus.

"My God! Where are we?"

It was the mate moaning at my elbow. He was thunderstruck, and as it were deprived of the moral support of his whiskers. He clapped his hands and absolutely cried out, "Lost!"

"Be quiet," I said, sternly.

He lowered his tone, but I saw the shadowy gesture of his despair. "What are we doing here?"

"Looking for the land wind."

He made as if to tear his hair, and addressed me recklessly.

"She will never get out. You have done it, sir. I knew it'd end in something like this. She will never weather, and you are too close now to stay. She'll drift ashore before she's round. O my God!"

I caught his arm as he was raising it to batter his poor devoted head, and shook it violently.

"She's ashore already," he wailed, trying to tear himself away.

"Is she? ... Keep good full there!"

"Good full, sir," cried the helmsman in a frightened, thin, childlike voice.

I hadn't let go the mate's arm and went on shaking it. "Ready about, do you hear? You go forward"—shake—"and stop there"—shake—"and hold your noise"—shake—"and see these head-sheets properly overhauled"—shake, shake—shake.

And all the time I dared not look towards the land lest my heart should fail me. I released my grip at last and he ran forward as if fleeing for dear life.

I wondered what my double there in the sail locker thought of this commotion. He was able to hear everything—and perhaps he was able to understand why, on my conscience, it had to be thus close—no less. My first order "Hard alee!" re-echoed ominously under the towering shadow of Koh-ring as if I had shouted in a mountain gorge. And then I watched the land intently. In that smooth water and light wind it was impossible to feel the ship coming-to. No! I could not feel her. And my second self was making now ready to ship out and lower himself overboard. Perhaps he was gone already ... ?

The great black mass brooding over our very mastheads began to pivot away from the ship's side silently. And now I forgot the secret stranger ready to depart, and remembered only that I was a total stranger to the ship. I did not know her. Would she do it? How was she to be handled?

I swung the mainyard and waited helplessly. She was perhaps stopped, and her very fate hung in the balance, with the black mass of Koh-ring like the gate of the everlasting night towering over her taffrail. What would she do now? Had she way on her yet? I stepped to the side swiftly, and on the shadowy water I could see nothing except a faint phosphorescent flash revealing the glassy smoothness of the sleeping surface. It was impossible to tell—and I had not learned yet the feel of my ship. Was she moving? What I needed was something easily seen, a piece of paper, which I could throw overboard and watch. I had nothing on me. To run down for it I didn't dare. There was no time. All at once my strained, yearning stare distinguished a white object floating within a yard of the ship's side. White on the black water. A phosphorescent flash passed under it. What was that thing? . . . I recognized my own floppy hat. It must have fallen off his head . . . and he didn't bother. Now I had what I wanted—the saving mark for my eyes. But I hardly thought of my other self, now gone from the ship, to be hidden forever from all friendly faces, to be a fugitive and a vagabond on the earth, with no brand of the curse on his sane forehead to stay a slaying hand . . . too proud to explain.

And I watched the hat—the expression of my sudden pity for his mere flesh. It had been meant to save his homeless head from the dangers of the sun. And now—behold—it was saving the ship, by serving me for a mark to help out the ignorance of my strangeness. Ha! It was drifting forward, warning me just in time that the ship had gathered sternway.

"Shift the helm," I said in a low voice to the seaman standing still like a statue.

The man's eyes glistened wildly in the binnacle light as he jumped round to the other side and spun round the wheel.

I walked to the break of the poop. On the overshadowed deck all hands stood by the forebraces waiting for my order. The stars ahead seemed to be gliding from right to left. And all was so still in the world that I heard the quiet remark, "She's round," passed in a tone of intense relief between two seamen.

"Let go and haul."

The foreyards ran round with a great noise, amidst cheery cries. And now the frightful whiskers made themselves heard giving various orders. Already the ship was drawing ahead. And I was alone with her. Nothing! no one in the world should stand now between us, throwing a shadow on the way of silent knowledge and mute affection, the perfect communion of a seaman with his first command.

Walking to the taffrail, I was in time to make out, on the very edge of a darkness thrown by a towering black mass like the very gateway of Erebus—yes, I was in time to catch an evanescent glimpse of my white hat left behind to mark the spot where the secret sharer of my cabin and of my thoughts, as though he were my second self, had lowered himself into the water to take his punishment: a free man, a proud swimmer striking out for a new destiny.

THOMAS MANN

The Infant Prodigy

*Thomas Mann (1875–1955) was born in Lübeck,
Germany, a son of wealthy merchant class people.
Many of his finest stories and novels deal with the
conflict between this burgher background and the
artistic temperament that demands such opposing
values. His best-known novels, Buddenbrooks, The
Magic Mountain, and the Joseph cycle, reveal his
intense interest in depth psychology, anthropology,
and Jung's theories of racial memory. His use of
the leitmotif—the repetition of certain themes,
words, and images—is a characteristic of his work
reminiscent of Wagnerian music.*

*Strongly opposed to the Nazi regime, Mann chose
to leave Germany, and spent his later years in the
United States.*

THE INFANT PRODIGY entered. The hall became quiet.

It became quiet and then the audience began to clap, because somewhere at the side a leader of mobs, a born organiz-
er, clapped first. The audience had heard nothing yet, but they
applauded; for a mighty publicity organization had heralded
the prodigy and people were already hypnotized, whether they
knew it or not.

The prodigy came from behind a splendid screen embroidered with Empire garlands and great conventionalized flowers,
and climbed nimbly up the steps to the platform, diving into
the applause as into a bath; a little chilly and shivering, but

yet as though into a friendly element. He advanced to the edge of the platform and smiled as though he were about to be photographed; he made a shy, charming gesture of greeting, like a little girl.

He was dressed entirely in white silk, which the audience found enchanting. The little white jacket was fancifully cut, with a sash underneath it, and even his shoes were made of white silk. But against the white socks his bare little legs stood out quite brown; for he was a Greek boy.

He was called Bibi Saccellaphylaccas. And such indeed was his name. No one knew what Bibi was the pet name for, nobody but the impresario, and he regarded it as a trade secret. Bibi had smooth black hair reaching to his shoulders; it was parted on the side and fastened back from the narrow domed forehead by a little silk bow. His was the most harmless childish countenance in the world, with an unfinished nose and guileless mouth. The area beneath his pitch-black mouselike eyes was already a little tired and visibly lined. He looked as though he were nine years old but was really eight and given out for seven. It was hard to tell whether to believe this or not. Probably everybody knew better and still believed it, as happens about so many things. The average man thinks that a little falseness goes with beauty. Where should we get any excitement out of our daily life if we were not willing to pretend a bit? And the average man is quite right, in his average brains!

The prodigy kept on bowing until the applause died down, then he went up to the grand piano, and the audience cast a last look at its programmes. First came a *Marche solonnelle*, then a *Rêverie*, and then *Le Hibou et les moineaux*—all by Bibi Saccellaphylaccas. The whole programme was by him, they were all his compositions. He could not score them, of course, but he had them all in his extraordinary little head and they possessed real artistic significance, or so it said, seriously and objectively, in the programme. The programme sounded as though the impresario had wrested these concessions from his critical nature after a hard struggle.

The prodigy sat down upon the revolving stool and felt with his feet for the pedals, which were raised by means of a clever device so that Bibi could reach them. It was Bibi's own piano, he took it everywhere with him. It rested upon wooden trestles and its polish was somewhat marred by the constant transportation—but all that only made things more interesting.

Bibi put his silk-shod feet on the pedals; then he made an artful little face, looked straight ahead of him, and lifted his right hand. It was a brown, childish little hand; but the wrist was strong and unlike a child's, with well-developed bones.

Bibi made his face for the audience because he was aware that he had to entertain them a little. But he had his own private enjoyment in the thing too, an enjoyment which he could never convey to anybody. It was that prickling delight, that secret shudder of bliss, which ran through him every time he sat at an open piano—it would always be with him. And here was the keyboard again, these seven black and white octaves, among which he had so often lost himself in abysmal and thrilling adventures—and yet it always looked as clean and untouched as a newly washed blackboard. This was the realm of music that lay before him. It lay spread out like an inviting ocean, where he might plunge in and blissfully swim, where he might let himself be borne and carried away, where he might go under in night and storm, yet keep the mastery: control, ordain—he held his right hand poised in the air.

A breathless stillness reigned in the room—the tense moment before the first note came. . . . How would it begin? It began so. And Bibi, with his index finger, fetched the first note out of the piano, a quite unexpectedly powerful first note in the middle register, like a trumpet blast. Others followed, an introduction developed—the audience relaxed.

The concert was held in the palatial hall of a fashionable first-class hotel. The walls were covered with mirrors framed in gilded arabesques, between frescoes of the rosy and fleshly school. Ornamental columns supported a ceiling that displayed a whole universe of electric bulbs, in clusters darting a brilliance far brighter than day and filling the whole space with thin, vibrating golden light. Not a seat was unoccupied, people were standing in the side aisles and at the back. The front seats cost twelve marks; for the impresario believed that anything worth having was worth paying for. And they were occupied by the best society, for it was in the upper classes, of course, that the greatest enthusiasm was felt. There were even some children, with their legs hanging down demurely from their chairs and their shining eyes staring at their gifted little white-clad contemporary.

Down in front on the left side sat the prodigy's mother, an extremely obese woman with a powdered double chin and a feather on her head. Beside her was the impresario,

a man of oriental appearance with large gold buttons on
his conspicuous cuffs. The princess was in the middle of the
front row—a wrinkled, shrivelled little old princess but still
a patron of the arts, especially everything full of sensibility.
She sat in a deep, velvet-upholstered arm-chair, and a Persian
carpet was spread before her feet. She held her hands folded
over her grey striped-silk breast, put her head on one side,
and presented a picture of elegant composure as she sat
looking up at the performing prodigy. Next her sat her lady-
in-waiting, in a green striped-silk gown. Being only a lady-
in-waiting she had to sit up very straight in her chair.

Bibi ended in a grand climax. With what power this wee
manikin belaboured the keyboard! The audience could scarcely
trust its ears. The march theme, an infectious, swinging tune,
broke out once more, fully harmonized, bold and showy;
with every note Bibi flung himself back from the waist as
though he were marching in a triumphal procession. He ended
fortissimo, bent over, slipped sideways off the stool, and stood
with a smile awaiting the applause.

And the applause burst forth, unanimously, enthusiastically;
the child made his demure little maidenly curtsy and people
in the front seat thought: "Look what slim little hips he has!
Clap, clap! Hurrah, bravo, little chap, Saccophylax or whatever your name is! Wait, let me take off my gloves—what
a little devil of a chap he is!"

Bibi had to come out three times from behind the screen
before they would stop. Some late-comers entered the hall
and moved about looking for seats. Then the concert continued. Bibi's *Rêverie* murmured its numbers, consisting almost entirely of arpeggios, above which a bar of melody
rose now and then, weak-winged. Then came *Le Hibou et
les moineaux.* This piece was brilliantly successful, it made
a strong impression; it was an effective childhood fantasy,
remarkably well envisaged. The bass represented the owl,
sitting morosely rolling his filmy eyes; while in the treble the
impudent, half-frightened sparrows chirped. Bibi received an
ovation when he finished, he was called out four times. A
hotel page with shiny buttons carried up three great laurel
wreaths onto the stage and proffered them from one side while
Bibi nodded and expressed his thanks. Even the princess
shared in the applause, daintily and noiselessly pressing her
palms together.

Ah, the knowing little creature understood how to make
people clap! He stopped behind the screen, they had to

wait for him; lingered a little on the steps of the platform, admired the long streamers on the wreaths—although actually such things bored him stiff by now. He bowed with the utmost charm, he gave the audience plenty of time to rave itself out, because applause is valuable and must not be cut short. "*Le Hibou* is my drawing card," he thought— this expression he had learned from the impresario. "Now I will play the fantasy, it is a lot better than *Le Hibou*, of course, especially the C-sharp passage. But you idiots dote on the *Hibou*, though it is the first and the silliest thing I wrote." He continued to bow and smile.

Next came a *Méditation* and then an *Étude*—the programme was quite comprehensive. The *Méditation* was very like the *Rêverie*—which was nothing against it—and the *Étude* displayed all of Bibi's virtuosity, which naturally fell a little short of his inventiveness. And then the *Fantaisie*. This was his favourite; he varied it a little each time, giving himself free rein and sometimes surprising even himself, on good evenings, by his own inventiveness.

He sat and played, so little, so white and shining, against the great black grand piano, elect and alone, above that confused sea of faces, above the heavy, insensitive mass soul, upon which he was labouring to work with his individual, differentiated soul. His lock of soft black hair with the white silk bow had fallen over his forehead, his trained and bony little wrists pounded away, the muscles stood out visibly on his brown childish cheeks.

Sitting there he sometimes had moments of oblivion and solitude, when the gaze of his strange little mouselike eyes with the big rings beneath them would lose itself and stare through the painted stage into space that was peopled with strange vague life. Then out of the corner of his eye he would give a quick look back into the hall and be once more with his audience.

"Joy and pain, the heights and the depths—that is my *Fantaisie*," he thought lovingly. "Listen, here is the C-sharp passage." He lingered over the approach, wondering if they would notice anything. But no, of course not, how should they? And he cast his eyes up prettily at the ceiling so that at least they might have something to look at.

All these people sat there in their regular rows, looking at the prodigy and thinking all sorts of things in their regular brains. An old gentleman with a white beard, a seal ring on his finger and a bulbous swelling on his bald spot, a

growth if you like, was thinking to himself: "Really, one
ought to be ashamed." He had never got any further than
"Ah, thou dearest Augustin" on the piano, and here he sat
now, a grey old man, looking on while this little hop-o'-my-
thumb performed miracles. Yes, yes, it is a gift of God,
we must remember that. God grants His gifts, or He with-
holds them, and there is no shame in being an ordinary
man. Like with the Christ Child.—Before a child one may
kneel without feeling ashamed. Strange that thoughts like
these should be so satisfying—he would even say so sweet,
if it was not too silly for a tough old man like him to use
the word. That was how he felt, anyhow.

Art . . . the business man with the parrot-nose was thinking.
"Yes, it adds something cheerful to life, a little good white
silk and a little tumty-ti-ti-tum. Really he does not play so
badly. Fully fifty seats, twelve marks apiece, that makes six
hundred marks—and everything else besides. Take off the
rent of the hall, the lighting and the programmes, you must
have fully a thousand marks profit. That is worth while."

That was Chopin he was just playing, thought the piano-
teacher, a lady with a pointed nose; she was of an age
when the understanding sharpens as the hopes decay. "But not
very original—I will say that afterwards, it sounds well.
And his hand position is entirely amateur. One must be able
to lay a coin on the back of the hand—I would use a ruler
on him."

Then there was a young girl, at that self-conscious and
chlorotic time of life when the most ineffable ideas come
into the mind. She was thinking to herself: "What is it he
is playing? It is expressive of passion, yet he is a child.
If he kissed me it would be as though my little brother
kissed me—no kiss at all. Is there such a thing as passion
all by itself, without any earthly object, a sort of child's-
play of passion? What nonsense! If I were to say such things
aloud they would just be at me with some more cod-liver
oil. Such is life."

An officer was leaning against a column. He looked on
at Bibi's success and thought: "Yes, you are something and
I am something, each in his own way." So he clapped his
heels together and paid to the prodigy the respect which
he felt to be due to all the powers that be.

Then there was a critic, an elderly man in a shiny black
coat and turned-up trousers splashed with mud. He sat in
his free seat and thought: "Look at him, this young beggar

of a Bibi. As an individual he has still to develop, but as a type he is already quite complete, the artist *par excellence*. He has in himself all the artist's exaltation and his utter worthlessness, his charlatanry and his sacred fire, his burning contempt and his secret raptures. Of course I can't write all that, it is too good. Of course, I should have been an artist myself if I had not seen through the whole business so clearly."

Then the prodigy stopped playing and a perfect storm arose in the hall. He had to come out again and again from behind his screen. The man with the shiny buttons carried up more wreaths: four laurel wreaths, a lyre made of violets, a bouquet of roses. He had not arms enough to convey all these tributes, the impresario himself mounted the stage to help him. He hung a laurel wreath round Bibi's neck, he tenderly stroked the black hair—and suddenly as though overcome he bent down and gave the prodigy a kiss, a resounding kiss, square on the mouth. And then the storm became a hurricane. That kiss ran through the room like an electric shock, it went direct to peoples' marrow and made them shiver down their backs. They were carried away by a helpless compulsion of sheer noise. Loud shouts mingled with the hysterical clapping of hands. Some of Bibi's commonplace little friends down there waved their handkerchiefs. But the critic thought: "Of course that kiss had to come—it's a good old gag. Yes, good Lord, if only one did not see through everything quite so clearly—"

And so the concert drew to a close. It began at half past seven and finished at half past eight. The platform was laden with wreaths and two little pots of flowers stood on the lamp-stands of the piano. Bibi played as his last number his *Rhapsodie grecque,* which turned into the Greek national hymn at the end. His fellow-countrymen in the audience would gladly have sung it with him if the company had not been so august. They made up for it with a powerful noise and hullabaloo, a hot-blooded national demonstration. And the aging critic was thinking: "Yes, the hymn had to come too. They have to exploit every vein—publicity cannot afford to neglect any means to its end. I think I'll criticize that as inartistic. But perhaps I am wrong, perhaps that is the most artistic thing of all. What is the artist? A jack-in-the-box. Criticism is on a higher plane. But I can't say that." And away he went in his muddy trousers.

After being called out nine or ten times the prodigy did

not come any more from behind the screen but went to his
mother and the impresario down in the hall. The audience
stood about among the chairs and applauded and pressed
forward to see Bibi close at hand. Some of them wanted
to see the princess too. Two dense circles formed, one
round the prodigy, the other round the princess, and you
could actually not tell which of them was receiving more
homage. But the court lady was commanded to go over to
Bibi; she smoothed down his silk jacket a bit to make it
look suitable for a court function, led him by the arm to
the princess, and solemnly indicated to him that he was to
kiss the royal hand. "How do you do it, child?" asked
the princess. "Does it come into your head of itself when
you sit down?" *"Oui, madame,"* answered Bibi. To himself
he thought: "Oh, what a stupid old princess!" Then he turned
round shyly and uncourtier-like and went back to his family.

Outside in the cloak-room there was a crowd. People held
up their numbers and received with open arms furs, shawls,
and galoshes. Somewhere among her acquaintances the piano-
teacher stood making her critique. "He is not very original,"
she said audibly and looked about her.

In front of one of the great mirrors an elegant young
lady was being arrayed in her evening cloak and fur shoes
by her brothers, two lieutenants. She was exquisitely beautiful,
with her steel-blue eyes and her clean-cut, well-bred face.
A really noble dame. When she was ready she stood waiting
for her brothers. "Don't stand so long in front of the glass,
Adolf," she said softly to one of them, who could not tear
himself away from the sight of his simple, good-looking young
features. But Lieutenant Adolf thinks: What cheek! He would
button his overcoat in front of the glass, just the same.
Then they went out on the street where the arc-lights gleamed
cloudily through the white mist. Lieutenant Adolf struck up
a little nigger-dance on the frozen snow to keep warm, with
his hands in his slanting overcoat pockets and his collar
turned up.

A girl with untidy hair and swinging arms, accompanied by
a gloomy-faced youth, came out just behind them. A child!
she thought. A charming child. But in there he was an
awe-inspiring . . . and aloud in a toneless voice she said:
"We are all infant prodigies, we artists."

"Well, bless my soul!" thought the old gentleman who had
never got further than Augustin on the piano, and whose
boil was now concealed by a top hat. "What does all that

mean? She sounds very oracular." But the gloomy youth understood. He nodded his head slowly.

Then they were silent and the untidy-haired girl gazed after the brothers and sister. She rather despised them, but she looked after them until they had turned the corner.

D. H. LAWRENCE

The Horse Dealer's Daughter

> *D. H. Lawrence (1885–1930) started life in Notting-*
> *hamshire, England, as the son of a coal miner. In his*
> *early years he taught school and studied to be a*
> *painter, but it was as a writer that he found his true*
> *vocation. Restless, unconventional, possessed himself*
> *with neurotic tendencies, he became one of the most*
> *original and powerful writers of the twentieth cen-*
> *tury. His frank analysis of the inner sexual conflicts*
> *of modern civilized man made him a highly contro-*
> *versial figure, but there is no question of their amaz-*
> *ing insight and psychological truth. Novelist, short*
> *story writer, essayist, and poet, Lawrence was re-*
> *markably versatile in practically every literary*
> *genre.*

"WELL MABEL, AND what are you going to do with yourself?" asked Joe, with foolish flippancy. He felt quite safe
himself. Without listening for an answer, he turned aside,
worked a grain of tobacco to the tip of his tongue, and spat
it out. He did not care about anything, since he felt safe
himself.

The three brothers and the sisters sat round the desolate
breakfast-table, attempting some sort of desultory consultation. The morning's post had given the final tap to the family
fortunes, and all was over. The dreary dining-room itself,
with its heavy mahogany furniture, looked as if it were
waiting to be done away with.

But the consultation amounted to nothing. There was a strange air of ineffectuality about the three men, as they sprawled at table, smoking and reflecting vaguely on their own condition. The girl was alone, a rather short, sullen-looking young woman of twenty-seven. She did not share the same life as her brothers. She would have been good-looking, save for the impressive fixity of her face, 'bull-dog', as her brothers called it.

There was a confused tramping of horses' feet outside. The three men all sprawled round in their chairs to watch. Beyond the dark holly bushes that separated the strip of lawn from the high-road, they could see a cavalcade of shire horses swinging out of their own yard, being taken for exercise. This was the last time. These were the last horses that would go through their hands. The young men watched with critical, callous looks. They were all frightened at the collapse of their lives, and the sense of disaster in which they were involved left them no inner freedom.

Yet they were three fine, well-set fellows enough. Joe, the eldest, was a man of thirty-three, broad and handsome in a hot, flushed way. His face was red, he twisted his black moustache over a thick finger, his eyes were shallow and restless. He had a sensual way of uncovering his teeth when he laughed, and his bearing was stupid. Now he watched the horses with a glazed look of helplessness in his eyes, a certain stupor of downfall.

The great draught-horses swung past. They were tied head to tail, four of them, and they heaved along to where a lane branched off from the high-road, planting their great hoofs floutingly in the fine black mud, swinging their great rounded haunches sumptuously, and trotting a few sudden stéps as they were led into the lane, round the corner. Every movement showed a massive, slumbrous strength, and a stupidity which held them in subjection. The groom at the head looked back, jerking the leading rope. And the cavalcade moved out of sight up the lane, the tail of the last horse, bobbed up tight and stiff, held out taut from the swinging great haunches as they rocked behind the hedges in a motion-like sleep.

Joe watched with glazed hopeless eyes. The horses were almost like his own body to him. He felt he was done for now. Luckily he was engaged to a woman as old as himself, and therefore her father, who was steward of a neighbouring estate, would provide him with a job. He would marry and go into harness. His life was over, he would be a subject animal now.

He turned uneasily aside, the retreating steps of the horses echoing in his ears. Then, with foolish restlessness, he reached for the scraps of bacon-rind from the plates, and making a faint whistling sound, flung them to the terrier that lay against the fender. He watched the dog swallow them, and waited till the creature looked into his eyes. Then a faint grin came on his face, and in a high, foolish voice he said:

"You won't get much more bacon, shall you, you little b——?"

The dog faintly and dismally wagged its tail, then lowered its haunches, circled round, and lay down again.

There was another helpless silence at the table. Joe sprawled uneasily in his seat, not willing to go till the family conclave was dissolved. Fred Henry, the second brother, was erect, clean-limbed, alert. He had watched the passing of the horses with more *sang-froid*. If he was an animal, like Joe, he was an animal which controls, not one which is controlled. He was master of any horse, and he carried himself with a well-tempered air of mastery. But he was not master of the situations of life. He pushed his coarse brown moustache upwards, off his lip, and glanced irritably at his sister, who sat impassive and inscrutable.

"You'll go and stop with Lucy for a bit, shan't you?" he asked. The girl did not answer.

"I don't see what else you can do," persisted Fred Henry.

"Go as a skivvy," Joe interpolated laconically.

The girl did not move a muscle.

"If I was her, I should go in for training for a nurse," said Malcolm, the youngest of them all. He was the baby of the family, a young man of twenty-two, with a fresh, jaunty *museau*.

But Mabel did not take any notice of him. They had talked at her and round her for so many years, that she hardly heard them at all.

The marble clock on the mantelpiece softly chimed the half-hour, the dog rose uneasily from the hearth-rug and looked at the party at the breakfast-table. But still they sat on in ineffectual conclave.

"Oh, all right," said Joe suddenly, apropos of nothing. "I'll get a move on."

He pushed back his chair, straddled his knees with a downward jerk, to get them free, in horsey fashion, and

went to the fire. Still he did not go out of the room; he
was curious to know what the others would do or say. He
began to charge his pipe, looking down at the dog and
saying in a high, affected voice:

"Going wi' me? Going wi' me are ter? Tha'rt goin' further
than tha counts on just now, dost hear?"

The dog faintly wagged its tail, the man stuck out his
jaw and covered his pipe with his hands, and puffed intently, losing himself in the tobacco, looking down all the
while at the dog with an absent brown eye. The dog looked
up at him in mournful distrust. Joe stood with his knees
stuck out, in real horsey fashion.

"Have you had a letter from Lucy?" Fred Henry asked of
his sister.

"Last week," came the neutral reply.

"And what does she say?"

There was no answer.

"Does she *ask* you to go and stop there?" persisted Fred
Henry.

"She says I can if I like."

"Well, then, you'd better. Tell her you'll come on Monday."

This was received in silence.

"That's what you'll do then, is it?" said Fred Henry, in
some exasperation.

But she made no answer. There was a silence of futility
and irritation in the room. Malcolm grinned fatuously.

"You'll have to make up your mind between now and next
Wednesday," said Joe loudly, "or else find yourself lodgings
on the kerbstone."

The face of the young woman darkened, but she sat on
immutable.

"Here's Jack Ferguson!" exclaimed Malcolm, who was looking aimlessly out of the window.

"Where?" exclaimed Joe loudly.

"Just gone past."

"Coming in?"

Malcolm craned his neck to see the gate.

"Yes," he said.

There was a silence. Mabel sat on like one condemned,
at the head of the table. Then a whistle was heard from
the kitchen. The dog got up and barked sharply. Joe opened
the door and shouted:

"Come on."

After a moment a young man entered. He was muffled up in overcoat and a purple woollen scarf, and his tweed cap, which he did not remove, was pulled down on his head. He was of medium height, his face was rather long and pale, his eyes looked tired.

"Hello, Jack! Well, Jack!" exclaimed Malcolm and Joe. Fred Henry merely said: "Jack."

"What's doing?" asked the newcomer, evidently addressing Fred Henry.

"Same. We've got to be out by Wednesday. Got a cold?"

"I have—got it bad, too."

"Why don't you stop in?"

"*Me* stop in? When I can't stand on my legs, perhaps I shall have a chance." The young man spoke huskily. He had a slight Scotch accent.

"It's a knock-out, isn't it," said Joe, boisterously, "if a doctor goes round croaking with a cold. Looks bad for the patients, doesn't it?"

The young doctor looked at him slowly.

"Anything the matter with *you,* then?" he asked sarcastically.

"Not as I know of. Damn your eyes, I hope not. Why?"

"I thought you were very concerned about the patients, wondered if you might be one yourself."

"Damn it, no, I've never been patient to no flaming doctor, and hope I never shall be," returned Joe.

At this point Mabel rose from the table, and they all seemed to become aware of her existence. She began putting the dishes together. The young doctor looked at her, but did not address her. He had not greeted her. She went out of the room with the tray, her face impassive and unchanged.

"When are you off then, all of you?" asked the doctor.

"I'm catching the eleven-forty," replied Malcolm. "Are you goin' down wi' th' trap, Joe?"

"Yes, I've told you I'm going down wi' th' trap, haven't I?"

"We'd better be getting her in then. So long, Jack, if I don't see you before I go," said Malcolm, shaking hands.

He went out, followed by Joe, who seemed to have his tail between his legs.

"Well, this is the devil's own," exclaimed the doctor, when he was left alone with Fred Henry. "Going before Wednesday, are you?"

"That's the orders," replied the other.

"Where, to Northampton?"

"That's it."

"The devil!" exclaimed Ferguson, with quiet chagrin.

And there was silence between the two.

"All settled up, are you?" asked Ferguson.

"About."

There was another pause.

"Well, I shall miss yer, Freddy, boy," said the young doctor.

"And I shall miss thee, Jack," returned the other.

"Miss you like hell," mused the doctor.

Fred Henry turned aside. There was nothing to say. Mabel came in again, to finish clearing the table.

"What are *you* going to do, then, Miss Pervin?" asked Ferguson. "Going to your sister's, are you?"

Mabel looked at him with her steady, dangerous eyes, that always made him uncomfortable, unsettling his superficial ease.

"No," she said.

"Well, what in the name of fortune *are* you going to do? Say what you mean to do," cried Fred Henry, with futile intensity.

But she only averted her head, and continued her work. She folded the white table-cloth, and put on the chenille cloth.

"The sulkiest bitch that ever trod!" muttered her brother.

But she finished her task with perfectly impassive face, the young doctor watching her interestedly all the while. Then she went out.

Fred Henry stared after her, clenching his lips, his blue eyes fixing in sharp antagonism, as he made a grimace of sour exasperation.

"You could bray her into bits, and that's all you'd get out of her," he said, in a small, narrowed tone.

The doctor smiled faintly.

"What's she *going* to do, then?" he asked.

"Strike me if *I* know!" returned the other.

There was a pause. Then the doctor stirred.

"I'll be seeing you to-night, shall I?" he said to his friend.

"Ay—where's it to be? Are we going over to Jessdale?"

"I don't know. I've got such a cold on me. I'll come round to the 'Moon and Stars', anyway."

"Let Lizzie and May miss their night for once, eh?"

"That's it—if I feel as I do now."

"All's one——"

The two young men went through the passage and down to the back door together. The house was large, but it was servantless now, and desolate. At the back was a small bricked houseyard and beyond that a big square, gravelled fine and red, and having stables on two sides. Sloping, dank, winter-dark fields stretched away on the open sides.

But the stables were empty. Joseph Pervin, the father of the family, had been a man of no education, who had become a fairly large horse dealer. The stables had been full of horses, there was a great turmoil and come-and-go of horses and of dealers and grooms. Then the kitchen was full of servants. But of late things had declined. The old man had married a second time, to retrieve his fortunes. Now he was dead and everything was gone to the dogs, there was nothing but debt and threatening.

For months, Mabel had been servantless in the big house, keeping the home together in penury for her ineffectual brothers. She had kept house for ten years. But previously it was with unstinted means. Then, however brutal and coarse everything was, the sense of money had kept her proud, confident. The men might be foul-mouthed, the women in the kitchen might have bad reputations, her brothers might have illegitimate children. But so long as there was money, the girl felt herself established, and brutally proud, reserved.

No company came to the house, save dealers and coarse men. Mabel had no associates of her own sex, after her sister went away. But she did not mind. She went regularly to church, she attended to her father. And she lived in the memory of her mother, who had died when she was fourteen, and whom she had loved. She had loved her father, too, in a different way, depending upon him, and feeling secure in him, until at the age of fifty-four he married again. And then she had set hard against him. Now he had died and left them all hopelessly in debt.

She had suffered badly during the period of poverty. Nothing, however, could shake the curious, sullen, animal pride that dominated each member of the family. Now, for Mabel, the end had come. Still she would not cast about her. She would follow her own way just the same. She would always hold the keys of her own situation. Mindless and persistent, she endured from day to day. Why should she think? Why should she answer anybody? It was enough that this was the end, and there was no way out. She need not pass any more darkly along the main street of the small town, avoiding every eye. She need not demean herself any more, going into the shops and buying the cheapest food. This was at an end. She thought of nobody, not even of herself. Mindless and persistent, she seemed in a sort of ecstasy to be coming nearer to her fulfilment, her own glorification, approaching her dead mother, who was glorified.

In the afternoon she took a little bag, with shears and sponge and a small scrubbing-brush, and went out. It was a grey, wintry day, with saddened, dark green fields and an atmosphere blackened by the smoke of foundries not far off. She went quickly, darkly along the causeway, heeding nobody, through the town to the churchyard.

There she always felt secure, as if no one could see her, although as a matter of fact she was exposed to the stare of everyone who passed along under the churchyard wall. Nevertheless, once under the shadow of the great looming church, among the graves, she felt immune from the world, reserved within the thick churchyard wall as in another country.

Carefully she clipped the grass from the grave, and arranged the pinky white, small chrysanthemums in the tin cross. When this was done, she took an empty jar from a neighbouring grave, brought water, and carefully, most scrupulously sponged the marble headstone and the coping-stone.

It gave her sincere satisfaction to do this. She felt in immediate contact with the world of her mother. She took minute pains, went through the park in a state bordering on pure happiness, as if in performing this task she came into a subtle, intimate connection with her mother. For the life she followed here in the world was far less real than the world of death she inherited from her mother.

The doctor's house was just by the church. Ferguson, being a mere hired assistant, was slave to the country-side. As he hurried now to attend to the out-patients in the surgery, glancing across the graveyard with his quick eye, he saw the girl at her task at the grave. She seemed so intent and remote, it was like looking into another world. Some mystical element was touched in him. He slowed down as he walked, watching her as if spellbound.

She lifted her eyes, feeling him looking. Their eyes met. And each looked away at once, each feeling, in some way, found out by the other. He lifted his cap and passed on down the road. There remained distinct in his consciousness, like a vision, the memory of her face, lifted from the tomb-stone in the churchyard, and looking at him with slow, large portentous eyes. It *was* portentous, her face. It seemed to mesmerise him. There was a heavy power in her eyes which laid hold of his whole being, as if he had drunk some power-ful drug. He had been feeling weak and done before. Now the life came back into him, he felt delivered from his own fretted, daily self.

He finished his duties at the surgery as quickly as might be, hastily filling up the bottles of the waiting people with cheap drugs. Then, in perpetual haste, he set off again to visit several cases in another part of his round, before tea-time. At all times he preferred to walk if he could, but particularly when he was not well. He fancied the motion restored him.

The afternoon was failing. It was grey, deadened, and wintry, with a slow, moist, heavy coldness sinking in and deadening all the faculties. But why should he think or notice? He hastily climbed the hill and turned across the dark green fields, following the black cinder-track. In the distance, across a shallow dip in the country, the small town was clustered like smouldering ash, a tower, a spire, a heap of low, raw, extinct houses. And on the nearest fringe of the town, sloping into the dip, was Oldmeadow, the Pervins' house. He could see the stables and the outbuildings distinctly, as they lay towards him on the slope. Well, he would not go there many more times! Another resource would be lost to him, another place gone: the only company he cared for in the alien, ugly little town he was losing. Nothing but work, drudgery, constant hastening from dwelling to dwelling among the colliers and the iron-workers. It wore him out, but at the same time he had a craving for it. It was a stimulant to him to be in the homes of the working people, moving, as it were, through the innermost body of their life. His nerves were excited and gratified. He could come so near, into the very lives of the rough, inarticulate, powerfully emotional men and women. He grumbled, he said he hated the hellish hole. But as a matter of fact it excited him, the contact with the rough, strongly-feeling people was a stimulant applied direct to his nerves.

Below Oldmeadow, in the green, shallow, soddened hollow of fields, lay a square, deep pond. Roving across the land-scape, the doctor's quick eye detected a figure in black pass-ing through the gate of the field, down towards the pond.

He looked again. It would be Mabel Pervin. His mind suddenly became alive and attentive.

Why was she going down there? He pulled up on the path on the slope above, and stood staring. He could just make sure of the small black figure moving in the hollow of the failing day. He seemed to see her in the midst of such obscurity, that he was like a clairvoyant, seeing rather with the mind's eye than with ordinary sight. Yet he could see her positively enough, whilst he kept his eye attentive. He felt, if he looked away from her, in the thick, ugly falling dusk, he would lose her altogether.

He followed her minutely as she moved, direct and intent, like something transmitted rather than stirring in voluntary activity, straight down the field towards the pond. There she stood on the bank for a moment. She never raised her head. Then she waded slowly into the water.

He stood motionless as the small black figure walked slowly and deliberately towards the centre of the pond, very slowly, gradually moving deeper into the motionless water, and still moving forward as the water got up to her breast. Then he could see her no more in the dusk of the dead afternoon.

"There!" he exclaimed. "Would you believe it?"

And he hastened straight down, running over the wet, soddened fields, pushing through the hedges, down into the depression of callous wintry obscurity. It took him several minutes to come to the pond. He stood on the bank, breathing heavily. He could see nothing. His eyes seemed to penetrate the dead water. Yes, perhaps that was the dark shadow of her black clothing beneath the surface of the water.

He slowly ventured into the pond. The bottom was deep, soft clay, he sank in, and the water clasped dead cold round his legs. As he stirred he could smell the cold, rotten clay that fouled up into the water. It was objectionable in his lungs. Still, repelled and yet not heeding, he moved deeper into the pond. The cold water rose over his thighs, over his loins, upon his abdomen. The lower part of his body was all sunk in the hideous cold element. And the bottom was so deeply soft and uncertain, he was afraid of pitching with his mouth underneath. He could not swim, and was afraid.

He crouched a little, spreading his hands under the water and moving them round, trying to feel for her. The dead cold pond swayed upon his chest. He moved again, a little deeper, and again, with his hands underneath, he felt all around under the water. And he touched her clothing. But it evaded his fingers. He made a desperate effort to grasp it.

And so doing he lost his balance and went under, horribly, suffocating in the foul earthy water, struggling madly for a few moments. At last, after what seemed an eternity, he got his footing, rose again into the air and looked around. He gasped, and knew he was in the world. Then he looked at the water. She had risen near him. He grasped her clothing, and drawing her nearer, turned to make his way to land again.

He went very slowly, carefully, absorbed in the slow progress. He rose higher, climbing out of the pond. The water was now only about his legs; he was thankful, full of relief to be out of the clutches of the pond. He lifted her and staggered on to the bank, out of the horror of wet, grey clay.

He laid her down on the bank. She was quite unconscious and running with water. He made the water come from her mouth, he worked to restore her. He did not have to work very long before he could feel the breathing begin again in her; she was breathing naturally. He worked a little longer. He could feel her live beneath his hands; she was coming back. He wiped her face, wrapped her in his overcoat, looked round into the dim, dark grey world, then lifted her and staggered down the bank and across the fields.

It seemed an unthinkably long way, and his burden so heavy he felt he would never get to the house. But at last he was in the stable-yard, and then in the house-yard. He opened the door and went into the house. In the kitchen he laid her down on the hearth-rug and called. The house was empty. But the fire was burning in the grate.

Then again he kneeled to attend to her. She was breathing regularly, her eyes were wide open and as if conscious, but there seemed something missing in her look. She was conscious in herself, but unconscious of her surroundings.

He ran upstairs, took blankets from a bed, and put them before the fire to warm. Then he removed her saturated, earthy-smelling clothing, rubbed her dry with a towel, and wrapped her naked in the blankets. Then he went into the dining-room, to look for spirits. There was a little whisky. He drank a gulp himself, and put some into her mouth.

The effect was instantaneous. She looked full into his face, as if she had been seeing him for some time, and yet had only just become conscious of him.

"Dr. Ferguson?" she said.

"What?" he answered.

He was divesting himself of his coat, intending to find some dry clothing upstairs. He could not bear the smell of the dead, clayey water, and he was mortally afraid for his own health.

"What did I do?" she asked.

"Walked into the pond," he replied. He had begun to shudder like one sick, and could hardly attend to her. Her eyes remained full on him, he seemed to be going dark in his mind, looking back at her helplessly. The shuddering became quieter in him, his life came back to him, dark and unknowing, but strong again.

"Was I out of my mind?" she asked, while her eyes were fixed on him all the time.

"Maybe, for the moment," he replied. He felt quiet, because his strength had come back. The strange fretful strain had left him.

"Am I out of my mind now?" she asked.

"Are you?" he reflected a moment. "No," he answered truthfully, "I don't see that you are." He turned his face aside. He was afraid now, because he felt dazed, and felt dimly that her power was stronger than his, in this issue. And she continued to look at him fixedly all the time. "Can you tell me where I shall find some dry things to put on?" he asked.

"Did you dive into the pond for me?" she asked.

"No," he answered. "I walked in. But I went in overhead as well."

There was silence for a moment. He hesitated. He very much wanted to go upstairs to get into dry clothing. But there was another desire in him. And she seemed to hold him. His will seemed to have gone to sleep, and left him, standing there slack before her. But he felt warm inside himself. He did not shudder at all, though his clothes were sodden on him.

"Why did you?" she asked.

"Because I didn't want you to do such a foolish thing," he said.

"It wasn't foolish," she said, still gazing at him as she lay on the floor, with a sofa cushion under her head. "It was the right thing to do. *I* knew best, then."

"I'll go and shift these wet things," he said. But still he had not the power to move out of her presence, until she sent him. It was as if she had the life of his body in her hands, and he could not extricate himself. Or perhaps he did not want to.

Suddenly she sat up. Then she became aware of her own immediate condition. She felt the blankets about her, she knew her own limbs. For a moment it seemed as if her reason were going. She looked round, with wild eye, as if seeking something. He stood still with fear. She saw her clothing lying scattered.

"Who undressed me?" she asked, her eyes resting full and inevitable on his face.

"I did," he replied, "to bring you round."

For some moments she sat and gazed at him awfully, her lips parted.

"Do you love me, then?" she asked.

He only stood and stared at her, fascinated. His soul seemed to melt.

She shuffled forward on her knees, and put her arms round him, round his legs, as he stood there, pressing her breasts against his knees and thighs, clutching him with strange, convulsive certainty, pressing his thighs against her, drawing him to her face, her throat, as she looked up at him with flaring, humble eyes of transfiguration, triumphant in first possession.

"You love me," she murmured, in strange transport, yearning and triumphant and confident. "You love me. I know you love me, I know."

And she was passionately kissing his knees, through the wet clothing, passionately and indiscriminately kissing his knees, his legs, as if unaware of everything.

He looked down at the tangled wet hair, the wild, bare, animal shoulders. He was amazed, bewildered, and afraid. He had never thought of loving her. He had never wanted to love her. When he rescued her and restored her, he was a doctor, and she was a patient. He had had no single personal thought of her. Nay, this introduction of the personal element was very distasteful to him, a violation of his professional honour. It was horrible to have her there embracing his knees. It was horrible. He revolted from it, violently. And yet—and yet—he had not the power to break away.

She looked at him again, with the same supplication of powerful love, and that same transcendent, frightening light of triumph. In view of the delicate flame which seemed to come from her face like a light, he was powerless. And yet he had never intended to love her. He had never intended. And something stubborn in him could not give way.

"You love me," she repeated, in a murmur of deep, rhapsodic assurance. "You love me."

Her hands were drawing him, drawing him down to her. He was afraid, even a little horrified. For he had, really, no intention of loving her. Yet her hands were drawing him towards her. He put out his hand quickly to steady himself, and grasped her bare shoulder. A flame seemed to burn the hand that grasped her soft shoulder. He had no intention of loving her: his whole will was against his yielding. It was horrible. And yet wonderful was the touch of her shoulders, beautiful the shining of her face. Was she perhaps mad? He had a horror of yielding to her. Yet something in him ached also.

He had been staring away at the door, away from her. But his hand remained on her shoulder. She had gone suddenly very still. He looked down at her. Her eyes were now wide with fear, with doubt, the light was dying from her face, a shadow of terrible greyness was returning. He could not bear the touch of her eyes' question upon him, and the look of death behind the question.

With an inward groan he gave way, and let his heart yield towards her. A sudden gentle smile came on his face. And her eyes, which never left his face, slowly, slowly filled with tears. He watched the strange water rise in her eyes, like some slow fountain coming up. And his heart seemed to burn and melt away in his breast.

He could not bear to look at her any more. He dropped on his knees and caught her head with his arms and pressed her face against his throat. She was very still. His heart, which seemed to have broken, was burning with a kind of agony in his breast. And he felt her slow, hot tears wetting his throat. But he could not move.

He felt the hot tears wet his neck and the hollows of his neck, and he remained motionless, suspended through one of man's eternities. Only now it had become indispensable to him to have her face pressed close to him; he could never let her go again. He could never let her head go away from the close clutch of his arm. He wanted to remain like that for ever, with his heart hurting him in a pain that was also life to him. Without knowing, he was looking down on her damp, soft brown hair.

Then, as it were suddenly, he smelt the horrid stagnant smell

of that water. And at the same moment she drew away
from him and looked at him. Her eyes were wistful and
unfathomable. He was afraid of them, and he fell to kissing
her, not knowing what he was doing. He wanted her eyes
not to have that terrible, wistful, unfathomable look.

When she turned her face to him again, a faint delicate
flush was glowing, and there was again dawning that terrible
shining of joy in her eyes, which really terrified him, and yet
which he now wanted to see, because he feared the look of
doubt still more.

"You love me?" she said, rather faltering.

"Yes." The word cost him a painful effort. Not because
it wasn't true. But because it was too newly true, the *saying*
seemed to tear open again his newly-torn heart. And he
hardly wanted it to be true, even now.

She lifted her face to him, and he bent forward and kissed
her on the mouth, gently, with the one kiss that is an
eternal pledge. And as he kissed her his heart strained again
in his breast. He never intended to love her. But now it was
over. He had crossed over the gulf to her, and all that he
had left behind had shrivelled and become void.

After the kiss, her eyes again slowly filled with tears. She
sat still, away from him, with her face drooped aside, and
her hands folded in her lap. The tears fell very slowly. There
was complete silence. He too sat there motionless and silent
on the hearth-rug. The strange pain of his heart that was
broken seemed to consume him. That he should love her?
That this was love! That he should be ripped open in this
way! Him, a doctor! How they would all jeer if they knew!
It was agony to him to think they might know.

In the curious naked pain of the thought he looked again
to her. She was sitting there drooped into a muse. He saw
a tear fall, and his heart flared hot. He saw for the first
time that one of her shoulders was quite uncovered, one
arm bare, he could see one of her small breasts; dimly,
because it had become almost dark in the room.

"Why are you crying?" he asked, in an altered voice.

She looked up at him, and behind her tears the consciousness of her situation for the first time brought a dark look
of shame to her eyes.

"I'm not crying, really," she said, watching him, half frightened.

He reached his hand, and softly closed it on her bare arm.

"I love you! I love you!" he said in a soft, low vibrating voice, unlike himself.

She shrank, and dropped her head. The soft, penetrating grip of his hand on her arm distressed her. She looked up at him.

"I want to go," she said. "I want to go and get you some dry things."

"Why?" he said. "I'm all right."

"But I want to go," she said. "And I want you to change your things."

He released her arm, and she wrapped herself in the blanket, looking at him rather frightened. And still she did not rise.

"Kiss me," she said wistfully.

He kissed her, but briefly, half in anger.

Then, after a second, she rose nervously, all mixed up in the blanket. He watched her in her confusion as she tried to extricate herself and wrap herself up so that she could walk. He watched her relentlessly, as she knew. And as she went, the blanket trailing, and as he saw a glimpse of her feet and her white leg, he tried to remember her as she was when he had wrapped her in the blanket. But then he didn't want to remember, because she had been nothing to him then, and his nature revolted from remembering her as she was when she was nothing to him.

A tumbling, muffled noise from within the dark house startled him. Then he heard her voice: "There are clothes." He rose and went to the foot of the stairs, and gathered up the garments she had thrown down. Then he came back to the fire, to rub himself down and dress. He grinned at his own appearance when he had finished.

The fire was sinking, so he put on coal. The house was now quite dark, save for the light of a street-lamp that shone in faintly from beyond the holly trees. He lit the gas with matches he found on the mantelpiece. Then he emptied the pockets of his own clothes, and threw all his wet things in a heap into the scullery. After which he gathered up her sodden clothes, gently, and put them in a separate heap on the coppertop in the scullery.

It was six o'clock on the clock. His own watch had stopped. He ought to go back to the surgery. He waited, and still she did not come down. So he went to the foot of the stairs and called:

"I shall have to go."

Almost immediately he heard her coming down. She had on her best dress of black voile, and her hair was tidy, but still damp. She looked at him—and in spite of herself, smiled.

"I don't like you in those clothes," she said.

"Do I look a sight?" he answered.

They were shy of one another.

"I'll make you some tea," she said.

"No, I must go."

"Must you?" And she looked at him again with the wide, strained, doubtful eyes. And again, from the pain of his breast, he knew how he loved her. He went and bent to kiss her, gently, passionately, with his heart's painful kiss.

"And my hair smells so horrible," she murmured in distraction. "And I'm so awful, I'm so awful! Oh no, I'm too awful." And she broke into bitter, heart-broken sobbing. "You can't want to love me, I'm horrible."

"Don't be silly, don't be silly," he said, trying to comfort her, kissing her, holding her in his arms. "I want you, I want to marry you, we're going to be married, quickly, quickly—to-morrow if I can."

But she only sobbed terribly, and cried:

"I feel awful. I feel awful. I feel I'm horrible to you."

"No, I want you, I want you," was all he answered, blindly, with that terrible intonation which frightened her almost more than her horror lest he should *not* want her.

W. SOMERSET MAUGHAM

The Colonel's Lady

*W. Somerset Maugham (1874-1966) called himself
only a "tale-teller," but he was a writer of far
more depth and psychological understanding than
this would imply. The son of a British diplomat,
Maugham was born in Paris and spoke French
before he spoke English. In a long lifetime he traveled widely, and his fiction often dealt with strange
places but never with unreal characters. A successful dramatist (The Circle, The Constant Wife, The
Letter . . .) before he wrote stories, he developed
a sharp feeling for form, and always felt it a kind
of literary snobbery to scorn strong plot structure.
His novel Of Human Bondage has become a literary
classic, and this, as well as a number of his other
novels and short stories, has been a highly successful
film.*

ALL THIS HAPPENED two or three years before the outbreak
of the war.

The Peregrines were having breakfast. Though they were
alone and the table was long they sat at opposite ends of
it. From the walls George Peregrine's ancestors, painted by
the fashionable painters of the day, looked down upon them.
The butler brought in the morning post. There were several
letters for the colonel, business letters, *The Times* and a
small parcel for his wife Evie. He looked at his letters and
then, opening *The Times*, began to read it. They finished

breakfast and rose from the table. He noticed that his wife hadn't opened the parcel.

"What's that?" he asked.

"Only some books."

"Shall I open it for you?"

"If you like."

He hated to cut string and so with some difficulty untied the knots.

"But they're all the same," he said when he had unwrapped the parcel. "What on earth d'you want six copies of the same book for?" He opened one of them. "Poetry." Then he looked at the title page. *When Pyramids Decay,* he read, by E. K. Hamilton. Eva Katherine Hamilton: that was his wife's maiden name. He looked at her with smiling surprise. "Have you written a book, Evie? You are a slyboots."

"I didn't think it would interest you very much. Would you like a copy?"

"Well, you know poetry isn't much in my line, but—yes, I'd like a copy; I'll read it. I'll take it along to my study. I've got a lot to do this morning."

He gathered up *The Times,* his letters and the book, and went out. His study was a large and comfortable room, with a big desk, leather arm-chairs and what he called "trophies of the chase" on the walls. On the bookshelves were works of reference, books on farming, gardening, fishing and shooting, and books on the last war, in which he had won an M.C. and a D.S.O. For before his marriage he had been in the Welsh Guards. At the end of the war he retired and settled down to the life of a country gentleman in the spacious house, some twenty miles from Sheffield, which one of his forebears had built in the reign of George III. George Peregrine had an estate of some fifteen hundred acres which he managed with ability; he was a Justice of the Peace and performed his duties conscientiously. During the season he rode to hounds two days a week. He was a good shot, a golfer and though now a little over fifty could still play a hard game of tennis. He could describe himself with propriety as an all-round sportsman.

He had been putting on weight lately, but was still a fine figure of a man; tall, with grey curly hair, only just beginning to grow thin on the crown, frank blue eyes, good features and a high colour. He was a public-spirited man, chairman of any number of local organisations and, as became his class and station, a loyal member of the Conserva-

tive Party. He looked upon it as his duty to see to the
welfare of the people on his estate and it was a satisfaction
to him to know that Evie could be trusted to tend the
sick and succour the poor. He had built a cottage hospital on
the outskirts of the village and paid the wages of a nurse
out of his own pocket. All he asked of the recipients of his
bounty was that at elections, county or general, they should
vote for his candidate. He was a friendly man, affable to
his inferiors, considerate with his tenants and popular with
the neighbouring gentry. He would have been pleased and at
the same time slightly embarrassed if someone had told him
he was a jolly good fellow. That was what he wanted to
be. He desired no higher praise.

It was hard luck that he had no children. He would have
been an excellent father, kindly but strict, and would have
brought up his sons as gentlemen's sons should be brought
up, sent them to Eton, you know, taught them to fish,
shoot and ride. As it was, his heir was a nephew, son of his
brother killed in a motor accident, not a bad boy, but not
a chip off the old block, no, sir, far from it; and would
you believe it, his fool of a mother was sending him to a
co-educational school. Evie had been a sad disappointment to
him. Of course she was a lady, and she had a bit of money
of her own; she managed the house uncommonly well and
she was a good hostess. The village people adored her. She
had been a pretty little thing when he married her, with
a creamy skin, light brown hair and a trim figure, healthy
too and not a bad tennis player; he couldn't understand
why she'd had no children; of course she was faded now,
she must be getting on for five and forty; her skin was drab,
her hair had lost its sheen and she was as thin as a rail.
She was always neat and suitably dressed, but she didn't
seem to bother how she looked, she wore no make-up and
didn't even use lipstick; sometimes at night when she dolled
herself up for a party you could tell that once she'd been
quite attractive, but ordinarily she was—well, the sort of
woman you simply didn't notice. A nice woman, of course, a
good wife, and it wasn't her fault if she was barren, but
it was tough on a fellow who wanted an heir of his own
loins; she hadn't any vitality, that's what was the matter with
her. He supposed he'd been in love with her when he asked
her to marry him, at least sufficiently in love for a man who
wanted to marry and settle down, but with time he discovered
that they had nothing much in common. She didn't care about

hunting, and fishing bored her. Naturally they'd drifted apart.
He had to do her the justice to admit that she'd never bothered
him. There'd been no scenes. They had no quarrels. She
seemed to take it for granted that he should go his own
way. When he went up to London now and then she never
wanted to come with him. He had a girl there, well, she
wasn't exactly a girl, she was thirty-five if she was a day,
but she was blonde and luscious and he only had to wire
ahead of time and they'd dine, do a show and spend the
night together. Well, a man, a healthy normal man had to
have some fun in his life. The thought crossed his mind that
if Evie hadn't been such a good woman she'd have been a
better wife; but it was not the sort of thought that he welcomed and he put it away from him.

George Peregrine finished his *Times* and being a considerate fellow rang the bell and told the butler to take it to
Evie. Then he looked at his watch. It was half-past ten and at
eleven he had an appointment with one of his tenants. He
had half an hour to spare.

"I'd better have a look at Evie's book," he said to himself.

He took it up with a smile. Evie had a lot of highbrow
books in her sitting-room, not the sort of books that interested him, but if they amused her he had no objection to her
reading them. He noticed that the volume he now held in
his hand contained no more than ninety pages. That was all
to the good. He shared Edgar Allan Poe's opinion that poems
should be short. But as he turned the pages he noticed that
several of Evie's had long lines of irregular length and didn't
rhyme. He didn't like that. At his first school, when he was a
little boy, he remembered learning a poem that began: *The
boy stood on the burning deck,* and later, at Eton, one that
started: *Ruin seize thee, ruthless king;* and then there was
Henry V; they'd had to take that, one half. He stared at
Evie's pages with consternation.

"That's not what I call poetry," he said.

Fortunately it wasn't all like that. Interspersed with the
pieces that looked so odd, lines of three or four words and
then a line of ten or fifteen, there were little poems, quite
short, that rhymed, thank God, with the lines all the same
length. Several of the pages were just headed with the word
Sonnet, and out of curiosity he counted the lines; there were
fourteen of them. He read them. They seemed all right, but
he didn't quite know what they were all about. He repeated
to himself: *Ruin seize thee, ruthless king.*

"Poor Evie," he sighed.

At that moment the farmer he was expecting was ushered into the study, and putting the book down he made him welcome. They embarked on their business.

"I read your book, Evie," he said as they sat down to lunch. "Jolly good. Did it cost you a packet to have it printed?"

"No, I was lucky. I sent it to a publisher and he took it."

"Not much money in poetry, my dear," he said in his good-natured, hearty way.

"No, I don't suppose there is. What did Bannock want to see you about this morning?"

Bannock was the tenant who had interrupted his reading of Evie's poems.

"He's asked me to advance the money for a pedigree bull he wants to buy. He's a good man and I've half a mind to do it."

George Peregrine saw that Evie didn't want to talk about her book and he was not sorry to change the subject. He was glad she had used her maiden name on the title page; he didn't suppose anyone would ever hear about the book, but he was proud of his own unusual name and he wouldn't have liked it if some damned penny-a-liner had made fun of Evie's effort in one of the papers.

During the few weeks that followed he thought it tactful not to ask Evie any questions about her venture into verse and she never referred to it. It might have been a discreditable incident that they had silently agreed not to mention. But then a strange thing happened. He had to go to London on business and he took Daphne out to dinner. That was the name of the girl with whom he was in the habit of passing a few agreeable hours whenever he went to town.

"Oh, George," she said, "is that your wife who's written a book they're all talking about?"

"What on earth d'you mean?"

"Well, there's a fellow I know who's a critic. He took me out to dinner the other night and he had a book with him. 'Got anything for me to read?' I said. 'What's that?' 'Oh, I don't think that's your cup of tea,' he said. 'It's poetry. I've just been reviewing it.' 'No poetry for me,' I said. 'It's about the hottest stuff I ever read,' he said. 'Selling like hot cakes. And it's damned good.'"

"Who's the book by?" asked George.

"A woman called Hamilton. My friend told me that wasn't

her real name. He said her real name was Peregrine. 'Funny,'
I said, 'I know a fellow called Peregrine.' 'Colonel in the
army,' he said. 'Lives near Sheffield.' "

"I'd just as soon you didn't talk about me to your friends,"
said George with a frown of vexation.

"Keep your shirt on, dearie. Who d'you take me for? I
just said: 'It's not the same one.' " Daphne giggled. "My friend
said: 'They say he's a regular Colonel Blimp.' "

George had a keen sense of humour.

"You could tell them better than that," he laughed. "If
my wife had written a book I'd be the first to know about it,
wouldn't I?"

"I suppose you would."

Anyhow the matter didn't interest her and when the colonel
began to talk of other things she forgot about it. He put it out
of his mind too. There was nothing to it, he decided, and that
silly fool of a critic had just been pulling Daphne's leg. He
was amused at the thought of her tackling that book because
she had been told it was hot stuff and then finding it just a lot
of bosh cut up into unequal lines.

He was a member of several clubs and next day he thought
he'd lunch at one in St. James's Street. He was catching a train back to Sheffield early in the afternoon. He was
sitting in a comfortable arm-chair having a glass of sherry before going into the dining-room when an old friend came up
to him.

"Well, old boy, how's life?" he said. "How d'you like being
the husband of a celebrity?"

George Peregrine looked at his friend. He thought he saw
an amused twinkle in his eyes.

"I don't know what you're talking about," he answered.

"Come off it, George. Everyone knows E. K. Hamilton is
your wife. Not often a book of verse has a success like that.
Look here, Henry Dashwood is lunching with me. He'd like to
meet you."

"Who the devil is Henry Dashwood and why should he want
to meet me?"

"Oh, my dear fellow, what do you do with yourself all the
time in the country? Henry's about the best critic we've got.
He wrote a wonderful review of Evie's book. D'you mean to
say she didn't show it you?"

Before George could answer his friend had called a man
over. A tall, thin man, with a high forehead, a beard, a long
nose and a stoop, just the sort of man whom George was

prepared to dislike at first sight. Introductions were effected.
Henry Dashwood sat down.

"Is Mrs. Peregrine in London by any chance? I should very
much like to meet her," he said.

"No, my wife doesn't like London. She prefers the country,"
said George stiffly.

"She wrote me a very nice letter about my review. I was
pleased. You know, we critics get more kicks than halfpence.
I was simply bowled over by her book. It's so fresh and
original, very modern without being obscure. She seems to be
as much at her ease in free verse as in the classical metres."
Then because he was a critic he thought he should criticise.
"Sometimes her ear is a trifle at fault, but you can say the
same of Emily Dickinson. There are several of those short
lyrics of hers that might have been written by Landor."

All this was gibberish to George Peregrine. The man was
nothing but a disgusting highbrow. But the colonel had good
manners and he answered with proper civility: Henry Dashwood went on as though he hadn't spoken.

"But what makes the book so outstanding is the passion that
throbs in every line. So many of these young poets are so
anaemic, cold, bloodless, dully intellectual, but here you
have real naked, earthy passion; of course deep, sincere emotion like that is tragic—ah, my dear Colonel, how right Heine
was when he said that the poet makes little songs out of his
great sorrows. You know, now and then, as I read and re-
read those heart-rending pages I thought of Sappho."

This was too much for George Peregrine and he got up.

"Well, it's jolly nice of you to say such nice things about
my wife's little book. I'm sure she'll be delighted. But I must
bolt, I've got to catch a train and I want to get a bite of
lunch."

"Damned fool," he said irritably to himself as he walked
upstairs to the dining-room.

He got home in time for dinner and after Evie had gone to
bed he went into his study and looked for her book. He
thought he'd just glance through it again to see for himself
what they were making such a fuss about, but he couldn't find
it. Evie must have taken it away.

"Silly," he muttered.

He'd told her he thought it jolly good. What more could a
fellow be expected to say? Well, it didn't matter. He lit his
pipe and read the *Field* till he felt sleepy. But a week or so
later it happened that he had to go into Sheffield for the day.

He lunched there at his club. He had nearly finished when the Duke of Haverel came in. This was the great local magnate and of course the colonel knew him, but only to say how d'you do to; and he was surprised when the Duke stopped at his table.

"We're so sorry your wife couldn't come to us for the week-end," he said, with a sort of shy cordiality. "We're expecting rather a nice lot of people."

George was taken aback. He guessed that the Haverels had asked him and Evie over for the week-end and Evie, without saying a word to him about it, had refused. He had the presence of mind to say he was sorry too.

"Better luck next time," said the Duke pleasantly and moved on.

Colonel Peregrine was very angry and when he got home he said to his wife:

"Look here, what's this about our being asked over to Haverel? Why on earth did you say we couldn't go? We've never been asked before and it's the best shooting in the county."

"I didn't think of that. I thought it would only bore you."

"Damn it all, you might at least have asked me if I wanted to go."

"I'm sorry."

He looked at her closely. There was something in her expression that he didn't quite understand. He frowned.

"I suppose *I* was asked?" he barked.

Evie flushed a little.

"Well, in point of fact you weren't."

"I call it damned rude of them to ask you without asking me."

"I suppose they thought it wasn't your sort of party. The Duchess is rather fond of writers and people like that, you know. She's having Henry Dashwood, the critic, and for some reason he wants to meet me."

"It was damned nice of you to refuse, Evie."

"It's the least I could do," she smiled. She hesitated a moment. "George, my publishers want to give a little dinner party for me one day towards the end of the month and of course they want you to come too."

"Oh, I don't think that's quite my mark. I'll come up to London with you if you like. I'll find someone to dine with."

Daphne.

"I expect it'll be very dull, but they're making rather a point of it. And the day after, the American publisher who's taken my book is giving a cocktail party at Claridge's. I'd like you to come to that if you wouldn't mind."

"Sounds like a crashing bore, but if you really want me to come I'll come."

"It would be sweet of you."

George Peregrine was dazed by the cocktail party. There were a lot of people. Some of them didn't look so bad, a few of the women were decently turned out, but the men seemed to him pretty awful. He was introduced to everyone as Colonel Peregrine, E. K. Hamilton's husband, you know. The men didn't seem to have anything to say to him, but the women gushed.

"You *must* be proud of your wife. Isn't it *wonderful?* You know, I read it right through at a sitting, I simply couldn't put it down, and when I'd finished I started again at the beginning and read it right through a second time. I was simply *thrilled.*"

The English publisher said to him:

"We've not had a success like this with a book of verse for twenty years. I've never seen such reviews."

The American publisher said to him:

"It's swell. It'll be a smash hit in America. You wait and see."

The American publisher had sent Evie a great spray of orchids. Damned ridiculous, thought George. As they came in, people were taken up to Evie, and it was evident that they said flattering things to her, which she took with a pleasant smile and a word or two of thanks. She was a trifle flushed with the excitement, but seemed quite at her ease. Though he thought the whole thing a lot of stuff and nonsense George noted with approval that his wife was carrying it off in just the right way.

"Well, there's one thing," he said to himself, "you can see she's a lady and that's a damned sight more than you can say of anyone else here."

He drank a good many cocktails. But there was one thing that bothered him. He had a notion that some of the people he was introduced to looked at him in rather a funny sort of way, he couldn't quite make out what it meant, and once when he strolled by two women who were sitting together on a sofa he had the impression that they were talking about him and after he passed he was almost certain they tittered. He was very glad when the party came to an end.

In the taxi on their way back to their hotel Evie said to him:

"You were wonderful, dear. You made quite a hit. The girls simply raved about you: they thought you so handsome."

"Girls," he said bitterly. "Old hags."

"Were you bored, dear?"

"Stiff."

She pressed his hand in a gesture of sympathy.

"I hope you won't mind if we wait and go down by the afternoon train. I've got some things to do in the morning."

"No, that's all right. Shopping?"

"I do want to buy one or two things, but I've got to go and be photographed. I hate the idea, but they think I ought to be. For America, you know."

He said nothing. But he thought. He thought it would be a shock to the American public when they saw the portrait of the homely, desiccated little woman who was his wife. He'd always been under the impression that they liked glamour in America.

He went on thinking, and next morning when Evie had gone out he went to his club and up to the library. There he looked up recent numbers of *The Times Literary Supplement,* *The New Statesman* and *The Spectator.* Presently he found reviews of Evie's book. He didn't read them very carefully, but enough to see that they were extremely favourable. Then he went to the bookseller's in Piccadilly where he occasionally bought books. He'd made up his mind that he had to read this damned thing of Evie's properly, but he didn't want to ask her what she'd done with the copy she'd given him. He'd buy one for himself. Before going in he looked in the window and the first thing he saw was a display of *When Pyramids Decay.* Damned silly title! He went in. A young man came forward and asked if he could help him.

"No, I'm just having a look round." It embarrassed him to ask for Evie's book and he thought he'd find it for himself and then take it to the salesman. But he couldn't see it anywhere and at last, finding the young man near him, he said in a carefully casual tone: "By the way, have you got a book called *When Pyramids Decay?*"

"The new edition came in this morning. I'll get a copy."

In a moment the young man returned with it. He was a short, rather stout young man, with a shock of untidy carroty hair and spectacles. George Peregrine, tall, upstanding, very military, towered over him.

"Is this a new edition then?" he asked.

"Yes, sir. The fifth. It might be a novel the way it's selling."

George Peregrine hesitated a moment.

"Why d'you suppose it's such a success? I've always been told no one reads poetry."

"Well, it's good, you know. I've read it meself." The young man, though obviously cultured, had a slight Cockney accent, and George quite instinctively adopted a patronising attitude. "It's the story they like. Sexy, you know, but tragic."

George frowned a little. He was coming to the conclusion that the young man was rather impertinent. No one had told him anything about there being a story in the damned book and he had not gathered that from reading the reviews. The young man went on:

"Of course it's only a flash in the pan, if you know what I mean. The way I look at it, she was sort of inspired like by a personal experience, like Housman was with *The Shropshire Lad*. She'll never write anything else."

"How much is the book?" said George coldly to stop his chatter. "You needn't wrap it up, I'll just slip it into my pocket."

The November morning was raw and he was wearing a greatcoat.

At the station he bought the evening papers and magazines and he and Evie settled themselves comfortably in opposite corners of a first-class carriage and read. At five o'clock they went along to the restaurant car to have tea and chatted a little. They arrived. They drove home in the car which was waiting for them. They bathed, dressed for dinner, and after dinner Evie, saying she was tired out, went to bed. She kissed him, as was her habit, on the forehead. Then he went into the hall, took Evie's book out of his greatcoat pocket and going into the study began to read it. He didn't read verse very easily and though he read with attention, every word of it, the impression he received was far from clear. Then he began at the beginning again and read it a second time. He read with increasing malaise, but he was not a stupid man and when he had finished he had a distinct understanding of what it was all about. Part of the book was in free verse, part in conventional metres, but the story it related was coherent and plain to the meanest intelligence. It was the story of a passionate love affair between an older woman, married, and a young man. George Peregrine made out the steps of it as easily as if he had been doing a sum in simple addition.

Written in the first person, it began with the tremulous surprise of the woman, past her youth, when it dawned upon

her that the young man was in love with her. She hesitated
to believe it. She thought she must be deceiving herself. And
she was terrified when on a sudden she discovered that she
was passionately in love with him. She told herself it was
absurd; with the disparity of age between them nothing but
unhappiness could come to her if she yielded to her emotion.
She tried to prevent him from speaking but the day came
when he told her that he loved her and forced her to tell him
that she loved him too. He begged her to run away with him.
She couldn't leave her husband, her home; and what life could
they look forward to, she an ageing woman, he so young?
How could she expect his love to last? She begged him to have
mercy on her. But his love was impetuous. He wanted her, he
wanted her with all his heart, and at last trembling, afraid,
desirous, she yielded to him. Then there was a period of
ecstatic happiness. The world, the dull, humdrum world of
every day, blazed with glory. Love songs flowed from her
pen. The woman worshipped the young, virile body of her
lover. George flushed darkly when she praised his broad
chest and slim flanks, the beauty of his legs and the flatness
of his belly.

Hot stuff, Daphne's friend had said. It was that all right.
Disgusting.

There were sad little pieces in which she lamented the
emptiness of her life when as must happen he left her, but
they ended with a cry that all she had to suffer would be
worth it for the bliss that for a while had been hers. She wrote
of the long, tremulous nights they passed together and the
languor that lulled them to sleep in one another's arms. She
wrote of the rapture of brief stolen moments when, braving
all danger, their passion overwhelmed them and they sur-
rendered to its call.

She thought it would be an affair of a few weeks, but
miraculously it lasted. One of the poems referred to three
years having gone by without lessening the love that filled
their hearts. It looked as though he continued to press her
to go away with him, far away, to a hill town in Italy, a
Greek island, a walled city in Tunisia, so that they could be
together always, for in another of the poems she besought
him to let things be as they were. Their happiness was pre-
carious. Perhaps it was owing to the difficulties they had to
encounter and the rarity of their meetings that their love had
retained for so long its first enchanting ardour. Then on a
sudden the young man died. How, when or where George

could not discover. There followed a long, heart-broken cry of bitter grief, grief she could not indulge in, grief that had to be hidden. She had to be cheerful, give dinner-parties and go out to dinner, behave as she had always behaved, though the light had gone out of her life and she was bowed down with anguish. The last poem of all was a set of four short stanzas in which the writer, sadly resigned to her loss, thanked the dark powers that rule man's destiny that she had been privileged at least for a while to enjoy the greatest happiness that we poor human beings can ever hope to know.

It was three o'clock in the morning when George Peregrine finally put the book down. It had seemed to him that he heard Evie's voice in every line, over and over again he came upon turns of phrase he had heard her use, there were details that were as familiar to him as to her: there was no doubt about it; it was her own story she had told, and it was as plain as anything could be that she had had a lover and her lover had died. It was not anger so much that he felt, nor horror or dismay, though he was dismayed and he was horrified, but amazement. It was as inconceivable that Evie should have had a love affair, and a wildly passionate one at that, as that the trout in a glass case over the chimney piece in his study, the finest he had ever caught, should suddenly wag its tail. He understood now the meaning of the amused look he had seen in the eyes of that man he had spoken to at the club, he understood why Daphne when she was talking about the book had seemed to be enjoying a private joke, and why those two women at the cocktail party had tittered when he strolled past them.

He broke out into a sweat. Then on a sudden he was seized with fury and he jumped up to go and awake Evie and ask her sternly for an explanation. But he stopped at the door. After all, what proof had he? A book. He remembered that he'd told Evie he thought it jolly good. True, he hadn't read it, but he'd pretended he had. He would look a perfect fool if he had to admit that.

"I must watch my step," he muttered.

He made up his mind to wait for two or three days and think it all over. Then he'd decide what to do. He went to bed, but he couldn't sleep for a long time.

"Evie," he kept on saying to himself. "Evie, of all people."

They met at breakfast next morning as usual. Evie was as she always was, quiet, demure and self-possessed, a middle-aged woman who made no effort to look younger than she was, a woman who had nothing of what he still called It. He looked at her as he hadn't looked at her for years. She had her usual placid serenity. Her pale blue eyes were untroubled. There was no sign of guilt on her candid brow. She made the same little casual remarks she always made.

"It's nice to get back to the country again after those two hectic days in London. What are you going to do this morning?"

It was incomprehensible.

Three days later he went to see his solicitor. Henry Blane was an old friend of George's as well as his lawyer. He had a place not far from Peregrine's and for years they had shot over one another's preserves. For two days a week he was a country gentleman and for the other five a busy lawyer in Sheffield. He was a tall, robust fellow, with a boisterous manner and a jovial laugh, which suggested that he liked to be looked upon essentially as a sportsman and a good fellow and only incidentally as a lawyer. But he was shrewd and worldly-wise.

"Well, George, what's brought you here today?" he boomed as the colonel was showed into his office. "Have a good time in London? I'm taking my missus up for a few days next week. How's Evie?"

"It's about Evie I've come to see you," said Peregrine, giving him a suspicious look. "Have you read her book?"

His sensitivity had been sharpened during those last days of troubled thought and he was conscious of a faint change in the lawyer's expression. It was as though he were suddenly on his guard.

"Yes, I've read it. Great success, isn't it? Fancy Evie breaking out into poetry. Wonders will never cease."

George Peregrine was inclined to lose his temper.

"It's made me look a perfect damned fool."

"Oh, what nonsense, George! There's no harm in Evie's writing a book. You ought to be jolly proud of her."

"Don't talk such rot. It's her own story. You know it and everyone else knows it. I suppose I'm the only one who doesn't know who her lover was."

"There is such a thing as imagination, old boy. There's no reason to suppose the whole thing isn't made up."

"Look here, Henry, we've known one another all our lives. We've had all sorts of good times together. Be honest with me. Can you look me in the face and tell me you believe it's a made-up story?"

Harry Blane moved uneasily in his chair. He was disturbed by the distress in old George's voice.

"You've got no right to ask me a question like that. Ask Evie."

"I daren't," George answered after an anguished pause. "I'm afraid she'd tell me the truth."

There was an uncomfortable silence.

"Who was the chap?"

Harry Blane looked at him straight in the eye.

"I don't know, and if I did I wouldn't tell you."

"You swine. Don't you see what a position I'm in? Do you think it's very pleasant to be made absolutely ridiculous?"

The lawyer lit a cigarette and for some moments silently puffed it.

"I don't see what I can do for you," he said at last.

"You've got private detectives you employ, I suppose. I want you to put them on the job and let them find everything out."

"It's not very pretty to put detectives on one's wife, old boy; and besides, taking for granted for a moment that Evie had an affair, it was a good many years ago and I don't suppose it would be possible to find out a thing. They seem to have covered their tracks pretty carefully."

"I don't care. You put the detectives on. I want to know the truth."

"I won't, George. If you're determined to do that you'd better consult someone else. And look here, even if you got evidence that Evie had been unfaithful to you what would you do with it? You'd look rather silly divorcing your wife because she'd committed adultery ten years ago."

"At all events I could have it out with her."

"You can do that now, but you know just as well as I do that if you do she'll leave you. D'you want her to do that?"

George gave him an unhappy look.

"I don't know. I always thought she'd been a damned good wife to me. She runs the house perfectly, we never have any servant trouble; she's done wonders with the garden and she's splendid with all the village people. But damn it, I have my self-respect to think of. How can I go on living with her when I know that she was grossly unfaithful to me?"

"Have you always been faithful to her?"

"More or less, you know. After all, we've been married

for nearly twenty-four years and Evie was never much for bed."

The solicitor slightly raised his eyebrows, but George was too intent on what he was saying to notice.

"I don't deny that I've had a bit of fun now and then. A man wants it. Women are different."

"We only have men's word for that," said Harry Blane, with a faint smile.

"Evie's absolutely the last woman I'd have suspected of kicking over the traces. I mean, she's a very fastidious, reticent woman. What on earth made her write the damned book?"

"I suppose it was a very poignant experience and perhaps it was a relief to her to get it off her chest like that."

"Well, if she had to write it why the devil didn't she write it under an assumed name?"

"She used her maiden name. I suppose she thought that was enough, and it would have been if the book hadn't had this amazing boom."

George Peregrine and the lawyer were sitting opposite one another with a desk between them. George, his elbow on the desk, his cheek on his hand, frowned at his thought.

"It's so rotten not to know what sort of a chap he was. One can't even tell if he was by way of being a gentleman. I mean, for all I know he may have been a farm-hand or a clerk in a lawyer's office."

Harry Blane did not permit himself to smile and when he answered there was in his eyes a kindly, tolerant look.

"Knowing Evie so well I think the probabilities are that he was all right. Anyhow I'm sure he wasn't a clerk in my office."

"It's been a shock to me," the colonel sighed. "I thought she was fond of me. She couldn't have written that book unless she hated me."

"Oh, I don't believe that. I don't think she's capable of hatred."

"You're not going to pretend that she loves me."

"No."

"Well, what does she feel for me?"

Harry Blane leaned back in his swivel chair and looked at George reflectively.

"Indifference, I should say."

The colonel gave a little shudder and reddened.

"After all, you're not in love with her, are you?"

George Peregrine did not answer directly.

"It's been a great blow to me not to have any children, but I've never let her see that I think she's let me down. I've always been kind to her. Within reasonable limits I've tried to do my duty by her."

The lawyer passed a large hand over his mouth to conceal the smile that trembled on his lips.

"It's been such an awful shock to me," Peregrine went on. "Damn it all, even ten years ago Evie was no chicken and God knows, she wasn't much to look at. It's so ugly." He sighed deeply. "What would *you* do in my place?"

"Nothing."

George Peregrine drew himself bolt upright in his chair and he looked at Harry with the stern set face that he must have worn when he inspected his regiment.

"I can't overlook a thing like this. I've been made a laughing-stock. I can never hold up my head again."

"Nonsense," said the lawyer sharply, and then in a pleasant, kindly manner, "Listen, old boy: the man's dead; it all happened a long while back. Forget it. Talk to people about Evie's book, rave about it, tell 'em how proud you are of her. Behave as though you had so much confidence in her, you *knew* she could never have been unfaithful to you. The world moves so quickly and people's memories are so short. They'll forget."

"I shan't forget."

"You're both middle-aged people. She probably does a great deal more for you than you think and you'd be awfully lonely without her. I don't think it matters if you don't forget. It'll be all to the good if you can get it into that thick head of yours that there's a lot more in Evie than you ever had the gumption to see."

"Damn it all, you talk as if *I* was to blame."

"No, I don't think you were to blame, but I'm not so sure that Evie was either. I don't suppose she wanted to fall in love with this boy. D'you remember those verses right at the end? The impression they gave me was that though she was shattered by his death, in a strange sort of way she welcomed it. All through she'd been aware of the fragility of the tie that bound them. He died in the full flush of his first love and had never known that love so seldom endures; he'd only known its bliss and beauty. In her own bitter grief she found solace in the thought that he'd been spared all sorrow."

"All that's a bit above my head, old boy. I see more or less what you mean."

George Peregrine stared unhappily at the inkstand on the desk. He was silent and the lawyer looked at him with curious, yet sympathetic, eyes.

"Do you realise what courage she must have had never by a sign to show how dreadfully unhappy she was?" he said gently.

Colonel Peregrine sighed.

"I'm broken. I suppose you're right; it's no good crying over spilt milk and it would only make things worse if I made a fuss."

"Well?"

George Peregrine gave him a pitiful little smile.

"I'll take your advice. I'll do nothing. Let them think me a damned fool and to hell with them. The truth is, I don't know what I'd do without Evie. But I'll tell you what, there's one thing I shall never understand till my dying day: What in the name of heaven did the fellow ever see in her?"

JEAN-PAUL SARTRE

The Wall

*Jean-Paul Sartre (1905—   ), foremost living
philosopher of the existentialist school, is also an
outstanding playwright, novelist, and short story
writer. A prisoner in Germany during World War
II, he escaped and became active in the French
Resistance movement. He was, and remains, a political activist, believing that in an absurd universe
man must, by his own acts and commitments, create
meaning for his life. Sartre's story "The Wall" is
generally agreed to be his masterpiece in this genre.
Its stark, probing, vivid portrait of men about to
die illustrates with immense power some of the basic
beliefs of existentialism.*

THEY PUSHED US into a large white room and my eyes began
to blink because the light hurt them. Then I saw a table
and four fellows seated at the table, civilians, looking at
some papers. The other prisoners were herded together at
one end and we were obliged to cross the entire room to
join them. There were several I knew, and others who must
have been foreigners. The two in front of me were blond
with round heads. They looked alike. I imagine they were
French. The smaller one kept pulling at his trousers, out of
nervousness.

This lasted about three hours. I was dog-tired and my
head was empty. But the room was well-heated, which struck

me as rather agreeable; we had not stopped shivering for twenty-four hours. The guards led the prisoners in one after the other in front of the table. Then the four fellows asked them their names and what they did. Most of the time that was all—or perhaps from time to time they would ask such questions as: "Did you help sabotage the munitions?" or, "Where were you on the morning of the ninth and what were you doing?" They didn't even listen to the replies, or at least they didn't seem to. They just remained silent for a moment and looked straight ahead, then they began to write. They asked Tom if it was true he had served in the International Brigade. Tom couldn't say he hadn't because of the papers they had found in his jacket. They didn't ask Juan anything, but after he told them his name, they wrote for a long while.

"It's my brother José who's the anarchist," Juan said. "You know perfectly well he's not here now. I don't belong to any party. I never did take part in politics." They didn't answer.

Then Juan said, "I didn't do anything. And I'm not going to pay for what the others did."

His lips were trembling. A guard told him to stop talking and led him away. It was my turn.

"Your name is Pablo Ibbieta?"

I said yes.

The fellow looked at his papers and said, "Where is Ramon Gris?"

"I don't know."

"You hid him in your house from the sixth to the nineteenth."

"I did not."

They continued to write for a moment and the guards led me away. In the hall, Tom and Juan were waiting between two guards. We started walking. Tom asked one of the guards, "What's the idea?" "How do you mean?" the guard asked. "Was that just the preliminary questioning, or was that the trial?" "That was the trial," the guard said. "So now what? What are they going to do with us?" The guard answered drily, "The verdict will be told you in your cell."

In reality, our cell was one of the cellars of the hospital. It was terribly cold there because it was very drafty. We had been shivering all night long and it had hardly been any better during the day. I had spent the preceding five days in a cellar in the archbishop's palace, a sort of dungeon that

must have dated back to the Middle Ages. There were lots
of prisoners and not much room, so they housed them just
anywhere. But I was not homesick for my dungeon. I hadn't
been cold there, but I had been alone, and that gets to be
irritating. In the cellar I had company. Juan didn't say a
word; he was afraid, and besides, he was too young to have
anything to say. But Tom was a good talker and knew Spanish
well.

In the cellar there were a bench and four straw mattresses. When they led us back we sat down and waited in
silence. After a while Tom said, "Our goose is cooked."

"I think so too," I said. "But I don't believe they'll do
anything to the kid."

Tom said, "They haven't got anything on him. He's the
brother of a fellow who's fighting, and that's all."

I looked at Juan. He didn't seem to have heard.

Tom continued, "You know what they do in Saragossa?
They lay the guys across the road and then they drive over
them with trucks. It was a Moroccan deserter who told us
that. They say it's just to save ammunition."

I said, "Well, it doesn't save gasoline."

I was irritated with Tom; he shouldn't have said that.

He went on, "There are officers walking up and down the
roads with their hands in their pockets, smoking, and they
see that it's done right. Do you think they'd put 'em out of
their misery? Like hell they do. They just let 'em holler.
Sometimes as long as an hour. The Moroccan said the first
time he almost puked."

"I don't believe they do that here," I said, "unless they
really are short of ammunition."

The daylight came in through four air vents and a round
opening that had been cut in the ceiling, to the left, and
which opened directly onto the sky. It was through this hole,
which was ordinarily closed by means of a trapdoor, that
they unloaded coal into the cellar. Directly under the hole,
there was a big pile of coal dust; it had been intended for
heating the hospital, but at the beginning of the war they
had evacuated the patients and the coal had stayed there
unused; it even got rained on from time to time, when they
forgot to close the trapdoor.

Tom started to shiver, "God damn it," he said, "I'm shivering. There, it is starting again."

He rose and began to do gymnastic exercises. At each movement, his shirt opened and showed his white, hairy chest.

He lay down on his back, lifted his legs in the air and began to do the scissors movement. I watched his big buttocks tremble. Tom was tough, but he had too much fat on him. I kept thinking that soon bullets and bayonet points would sink into that mass of tender flesh as though it were a pat of butter.

I wasn't exactly cold, but I couldn't feel my shoulders or my arms. From time to time, I had the impression that something was missing and I began to look around for my jacket. Then I would suddenly remember they hadn't given me a jacket. It was rather awkward. They had taken our clothes to give them to their own soldiers and had left us only our shirts and these cotton trousers the hospital patients wore in mid-summer. After a moment, Tom got up and sat down beside me, breathless.

"Did you get warmed up?"

"Damn it, no. But I'm all out of breath."

Around eight o'clock in the evening, a Major came in with two falangists.

"What are the names of those three over there?" he asked the guard.

"Steinbock, Ibbieta and Mirbal," said the guard.

The Major put on his glasses and examined his list.

"Steinbock—Steinbock . . . Here it is. You are condemned to death. You'll be shot tomorrow morning."

He looked at his list again.

"The other two, also," he said.

"That's not possible," said Juan. "Not me."

The Major looked at him with surprise. "What's your name?"

"Juan Mirbal."

"Well, your name is here," said the Major, "and you're condemned to death."

"I didn't do anything," said Juan.

The Major shrugged his shoulders and turned toward Tom and me.

"You are both Basque."

"No, nobody's Basque."

He appeared exasperated.

"I was told there were three Basques. I'm not going to waste my time running after them. I suppose you don't want a priest?"

We didn't even answer.

Then he said, "A Belgian doctor will be around in a little while. He has permission to stay with you all night."

He gave a military salute and left.

"What did I tell you?" Tom said. "We're in for something swell."

"Yes," I said. "It's a damned shame for the kid."

I said that to be fair, but I really didn't like the kid. His face was too refined and it was disfigured by fear and suffering, which had twisted all his features. Three days ago, he was just a kid with a kind of affected manner some people like. But now he looked like an aging fairy, and I thought to myself he would never be young again, even if they let him go. It wouldn't have been a bad thing to show him a little pity, but pity makes me sick, and besides, I couldn't stand him. He hadn't said anything more, but he had turned gray. His face and hands were gray. He sat down again and stared, round-eyed, at the ground. Tom was good-hearted and tried to take him by the arm, but the kid drew himself away violently and made an ugly face. "Leave him alone," I said quietly. "Can't you see he's going to start to bawl?" Tom obeyed regretfully. He would have liked to console the kid; that would have kept him occupied and he wouldn't have been tempted to think about himself. But it got on my nerves. I had never thought about death, for the reason that the question had never come up. But now it had come up, and there was nothing else to do but think about it.

Tom started talking. "Say, did you ever bump anybody off?" he asked me. I didn't answer. He started to explain to me that he had bumped off six fellows since August. He hadn't yet realized what we were in for, and I saw clearly he didn't *want* to realize it. I myself hadn't quite taken it in. I wondered if it hurt very much. I thought about the bullets; I imagined their fiery hail going through my body. All that was beside the real question; but I was calm, we had all night in which to realize it. After a while Tom stopped talking and I looked at him out of the corner of my eye. I saw that he, too, had turned gray and that he looked pretty miserable. I said to myself, "It's starting." It was almost dark, a dull light filtered through the air vents across the coal pile and made a big spot under the sky. Through the hole in the ceiling I could already see a star. The night was going to be clear and cold.

The door opened and two guards entered. They were followed by a blond man in a tan uniform. He greeted us.

"I'm the doctor," he said. "I've been authorized to give you any assistance you may require in these painful circumstances."

He had an agreeable, cultivated voice.

I said to him, "What are you going to do here?"

"Whatever you want me to do. I shall do everything in my power to lighten these few hours."

"Why did you come to us? There are lots of others: the hospital's full of them."

"I was sent here," he answered vaguely. "You'd probably like to smoke, wouldn't you?" he added suddenly. "I've got some cigarettes and even some cigars."

He passed around some English cigarettes and some *puros*, but we refused them. I looked him straight in the eye and he appeared uncomfortable.

"You didn't come here out of compassion," I said to him. "In fact, I know who you are. I saw you with some fascists in the barracks yard the day I was arrested."

I was about to continue, when all at once something happened to me which surprised me: the presence of this doctor had suddenly ceased to interest me. Usually, when I've got hold of a man I don't let go. But somehow the desire to speak had left me. I shrugged my shoulders and turned away. A little later, I looked up and saw he was watching me with an air of curiosity. The guards had sat down on one of the mattresses. Pedro, the tall thin one, was twiddling his thumbs, while the other one shook his head occasionally to keep from falling asleep.

"Do you want some light?" Pedro suddenly asked the doctor. The other fellow nodded, "Yes." I think he was not over-intelligent, but doubtless he was not malicious. As I looked at his big, cold, blue eyes, it seemed to me the worst thing about him was his lack of imagination. Pedro went out and came back with an oil lamp which he set on the corner of the bench. It gave a poor light, but it was better than nothing; the night before we had been left in the dark. For a long while I stared at the circle of light the lamp threw on the ceiling. I was fascinated. Then, suddenly, I came to, the light circle paled, and I felt as if I were being crushed under an enormous weight. It wasn't the thought of death, and it wasn't fear; it was something anonymous. My cheeks were burning hot and my head ached.

I roused myself and looked at my two companions. Tom had his head in his hands and only the fat, white nape of

his neck was visible. Juan was by far the worst off; his mouth
was wide open and his nostrils were trembling. The doctor
came over to him and touched him on the shoulder, as
though to comfort him; but his eyes remained cold. Then
I saw the Belgian slide his hand furtively down Juan's arm
to his wrist. Indifferent, Juan let himself be handled. Then,
as though absent-mindedly, the Belgian laid three fingers over
his wrist; at the same time, he drew away somewhat and
managed to turn his back to me. But I leaned over backward
and saw him take out his watch and look at it a moment
before relinquishing the boy's wrist. After a moment, he let
the inert hand fall and went and leaned against the wall.
Then, as if he had suddenly remembered something very
important that had to be noted down immediately, he took
a notebook from his pocket and wrote a few lines in it.
"The son-of-a-bitch," I thought angrily. "He better not come
and feel my pulse; I'll give him a punch in his dirty jaw."

He didn't come near me, but I felt he was looking at
me. I raised my head and looked back at him. In an im-
personal voice, he said, "Don't you think it's frightfully
cold here?"

He looked purple with cold.

"I'm not cold," I answered him.

He kept looking at me with a hard expression. Suddenly
I understood, and I lifted my hands to my face. I was
covered with sweat. Here, in this cellar, in mid-winter, right
in a draft, I was sweating. I ran my fingers through my
hair, which was stiff with sweat; at the same time, I realized
my shirt was damp and sticking to my skin. I had been streaming with perspiration for an hour, at least, and had felt
nothing. But this fact hadn't escaped that Belgian swine. He
had seen the drops rolling down my face and had said to
himself that it showed an almost pathological terror; and
he himself had felt normal and proud of it because he was
cold. I wanted to get up and go punch his face in, but I
had hardly started to make a move before my shame and
anger had disappeared. I dropped back onto the bench with
indifference.

I was content to rub my neck with my handkerchief because now I felt the sweat dripping from my hair onto the
nape of my neck and that was disagreeable. I soon gave
up rubbing myself, however, for it didn't do any good; my
handkerchief was already wringing wet and I was still sweat-

ing. My buttocks, too, were sweating, and my damp trousers stuck to the bench.

Suddenly, Juan said, "You're a doctor, aren't you?"

"Yes," said the Belgian.

"Do people suffer—very long?"

"Oh! When . . . ? No, no," said the Belgian, in a paternal voice, "it's quickly over."

His manner was as reassuring as if he had been answering a paying patient.

"But I . . . Somebody told me—they often have to fire two volleys."

"Sometimes," said the Belgian, raising his head, "it just happens that the first volley doesn't hit any of the vital organs."

"So then they have to reload their guns and aim all over again?" Juan thought for a moment, then added hoarsely, "But that takes time!"

He was terribly afraid of suffering. He couldn't think about anything else, but that went with his age. As for me, I hardly thought about it any more and it certainly was not fear of suffering that made me perspire.

I rose and walked toward the pile of coal dust. Tom gave a start and looked at me with a look of hate. I irritated him because my shoes squeaked. I wondered if my face was as putty-colored as his. Then I noticed that he, too, was sweating. The sky was magnificent; no light at all came into our dark corner and I had only to lift my head to see the Big Bear. But it didn't look the way it had looked before. Two days ago, from my cell in the archbishop's palace, I could see a big patch of sky and each time of day brought back a different memory. In the morning, when the sky was a deep blue, and light, I thought of beaches along the Atlantic; at noon, I could see the sun, and I remembered a bar in Seville where I used to drink manzanilla and eat anchovies and olives; in the afternoon, I was in the shade, and I thought of the deep shadow which covers half of the arena while the other half gleams in the sunlight: it really gave me a pang to see the whole earth reflected in the sky like that. Now, however, no matter how much I looked up in the air, the sky no longer recalled anything. I liked it better that way. I came back and sat down next to Tom. There was a long silence.

Then Tom began to talk in a low voice. He had to keep talking, otherwise he lost his way in his own thoughts. I

believe he was talking to me, but he didn't look at me. No
doubt he was afraid to look at me, because I was gray
and sweating. We were both alike and worse than mirrors
for each other. He looked at the Belgian, the only one who
was alive.

"Say, do you understand? I don't."

Then I, too, began to talk in a low voice. I was watching
the Belgian.

"Understand what? What's the matter?"

"Something's going to happen to us that I don't understand."

There was a strange odor about Tom. It seemed to me that
I was more sensitive to odors than ordinarily. With a sneer,
I said, "You'll understand, later."

"That's not so sure," he said stubbornly. "I'm willing to be
courageous, but at least I ought to know . . . Listen, they're
going to take us out into the courtyard. All right. The fellows
will be standing in line in front of us. How many of them
will there be?"

"Oh, I don't know. Five, or eight. Not more."

"That's enough. Let's say there'll be eight of them. Somebody will shout 'Shoulder arms!' and I'll see all eight rifles
aimed at me. I'm sure I'm going to feel like going through
the wall. I'll push against the wall as hard as I can with
my back, and the wall won't give in. The way it is in a
nightmare. . . . I can imagine all that. Ah, if you only
knew how well I can imagine it!"

"Skip it!" I said. "I can imagine it too."

"It must hurt like the devil. You know they aim at your
eyes and mouth so as to disfigure you," he added maliciously.
"I can feel the wounds already. For the last hour I've been
having pains in my head and neck. Not real pains—it's
worse still. They're the pains I'll feel tomorrow morning.
And after that, then what?"

I understood perfectly well what he meant, but I didn't
want to seem to understand. As for the pains, I, too, felt
them all through my body, like a lot of little gashes. I
couldn't get used to them, but I was like him, I didn't
think they were very important.

"After that," I said roughly, "you'll be eating daisies."

He started talking to himself, not taking his eyes off the
Belgian, who didn't seem to be listening to him. I knew
what he had come for, and that what we were thinking didn't

interest him. He had come to look at our bodies, our bodies
which were dying alive.

"It's like in a nightmare," said Tom. "You want to think
of something, you keep having the impression you've got it,
that you're going to understand, and then it slips away from
you, it eludes you and it's gone again. I say to myself,
afterwards, there won't be anything. But I don't really understand what that means. There are moments when I almost
do—and then it's gone again. I start to think of the pains,
the bullets, the noise of the shooting. I am a materialist, I
swear it; and I'm not going crazy, either. But there's something wrong. I see my own corpse. That's not hard, but
it's *I* who see it, with *my* eyes. I'll have to get to the point
where I think—where I think I won't see anything more.
I won't hear anything more, and the world will go on for
the others. We're not made to think that way, Pablo. Believe me, I've already stayed awake all night waiting for
something. But this is not the same thing. This will grab
us from behind, Pablo, and we won't be ready for it."

"Shut up," I said. "Do you want me to call a father
confessor?"

He didn't answer. I had already noticed that he had a
tendency to prophesy and call me "Pablo" in a kind of pale
voice. I didn't like that very much, but it seems all the
Irish are like that. I had a vague impression that he smelled
of urine. Actually, I didn't like Tom very much, and I
didn't see why, just because we were going to die together,
I should like him any better. There are certain fellows with
whom it would be different—with Ramon Gris, for instance.
But between Tom and Juan, I felt alone. In fact, I liked
it better that way. With Ramon I might have grown soft.
But I felt terribly hard at that moment, and I wanted to
stay hard.

Tom kept on muttering, in a kind of absent-minded way.
He was certainly talking to keep from thinking. Naturally,
I agreed with him, and I could have said everything he was
saying. It's not *natural* to die. And since I was going to
die, nothing seemed natural any more: neither the coal pile,
nor the bench, nor Pedro's dirty old face. Only it was disagreeable for me to think the same things Tom thought.
And I knew perfectly well that all night long, within five
minutes of each other, we would keep on thinking things
at the same time, sweating or shivering at the same time.
I looked at him sideways and, for the first time, he seemed

strange to me. He had death written on his face. My
pride was wounded. For twenty-four hours I had lived
side by side with Tom, I had listened to him, I had talked
to him, and I knew we had nothing in common. And now
we were as alike as twin brothers, simply because we were
going to die together. Tom took my hand without looking
at me.

"Pablo, I wonder . . . I wonder if it's true that we just
cease to exist."

I drew my hand away.

"Look between your feet, you dirty dog."

There was a puddle between his feet and water was dripping
from his trousers.

"What's the matter?" he said, frightened.

"You're wetting your pants," I said to him.

"It's not true," he said furiously. "I can't be . . . I don't
feel anything."

The Belgian had come closer to him. With an air of false
concern, he asked, "Aren't you feeling well?"

Tom didn't answer. The Belgian looked at the puddle without comment.

"I don't know what that is," Tom said savagely, "but I'm
not afraid. I swear to you, I'm not afraid."

The Belgian made no answer. Tom rose and went to the
corner. He came back, buttoning his fly, and sat down, without a word. The Belgian was taking notes.

We were watching the doctor. Juan was watching him too.
All three of us were watching him because he was alive.
He had the gestures of a living person, the interests of a
living person; he was shivering in this cellar the way living
people shiver; he had an obedient, well-fed body. We, on
the other hand, didn't feel our bodies any more—not the
same way, in any case. I felt like touching my trousers, but
I didn't dare to. I looked at the Belgian, well-planted on
his two legs, master of his muscles—and able to plan for
tomorrow. We were like three shadows deprived of blood;
we were watching him and sucking his life like vampires.

Finally he came over to Juan. Was he going to lay his
hand on the nape of Juan's neck for some professional reason,
or had he obeyed a charitable impulse? If he had acted out
of charity, it was the one and only time during the whole
night. He fondled Juan's head and the nape of his neck.
The kid let him do it, without taking his eyes off him. Then,
suddenly, he took hold of the doctor's hand and looked

at it in a funny way. He held the Belgian's hand between his own two hands and there was nothing pleasing about them, those two gray paws squeezing that fat red hand. I sensed what was going to happen and Tom must have sensed it, too. But all the Belgian saw was emotion, and he smiled paternally. After a moment, the kid lifted the big red paw to his mouth and started to bite it. The Belgian drew back quickly and stumbled toward the wall. For a second, he looked at us with horror. He must have suddenly understood that we were not men like himself. I began to laugh, and one of the guards started up. The other had fallen asleep with his eyes wide open, showing only the whites.

I felt tired and over-excited at the same time. I didn't want to think any more about what was going to happen at dawn—about death. It didn't make sense, and I never got beyond just words, or emptiness. But whenever I tried to think about something else I saw the barrels of rifles aimed at me. I must have lived through my execution twenty times in succession; one time I thought it was the real thing; I must have dozed off for a moment. They were dragging me toward the wall and I was resisting; I was imploring their pardon. I woke with a start and looked at the Belgian. I was afraid I had cried out in my sleep. But he was smoothing his mustache; he hadn't noticed anything. If I had wanted to, I believe I could have slept for a while. I had been awake for the last forty-eight hours, and I was worn out. But I didn't want to lose two hours of life. They would have had to come and wake me at dawn. I would have followed them, drunk with sleep, and I would have gone off without so much as "Gosh!" I didn't want it that way, I didn't want to die like an animal. I wanted to understand. Besides, I was afraid of having nightmares. I got up and began to walk up and down and, so as to think about something else, I began to think about my past life. Memories crowded in on me, helter-skelter. Some were good and some were bad—at least that was how I had thought of them before. There were faces and happenings. I saw the face of a little *novilero* who had gotten himself horned during the *Feria*, in Valencia. I saw the face of one of my uncles, of Ramon Gris. I remembered all kinds of things that had happened: how I had been on strike for three months in 1926, and had almost died of hunger. I recalled a night I had spent on a bench in Granada; I hadn't eaten for three days, I was nearly wild, I didn't want to give up the sponge. I had to

smile. With what eagerness I had run after happiness, and
women, and liberty! And to what end? I had wanted to
liberate Spain, I admired Py Margall, I had belonged to the
anarchist movement, I had spoken at public meetings. I took
everything as seriously as if I had been immortal.

At that time I had the impression that I had my whole life
before me, and I thought to myself, "It's all a god-damned
lie." Now it wasn't worth anything because it was finished. I
wondered how I had ever been able to go out and have a
good time with girls. I wouldn't have lifted my little finger
if I had ever imagined that I would die like this. I saw
my life before me, finished, closed, like a bag, and yet what
was inside was not finished. For a moment I tried to appraise
it. I would have liked to say to myself, "It's been a good
life." But it couldn't be appraised, it was only an outline.
I had spent my time writing checks on eternity, and had
understood nothing. Now, I didn't miss anything. There were
a lot of things I might have missed: the taste of manzanilla, for instance, or the swims I used to take in summer
in a little creek near Cadiz. But death had taken the charm
out of everything.

Suddenly the Belgian had a wonderful idea.

"My friends," he said to us, "if you want me to—and pro-
viding the military authorities give their consent—I could
undertake to deliver a word or some token from you to
your loved ones. . . ."

Tom growled, "I haven't got anybody."

I didn't answer. Tom waited for a moment, then he looked
at me with curiosity. "Aren't you going to send any message
to Concha?"

"No."

I hated that sort of sentimental conspiracy. Of course, it
was my fault, since I had mentioned Concha the night
before, and I should have kept my mouth shut. I had been
with her for a year. Even as late as last night, I would
have cut my arm off with a hatchet just to see her again
for five minutes. That was why I had mentioned her. I
couldn't help it. Now I didn't care any more about seeing
her. I hadn't anything more to say to her. I didn't even
want to hold her in my arms. I loathed my body because
it had turned gray and was sweating—and I wasn't even sure
that I didn't loathe hers too. Concha would cry when she
heard about my death; for months she would have no more
interest in life. But still it was I who was going to die.

I thought of her beautiful, loving eyes. When she looked at me something went from her to me. But I thought to myself that it was all over; if she looked at me *now* her gaze would not leave her eyes, it would not reach out to me. I was alone.

Tom, too, was alone, but not the same way. He was seated astride his chair and had begun to look at the bench with a sort of smile, with surprise, even. He reached out his hand and touched the wood cautiously, as though he were afraid of breaking something, then he drew his hand back hurriedly, and shivered. I wouldn't have amused myself touching that bench, if I had been Tom, that was just some more Irish playacting. But somehow it seemed to me too that the different objects had something funny about them. They seemed to have grown paler, less massive than before. I had only to look at the bench, the lamp or the pile of coal dust to feel I was going to die. Naturally, I couldn't think clearly about my death, but I saw it everywhere, even on the different objects, the way they had withdrawn and kept their distance, tactfully, like people talking at the bedside of a dying person. It was *his own death* Tom had just touched on the bench.

In the state I was in, if they had come and told me I could go home quietly, that my life would be saved, it would have left me cold. A few hours, or a few years of waiting are all the same, when you've lost the illusion of being eternal. Nothing mattered to me any more. In a way, I was calm. But it was a horrible kind of calm—because of my body. My body—I saw with its eyes and I heard with its ears, but it was no longer I. It sweat and trembled independently, and I didn't recognize it any longer. I was obliged to touch it and look at it to know what was happening to it, just as if it had been someone else's body. At times I still felt it, I felt a slipping, a sort of headlong plunging, as in a falling airplane, or else I heard my heart beating. But this didn't give me confidence. In fact, everything that came from my body had something damned dubious about it. Most of the time it was silent, it stayed put and I didn't feel anything other than a sort of heaviness, a loathsome presence against me. I had the impression of being bound to an enormous vermin.

The Belgian took out his watch and looked at it.

"It's half-past three," he said.

The son-of-a-bitch! He must have done it on purpose. Tom

jumped up. We hadn't yet realized the time was passing. The night surrounded us like a formless, dark mass; I didn't even remember it had started.

Juan started to shout. Wringing his hands, he implored, "I don't want to die! I don't want to die!"

He ran the whole length of the cellar with his arms in the air, then he dropped down onto one of the mattresses, sobbing. Tom looked at him with dismal eyes and didn't even try to console him any more. The fact was, it was no use; the kid made more noise than we did, but he was less affected, really. He was like a sick person who defends himself against his malady with a high fever. When there's not even any fever left, it's much more serious.

He was crying. I could tell he felt sorry for himself; he was thinking about death. For one second, one single second, I too felt like crying, crying out of pity for myself. But just the contrary happened. I took one look at the kid, saw his thin, sobbing shoulders, and I felt I was inhuman. I couldn't feel pity either for these others or for myself. I said to myself, "I want to die decently."

Tom had gotten up and was standing just under the round opening looking out for the first signs of daylight. I was determined, I wanted to die decently, and I only thought about that. But underneath, ever since the doctor had told us the time, I felt time slipping, flowing by, one drop at a time.

It was still dark when I heard Tom's voice.

"Do you hear them?"

"Yes."

People were walking in the courtyard.

"What the hell are they doing? After all, they can't shoot in the dark."

After a moment, we didn't hear anything more. I said to Tom, "There's the daylight."

Pedro got up yawning, and came and blew out the lamp. He turned to the man beside him. "It's hellish cold."

The cellar had grown gray. We could hear shots at a distance.

"It's about to start," I said to Tom. "That must be in the back courtyard."

Tom asked the doctor to give him a cigarette. I didn't want any; I didn't want either cigarettes or alcohol. From that moment on, the shooting didn't stop.

"Can you take it in?" Tom said.

He started to add something, then he stopped and began to watch the door. The door opened and a lieutenant came in with four soldiers. Tom dropped his cigarette.

"Steinbock?"

Tom didn't answer. Pedro pointed him out.

"Juan Mirbal?"

"He's the one on the mattress."

"Stand up," said the Lieutenant.

Juan didn't move. Two soldiers took hold of him by the armpits and stood him up on his feet. But as soon as they let go of him he fell down.

The soldiers hesitated a moment.

"He's not the first one to get sick," said the Lieutenant. "You'll have to carry him, the two of you. We'll arrange things when we get there." He turned to Tom. "All right, come along."

Tom left between two soldiers. Two other soldiers followed, carrying the kid by his arms and legs. He was not unconscious; his eyes were wide open and tears were rolling down his cheeks. When I started to go out, the Lieutenant stopped me.

"Are you Ibbieta?"

"Yes."

"You wait here. They'll come and get you later on."

They left. The Belgian and the two jailers left too, and I was alone. I didn't understand what had happened to me, but I would have liked it better if they had ended it all right away. I heard the volleys at almost regular intervals; at each one, I shuddered. I felt like howling and tearing my hair. But instead, I gritted my teeth and pushed my hands deep into my pockets, because I wanted to stay decent.

An hour later, they came to fetch me and took me up to the first floor in a little room which smelt of cigar smoke and was so hot it seemed to me suffocating. Here there were two officers sitting in comfortable chairs, smoking, with papers spread out on their knees.

"Your name is Ibbieta?"

"Yes."

"Where is Ramon Gris?"

"I don't know."

The man who questioned me was small and stocky. He had hard eyes behind his glasses.

"Come nearer," he said to me.

I went nearer. He rose and took me by the arms, looking

at me in a way calculated to make me go through the floor.
At the same time he pinched my arms with all his might.
He didn't mean to hurt me; it was quite a game; he wanted
to dominate me. He also seemed to think it was necessary
to blow his fetid breath right into my face. We stood like
that for a moment, only I felt more like laughing than anything else. It takes a lot more than that to intimidate a man
who's about to die: it didn't work. He pushed me away
violently and sat down again.

"It's your life or his," he said. "You'll be allowed to go
free if you tell us where he is."

After all, these two bedizened fellows with their riding
crops and boots were just men who were going to die one
day. A little later than I, perhaps, but not a great deal.
And there they were, looking for names among their papers,
running after other men in order to put them in prison
or do away with them entirely. They had their opinions on
the future of Spain and on other subjects. Their petty activities seemed to me to be offensive and ludicrous. I could
no longer put myself in their place. I had the impression
they were crazy.

The little fat fellow kept looking at me, tapping his boots
with his riding crop. All his gestures were calculated to make
him appear like a spirited, ferocious animal.

"Well? Do you understand?"

"I don't know where Gris is," I said. "I thought he was in
Madrid."

The other officer lifted his pale hand indolently. This in-
dolence was also calculated. I saw through all their little
tricks, and I was dumbfounded that men should still exist
who took pleasure in that kind of thing.

"You have fifteen minutes to think it over," he said slowly.
"Take him to the linen-room, and bring him back here in
fifteen minutes. If he continues to refuse, he'll be executed
at once."

They knew what they were doing. I had spent the night
waiting. After that, they had made me wait another hour
in the cellar, while they shot Tom and Juan, and now they
locked me in the linen-room. They must have arranged the
whole thing the night before. They figured that sooner or
later people's nerves wear out and they hoped to get me
that way.

They made a big mistake. In the linen-room I sat down
on a ladder because I felt very weak, and I began to think

things over. Not their proposition, however. Naturally I knew where Gris was. He was hiding in his cousins' house, about two miles outside of the city. I knew, too, that I would not reveal his hiding place, unless they tortured me (but they didn't seem to be considering that). All that was definitely settled and didn't interest me in the least. Only I would have liked to understand the reasons for my own conduct. I would rather die than betray Gris. Why? I no longer liked Ramon Gris. My friendship for him had died shortly before dawn along with my love for Concha, along with my own desire to live. Of course I still admired him—he was hard. But it was not for that reason that I was willing to die in his place; his life was no more valuable than mine. No life was of any value. A man was going to be stood up against a wall and fired at till he dropped dead. It didn't make any difference whether it was I or Gris or somebody else. I knew perfectly well he was more useful to the Spanish cause than I was, but I didn't give a God damn about Spain or anarchy, either; nothing had any importance now. And yet, there I was. I could save my skin by betraying Gris and I refused to do it. It seemed more ludicrous to me than anything else; it was stubbornness.

I thought to myself, "Am I hard-headed!" And I was seized with a strange sort of cheerfulness.

They came to fetch me and took me back to the two officers. A rat darted out under our feet and that amused me. I turned to one of the falangists and said to him, "Did you see that rat?"

He made no reply. He was gloomy, and took himself very seriously. As for me, I felt like laughing, but I restrained myself because I was afraid that if I started, I wouldn't be able to stop. The falangist wore mustaches. I kept after him. "You ought to cut off those mustaches, you fool."

I was amused by the fact that he let hair grow all over his face while he was still alive. He gave me a kind of half-hearted kick, and I shut up.

"Well," said the fat officer, "have you thought things over?"

I looked at them with curiosity, like insects of a very rare species.

"I know where he is," I said. "He's hiding in the cemetery. Either in one of the vaults, or in the gravediggers' shack."

I said that just to make fools of them. I wanted to see them get up and fasten their belts and bustle about giving orders.

They jumped to their feet.

"Fine. Moles, go ask Lieutenant Lopez for fifteen men. And as for you," the little fat fellow said to me, "if you've told the truth, I don't go back on my word. But you'll pay for this, if you're pulling our leg."

They left noisily and I waited in peace, still guarded by the falangists. From time to time I smiled at the thought of the face they were going to make. I felt dull and malicious. I could see them lifting up the gravestones, or opening the doors of the vaults one by one. I saw the whole situation as though I were another person: the prisoner determined to play the hero, the solemn falangists with their mustaches and the men in uniform running around among the graves. It was irresistibly funny.

After half an hour, the little fat fellow came back alone. I thought he had come to give the order to execute me. The others must have stayed in the cemetery.

The officer looked at me. He didn't look at all foolish.

"Take him out in the big courtyard with the others," he said. "When military operations are over, a regular tribunal will decide his case."

I thought I must have misunderstood.

"So they're not—they're not going to shoot me?" I asked.

"Not now, in any case. Afterwards, that doesn't concern me."

I still didn't understand.

"But why?" I said to him.

He shrugged his shoulders without replying, and the soldiers led me away. In the big courtyard there were a hundred or so prisoners, women, children and a few old men. I started to walk around the grass plot in the middle. I felt absolutely idiotic. At noon we were fed in the dining hall. Two or three fellows spoke to me. I must have known them, but I didn't answer. I didn't even know where I was.

Toward evening, about ten new prisoners were pushed into the courtyard. I recognized Garcia, the baker.

He said to me, "Lucky dog! I didn't expect to find you alive."

"They condemned me to death," I said, "and then they changed their minds. I don't know why."

"I was arrested at two o'clock," Garcia said.

"What for?"

Garcia took no part in politics.

"I don't know," he said. "They arrest everybody who doesn't think the way they do."

He lowered his voice.

"They got Gris."

I began to tremble.

"When?"

"This morning. He acted like a damned fool. He left his cousins' house Tuesday because of a disagreement. There were any number of fellows who would have hidden him, but he didn't want to be indebted to anybody any more. He said, 'I would have hidden at Ibbieta's, but since they've got him, I'll go hide in the cemetery.'"

"In the cemetery?"

"Yes. It was the god-damnedest thing. Naturally they passed by there this morning; that had to happen. They found him in the gravediggers' shack. They opened fire at him and they finished him off."

"In the cemetery!"

Everything went around in circles, and when I came to I was sitting on the ground. I laughed so hard the tears came to my eyes.

ALBERT CAMUS

The Adulterous Woman

Albert Camus (1913-1960) was born in Algeria, a son of peasant parents. He was involved in theatrical work as well as in the writing of his now famous existentialist novels The Stranger *and* The Plague. *During the German occupation of France he was active in the Resistance and in political journalism. His works include philosophical essays and a number of remarkable short stories. In 1957 he was awarded the Nobel Prize for literature. He was killed in an automobile accident in 1960.*

Camus was one of the outstanding writers of the existentialist philosophy. Almost all of his work is an attempt to come to terms with the absurd nature of the world and to find some moral commitment for the atheistic humanist. In "The Adulterous Woman" the isolation and emptiness of the protagonist finds an answer in a mystical union with the indifferent universe.

A HOUSEFLY HAD been circling for the last few minutes in the bus, though the windows were closed. An odd sight here, it had been silently flying back and forth on tired wings. Janine lost track of it, then saw it light on her husband's motionless hand. The weather was cold. The fly shuddered with each gust of sandy wind that scratched against the windows. In the meager light of the winter morning, with a great fracas of sheet metal and axles, the vehicle was rolling, pitching, and making hardly any progress. Janine looked at her husband. With wisps of graying hair growing low on a narrow forehead, a broad nose, a flabby mouth, Marcel looked like a pouting faun. At each hollow in the pavement she felt him jostle against her. Then his heavy torso would slump back on his widespread legs and he would become inert again and absent, with vacant stare. Nothing about him seemed active but his thick hairless hands, made even shorter by the flannel underwear extending below his cuffs and covering his wrists. His hands were holding so tight to a little canvas suitcase set between his knees that they appeared not to feel the fly's halting progress.

Suddenly the wind was distinctly heard to howl and the gritty fog surrounding the bus became even thicker. The sand now struck the windows in packets as if hurled by invisible hands. The fly shook a chilled wing, flexed its legs, and took flight. The bus slowed and seemed on the point of stopping. But the wind apparently died down, the fog lifted slightly, and the vehicle resumed speed. Gaps of light opened up in the dust-drowned landscape. Two or three frail, whitened palm trees which seemed cut out of metal flashed into sight in the window only to disappear the next moment.

"What a country!" Marcel said.

The bus was full of Arabs pretending to sleep, shrouded in their burnooses. Some had folded their legs on the seat and swayed more than the others in the car's motion. Their silence and impassivity began to weigh upon Janine; it seemed to her as if she had been traveling for days with that mute escort. Yet the bus had left only at dawn from the end of the rail line and for two hours in the cold morning it had been advancing on a stony, desolate plateau which, in the beginning at least, extended its straight lines all the way to reddish horizons. But the wind had risen and gradually swallowed up the vast expanse. From that moment on, the passengers had seen nothing more; one after another, they had ceased talking and were silently progressing in a sort of sleepless night, occasionally wiping their lips and eyes irritated by the sand that filtered into the car.

"Janine!" She gave a start at her husband's call. Once again she thought how ridiculous that name was for someone tall and sturdy like her. Marcel wanted to know where his sample case was. With her foot she explored the empty space under the seat and encountered an object which she decided must be it. She could not stoop over without gasping somewhat. Yet

in school she had won the first prize in gymnastics and hadn't
known what it was to be winded. Was that so long ago?
Twenty-five years. Twenty-five years were nothing, for it
seemed to her only yesterday when she was hesitating between an independent life and marriage, just yesterday when
she was thinking anxiously of the time she might be
growing old alone. She was not alone and that law-student
who always wanted to be with her was now at her side. She
had eventually accepted him although he was a little shorter
than she and she didn't much like his eager, sharp laugh or
his black protruding eyes. But she liked his courage in facing
up to life, which he shared with all the French of this country.
She also liked his crestfallen look when events or men failed
to live up to his expectations. Above all, she liked being
loved, and he had showered her with attentions. By so often
making her aware that she existed for him he made her exist
in reality. No, she was not alone. . . .

The bus, with many loud honks, was plowing its way through
invisible obstacles. Inside the car, however, no one stirred.
Janine suddenly felt someone staring at her and turned toward
the seat across the aisle. He was not an Arab, and she was
surprised not to have noticed him from the beginning. He was
wearing the uniform of the French regiments of the Sahara
and an unbleached linen cap above his tanned face, long and
pointed like a jackal's. His gray eyes were examining her
with a sort of glum disapproval, in a fixed stare. She suddenly
blushed and turned back to her husband, who was still looking
straight ahead in the fog and wind. She snuggled down in her
coat. But she could still see the French soldier, long and thin,
so thin in his fitted tunic that he seemed constructed of a dry,
friable material, a mixture of sand and bone. Then it was that
she saw the thin hands and burned faces of the Arabs in
front of her and noticed that they seemed to have plenty of
room, despite their ample garments, on the seat where she
and her husband felt wedged in. She pulled her coat around
her knees. Yet she wasn't so fat—tall and well rounded
rather, plump and still desirable, as she was well aware when
men looked at her, with her rather childish face, her bright,
naïve eyes contrasting with this big body she knew to be warm
and inviting.

No, nothing had happened as she had expected. When
Marcel had wanted to take her along on his trip she had
protested. For some time he had been thinking of this trip—
since the end of the war, to be precise, when business had

returned to normal. Before the war the small dry-goods business he had taken over from his parents on giving up his study of law had provided a fairly good living. On the coast the years of youth can be happy ones. But he didn't much like physical effort and very soon had given up taking her to the beaches. The little car took them out of town solely for the Sunday afternoon ride. The rest of the time he preferred his shop full of multicolored piece-goods shaded by the arcades of this half-native, half-European quarter. Above the shop they lived in three rooms furnished with Arab hangings and furniture from the Galerie Barbès. They had not had children. The years had passed in the semi-darkness behind the half-closed shutters. Summer, the beaches, excursions, the mere sight of the sky were things of the past. Nothing seemed to interest Marcel but business. She felt she had discovered his true passion to be money, and, without really knowing why, she didn't like that. After all, it was to her advantage. Far from being miserly, he was generous, especially where she was concerned. "If something happened to me," he used to say, "you'd be provided for." And, in fact, it is essential to provide for one's needs. But for all the rest, for what is not the most elementary need, how to provide? This is what she felt vaguely, at infrequent intervals. Meanwhile she helped Marcel keep his books and occasionally substituted for him in the shop. Summer was always the hardest, when the heat stifled even the sweet sensation of boredom.

Suddenly, in summer as it happened, the war, Marcel called up then rejected on grounds of health, the scarcity of piece-goods, business at a standstill, the streets empty and hot. If something happened now, she would no longer be provided for. This is why, as soon as piece-goods came back on the market, Marcel had thought of covering the villages of the Upper Plateaus and of the South himself in order to do without a middleman and sell directly to the Arab merchants. He had wanted to take her along. She knew that travel was difficult, she had trouble breathing, and she would have preferred staying at home. But he was obstinate and she had accepted because it would have taken too much energy to refuse. Here they were and, truly, nothing was like what she had imagined. She had feared the heat, the swarms of flies, the filthy hotels reeking of aniseed. She had not thought of the cold, of the biting wind, of these semi-polar plateaus cluttered with moraines. She had dreamed too of palm trees and soft sand. Now she saw that the desert was not that

at all, but merely stone, stone everywhere, in the sky full of
nothing but stone-dust, rasping and cold, as on the ground,
where nothing grew among the stones except dry grasses.

The bus stopped abruptly. The driver shouted a few words
in that language she had heard all her life without ever
understanding it. "What's the matter?" Marcel asked. The
driver, in French this time, said that the sand must have
clogged the carburetor, and again Marcel curséd this country.
The driver laughed hilariously and asserted that it was nothing,
that he would clean the carburetor and they'd be off again.
He opened the door and the cold wind blew into the bus,
lashing their faces with myriad grains of sand. All the
Arabs silently plunged their noses into their burnooses and
huddled up. "Shut the door," Marcel shouted. The driver
laughed as he came back to the door. Without hurrying, he
took some tools from under the dashboard, then, tiny in the
fog, again disappeared ahead without closing the door. Marcel sighed. "You may be sure he's never seen a motor in his
life." "Oh, be quiet!" said Janine. Suddenly she gave a start.
On the shoulder of the road close to the bus, draped forms
were standing still. Under the burnoose's hood and behind a
rampart of veils, only their eyes were visible. Mute, come
from nowhere, they were staring at the travelers. "Shepherds," Marcel said.

Inside the car there was total silence. All the passengers,
heads lowered, seemed to be listening to the voice of the
wind loosed across these endless plateaus. Janine was all of a
sudden struck by the almost complete absence of luggage.
At the end of the railroad line the driver had hoisted their
trunk and a few bundles onto the roof. In the racks inside
the bus could be seen nothing but gnarled sticks and shopping-
baskets. All these people of the South apparently were traveling empty-handed.

But the driver was coming back, still brisk. His eyes alone
were laughing above the veils with which he too had masked
his face. He announced that they would soon be under way.
He closed the door, the wind became silent, and the rain of
sand on the windows could be heard better. The motor
coughed and died. After having been urged at great length by
the starter, it finally sparked and the driver raced it by
pressing on the gas. With a big hiccough the bus started off.
From the ragged clump of shepherds, still motionless, a hand
rose and then faded into the fog behind them. Almost at
once the vehicle began to bounce on the road, which had

become worse. Shaken up, the Arabs constantly swayed.
Nonetheless, Janine was feeling overcome with sleep when
there suddenly appeared in front of her a little yellow box
filled with lozenges. The jackal-soldier was smiling at her.
She hesitated, took one, and thanked him. The jackal pock-
eted the box and simultaneously swallowed his smile. Now
he was staring at the road, straight in front of him. Janine
turned toward Marcel and saw only the solid back of his
neck. Through the window he was watching the denser fog
rising from the crumbly embankment.

They had been traveling for hours and fatigue had extinguished all life in the car when shouts burst forth outside.
Children wearing burnooses, whirling like tops, leaping, clapping their hands, were running around the bus. It was now
going down a long street lined with low houses; they were
entering the oasis. The wind was still blowing, but the walls
intercepted the grains of sand which had previously cut off
the light. Yet the sky was still cloudy. Amidst shouts, in a
great screeching of brakes, the bus stopped in front of the
adobe arcades of a hotel with dirty windows. Janine got out
and, once on the pavement, staggered. Above the houses
she could see a slim minaret. On her left rose the first palm
trees of the oasis, and she would have liked to go toward them.
But although it was close to noon, the cold was bitter; the
wind made her shiver. She turned toward Marcel and saw
the soldier coming toward her. She was expecting him to
smile or salute. He passed without looking at her and disappeared. Marcel was busy getting down the trunk of piece-
goods, a black foot-locker perched on the bus's roof. It
would not be easy. The driver was the only one to take care
of the luggage and he had already stopped, standing on the
roof, to hold forth to the circle of burnooses gathered
around the bus. Janine, surrounded with faces that seemed
cut out of bone and leather, besieged by guttural shouts,
suddenly became aware of her fatigue. "I'm going in," she
said to Marcel, who was shouting impatiently at the driver.

She entered the hotel. The manager, a thin, laconic French-
man, came to meet her. He led her to a second-floor balcony overlooking the street and into a room which seemed
to have but an iron bed, a white-enameled chair, an un-
curtained wardrobe, and, behind a rush screen, a washbasin
covered with fine sand-dust. When the manager had closed
the door, Janine felt the cold coming from the bare, whitewashed walls. She didn't know where to put her bag, where

to put herself. She had either to lie down or to remain standing, and to shiver in either case. She remained standing, holding her bag and staring at a sort of window-slit that opened onto the sky near the ceiling. She was waiting, but she didn't know for what. She was aware only of her solitude, and of the penetrating cold, and of a greater weight in the region of her heart. She was in fact dreaming, almost deaf to the sounds rising from the street along with Marcel's vocal outbursts, more aware on the other hand of that sound of a river coming from the window-slit and caused by the wind in the palm trees, so close now, it seemed to her. Then the wind seemed to increase and the gentle ripple of waters became a hissing of waves. She imagined, beyond the walls, a sea of erect, flexible palm trees unfurling in the storm. Nothing was like what she had expected, but those invisible waves refreshed her tired eyes. She was standing, heavy, with dangling arms, slightly stooped, as the cold climbed her thick legs. She was dreaming of the erect and flexible palm trees and of the girl she had once been.

After having washed, they went down to the dining-room. On the bare walls had been painted camels and palm trees drowned in a sticky background of pink and lavender. The arcaded windows let in a meager light. Marcel questioned the hotel manager about the merchants. Then an elderly Arab wearing a military decoration on his tunic served them. Marcel, preoccupied, tore his bread into little pieces. He kept his wife from drinking water. "It hasn't been boiled. Take wine." She didn't like that, for wine made her sleepy. Besides, there was pork on the menu. "They don't eat it because of the Koran. But the Koran didn't know that well-done pork doesn't cause illness. We French know how to cook. What are you thinking about?" Janine was not thinking of anything, or perhaps of that victory of the cooks over the prophets. But she had to hurry. They were to leave the next morning for still farther south; that afternoon they had to see all the important merchants. Marcel urged the elderly Arab to hurry the coffee. He nodded without smiling and pattered out. "Slowly in the morning, not too fast in the afternoon," Marcel said, laughing. Yet eventually the coffee came. They barely took time to swallow it and went out into the dusty, cold street. Marcel called a young Arab to help him carry the trunk, but as a matter of principle quibbled about the payment. His opinion, which he once more expressed to Janine, was in fact

based on the vague principle that they always asked for twice
as much in the hope of settling for a quarter of the amount.
Janine, ill at ease, followed the two trunk-bearers. She had
put on a wool dress under her heavy coat and would have
liked to take up less space. The pork, although well done,
and the small quantity of wine she had drunk also bothered
her somewhat.

They walked along a diminutive public garden planted with
dusty trees. They encountered Arabs who stepped out of their
way without seeming to see them, wrapping themselves in
their burnooses. Even when they were wearing rags, she
felt they had a look of dignity unknown to the Arabs of
her town. Janine followed the trunk, which made a way for
her through the crowd. They went through the gate in an
earthen rampart and emerged on a little square planted with
the same mineral trees and bordered on the far side, where
it was widest, with arcades and shops. But they stopped on
the square itself in front of a small construction shaped like
an artillery shell and painted chalky blue. Inside, in the single
room lighted solely by the entrance, an old Arab with white
mustaches stood behind a shiny plank. He was serving tea,
raising and lowering the teapot over three tiny multicolored
glasses. Before they could make out anything else in the darkness, the cool scent of mint tea greeted Marcel and Janine
at the door. Marcel had barely crossed the threshold and
dodged the garlands of pewter teapots, cups and trays, and
the postcard displays when he was up against the counter.
Janine stayed at the door. She stepped a little aside so as not
to cut off the light. At that moment she perceived in the
darkness behind the old merchant two Arabs smiling at them,
seated on the bulging sacks that filled the back of the shop.
Red-and-black rugs and embroidered scarves hung on the
walls; the floor was cluttered with sacks and little boxes filled
with aromatic seeds. On the counter, beside a sparkling
pair of brass scales and an old yardstick with figures effaced,
stood a row of loaves of sugar. One of them had been unwrapped from its coarse blue paper and cut into on top. The
smell of wool and spices in the room became apparent behind the scent of tea when the old merchant set down the
teapot and said good-day.

Marcel talked rapidly in the low voice he assumed when
talking business. Then he opened the trunk, exhibited the
wools and silks, pushed back the scale and yardstick to
spread out his merchandise in front of the old merchant. He

got excited, raised his voice, laughed nervously, like a woman who wants to make an impression and is not sure of herself. Now, with hands spread wide, he was going through the gestures of selling and buying. The old man shook his head, passed the tea tray to the two Arabs behind him, and said just a few words that seemed to discourage Marcel. He picked up his goods, piled them back into the trunk, then wiped an imaginary sweat from his forehead. He called the little porter and they started off toward the arcades. In the first shop, although the merchant began by exhibiting the same Olympian manner, they were a little luckier. "They think they're God almighty," Marcel said, "but they're in business too! Life is hard for everyone."

Janine followed without answering. The wind had almost ceased. The sky was clearing in spots. A cold, harsh light came from the deep holes that opened up in the thickness of the clouds. They had now left the square. They were walking in narrow streets along earthen walls over which hung rotted December roses, or from time to time, a pomegranate, dried and wormy. An odor of dust and coffee, the smoke of a wood fire, the smell of stone and of sheep permeated this quarter. The shops, hollowed out of the walls, were far from one another; Janine felt her feet getting heavier. But her husband was gradually becoming more cheerful. He was beginning to sell and was feeling more kindly; he called Janine "Baby"; the trip would not be wasted. "Of course," Janine said mechanically, "it's better to deal directly with them."

They came back by another street, toward the center. It was late in the afternoon; the sky was now almost completely clear. They stopped in the square. Marcel rubbed his hands and looked affectionately at the trunk in front of them. "Look," said Janine. From the other end of the square was coming a tall Arab, thin, vigorous, wearing a sky-blue burnoose, soft brown boots and gloves, and bearing his bronzed aquiline face loftily. Nothing but the *chèche* that he was wearing swathed as a turban distinguished him from those French officers in charge of native affairs whom Janine had occasionally admired. He was advancing steadily toward them, but seemed to be looking beyond their group as he slowly removed the glove from one hand. "Well," said Marcel as he shrugged his shoulders, "there's one who thinks he's a general." Yes, all of them here had that look of pride; but this one, really, was going too far. Although they were surrounded by the empty space of the square, he was walking straight

toward the trunk without seeing it, without seeing them. Then
the distance separating them decreased rapidly and the Arab
was upon them when Marcel suddenly seized the handle of
the foot-locker and pulled it out of the way. The Arab
passed without seeming to notice anything and headed with
the same regular step toward the ramparts. Janine looked at
her husband; he had his crestfallen look. "They think they can
get away with anything now," he said. Janine did not reply.
She loathed that Arab's stupid arrogance and suddenly felt
unhappy. She wanted to leave and thought of her little
apartment. The idea of going back to the hotel, to that icy
room, discouraged her. It suddenly occurred to her that the
manager had advised her to climb up to the terrace around
the fort to see the desert. She said this to Marcel and that
he could leave the trunk at the hotel. But he was tired and
wanted to sleep a little before dinner. "Please," said Janine.
He looked at her, suddenly attentive. "Of course, my dear,"
he said.

She waited for him in the street in front of the hotel. The
white-robed crowd was becoming larger and larger. Not a
single woman could be seen, and it seemed to Janine that
she had never seen so many men. Yet none of them looked
at her. Some of them, without appearing to see her, slowly
turned toward her that thin, tanned face that made them all
look alike to her, the face of the French soldier in the bus
and that of the gloved Arab, a face both shrewd and proud.
They turned that face toward the foreign woman, they didn't
see her, and then, light and silent, they walked around her as
she stood there with swelling ankles. And her discomfort,
her need of getting away increased. "Why did I come?" But
already Marcel was coming back.

When they climbed the stairs to the fort, it was five
o'clock. The wind had died down altogether. The sky, completely clear, was now periwinkle blue. The cold, now drier,
made their cheeks smart. Halfway up the stairs an old Arab,
stretched out against the wall, asked them if they wanted a
guide, but didn't budge, as if he had been sure of their refusal
in advance. The stairs were long and steep despite several
landings of packed earth. As they climbed, the space widened
and they rose into an ever broader light, cold and dry, in
which every sound from the oasis reached them pure and
distinct. The bright air seemed to vibrate around them with a
vibration increasing in length as they advanced, as if
their progress struck from the crystal of light a sound wave

that kept spreading out. And as soon as they reached the
terrace and their gaze was lost in the vast horizon beyond
the palm grove, it seemed to Janine that the whole sky rang
with a single short and piercing note, whose echoes gradually
filled the space above her, then suddenly died and left her
silently facing the limitless expanse.

From east to west, in fact, her gaze swept slowly, without
encountering a single obstacle, along a perfect curve. Beneath her, the blue-and-white terraces of the Arab town
overlapped one another, splattered with the dark-red spots
of peppers drying in the sun. Not a soul could be seen, but
from the inner courts, together with the aroma of roasting
coffee, there rose laughing voices or incomprehensible stamping of feet. Farther off, the palm grove, divided into uneven
squares by clay walls, rustled its upper foliage in a wind
that could not be felt upon the terrace. Still farther off and
all the way to the horizon extended the ocher-and-gray realm
of stones, in which no life was visible. At some distance
from the oasis, however, near the wadi that bordered the
palm grove on the west could be seen broad black tents. All
around them a flock of motionless dromedaries, tiny at that
distance, formed against the gray ground the black signs of a
strange handwriting, the meaning of which had to be de-
ciphered. Above the desert, the silence was as vast as the
space.

Janine, leaning her whole body against the parapet, was
speechless, unable to tear herself away from the void opening
before her. Beside her, Marcel was getting restless. He was
cold; he wanted to go back down. What was there to see
here, after all? But she could not take her gaze from the
horizon. Over yonder, still farther south, at that point where
sky and earth met in a pure line—over yonder it suddenly
seemed there was awaiting her something of which, though
it had always been lacking, she had never been aware until
now. In the advancing afternoon the light relaxed and softened; it was passing from the crystalline to the liquid. Simultaneously, in the heart of a woman brought there by pure
chance a knot tightened by the years, habit, and boredom
was slowly loosening. She was looking at the nomads' encamp-
ment. She had not even seen the men living in it; nothing
was stirring among the black tents, and yet she could think
only of them whose existence she had barely known until this
day. Homeless, cut off from the world, they were a handful
wandering over the vast territory she could see, which however

was but a paltry part of an even greater expanse whose
dizzying course stopped only thousands of miles farther south,
where the first river finally waters the forest. Since the beginning of time, on the dry earth of this limitless land scraped
to the bone, a few men had been ceaselessly trudging, pos-
sessing nothing but serving no one, poverty-stricken but free
lords of a strange kingdom. Janine did not know why this
thought filled her with such a sweet, vast melancholy that it
closed her eyes. She knew that this kingdom had been eternally
promised her and yet that it would never be hers, never again,
except in this fleeting moment perhaps when she opened her
eyes again on the suddenly motionless sky and on its waves
of steady light, while the voices rising from the Arab town
suddenly fell silent. It seemed to her that the world's course
had just stopped and that, from that moment on, no one
would ever age any more or die. Everywhere, henceforth,
life was suspended—except in her heart, where, at the same
moment, someone was weeping with affliction and wonder.

But the light began to move; the sun, clear and devoid of
warmth, went down toward the west, which became slightly
pink, while a gray wave took shape in the east ready to roll
slowly over the vast expanse. A first dog barked and its
distant bark rose in the now even colder air. Janine noticed
that her teeth were chattering. "We are catching our death
of cold," Marcel said. "You're a fool. Let's go back." But he
took her hand awkwardly. Docile now, she turned away
from the parapet and followed him. Without moving, the old
Arab on the stairs watched them go down toward the town.
She walked along without seeing anyone, bent under a tremendous and sudden fatigue, dragging her body, whose weight
now seemed to her unbearable. Her exaltation had left her.
Now she felt too tall, too thick, too white too, for this world
she had just entered. A child, the girl, the dry man, the
furtive jackal were the only creatures who could silently walk
that earth. What would she do there henceforth except
to drag herself toward sleep, toward death?

She dragged herself, in fact, toward the restaurant with a
husband suddenly taciturn unless he was telling how tired
he was, while she was struggling weakly against a cold,
aware of a fever rising within her. Then she dragged herself
toward her bed, where Marcel came to join her and put the
light out at once without asking anything of her. The room
was frigid. Janine felt the cold creeping up while the fever
was increasing. She breathed with difficulty, her blood pumped

without warming her; a sort of fear grew within her. She turned over and the old iron bedstead groaned under her weight. No, she didn't want to fall ill. Her husband was already asleep; she too had to sleep; it was essential. The muffled sounds of the town reached her through the window-slit. With a nasal twang old phonographs in the Moorish cafés ground out tunes she recognized vaguely; they reached her borne on the sound of a slow-moving crowd. She must sleep. But she was counting black tents; behind her eyelids motionless camels were grazing; immense solitudes were whirling within her. Yes, why had she come? She fell asleep on that question.

She awoke a little later. The silence around her was absolute. But, on the edges of town, hoarse dogs were howling in the soundless night. Janine shivered. She turned over, felt her husband's hard shoulder against hers, and suddenly, half asleep, huddled against him. She was drifting on the surface of sleep without sinking in and she clung to that shoulder with unconscious eagerness as her safest haven. She was talking, but no sound issued from her mouth. She was talking, but she herself hardly heard what she was saying. She could feel only Marcel's warmth. For more than twenty years every night thus, in his warmth, just the two of them, even when ill, even when traveling, as at present . . . Besides, what would she have done alone at home? No child! Wasn't that what she lacked? She didn't know. She simply followed Marcel, pleased to know that someone needed her. The only joy he gave her was the knowledge that she was necessary. Probably he didn't love her. Love, even when filled with hate, doesn't have that sullen face. But what is his face like? They made love in the dark by feel, without seeing each other. Is there another love than that of darkness, a love that would cry aloud in daylight? She didn't know, but she did know that Marcel needed her and that she needed that need, that she lived on it night and day, at night especially—every night, when he didn't want to be alone, or to age or die, with that set expression he assumed which she occasionally recognized on other men's faces, the only common expression of those madmen hiding under an appearance of wisdom until the madness seizes them and hurls them desperately toward a woman's body to bury in it, without desire, everything terrifying that solitude and night reveals to them.

Marcel stirred as if to move away from her. No, he didn't love her; he was merely afraid of what was not she, and she

and he should long ago have separated and slept alone until
the end. But who can always sleep alone? Some men do, cut
off from others by a vocation or misfortune, who go to bed
every night in the same bed as death. Marcel never could do
so—he above all, a weak and disarmed child always frightened by suffering, her own child indeed who needed her and
who, just at that moment, let out a sort of whimper. She
cuddled a little closer and put her hand on his chest. And to
herself she called him with the little love-name she had once
given him, which they still used from time to time without
even thinking of what they were saying.

She called him with all her heart. After all, she too needed
him, his strength, his little eccentricities, and she too was
afraid of death. "If I could overcome that fear, I'd be happy.
. . ." Immediately, a nameless anguish seized her. She drew
back from Marcel. No, she was overcoming nothing, she was
not happy, she was going to die, in truth, without having been
liberated. Her heart pained her; she was stifling under a huge
weight that she suddenly discovered she had been dragging
around for twenty years. Now she was struggling under it with
all her strength. She wanted to be liberated even if Marcel,
even if the others, never were! Fully awake, she sat up in bed
and listened to a call that seemed very close. But from the
edges of night the exhausted and yet indefatigable voices
of the dogs of the oasis were all that reached her ears. A
slight wind had risen and she heard its light waters flow in
the palm grove. It came from the south, where desert and
night mingled now under the again unchanging sky, where life
stopped, where no one would ever age or die any more. Then
the waters of the wind dried up and she was not even sure
of having heard anything except a mute call that she could,
after all, silence or notice. But never again would she know its
meaning unless she responded to it at once. At once—yes,
that much was certain at least!

She got up gently and stood motionless beside the bed,
listening to her husband's breathing. Marcel was asleep. The
next moment, the bed's warmth left her and the cold gripped
her. She dressed slowly, feeling for her clothes in the faint
light coming through the blinds from the streetlamps. Her
shoes in her hand, she reached the door. She waited a moment
more in the darkness, then gently opened the door. The knob
squeaked and she stood still. Her heart was beating madly.
She listened with her body tense and, reassured by the silence,
turned her hand a little more. The knob's turning seemed

to her interminable. At last she opened the door, slipped
outside, and closed the door with the same stealth. Then, with
her cheek against the wood, she waited. After a moment she
made out, in the distance, Marcel's breathing. She faced
about, felt the icy night air against her cheek, and ran the
length of the balcony. The outer door was closed. While she
was slipping the bolt, the night watchman appeared at the top
of the stairs, his face blurred with sleep, and spoke to her in
Arabic. "I'll be back," said Janine as she stepped out into
the night.

Garlands of stars hung down from the black sky over the
palm trees and houses. She ran along the short avenue, now
empty, that led to the fort. The cold, no longer having to
struggle against the sun, had invaded the night; the icy air
burned her lungs. But she ran, half blind, in the darkness.
At the top of the avenue, however, lights appeared, then descended toward her zizagging. She stopped, caught the whir
of turning sprockets and, behind the enlarging lights, soon saw
vast burnooses surmounting fragile bicycle wheels. The burnooses flapped against her; then three red lights sprang out of
the black behind her and disappeared at once. She continued
running toward the fort. Halfway up the stairs, the air burned
her lungs with such cutting effect that she wanted to stop. A
final burst of energy hurled her despite herself onto the
terrace, against the parapet, which was now pressing her
belly. She was panting and everything was hazy before her
eyes. Her running had not warmed her and she was still
trembling all over. But the cold air she was gulping down
soon flowed evenly inside her and a spark of warmth began
to glow amidst her shivers. Her eyes opened at last on the
expanse of night.

Not a breath, not a sound—except at intervals the muffled
crackling of stones that the cold was reducing to sand—disturbed the solitude and silence surrounding Janine. After a
moment, however, it seemed to her that the sky above her
was moving in a sort of slow gyration. In the vast reaches
of the dry, cold night, thousands of stars were constantly
appearing, and their sparkling icicles, loosened at once, began to slip gradually toward the horizon. Janine could not
tear herself away from contemplating those drifting flares.
She was turning with them, and the apparently stationary
progress little by little identified her with the core of her being,
where cold and desire were now vying with each other. Before
her the stars were falling one by one and being snuffed out

among the stones of the desert, and each time Janine opened
a little more to the night. Breathing deeply, she forgot the
cold, the dead weight of others, the craziness or stuffiness of
life, the long anguish of living and dying. After so many years
of mad, aimless fleeing from fear, she had come to a stop at
last. At the same time, she seemed to recover her roots and
the sap again rose in her body, which had ceased trembling.
Her whole belly pressed against the parapet as she strained
toward the moving sky; she was merely waiting for her fluttering heart to calm down and establish silence within her. The
last stars of the constellations dropped their clusters a little
lower on the desert horizon and became still. Then, with
unbearable gentleness, the water of night began to fill Janine,
drowned the cold, rose gradually from the hidden core of
her being and overflowed in wave after wave, rising up even
to her mouth full of moans. The next moment, the whole sky
stretched out over her, fallen on her back on the cold
earth.

When Janine returned to the room, with the same pre-
cautions, Marcel was not awake. But he whimpered as she
got back in bed and a few seconds later sat up suddenly.
He spoke and she didn't understand what he was saying. He
got up, turned on the light, which blinded her. He staggered
toward the washbasin and drank a long draught from the
bottle of mineral water. He was about to slip between the
sheets when, one knee on the bed, he looked at her without
understanding. She was weeping copiously, unable to restrain
herself. "It's nothing, dear," she said, "it's nothing."

FRANZ KAFKA

Jackals and Arabs

Franz Kafka (1883-1924) wrote, in his short and unhappy lifetime, a body of work so original, so remarkably anguished in its nightmare search for an elusive God, that his has become the central voice for a whole literature of existentialism. A Jew born in Prague, he was the son of a domineering father who had neither understanding nor sympathy for the artistic interests of his son. Kafka's three novels, The Trial, The Castle, and Amerika, were all published posthumously. In these and in his stories, Kafka explores a world of guilt and frustration, seeking below the threshold of the conscious, rational mind. Kafka's stories exist on multi-levels of meaning. They are the voice of the "age of anxiety."

WE WERE CAMPING in the oasis. My companions were asleep. The tall, white figure of an Arab passed by; he had been seeing to the camels and was on his way to his own sleeping place.

I threw myself on my back in the grass; I tried to fall asleep; I could not; a jackal howled in the distance; I sat up again. And what had been so far away was all at once quite near. Jackals were swarming round me, eyes gleaming dull gold and vanishing again, lithe bodies moving nimbly and rhythmically, as if at the crack of a whip.

One jackal came from behind me, nudging right under my arm, pressing against me, as if he needed my warmth, and then stood before me and spoke to me almost eye to eye.

"I am the oldest jackal far and wide. I am delighted to
have met you here at last. I had almost given up hope, since
we have been waiting endless years for you; my mother
waited for you, and her mother, and all our fore-mothers
right back to the first mother of all the jackals. It is true,
believe me!"

"That is surprising," said I, forgetting to kindle the pile
of firewood which lay ready to smoke away jackals, "that is
very surprising for me to hear. It is by pure chance that I
have come here from the far North, and I am making only a
short tour of your country. What do you jackals want, then?"

As if emboldened by this perhaps too friendly inquiry the
ring of jackals closed in on me; all were panting and open-
mouthed.

"We know," began the eldest, "that you have come from
the North; that is just what we base our hopes on. You
Northerners have the kind of intelligence that is not to be
found among Arabs. Not a spark of intelligence, let me tell
you, can be struck from their cold arrogance. They kill
animals for food, and carrion they despise."

"Not so loud," said I, "there are Arabs sleeping near by."

"You are indeed a stranger here," said the jackal, "or
you would know that never in the history of the world has
any jackal been afraid of an Arab. Why should we fear them?
Is it not misfortune enough for us to be exiled among such
creatures?"

"Maybe, maybe," said I, "matters so far outside my prov-
ince I am not competent to judge; it seems to me a very
old quarrel; I suppose it's in the blood, and perhaps will only
end with it."

"You are very clever," said the old jackal; and they all
began to pant more quickly; the air pumped out of their
lungs although they were standing still; a rank smell which
at times I had to set my teeth to endure streamed from their
open jaws, "you are very clever; what you have just said
agrees with our old tradition. So we shall draw blood from
them and the quarrel will be over."

"Oh!" said I, more vehemently than I intended, "they'll
defend themselves; they'll shoot you down in dozens with their
muskets."

"You misunderstand us," said he, "a human failing which
persists apparently even in the far North. We're not proposing
to kill them. All the water in the Nile couldn't cleanse us of

that. Why, the mere sight of their living flesh makes us turn tail and flee into cleaner air, into the desert, which for that very reason is our home."

And all the jackals around, including many newcomers from farther away, dropped their muzzles between their forelegs and wiped them with their paws; it was as if they were trying to conceal a disgust so overpowering that I felt like leaping over their heads to get away.

"Then what are you proposing to do?" I asked, trying to rise to my feet; but I could not get up; two young beasts behind me had locked their teeth through my coat and shirt; I had to go on sitting. "These are your trainbearers," explained the old jackal, quite seriously, "a mark of honor." "They must let go!" I cried, turning now to the old jackal, now to the youngsters. "They will, of course," said the old one, "if that is your wish. But it will take a little time, for they have got their teeth well in, as is our custom, and must first loosen their jaws bit by bit. Meanwhile, give ear to our petition." "Your conduct hasn't exactly inclined me to grant it," said I. "Don't hold it against us that we are clumsy," said he, and now for the first time had recourse to the natural plaintiveness of his voice, "we are poor creatures, we have nothing but our teeth; whatever we want to do, good or bad, we can tackle it only with our teeth." "Well, what do you want?" I asked, not much mollified.

"Sir," he cried, and all the jackals howled together; very remotely it seemed to resemble a melody. "Sir, we want you to end this quarrel that divides the world. You are exactly the man whom our ancestors foretold as born to do it. We want to be troubled no more by Arabs; room to breathe; a skyline cleansed of them; no more bleating of sheep knifed by an Arab; every beast to die a natural death; no interference till we have drained the carcass empty and picked its bones clean. Cleanliness, nothing but cleanliness is what we want"—and now they were all lamenting and sobbing—"how can you bear to live in such a world, O noble heart and kindly bowels? Filth is their white; filth is their black; their beards are a horror; the very sight of their eye sockets makes one want to spit; and when they lift an arm, the murk of hell yawns in the armpit. And so, sir, and so, dear sir, by means of your all-powerful hands slit their throats through with these scissors!" And in answer to a jerk of his head a jackal came trotting up with a small pair of sewing scissors, covered with ancient rust, dangling from an eye-tooth.

"Well, here's the scissors at last, and high time to stop!" cried the Arab leader of our caravan who had crept upwind towards us and now cracked his great whip.

The jackals fled in haste, but at some little distance rallied in a close huddle, all the brutes so tightly packed and rigid that they looked as if penned in a small fold girt by flickering will-o'-the-wisps.

"So you've been treated to this entertainment too, sir," said the Arab, laughing as gaily as the reserve of his race permitted. "You know, then, what the brutes are after?" I asked. "Of course," said he, "it's common knowledge; so long as Arabs exist, that pair of scissors goes wandering through the desert and will wander with us to the end of our days. Every European is offered it for the great work; every European is just the man that fate has chosen for them. They have the most lunatic hopes, these beasts; they're just fools, utter fools. That's why we like them; they are our dogs; finer dogs than any of yours. Watch this, now, a camel died last night and I have had it brought here."

Four men came up with the heavy carcass and threw it down before us. It had hardly touched the ground before the jackals lifted up their voices. As if irresistibly drawn by cords each of them began to waver forward, crawling on his belly. They had forgotten the Arabs, forgotten their hatred, the all-obliterating immediate presence of the stinking carrion bewitched them. One was already at the camel's throat, sinking his teeth straight into an artery. Like a vehement small pump endeavoring with as much determination as hopefulness to extinguish some raging fire, every muscle in his body twitched and labored at the task. In a trice they were all on top of the carcass, laboring in common, piled mountain-high.

And now the caravan leader lashed his cutting whip criss-cross over their backs. They lifted their heads; half swooning in ecstasy; saw the Arabs standing before them; felt the sting of the whip on their muzzles; leaped and ran backwards a stretch. But the camel's blood was already lying in pools, reeking to heaven, the carcass was torn wide open in many places. They could not resist it; they were back again; once more the leader lifted his whip; I stayed his arm. "You are right, sir," said he, "we'll leave them to their business; besides, it's time to break camp. Well, you've seen them. Marvelous creatures, aren't they? And how they hate us!"

ISAK DINESEN

Sorrow-Acre

Isak Dinesen (1885-1962) is a "sport" among writ-ers, fitting no easy classification. Her stories are philosophic, moralistic, and gothic, an unusual com-bination that makes them seem distant in time but universal and fascinating in the values they explore. Born in Denmark, Isak Dinesen's early interest in the arts expressed itself in painting. She began to write after she went to live in Kenya with her hus-band, Baron Blixen. Her novel The Angelic Aveng-ers, *published under a pseudonym during the war, was an attack on Nazism too subtle to be recognized as such by Nazi censors. Her fame chiefly rests, however, on her two remarkable and original col-lections of short stories,* Seven Gothic Tales *and* Winter's Tales.

THE LOW, UNDULATING Danish landscape was silent and serene, mysteriously wide-awake in the hour before sunrise. There was not a cloud in the pale sky, not a shadow along the dim, pearly fields, hills and woods. The mist was lifting from the valleys and hollows, the air was cool, the grass and the foliage dripping wet with morning-dew. Unwatched by the eyes of man, and undisturbed by his activity, the country breathed a timeless life, to which language was inadequate.

All the same, a human race had lived on this land for a thousand years, had been formed by its soil and weather, and had marked it with its thoughts, so that now no one could tell where the existence of the one ceased and the other be-

From WINTER'S TALES, by Isak Dinesen. Copyright 1942 by Random House, Inc. Reprinted by permission.

gan. The thin grey line of a road, winding across the plain
and up and down hills, was the fixed materialisation of human
longing, and of the human notion that it is better to be in
one place than another.

A child of the country would read this open landscape
like a book. The irregular mosaic of meadows and cornlands
was a picture, in timid green and yellow, of the people's
struggle for its daily bread; the centuries had taught it to
plough and sow in this way. On a distant hill the immovable
wings of a windmill, in a small blue cross against the sky,
delineated a later stage in the career of bread. The blurred
outline of thatched roofs—a low, brown growth of the earth
—where the huts of the village thronged together, told the
history, from his cradle to his grave, of the peasant, the
creature nearest to the soil and dependent on it, prospering
in a fertile year and dying in years of drought and pests.

A little higher up, with the faint horizontal line of the
white cemetery-wall round it, and the vertical contour of tall
poplars by its side, the red-tiled church bore witness, as far
as the eye reached, that this was a Christian country. The
child of the land knew it as a strange house, inhabited only
for a few hours every seventh day, but with a strong, clear
voice in it to give out the joys and sorrows of the land:
a plain, square embodiment of the nation's trust in the justice
and mercy of heaven. But where, amongst cupular woods
and groves, the lordly, pyramidal silhouette of the cut lime
avenues rose in the air, there a big country house lay.

The child of the land would read much within these elegant, geometrical ciphers on the hazy blue. They spoke of
power, the lime trees paraded round a stronghold. Up here
was decided the destiny of the surrounding land and of the
men and beasts upon it, and the peasant lifted his eyes to the
green pyramids with awe. They spoke of dignity, decorum
and taste. Danish soil grew no finer flower than the mansion
to which the long avenue led. In its lofty rooms life and
death bore themselves with stately grace. The country house
did not gaze upward, like the church, nor down to the ground
like the huts; it had a wider earthly horizon than they, and
was related to much noble architecture all over Europe.
Foreign artisans had been called in to panel and stucco it,
and its own inhabitants travelled and brought back ideas,
fashions and things of beauty. Paintings, tapestries, silver and
glass from distant countries had been made to feel at home
here and now formed part of Danish country life.

The big house stood as firmly rooted in the soil of Denmark
the peasants' huts, and was as faithfully allied to her four
inds and her changing seasons, to her animal life, trees and
owers. Only its interests lay in a higher plane. Within the
omain of the lime trees it was no longer cows, goats and pigs
a which the minds and the talk ran, but horses and dogs. The
ild fauna, the game of the land, that the peasant shook his fist
, when he saw it on his young green rye or in his ripening
heat field, to the residents of the country houses were the main
ursuit and the joy of existence.

The writing in the sky solemnly proclaimed continuance, a
orldly immortality. The great country houses had held their
round through many generations. The families who lived in
iem revered the past as they honoured themselves, for the his-
ory of Denmark was their own history.

A Rosenkrantz had sat at Rosenholm, a Juel at Hverringe, a
keel at Gammel-Estrup as long as people remembered. They
ad seen kings and schools of style succeed one another and,
roudly and humbly, had made over their personal existence to
aat of their land, so that amongst their equals and with the
easants they passed by its name: Rosenholm, Hverringe, Gam-
iel-Estrup. To the King and the country, to his family and to
ie individual lord of the manor himself it was a matter of minor
onsequence which particular Rosenkrantz, Juel and Skeel, out
f a long row of fathers and sons, at the moment in his person
icarnated the fields and woods, the peasants, cattle and game of
he estate. Many duties rested on the shoulders of the big land-
wners—towards God in heaven, towards the King, his neigh-
our and himself—and they were all harmoniously consolidated
nto the idea of his duties towards his land. Highest amongst
hese ranked his obligation to uphold the sacred continuance,
nd to produce a new Rosenkrantz, Juel or Skeel for the service
f Rosenholm, Hverringe and Gammel-Estrup.

Female grace was prized in the manors. Together with good
unting and fine wine it was the flower and emblem of the
igher existence led there, and in many ways the families prided
hemselves more on their daughters than on their sons.

The ladies who promenaded in the lime avenues, or drove
hrough them in heavy coaches with four horses, carried the
uture of the name in their laps and were, like dignified and
ebonair caryatides, holding up the houses. They were them-
elves conscious of their value, kept up their price, and

moved in a sphere of pretty worship and self-worship. They might even be thought to add to it, on their own, a graceful, arch, paradoxical haughtiness. For how free were they, how powerful! Their lords might rule the country, and allow themselves many liberties, but when it came to that supreme matter of legitimacy which was the vital principle of their world, the centre of gravity lay with them.

The lime trees were in bloom. But in the early morning only a faint fragrance drifted through the garden, an airy message, an aromatic echo of the dreams during the short summer night.

In a long avenue that led from the house all the way to the end of the garden, where, from a small white pavilion in the classic style, there was a great view over the fields, a young man walked. He was plainly dressed in brown, with pretty linen and lace, bare-headed, with his hair tied by a ribbon. He was dark, a strong and sturdy figure with fine eyes and hands; he limped a little on one leg.

The big house at the top of the avenue, the garden and the fields had been his childhood's paradise. But he had travelled and lived out of Denmark, in Rome and Paris, and he was at present appointed to the Danish Legation to the Court of King George, the brother of the late, unfortunate young Danish Queen. He had not seen his ancestral home for nine years. It made him laugh to find, now, everything so much smaller than he remembered it, and at the same time he was strangely moved by meeting it again. Dead people came towards him and smiled at him; a small boy in a ruff ran past him with his hoop and kite, in passing gave him a clear glance and laughingly asked: "Do you mean to tell me that you are I?" He tried to catch him in the flight, and to answer him: "Yes, I assure you that I am you," but the light figure did not wait for a reply.

The young man, whose name was Adam, stood in a particular relation to the house and the land. For six months he had been heir to it all; nominally he was so even at this moment. It was this circumstance which had brought him from England, and on which his mind was dwelling, as he walked along slowly.

The old lord up at the manor, his father's brother, had had much misfortune in his domestic life. His wife had died young, and two of his children in infancy. The one son then left to him, his cousin's playmate, was a sickly and morose boy. For ten years the father travelled with him from one water-

ing place to another, in Germany and Italy, hardly ever in
other company than that of his silent, dying child, sheltering
the faint flame of life with both hands, until such time as it
could be passed over to a new bearer of the name. At the
same time another misfortune had struck him: he fell into
disfavour at Court, where till now he had held a fine position.
He was about to rehabilitate his family's prestige through the
marriage which he had arranged for his son, when before it
could take place the bridegroom died, not yet twenty years
old.

Adam learned of his cousin's death, and his own changed
fortune, in England, through his ambitious and triumphant
mother. He sat with her letter in his hand and did not know
what to think about it.

If this, he reflected, had happened to him while he was
still a boy, in Denmark, it would have meant all the world
to him. It would be so now with his friends and schoolfel-
lows, if they were in his place, and they would, at this moment, be congratulating or envying him. But he was neither
covetous nor vain by nature; he had faith in his own talents
and had been content to know that his success in life de-
pended on his personal ability. His slight infirmity had always
set him a little apart from other boys; it had, perhaps,
given him a keener sensibility of many things in life, and he
did not, now, deem it quite right that the head of the family
should limp on one leg. He did not even see his prospects
in the same light as his people at home. In England he had
met with greater wealth and magnificence than they dreamed
of; he had been in love with, and made happy by, an English
lady of such rank and fortune that to her, he felt, the finest
estate of Denmark would look but like a child's toy farm.

And in England, too, he had come in touch with the great
new ideas of the age: of nature, of the right and freedom
of man, of justice and beauty. The universe, through them,
had become infinitely wider to him; he wanted to find out
still more about it and was planning to travel to America,
to the new world. For a moment he felt trapped and imprisoned, as if the dead people of his name, from the family
vault at home, were stretching out their parched arms for him.

But at the same time he began to dream at night of the
old house and garden. He had walked in these avenues in
dream, and had smelled the scent of the flowering limes.
When at Ranelagh an old gypsy woman looked at his hand
and told him that a son of his was to sit in the seat of his

fathers, he felt a sudden, deep satisfaction, queer in a young man who till now had never given his sons a thought.

Then, six months later, his mother again wrote to tell him that his uncle had himself married the girl intended for his dead son. The head of the family was still in his best age, not over sixty, and although Adam remembered him as a small, slight man, he was a vigorous person; it was likely that his young wife would bear him sons.

Adam's mother in her disappointment lay the blame on him. If he had returned to Denmark, she told him, his uncle might have come to look upon him as a son, and would not have married; nay, he might have handed the bride over to him. Adam knew better. The family estate, differing from the neighbouring properties, had gone down from father to son ever since a man of their name first sat there. The tradition of direct succession was the pride of the clan and a sacred dogma to his uncle; he would surely call for a son of his own flesh and bone.

But at the news the young man was seized by a strange, deep, aching remorse towards his old home in Denmark. It was as if he had been making light of a friendly and generous gesture, and disloyal to someone unfailingly loyal to him. It would be but just, he thought, if from now the place should disown and forget him. Nostalgia, which before he had never known, caught hold of him; for the first time he walked in the streets and parks of London as a stranger.

He wrote to his uncle and asked if he might come and stay with him, begged leave from the Legation and took ship for Denmark. He had come to the house to make his peace with it; he had slept little in the night, and was up so early and walking in the garden, to explain himself, and to be forgiven.

While he walked, the still garden slowly took up its day's work. A big snail, of the kind that his grandfather had brought back from France, and which he remembered eating in the house as a child, was already, with dignity, dragging a silver train down the avenue. The birds began to sing; in an old tree under which he stopped a number of them were worrying an owl; the rule of the night was over.

He stood at the end of the avenue and saw the sky lightening. An ecstatic clarity filled the world; in half an hour the sun would rise. A rye field here ran along the garden; two roe-deer were moving in it and looked roseate in the dawn. He gazed out over the fields, where as a small boy he had

ridden his pony, and towards the wood where he had killed
his first stag. He remembered the old servants who had taught
him; some of them were now in their graves.

The ties which bound him to this place, he reflected, were
of a mystic nature. He might never again come back to it,
and it would make no difference. As long as a man of his
own blood and name should sit in the house, hunt in the
fields and be obeyed by the people in the huts, wherever he
travelled on earth, in England or amongst the red Indians
of America, he himself would still be safe, would still have
a home, and would carry weight in the world.

His eyes rested on the church. In old days, before the
time of Martin Luther, younger sons of great families, he
knew, had entered the Church of Rome, and had given up
individual wealth and happiness to serve the greater ideals.
They, too, had bestowed honour upon their homes and were
remembered in its registers. In the solitude of the morning,
half in jest he let his mind run as it listed; it seemed to
him that he might speak to the land as to a person, as to
the mother of his race. "Is it only my body that you want,"
he asked her, "while you reject my imagination, energy and
emotions? If the world might be brought to acknowledge that
the virtue of our name does not belong to the past only, will
it give you no satisfaction?" The landscape was so still that
he could not tell whether it answered him yes or no.

After a while he walked on, and came to the new French
rose garden laid out for the young mistress of the house.
In England he had acquired a freer taste in gardening, and
he wondered if he could liberate these blushing captives, and
make them thrive outside their cut hedges. Perhaps, he med-
itated, the elegantly conventional garden would be a floral
portrait of his young aunt from Court, whom he had not
yet seen.

As once more he came to the pavilion at the end of the
avenue his eyes were caught by a bouquet of delicate colours
which could not possibly belong to the Danish summer morning. It was in fact his uncle himself, powdered and silk-stock-
inged, but still in a brocade dressing-gown, and obviously
sunk in deep thought. "And what business, or what medita-
tions," Adam asked himself, "drags a connoisseur of the
beautiful, but three months married to a wife of seventeen,
from his bed into his garden before sunrise?" He walked
up to the small, slim, straight figure.

His uncle on his side showed no surprise at seeing him,

but then he rarely seemed surprised at anything. He greeted him, with a compliment on his matunality, as kindly as he had done on his arrival last evening. After a moment he looked to the sky, and solemnly proclaimed: "It will be a hot day." Adam, as a child, had often been impressed by the grand, ceremonial manner in which the old lord would state the common happenings of existence; it looked as if nothing had changed here, but all was what it used to be.

The uncle offered the nephew a pinch of snuff. "No, thank you, Uncle," said Adam, "it would ruin my nose to the scent of your garden, which is as fresh as the Garden of Eden, newly created." "From every tree of which," said his uncle, smiling, "thou, my Adam, mayest freely eat." They slowly walked up the avenue together.

The hidden sun was now already gilding the top of the tallest trees. Adam talked of the beauties of nature, and of the greatness of Nordic scenery, less marked by the hand of man than that of Italy. His uncle took the praise of the landscape as a personal compliment, and congratulated him because he had not, in likeness to many young travellers in foreign countries, learned to despise his native land. No, said Adam, he had lately in England longed for the fields and woods of his Danish home. And he had there become acquainted with a new piece of Danish poetry which had enchanted him more than any English or French work. He named the author, Johannes Ewald, and quoted a few of the mighty, turbulent verses.

"And I have wondered, while I read," he went on after a pause, still moved by the lines he himself had declaimed, "that we have not till now understood how much our Nordic mythology in moral greatness surpasses that of Greece and Rome. If it had not been for the physical beauty of the ancient gods, which has come down to us in marble, no modern mind could hold them worthy of worship. They were mean, capricious and treacherous. The gods of our Danish forefathers are as much more divine than they as the Druid is nobler than the Augur. For the fair gods of Asgaard did possess the sublime human virtues; they were righteous, trustworthy, benevolent and even, within a barbaric age, chivalrous." His uncle here for the first time appeared to take any real interest in the conversation. He stopped, his majestic nose a little in the air. "Ah, it was easier to them," he said.

"What do you mean, Uncle?" Adam asked. "It was a great deal easier," said his uncle, "to the northern gods than

to those of Greece to be, as you will have it, righteous and
benevolent. To my mind it even reveals a weakness in the
souls of our ancient Danes that they should consent to adore
such divinities." "My dear uncle," said Adam, smiling, "I
have always felt that you would be familiar with the modes
of Olympus. Now please let me share your insight, and tell
me why virtue should come easier to our Danish gods than
to those of milder climates." "They were not as powerful,"
said his uncle.

"And does power," Adam again asked, "stand in the way
of virtue?" "Nay," said his uncle gravely. "Nay, power is
in itself the supreme virtue. But the gods of which you speak
were never all-powerful. They had, at all times, by their side
those darker powers which they named the Jotuns, and who
worked the suffering, the disasters, the ruin of our world. They
might safely give themselves up to temperance and kindness.
The omnipotent gods," he went on, "have no such facilitation.
With their omnipotence they take over the woe of the universe."

They had walked up the avenue till they were in view of
the house. The old lord stopped and ran his eyes over it.
The stately building was the same as ever; behind the two
tall front windows, Adam knew, was now his young aunt's
room. His uncle turned and walked back.

"Chivalry," he said, "chivalry, of which you were speaking,
is not a virtue of the omnipotent. It must needs imply mighty
rival powers for the knight to defy. With a dragon inferior
to him in strength, what figure will St. George cut? The
knight who finds no superior forces ready to hand must in-
vent them, and combat wind-mills; his knighthood itself stip-
ulates dangers, vileness, darkness on all sides of him. Nay,
believe me, my nephew, in spite of his moral worth, your
chivalrous Odin of Asgaard as a Regent must take rank
below that of Jove who avowed his sovereignty, and accepted the world which he ruled. But you are young," he
added, "and the experience of the aged to you will sound
pedantic."

He stood immovable for a moment and then with deep
gravity proclaimed: "The sun is up."

The sun did indeed rise above the horizon. The wide landscape was suddenly animated by its splendour, and the
dewy grass shone in a thousand gleams.

"I have listened to you, Uncle," said Adam, "with great
interest. But while we have talked you yourself have seemed

to me preoccupied; your eyes have rested on the field outside the garden, as if something of great moment, a matter
of life and death, was going on there. Now that the sun
is up, I see the mowers in the rye and hear them whetting
their sickles. It is, I remember you telling me, the first day
of the harvest. That is a great day to a landowner and
enough to take his mind away from the gods. It is very
fine weather, and I wish you a full barn."

The elder man stood still, his hands on his walking-stick.
"There is indeed," he said at last, "something going on in
that field, a matter of life and death. Come, let us sit down
here, and I will tell you the whole story." They sat down
on the seat that ran all along the pavilion, and while he
spoke the old lord of the land did not take his eyes off the
rye field.

"A week ago, on Thursday night," he said, "someone set
fire to my barn at Rødmosegaard—you know the place, close
to the moor—and burned it all down. For two or three
days we could not lay hands on the offender. Then on Monday morning the keeper at Rødmose, with the wheelwright
over there, came up to the house; they dragged with them
a boy, Goske Piil, a widow's son, and they made their Bible
oath that he had done it; they had themselves seen him
sneaking round the barn by nightfall on Thursday. Goske
had no good name on the farm; the keeper bore him a
grudge upon an old matter of poaching, and the wheelwright did not like him either, for he did, I believe, suspect
him with his young wife. The boy, when I talked to him,
swore to his innocence, but he could not hold his own against
the two old men. So I had him locked up, and meant to
send him in to our judge of the district, with a letter.

"The judge is a fool, and would naturally do nothing but
what he thought I wished him to do. He might have the
boy sent to the convict prison for arson, or put amongst
the soldiers as a bad character and a poacher. Or again,
if he thought that that was what I wanted, he could let
him off.

"I was out riding in the fields, looking at the corn that
was soon ripe to be mowed, when a woman, the widow,
Goske's mother, was brought up before me, and begged to
speak to me. Anne-Marie is her name. You will remember
her; she lives in the small house east of the village. She
has not got a good name in the place either. They tell as a
girl she had a child and did away with it.

"From five days' weeping her voice was so cracked that it was difficult for me to understand what she said. Her son, she told me at last, had indeed been over at Rødmose on Thursday, but for no ill purpose; he had gone to see someone. He was her only son, she called the Lord God to witness on his innocence, and she wrung her hands to me that I should save the boy for her.

"We were in the rye field that you and I are looking at now. That gave me an idea. I said to the widow: 'If in one day, between sunrise and sunset, with your own hands you can mow this field, and it be well done, I will let the case drop and you shall keep your son. But if you cannot do it, he must go, and it is not likely that you will then ever see him again.'

"She stood up then and gazed over the field. She kissed my riding boot in gratitude for the favour shown to her."

The old lord here made a pause, and Adam said: "Her son meant much to her?" "He is her only child," said his uncle. "He means to her her daily bread and support in old age. It may be said that she holds him as dear as her own life. As," he added, "within a higher order of life, a son to his father means the name and the race, and he holds him as dear as life everlasting. Yes, her son means much to her. For the mowing of that field is a day's work to three men, or three days' work to one man. Today, as the sun rose, she set to her task. And down there, by the end of the field, you will see her now, in a blue head-cloth, with the man I have set to follow her and to ascertain that she does the work unassisted, and with two or three friends by her, who are comforting her."

Adam looked down, and did indeed see a woman in a blue head-cloth, and a few other figures in the corn.

They sat for a while in silence. "Do you yourself," Adam then said, "believe the boy to be innocent?" "I cannot tell," said his uncle. "There is no proof. The word of the keeper and the wheelwright stand against the boy's word. If indeed I did believe the one thing or the other, it would be merely a matter of chance, or maybe of sympathy. The boy," he said after a moment, "was my son's playmate, the only other child that I ever knew him to like or to get on with." "Do you," Adam again asked, "hold it possible to her to fulfill your condition?" "Nay, I cannot tell," said the old lord. "To an ordinary person it would not be possible. No ordinary person would ever have taken it on at all. I chose it so. We are not quibbling with the law, Anne-Marie and I."

Adam for a few minutes followed the movement of the
small group in the rye. "Will you walk back?" he asked.
"No," said his uncle, "I think that I shall stay here till I
have seen the end of the thing." "Until sunset?" Adam asked
with surprise. "Yes," said the old lord. Adam said: "It will
be a long day." "Yes," said his uncle, "a long day. But,"
he added, as Adam rose to walk away, "if, as you said,
you have got that tragedy of which you spoke in your pocket,
be so kind as to leave it here, to keep me company." Adam
handed him the book.

In the avenue he met two footmen who carried the old
lord's morning chocolate down to the pavilion on large silver
trays.

As now the sun rose in the sky, and the day grew hot, the
lime trees gave forth their exuberance of scent, and the
garden was filled with unsurpassed, unbelievable sweetness.
Towards the still hour of midday the long avenue reverberated like a soundboard with a low, incessant murmur: the
humming of a million bees that clung to the pendulous,
thronging clusters of blossoms and were drunk with bliss.

In all the short lifetime of Danish summer there is no
richer or more luscious moment than that week wherein the
lime trees flower. The heavenly scent goes to the head and
to the heart; it seems to unite the fields of Denmark with
those of Elysium; it contains both hay, honey and holy in-
cense, and is half fairy-land and half apothecary's locker.
The avenue was changed into a mystic edifice, a dryad's
cathedral, outward from summit to base lavishly adorned,
set with multitudinous ornaments, and golden in the sun.
But behind the walls the vaults were benignly cool and sombre, like ambrosial sanctuaries in a dazzling and burning
world, and in here the ground was still moist.

Up in the house, behind the silk curtains of the two front
windows, the young mistress of the estate from the wide bed
stuck her feet into two little high-heeled slippers. Her lace-
trimmed nightgown had slid up above her knees and down
from the shoulder; her hair, done up in curling-pins for the
night, was still frosty with the powder of yesterday, her
round face flushed with sleep. She stepped out to the middle
of the floor and stood there, looking extremely grave and
thoughtful, yet she did not think at all. But through her
head a long procession of pictures marched, and she was

unconsciously endeavouring to put them in order, as the pictures of her existence had used to be.

She had grown up at Court; it was her world, and there was probably not in the whole country a small creature more exquisitely and innocently drilled to the stately measure of a palace. By favour of the old Dowager Queen she bore her name and that of the King's sister, the Queen of Sweden: Sophie Magdalena. It was with a view to these things that her husband, when he wished to restore his status in high places, had chosen her as a bride, first for his son and then for himself. But her own father, who held an office in the Royal Household and belonged to the new Court aristocracy, in his day had done the same thing the other way round, and had married a country lady, to get a foothold within the old nobility of Denmark. The little girl had her mother's blood in her veins. The country to her had been an immense surprise and delight.

To get into her castle-court she must drive through the farm yard, through the heavy stone gateway in the barn itself, wherein the rolling of her coach for a few seconds re-echoed like thunder. She must drive past the stables and the timber-mare, from which sometimes a miscreant would follow her with sad eyes, and might here startle a long string of squalling geese, or pass the heavy, scowling bull, led on by a ring in his nose and kneading the earth in dumb fury. At first this had been to her, every time, a slight shock and a jest. But after a while all these creatures and things, which belonged to her, seemed to become part of herself. Her mothers, the old Danish country ladies, were robust persons, undismayed by any kind of weather; now she herself had walked in the rain and had laughed and glowed in it like a green tree.

She had taken her great new home in possession at a time when all the world was unfolding, mating and propagating. Flowers, which she had known only in bouquets and festoons, sprung from the earth round her; birds sang in all the trees. The new-born lambs seemed to her daintier than her dolls had been. From her husband's Hanoverian stud, foals were brought to her to give names; she stood and watched as they poked their soft noses into their mothers' bellies to drink. Of this strange process she had till now only vaguely heard. She had happened to witness, from a path in the park, the rearing and screeching stallion on the mare. All this luxuriance, lust and fecundity was displayed before her eyes, as for her pleasure.

And for her own part, in the midst of it, she was given an old husband who treated her with punctilious respect because she was to bear him a son. Such was the compact; she had known of it from the beginning. Her husband, she found, was doing his best to fulfill his part of it, and she herself was loyal by nature and strictly brought up. She would not shirk her obligation. Only she was vaguely aware of a discord or an incompatibility within her majestic existence, which prevented her from being as happy as she had expected to be.

After a time her chagrin took a strange form: as the consciousness of an absence. Someone ought to have been with her who was not. She had no experience in analysing her feelings; there had not been time for that at Court. Now, as she was more often left to herself, she vaguely probed her own mind. She tried to set her father in that void place, her sisters, her music master, an Italian singer whom she had admired; but none of them would fill it for her. At times she felt lighter at heart, and believed the misfortune to have left her. And then again it would happen, if she were alone, or in her husband's company, and even within his embrace, that everything round her would cry out: Where? Where? so that she let her wild eyes run about the room in search for the being who should have been there, and who had not come.

When, six months ago, she was informed that her first young bridegroom had died and that she was to marry his father in his place, she had not been sorry. Her youthful suitor, the one time she had seen him, had appeared to her infantile and insipid; the father would make a statelier consort. Now she had sometimes thought of the dead boy, and wondered whether with him life would have been more joyful. But she soon again dismissed the picture, and that was the sad youth's last recall to the stage of this world.

Upon one wall of her room there hung a long mirror. As she gazed into it new images came along. The day before, driving with her husband, she had seen, at a distance, a party of village girls bathe in the river, and the sun shining on them. All her life she had moved amongst naked marble deities, but it had till now never occurred to her that the people she knew should themselves be naked under their bodices and trains, waistcoats and satin breeches, that indeed she herself felt naked within her clothes. Now, in front of the looking-glass, she tardily untied the ribbons of her nightgown, and let it drop to the floor.

The room was dim behind the drawn curtains. In the mirror her body was silvery like a white rose; only her cheeks and mouth, and the tips of her fingers and breasts had a faint carmine. Her slender torso was formed by the whalebones that had clasped it tightly from her childhood; above the slim, dimpled knee a gentle narrowness marked the place of the garter. Her limbs were rounded as if, at whatever place they might be cut through with a sharp knife, a perfectly circular transverse incision would be obtained. The side and belly were so smooth that her own gaze slipped and glided, and grasped for a hold. She was not altogether like a statue, she found, and lifted her arms above her head. She turned to get a view of her back, the curves below the waistline were still blushing from the pressure of the bed. She called to mind a few tales about nymphs and goddesses, but they all seemed a long way off, so her mind returned to the peasant girls in the river. They were, for a few minutes, idealized into playmates, or sisters even, since they belonged to her as did the meadow and the blue river itself. And within the next moment the sense of forlornness once more came upon her, a *horror vacui* like a physical pain. Surely, surely someone should have been with her now, her other self, like the image in the glass, but nearer, stronger, alive. There was no one, the universe was empty round her.

A sudden, keen itching under her knee took her out of her reveries, and awoke in her the hunting instincts of her breed. She wetted a finger on her tongue, slowly brought it down and quickly slapped it to the spot. She felt the diminutive, sharp body of the insect against the silky skin, pressed the thumb to it, and triumphantly lifted up the small prisoner between her fingertips. She stood quite still, as if meditating upon the fact that a flea was the only creature risking its life for her smoothness and sweet blood.

Her maid opened the door and came in, loaded with the attire of the day—shift, stays, hoop and petticoats. She remembered that she had a guest in the house, the new nephew arrived from England. Her husband had instructed her to be kind to their young kinsman, disinherited, so to say, by her presence in the house. They would ride out on the land together.

In the afternoon the sky was no longer blue as in the

morning. Large clouds slowly towered up on it, and the great vault itself was colourless, as if diffused into vapours round the white-hot sun in zenith. A low thunder ran along the western horizon; once or twice the dust of the roads rose in tall spirals. But the fields, the hills and the woods were as still as a painted landscape.

Adam walked down the avenue to the pavilion, and found his uncle there, fully dressed, his hands upon his walking-stick and his eyes on the rye field. The book that Adam had given him lay by his side. The field now seemed alive with people. Small groups stood here and there in it, and a long row of men and women were slowly advancing towards the garden in the line of the swath.

The old lord nodded to his nephew, but did not speak or change his position. Adam stood by him as still as himself.

The day to him had been strangely disquieting. At the meeting again with old places the sweet melodies of the past had filled his senses and his mind, and had mingled with new, bewitching tunes of the present. He was back in Denmark, no longer a child but a youth, with a keener sense of the beautiful, with tales of other countries to tell, and still a true son of his own land and enchanted by its loveliness as he had never been before.

But through all these harmonies the tragic and cruel tale which the old lord had told him in the morning, and the sad contest which he knew to be going on so near by, in the corn field, had re-echoed, like the recurrent, hollow throbbing of a muffled drum, a redoubtable sound. It came back time after time, so that he had felt himself to change colour and to answer absently. It brought with it a deeper sense of pity with all that lived than he had ever known. When he had been riding with his young aunt, and their road ran along the scene of the drama, he had taken care to ride between her and the field, so that she should not see what was going on there, or question him about it. He had chosen the way home through the deep, green wood for the same reason.

More dominantly even than the figure of the woman struggling with her sickle for her son's life, the old man's figure, as he had seen it at sunrise, kept him company through the day. He came to ponder on the part which that lonely, determinate form had played in his own life. From the time when his father died, it had impersonated to the boy law and order, wisdom of life and kind guardianship. What was he to do, he thought, if after eighteen years these filial feelings must change, and his second father's figure take on to him a horrible aspect, as a symbol of the tyranny and oppression of the world? What was he to do if ever the two should come to stand in opposition to each other as adversaries?

At the same time an unaccountable, a sinister alarm and dread on behalf of the old man himself took hold of him. For surely here the Goddess Nemesis could not be far away. This man had ruled the world round him for a longer period than Adam's own lifetime and had never been gainsaid by anyone. During the years when he had wandered through Europe with a sick boy of his own blood as his sole companion he had learned to set himself apart from his surroundings, and to close himself up to all outer life, and he had become insusceptible to the ideas and feelings of other human beings. Strange fancies might there have run in his mind, so that in the end he had seen himself as the only person really existing, and the world as a poor and vain shadow-play, which had no substance to it.

Now, in senile wilfullness, he would take in his hand the life of those simpler and weaker than himself, of a woman, using it to his own ends, and he feared of no retributive justice. Did he not know, the young man thought, that there were powers in the world, different from and more formidable than the short-lived might of a despot?

With the sultry heat of the day this foreboding of impending disaster grew upon him, until he felt ruin threatening not the old lord only, but the house, the name and himself with him. It seemed to him that he must cry out a warning to the man he had loved, before it was too late.

But as now he was once more in his uncle's company, the green calm of the garden was so deep that he did not find his voice to cry out. Instead a little French air which his aunt had sung to him up in the house kept running in his mind.—*"C'est un trop doux effort . . ."* He had good knowledge of music; he had heard the air before, in Paris, but not so sweetly sung.

After a time he asked: "Will the woman fulfill her bargain?" His uncle unfolded his hands. "It is an extraordinary thing," he said animatedly, "that it looks as if she might fulfill it. If you count the hours from sunrise till now, and from now till sunset, you will find the time left her to be half of that already gone. And see! She has now mowed two-thirds of the field. But then we will naturally have to reckon with her strength declining as she works on. All in all, it is an idle pursuit in you or me to bet on the issue of the matter; we must wait and see. Sit down, and keep me company in my watch." In two minds Adam sat down.

"And here," said his uncle, and took up the book from the seat, "is your book, which has passed the time finely. It is great poetry, ambrosia to the ear and the heart. And it has, with our discourse on divinity this morning, given me stuff for thought. I have been reflecting upon the law of retributive justice." He took a pinch of snuff, and went on. "A new age," he said, "has made to itself a god in its own image, an emotional god. And now you are already writing a tragedy on your god."

Adam had no wish to begin a debate on poetry with his uncle, but he also somehow dreaded a silence, and said: "It may be, then, that we hold tragedy to be, in the scheme of life, a noble, a divine phenomenon."

"Aye," said his uncle solemnly, "a noble phenomenon, the noblest on earth. But of the earth only, and never divine. Tragedy is the privilege of man, his highest privilege. The God of the Christian Church Himself, when He wished to experience tragedy, had to assume human form. And even at that," he added thoughtfully, "the tragedy was not wholly valid, as it would have become had the hero of it been, in very truth, a man. The divinity of Christ conveyed to it a divine note, the moment of comedy. The real tragic part, by the nature of things, fell to the executors, not to the victim. Nay, my nephew, we should not adulterate the pure elements of the cosmos. Tragedy should remain the right of human beings, subject, in their conditions or in their own nature, to the dire law of necessity. To them it is salvation and beautification. But the gods, whom we must believe to be unacquainted with and incomprehensive of necessity, can have no knowledge of the tragic. When they are brought face to face with it they will, according to my experience, have the good taste and decorum to keep still, and not interfere.

"No," he said after a pause, "the true art of the gods is the comic. The comic is a condescension of the divine to the world of man; it is the sublime vision, which cannot be studied, but must ever be celestially granted. In the comic the gods see their own being reflected as in a mirror, and while the tragic poet is bound by strict laws, they will allow the comic artist a freedom as unlimited as their own. They do not even withhold their own existence from his sports. Jove may favour Lucianos of Samosata. As long as your

mockery is in true godly taste you may mock at the gods and
still remain a sound devotee. But in pitying, or condoling with
your god, you deny and annihilate him, and such is the most
horrible of atheisms.

"And here on earth, too," he went on, "we, who stand in
lieu of the gods and have emancipated ourselves from the
tyranny of necessity, should leave to our vassals their monopoly of tragedy, and for ourselves accept the comic with
grace. Only a boorish and cruel master—a parvenu, in fact—
will make a jest of his servants' necessity, or force the comic
upon them. Only a timid and pedantic ruler, a *petit-maître*,
will fear the ludicrous on his own behalf. Indeed," he finished
his long speech, "the very same fatality, which, in striking
the burgher or peasant, will become tragedy, with the aristo-
crat is exalted to the comic. By the grace and wit of our ac-
ceptance hereof our aristocracy is known."

Adam could not help smiling a little as he heard the
apotheosis of the comic on the lips of the erect, ceremonious
prophet. In this ironic smile he was, for the first time, estrang-
ing himself from the head of his house.

A shadow fell across the landscape. A cloud had crept over
the sun; the country changed colour beneath it, faded and
bleached, and even all sounds for a minute seemed to die out
of it.

"Ah, now," said the old lord, "if it is going to rain, and
the rye gets wet, Anne-Marie will not be able to finish in
time. And who comes there?" he added, and turned his head
a little.

Preceded by a lackey a man in riding boots and a striped
waistcoat with silver buttons, and with his hat in his hand,
came down the avenue. He bowed deeply, first to the old
lord and then to Adam.

"My bailiff," said the old lord. "Good afternoon, Bailiff.
What news have you to bring?" The bailiff made a sad gesture.
"Poor news only, my lord," he said. "And how poor news?"
asked his master. "There is," said the bailiff with weight,
"not a soul at work on the land, and not a sickle going except
that of Anne-Marie in this rye field. The mowing has stopped;
they are all at her heels. It is a poor day for a first day of
the harvest." "Yes, I see," said the old lord. The bailiff went
on. "I have spoken kindly to them," he said, "and I have
sworn at them; it is all one. They might as well all be deaf."

"Good bailiff," said the old lord, "leave them in peace; let
them do as they like. This day may, all the same, do them

more good than many others. Where is Goske, the boy, Anne-
Marie's son?" "We have set him in the small room by the
barn," said the bailiff. "Nay, let him be brought down," said
the old lord; "let him see his mother at work. But what do
you say—will she get the field mowed in time?" "If you ask
me, my lord," said the bailiff, "I believe that she will. Who
would have thought so? She is only a small woman. It is as
hot a day today as, well, as I do ever remember. I myself,
you yourself, my lord, could not have done what Anne-Marie
has done today." "Nay, nay, we could not, Bailiff," said the
old lord.

The bailiff pulled out a red handkerchief and wiped his
brow, somewhat calmed by venting his wrath. "If," he remarked with bitterness, "they would all work as the widow
works now, we would make a profit on the land." "Yes,"
said the old lord, and fell into thought, as if calculating the
profit it might make. "Still," he said, "as to the question of
profit and loss, that is more intricate than it looks. I will tell
you something that you may not know: The most famous
tissue ever woven was ravelled out again every night. But
come," he added, "she is close by now. We will go and have
a look at her work ourselves." With these words he rose and
set his hat on.

The cloud had drawn away again; the rays of the sun once
more burned the wide landscape, and as the small party walked
out from under the shade of the trees the dead-still heat was
heavy as lead; the sweat sprang out on their faces and their
eyelids smarted. On the narrow path they had to go one by
one, the old lord stepping along first, all black, and the footman, in his bright livery, bringing up the rear.

The field was indeed filled with people like a market-place;
there were probably a hundred or more men and women in it.
To Adam the scene recalled pictures from his Bible: the meeting between Esau and Jacob in Edom, or Boas' reapers in
his barley field near Bethlehem. Some were standing by the
side of the field, others pressed in small groups close to the
mowing woman, and a few followed in her wake, binding up
sheaves where she had cut the corn, as if thereby they
thought to help her, or as if by all means they meant to
have part in her work. A younger woman with a pail on her
head kept close to her side, and with her a number of half-
grown children. One of these first caught sight of the lord of
the estate and his suite, and pointed to him. The binders let

their sheaves drop, and as the old man stood still many of the onlookers drew close round him.

The woman on whom till now the eyes of the whole field had rested—a small figure on the large stage—was advancing slowly and unevenly, bent double as if she were walking on her knees, and stumbling as she walked. Her blue head-cloth had slipped back from her head; the grey hair was plastered to the skull with sweat, dusty and stuck with straw. She was obviously totally unaware of the multitude round her; neither did she now once turn her head or her gaze towards the new arrivals.

Absorbed in her work she again and again stretched out her left hand to grasp a handful of corn, and her right hand with the sickle in it to cut it off close to the soil, in wavering, groping pulls, like a tired swimmer's strokes. Her course took her so close to the feet of the old lord that his shadow fell on her. Just then she staggered and swayed sideways, and the woman who followed her lifted the pail from her head and held it to her lips. Anne-Marie drank without leaving her hold on her sickle, and the water ran from the corners of her mouth. A boy, close to her, quickly bent one knee, seized her hands in his own and, steadying and guiding them, cut off a gripe of rye. "No, no," said the old lord, "you must not do that, boy. Leave Anne-Marie in peace to her work." At the sound of his voice the woman, falteringly, lifted her face in his direction.

The bony and tanned face was streaked with sweat and dust; the eyes were dimmed. But there was not in its expression the slightest trace of fear or pain. Indeed amongst all the grave and concerned faces of the field hers was the only one perfectly calm, peaceful and mild. The mouth was drawn together in a thin line, a prim, keen, patient little smile, such as will be seen in the face of an old woman at her spinning-wheel or her knitting, eager on her work, and happy in it. And as the younger women lifted back the pail, she immediately again fell to her mowing, with an ardent, tender craving, like that of a mother who lays a baby to the nipple. Like an insect that bustles along in high grass, or like a small vessel in a heavy sea, she butted her way on, her quiet face once more bent upon her task.

The whole throng of onlookers, and with them the small group from the pavilion, advanced as she advanced, slowly and as if drawn by a string. The bailiff, who felt the intense silence of the field heavy on him, said to the old lord: "The rye will yield better this year than last," and got no reply. He repeated his remark to Adam, and at last to the footman, who felt himself above a discussion on agriculture, and only cleared his throat in answer. In a while the bailiff again broke the silence. "There is the boy," he said and pointed with his thumb. "They have brought him down." At that moment the woman fell forward on her face and was lifted up by those nearest to her.

Adam suddenly stopped on the path, and covered his eyes with his hand. The old lord without turning asked him if he felt incommoded by the heat. "No," said Adam, "but stay. Let me speak to you." His uncle stopped, with his hand on the stick and looking ahead, as if regretful of being held back.

"In the name of God," cried the young man in French, "force not this woman to continue." There was a short pause. "But I force her not, my friend," said his uncle in the same language. "She is free to finish at any moment." "At the cost of her child only," again cried Adam. "Do you not see that she is dying? You know not what you are doing, or what it may bring upon you."

The old lord, perplexed by this unexpected animadversion, after a second turned all round, and his pale, clear eyes sought his nephew's face with stately surprise. His long, waxen face, with two symmetrical curls at the sides, had something of the mien of an idealized and ennobled old sheep or ram. He made sign to the bailiff to go on. The footman also withdrew a little, and the uncle and nephew were, so to say, alone on the path. For a minute neither of them spoke.

"In this very place where we now stand," said the old lord, then, with hauteur, "I gave Anne-Marie my word."

"My uncle!" said Adam. "A life is a greater thing even than a word. Recall that word, I beseech you, which was given in caprice, as a whim. I am praying you more for your sake than for my own, yet I shall be grateful to you all my life if you will grant me my prayer."

"You will have learned in school," said his uncle, "that in the beginning was the word. It may have been pronounced in caprice, as a whim, the Scripture tells us nothing about it. It is still the principle of our world, its law of gravitation. My own humble word has been the principle of the land on which we stand, for an age of man. My father's word was the same, before my day."

"You are mistaken," cried Adam. "The word is creative— it is imagination, daring and passion. By it the world was made. How much greater are these powers which bring into being than any restricting or controlling law! You wish the land on which we look to produce and propagate; you should not banish from it the forces which cause, and which keep up life, nor turn it into a desert by dominance of law. And when you look at the people, simpler than we and nearer to the heart of nature, who do not analyse their feelings, whose life is one with the life of the earth, do they not inspire in you tenderness, respect, reverence even? This woman is ready to die for her son; will it ever happen to you or me that a woman willingly gives up her life for us? And if it did indeed come to pass, should we make so light of it as not to give up a dogma in return?"

"You are young," said the old lord. "A new age will undoubtedly applaud you. I am old-fashioned, I have been quoting to you texts a thousand years old. We do not, perhaps, quite understand one another. But with my own people I am, I believe, in good understanding. Anne-Marie might well feel that I am making light of her exploit, if now, at the eleventh hour, I did nullify it by a second word. I myself should feel so in her place. Yes, my nephew, it is possible, did I grant you your prayer and pronounce such an amnesty, that I should find it void against her faithfulness, and that we would still see her at her work, unable to give it up, as a shuttle in the rye field, until she had it all mowed. But she would then be a shocking, a horrible sight, a figure of unseemly fun, like a small planet running wild in the sky, when the law of gravitation had been done away with."

"And if she dies at her task," Adam exclaimed, "her death, and its consequences will come upon your head."

The old lord took off his hat and gently ran his hand over his powdered head. "Upon my head?" he said. "I have kept up my head in many weathers. Even," he added proudly, "against the cold wind from high places. In what shape will it come upon my head, my nephew?" "I cannot tell," cried Adam in despair. "I have spoken to warn you. God only knows." "Amen," said the old lord with a little delicate smile. "Come, we will walk on." Adam drew in his breath deeply.

"No," he said in Danish. "I cannot come with you. This field is yours; things will happen here as you decide. But I myself must go away. I beg you to let me have, this evening, a coach as far as town. For I could not sleep another night under your roof, which I have honoured beyond any on earth." So many conflicting feelings at his own speech thronged in his breast

that it would have been impossible for him to give them
words.

The old lord, who had already begun to walk on, stood still,
and with him the lackey. He did not speak for a minute, as
if to give Adam time to collect his mind. But the young man's
mind was in uproar and would not be collected.

"Must we," the old man asked, in Danish, "take leave here,
in the rye field? I have held you dear, next to my own son.
I have followed your career in life from year to year, and
have been proud of you. I was happy when you wrote
to say that you were coming back. If now you will go away,
I wish you well." He shifted his walking-stick from the right
hand to the left and gravely looked his nephew in the face.

Adam did not meet his eyes. He was gazing out over the
landscape. In the late mellow afternoon it was resuming its
colours, like a painting brought into proper light; in the meadows the little black stacks of peat stood gravely distinct
upon the green sward. On this same morning he had greeted
it all, like a child running laughingly to its mother's bosom;
now already he must tear himself from it, in discordance,
and forever. And at the moment of parting it seemed infinitely
dearer than any time before, so much beautified and solem-
nized by the coming separation that it looked like the place
in a dream, a landscape out of paradise, and he wondered if it
was really the same. But, yes—there before him was, once
more, the hunting-ground of long ago. And there was the road
on which he had ridden today.

"But tell me where you mean to go from here," said the old
lord slowly. "I myself have travelled a good deal in my days.
I know the word of leaving, the wish to go away. But I have
learned by experience that, in reality, the word has a meaning
only to the place and the people which one leaves. When you
have left my house—although it will see you go with sadness
—as far as it is concerned the matter is finished and done with.
But to the person who goes away it is a different thing, and
not so simple. At the moment that he leaves one place he will
be already, by the laws of life, on his way to another, upon
this earth. Let me know, then, for the sake of our old acquaintance, to which place you are going when you leave here. To
England?"

"No," said Adam. He felt in his heart that he could never
again go back to England or to his easy and carefree life
there. It was not far enough away; deeper waters than the
North Sea must now be laid between him and Denmark. "No,

not to England," he said. "I shall go to America, to the new
world." For a moment he shut his eyes, trying to form to
himself a picture of existence in America, with the grey
Atlantic Ocean between him and these fields and woods.

"To America?" said his uncle and drew up his eyebrows.
"Yes, I have heard of America. They have got freedom there,
a big waterfall, savage red men. They shoot turkeys, I have
read, as we shoot partridges. Well, if it be your wish, go to
America, Adam, and be happy in the new world."

He stood for some time, sunk in thought, as if he had
already sent off the young man to America, and had done
with him. When at last he spoke, his words had the character
of a monologue, enunciated by the person who watches things
come and go, and himself stays on.

"Take service, there," he said, "with the power which will
give you an easier bargain than this: That with your own life
you may buy the life of your son."

Adam had not listened to his uncle's remarks about America, but the conclusive, solemn words caught his ear. He looked
up. As if for the first time in his life, he saw the old man's
figure as a whole, and conceived how small it was, so much
smaller than himself, pale, a thin black anchorite upon his
own land. A thought ran through his head: "How terrible to
be old!" The abhorrence of the tyrant, and the sinister dread
on his behalf, which had followed him all day, seemed to die
out of him, and his pity with all creation to extend even to
the sombre form before him.

His whole being had cried out for harmony. Now, with the
possibility of forgiving, of a reconciliation, a sense of relief
went through him; confusedly he bethought himself of Anne-
Marie drinking the water held to her lips. He took off his hat,
as his uncle had done a moment ago, so that to a beholder
at a distance it would seem that the two dark-clad gentlemen on the path were repeatedly and respectfully saluting
one another, and brushed the hair from his forehead. Once
more the tune of the garden-room rang in his mind:

> "Mourir pour ce qu'on aime
> C'est un trop doux effort . . ."

He stood for a long time immobile and dumb. He broke
off a few ears of rye, kept them in his hand and looked at
them.

He saw the ways of life, he thought, as a twined and tangled design, complicated and mazy; it was not given him or any mortal to command or control it. Life and death, happiness and woe, the past and the present, were interlaced within the pattern. Yet to the initiated it might be read as easily as our ciphers—which to the savage must seem confused and incomprehensible—will be read by the schoolboy. And out of the contrasting elements concord rose. All that lived must suffer; the old man, whom he had judged hardly, had suffered, as he had watched his son die, and had dreaded the obliteration of his being. He himself would come to know ache, tears and remorse, and, even through these, the fullness of life. So might now, to the woman in the rye field, her ordeal be a triumphant procession. For to die for the one you loved was an effort too sweet for words.

As now he thought of it, he knew that all his life he had sought the unity of things, the secret which connects the phenomena of existence. It was this strife, this dim presage, which had sometimes made him stand still and inert in the midst of the games of his playfellows, or which had, at other moments—on moonlight nights, or in his little boat on the sea—lifted the boy to ecstatic happiness. Where other young people, in their pleasures or their amours, had searched for contrast and variety, he himself had yearned only to comprehend in full the oneness of the world. If things had come differently to him, if his young cousin had not died, and the events that followed his death had not brought him to Denmark, his search for understanding and harmony might have taken him to America, and he might have found them there, in the virgin forests of a new world. Now they had been disclosed to him today, in the place where he had played as a child. As the song is one with the voice that sings it, as the road is one with the goal, as lovers are made one in their embrace, so is man one with his destiny, and he shall love it as himself.

He looked up again, towards the horizon. If he wished to, he felt, he might find out what it was that had brought to him, here, the sudden conception of the unity of the universe. When this same morning he had philosophized, lightly and for his own sake, on his feeling of belonging to this land and soil, it had been the beginning of it. But since then it had grown; it had become a mightier thing, a revelation to his soul. Some time he would look into it, for the law of cause and effect was a wonderful and fascinating study. But not now. This hour

was consecrated to greater emotions, to a surrender to fate
and to the will of life.

"No," he said at last. "If you wish it I shall not go. I shall
stay here."

At that moment a long, loud roll of thunder broke the
stillness of the afternoon. It re-echoed for a while amongst
the low hills, and it reverberated within the young man's
breast as powerfully as if he had been seized and shaken by
hands. The landscape had spoken. He remembered that twelve
hours ago he had put a question to it, half in jest, and not
knowing what he did. Here it gave him its answer.

What it contained he did not know; neither did he inquire.
In his promise to his uncle he had given himself over to the
mightier powers of the world. Now what must come must
come.

"I thank you," said the old lord, and made a little stiff
gesture with his hand. "I am happy to hear you say so. We
should not let the difference in our ages, or of our views,
separate us. In our family we have been wont to keep peace
and faith with one another. You have made my heart lighter."

Something within his uncle's speech faintly recalled to
Adam the misgivings of the afternoon. He rejected them; he
would not let them trouble the new, sweet felicity which his
resolution to stay had brought him.

"I shall go on now," said the old lord. "But there is no
need for you to follow me. I will tell you tomorrow how the
matter has ended." "No," said Adam, "I shall come back by
sunset, to see the end of it myself."

All the same he did not come back. He kept the hour in
his mind, and all through the evening the consciousness of
the drama, and the profound concern and compassion with
which, in his thoughts, he followed it, gave to his speech,
glance and movements a grave and pathetic substance. But
he felt that he was, in the rooms of the manor, and even by
the harpsichord on which he accompanied his aunt to her air
from *Alceste*, as much in the centre of things as if he had
stood in the rye field itself, and as near to those human
beings whose fate was now decided there. Anne-Marie and
he were both in the hands of destiny, and destiny would, by
different ways, bring each to the designated end.

Later on he remembered what he had thought that evening.

But the old lord stayed on. Late in the afternoon he even
had an idea; he called down his valet to the pavilion and
made him shift his clothes on him and dress him up in a

brocaded suit that he had worn at Court. He let a lace-trimmed shirt be drawn over his head and stuck out his slim legs to have them put into thin silk stockings and buckled shoes. In this majestic attire he dined alone, of a frugal meal, but took a bottle of Rhenish wine with it, to keep up his strength. He sat on for a while, a little sunk in his seat; then, as the sun neared the earth, he straightened himself, and took the way down to the field.

The shadows were now lengthening, azure blue along all the eastern slopes. The lonely trees in the corn marked their site by narrow blue pools running out from their feet, and as the old man walked a thin, immensely elongated reflection stirred behind him on the path. Once he stood still; he thought he heard a lark singing over his head, a spring-like sound; his tired head held no clear perception of the season; he seemed to be walking, and standing, in a kind of eternity.

The people in the field were no longer silent, as they had been in the afternoon. Many of them talked loudly among themselves, and a little farther away a woman was weeping.

When the bailiff saw his master, he came up to him. He told him, in great agitation, that the widow would, in all likelihood, finish the mowing of the field within a quarter of an hour.

"Are the keeper and the wheelwright here?" the old lord asked him. "They have been here," said the bailiff, "and have gone away, five times. Each time they have said that they would not come back. But they have come back again, all the same, and they are here now." "And where is the boy?" the old lord asked again. "He is with her," said the bailiff. "I have given him leave to follow her. He has walked close to his mother all the afternoon, and you will see him now by her side, down there."

Anne-Marie was now working her way up towards them more evenly than before, but with extreme slowness, as if at any moment she might come to a standstill. This excessive tardiness, the old lord reflected, if it had been purposely performed, would have been an inimitable, dignified exhibition of skilled art; one might fancy the Emperor of China advancing in like manner on a divine procession or rite. He shaded his eyes with his hand, for the sun was now just beyond the horizon, and its last rays made light, wild, many-coloured specks dance before his sight. With such splendour did the sunset emblazon the earth and the air that the landscape was turned into a melting-pot of glorious metals.

The meadows and the grasslands became pure gold; the barley
field near by, with its long ears, was a live lake of shining
silver.

There was only a small patch of straw standing in the
rye field, when the woman, alarmed by the change in the
light, turned her head a little to get a look at the sun. The
while she did not stop her work, but grasped one handful of
corn and cut it off, then another, and another. A great stir,
and a sound like a manifold, deep sigh, ran through the
crowd. The field was now mowed from one end to the other.
Only the mower herself did not realize the fact; she stretched
out her hand anew, and when she found nothing in it, she
seemed puzzled or disappointed. Then she let her arms drop,
and slowly sank to her knees.

Many of the women burst out weeping, and the swarm drew
close round her, leaving only a small open space at the side
where the old lord stood. Their sudden nearness frightened
Anne-Marie; she made a slight, uneasy movement, as if terrified that they should put their hands on her.

The boy, who had kept by her all day, now fell on his
knees beside her. Even he dared not touch her, but held one
arm low behind her back and the other before her, level
with her collar-bone, to catch hold of her if she should fall,
and all the time he cried aloud. At that moment the sun went
down.

The old lord stepped forward and solemnly took off his
hat. The crowd became silent, waiting for him to speak. But
for a minute or two he said nothing. Then he addressed her,
very slowly.

"Your son is free, Anne-Marie," he said. He again waited
a little, and added: "You have done a good day's work, which
will long be remembered."

Anne-Marie raised her gaze only as high as his knees, and
he understood that she had not heard what he said. He
turned to the boy. "You tell your mother, Goske," he said,
gently, "what I have told her."

The boy had been sobbing wildly, in raucous, broken moans.
It took him some time to collect and control himself. But
when at last he spoke, straight into his mother's face, his
voice was low, a little impatient, as if he were conveying an
everyday message to her. "I am free, Mother," he said. "You
have done a good day's work that will long be remembered."

At the sound of his voice she lifted her face to him. A
faint, bland shadow of surprise ran over it, but still she gave

no sign of having heard what he said, so that the people round them began to wonder if the exhaustion had turned her deaf. But after a moment she slowly and waveringly raised her hand, fumbling in the air as she aimed at his face, and with her fingers touched his cheek. The cheek was wet with tears, so that at the contact her fingertips lightly stuck to it, and she seemed unable to overcome the infinitely slight resistance, or to withdraw her hand. For a minute the two looked each other in the face. Then, softly and lingeringly, like a sheaf of corn that falls to the ground, she sank forward onto the boy's shoulder, and he closed his arms round her.

He held her thus, pressed against him, his own face buried in her hair and head-cloth, for such a long time that those nearest to them, frightened because her body looked so small in his embrace, drew closer, bent down and loosened his grip. The boy let them do so without a word or a movement. But the woman who held Anne-Marie in her arms to lift her up, turned her face to the old lord. "She is dead," she said.

The people who had followed Anne-Marie all through the day kept standing and stirring in the field for many hours, as long as the evening light lasted, and longer. Long after some of them had made a stretcher from branches of the trees and had carried away the dead woman, others wandered on, up and down the stubble, imitating and measuring her course from one end of the rye field to the other, and binding up the last sheaves, where she had finished her mowing.

The old lord stayed with them for a long time, stepping along a little, and again standing still.

In the place where the woman had died the old lord later on had a stone set up, with a sickle engraved on it. The peasants on the land then named the rye field "Sorrow-Acre." By this name it was known a long time after the story of the woman and her son had itself been forgotten.

ISAAC BABEL

In the Basement

*Isaac Babel (1894-1939?) was born in Odessa of
Jewish parentage. He lived for a time in St. Peters-
burg in impoverished circumstances, helped only by
the encouragement of Maxim Gorki. He won early
fame in 1923 when his stories began to appear in
magazines. Odessa Tales and Red Cavalry, brilliant
collections of his stories, appeared in 1924 and 1926.
There is no mention of his name in Soviet publications after 1936, and it is believed he may have died
in a concentration camp in 1939.*

*Babel's stories trace the interior life of an op-
pressed minority with remarkable warmth and tenderness, but their intimacy is always edged with
sharp awareness of a hostile outer world.*

I WAS AN untruthful little boy. It was because of my reading: my imagination was always working overtime. I read
during lessons, during recess, on my way home, at night
under the table, hidden by the hanging tablecloth. My nose
buried in a book, I let slide everything that really mattered,
such as playing truant in the harbor, learning the art of
billiards in the coffeehouses on Greek Street, going swimming
at Langeron. I had no pals. Who would have wanted to
waste his time with a boy like me?

One day I noticed that Mark Borgman, our top student,
had got hold of a book on Spinoza. He had just read it,
and simply had to tell the other boys about the Spanish

Reprinted by permission of S. G. Phillips, Inc. from THE COLLECTED
STORIES OF ISAAC BABEL. Copyright © 1955 by S. G. Phillips,
Inc.

Inquisition. What he told them was just a mumble of long words: there was no poetry in what he said. I couldn't help butting in. I told those willing to listen to me about old Amsterdam, the twilight of the ghetto, the philosophers who cut diamonds. To what I had read I added much of my own. I just had to. My imagination heightened the drama, altered the endings, made the beginnings more mysteriously involved. The death of Spinoza, his free and lonely death, appeared to me like a battle. The Sanhedrin was trying to make the dying man repent, but he wouldn't. I worked in Rubens. It seemed to me that Rubens was standing by Spinoza's deathbed taking a mask of the dead man's face.

My schoolmates listened mouths agape to the fantastic tale I told with so much brio, and dispersed unwillingly when the bell went. In the next recess Borgman came over to me and took me by the arm, and we started strolling about together. Soon we had come to terms. Borgman wasn't bad as top students go. To his powerful mind, secondary-school wisdom seemed mere scribbles in the margin of the real book, and this book he sought avidly. Twelve-year-old ninnies as we were, we could tell that an unusual, a learned life awaited Borgman. He didn't even do his lessons, but just listened to them. This sober, self-controlled boy became attached to me because of the way I had of garbling every possible thing, things that couldn't have been simpler.

That year we moved up to the third class. My report card consisted chiefly of the remark "poor." I was such a queer, fanciful lad that after much thought the teachers decided not to mark me "very poor," and so I moved up with the rest. At the beginning of the summer Borgman invited me to the family villa outside Odessa. His father was manager of the Russian Bank for Foreign Trade. He was one of the men who were turning Odessa into a Marseille or a Naples. The leaven of the old-time Odessa trader worked in him; he was one of those sceptical, amiable rakes. Borgman Senior didn't speak Russian if he could help it, preferring to express himself in the coarse and fragmentary language of Liverpool captains. When the Italian Opera visited our city in April, a dinner for the members of the company was arranged at Borgman's house. The obese banker, last of the Odessa traders, started a two-months' affair with the large-bosomed prima donna. She departed with memories that did not burden her conscience, and a necklace chosen with taste and not too expensive.

The old man was Argentine consul and president of the stock exchange committee. It was to his house I was invited. My Aunt Bobka announced this in a loud voice to the whole courtyard. She dressed me up as best she could, and I took the little steam streetcar to the sixteenth Great Fountain stop. The villa stood on a low red bluff right by the shore. On the bluff a flower garden was laid out, with fuchsias and clipped globes of thuja.

I came of a poverty-stricken and ramshackle family, and the setup at the Borgman villa shook me. In verdure-hidden walks wicker chairs gleamed whitely. The dining table was a mass of flowers, the windows had green frames outside. Before the house a low wooden colonnade stood spaciously.

Toward evening the bank-manager came home. After dinner he placed a wicker chair right on the edge of the bluff overlooking the moving plain of the sea, tucked up his legs in their white trousers, lit a cigar, and started reading the *Manchester Guardian*. The guests, ladies from Odessa, started a poker game on the veranda. On the corner of the table a slender tea urn with ivory handles hissed and bubbled.

Card addicts and sweet-tooths, untidy female fops with secret vices, scented lingerie and enormous thighs, the women snapped their black fans and staked gold coins. Through the fence of wild vine the sun reached at them, its fiery disc enormous. Bronze gleams lent weight to the women's black hair. Drops of the sunset sparkled in diamonds—diamonds disposed in every possible place: in the profundities of splayed bosoms, in painted ears, on puffy bluish she-animal fingers.

Evening fell. A bat whispered past. Blacker than before, the sea rolled up onto the red rocks. My twelve-year-old heart swelled with the joy and lightness of other people's wealth. My friend and I walked arm in arm up and down a distant and secluded path. Borgman was telling me that he was going to be an aircraft engineer. It was rumored that his father was to be sent to represent the Russian Bank for Foreign Trade in London. Mark would be able to study in England.

In our house, Aunt Bobka's house, such things were never talked of. I had nothing to give in return for all this measureless magnificence. So I told Mark that though everything at our place was quite different, grandfather Leivi-Itzkhok and my uncle had traveled all around the world and had thousands of adventures. I narrated these adventures one after the other. All awareness of the possible abandoned me; I took Uncle

Simon-Wolf through the Russo-Turkish War, to Alexandria, to Egypt.

Night towered in the poplars, stars lay heavy on the bowed leaves. Waving my hands, I talked on and on. The fingers of the future aircraft engineer shuddered in mine. Struggling awake from his trance, he promised to come and see me on the following Sunday, and hoarding this promise, I took the little steam streetcar home, to Aunt Bobka's.

All the week following my visit I kept picturing myself as a bank-manager. I did deals with Singapore and Port Said running into millions. I bought a yacht and made solitary voyages. On Saturday it was time to wake from my dreams. Next day young Borgman was coming, and nothing I had told him about really existed. What did exist was different, and much more surprising than anything I had invented, but at the age of twelve I had no idea how things stood with me and reality. Grandfather Leivi-Itzkhok, the rabbi expelled from his little town for forging Count Branicki's signature on bills of exchange, was reckoned crazy by the neighbors and all the urchins of the locality. My Uncle Simon I just couldn't stick on account of his loudmouthed eccentricity, his crazy fits of enthusiasm, the way he shouted and bullied. Aunt Bobka was the only sensible one. But Aunt Bobka was proud of my friendship with a bank-manager's son. She felt that this meant the beginning of a brilliant career, and she baked apple strudel with jam and poppy-seed tarts for the guest. The whole heart of our tribe, a heart so inured to stubborn resistance, was cooked into those tarts. Grandfather, with his battered top hat and the old boots on his swollen feet, we stowed away with our neighbors the Apelkhots, after I had begged him not to show his face till our visitor had left. Uncle Simon was also arranged for: he went off with his broker friends to drink tea at the Bear tavern. At this place of refreshment they used to lace their tea with vodka, so one could rely on Uncle taking his time. Here it is necessary to observe that the family I spring from was not like other Jewish families. We had drunkards amongst us, and some of us had gone in for seducing the daughters of generals and abandoning them before reaching the frontier. Grandfather, as I have said, had done a bit of forging in his day, and had composed blackmailing letters for women who had been thrown over.

To make sure that Uncle Simon would stay away the whole day, I gave him three roubles I had saved up. Three roubles take a deal of spending. Uncle would be back late, and the bank-manager's son would never learn that the tale of my uncle's strength and magnanimity was untrue from beginning to end. Though to tell the truth, if you go by the heart, it wasn't all that untrue, but it must be admitted that one's first sight of the filthy, loudmouthed fellow did nothing to corroborate this transcendent truth.

On Sunday morning Aunt Bobka decked herself in a brown frock. Her kindly fat bosom lay all over the place. She put on a kerchief with black print blossoms, the kerchief they put on in the synagogue at Atonement and Rosh Hashana. On the table she set pies, jam, and cracknels. Then she started to wait. We lived in a basement; Borgman raised his brows as he passed along the humpbacked floor of the corridor. I showed him the alarm clock made by grandfather down to the last screw. A lamp was fitted to the clock, and when the clock marked the half-hour or the hour the lamp lit up. I also showed him the barrel of boot-polish. The recipe for this polish had been invented by Leivi-Itzkhok, and he would reveal the secret to no living soul. Then Borgman and I read a few pages of grandfather's manuscript. It was written in Hebrew on square yellow sheets of paper as large as maps. The manuscript was entitled "The Headless Man," and in it were described all the neighbors he had had in his seventy years, first at Skvira and Belaya Tserkov and later on at Odessa. Gravediggers, cantors, Jewish drunkards, cooks at circumcisions, and the quacks who performed the ritual operation—such were Leivi-Itzkhok's heroes. They were all as mad as hatters, tongue-tied, with lumpy noses, pimples on their bald pates, and backsides askew.

While we were reading, Aunt Bobka appeared in her brown dress. She floated in surrounded by her great bosom and bearing a tea urn on a tray. I performed the introductions. Aunt Bobka said "Pleased to meet you," thrust out her stiff, sweaty fingers and scuffled both feet. Everything was going better than one could have hoped. The Apelkhots kept grandfather safely tucked away. I pulled out his treasures one after the other: grammars in all languages, sixty-six volumes of the Talmud. Mark was dazzled by the barrel of polish, by the ingenious alarm clock and the mountain of Talmud: things that were not to be seen in any other house in town.

We had two glasses of tea each with the strudel, then Aunt Bobka, nodding her head and retreating backward, disappeared. I grew light of heart, struck a pose, and started reciting poetry. Never in my life have I loved anything more

than the lines I then started spouting. Antony, bending over
Caesar's corpse, addresses the Roman crowd:

> *Friends, Romans, countrymen, lend me your ears;*
> *I come to bury Caesar, not to praise him.*

So Antony begins his stuff. I choked with excitement and
pressed my hands to my breast.

> *He was my friend, faithful and just to me;*
> *But Brutus says he was ambitious;*
> *And Brutus is an honourable man.*
> *He hath brought many captives home to Rome,*
> *Whose ransoms did the general coffers fill.*
> *Did this in Caesar seem ambitious?*
> *When that the poor have cried, Caesar hath wept;*
> *Ambition should be made of sterner stuff.*
> *Yet Brutus says he was ambitious;*
> *And Brutus is an honourable man.*
> *You all did see that on the Lupercal*
> *I thrice presented him a kingly crown,*
> *Which he did thrice refuse. Was this ambition?*
> *Yet Brutus says he was ambitious;*
> *And sure he is an honourable man.*

Before my eyes, in the vapors of the universe, the face of
Brutus hung. It grew whiter than chalk. The Roman people
moved muttering upon me. I raised my hand, and Borgman's
eyes obediently followed it. My clenched fist trembled, I
raised my hand—and through the window saw Uncle Simon
crossing the courtyard accompanied by Leikakh the broker.
They were staggering beneath the weight of a clothes hangar
made of antlers and a red trunk with fittings shaped like
lions' jaws. Through the window Aunt Bobka also saw them.
Forgetting about our visitor, she dashed into the room and
seized me in her trembling arms.

"My precious, he's been buying furniture again!"

Borgman started to get up, neat in his school uniform, and
bowed uncertainly to Aunt Bobka. The door was being as-
saulted. In the corridor there was the stamping of boots, the
noise of the trunk being shunted. The voices of Uncle Simon
and the red-haired Leikakh thundered deafeningly. They
had been drinking.

"Bobka," shouted Uncle Simon, "guess how much I paid for these horns!"

He was blaring like a trumpet, but there was uncertainty in his voice. Even though he was drunk, he knew how we hated the red-haired Leikakh, who instigated all his purchases and inundated us with ridiculous bits of furniture that we didn't want.

Aunt Bobka said nothing. Leikakh hissed something at Uncle Simon. To drown his serpentine susurration, to deaden my dismay, I cried with the voice of Antony:

> But yesterday the word of Caesar might
> Have stood against the world. Now lies he there,
> And none so poor to do him reverence.
> O masters! If I were dispos'd to stir
> Your hearts and minds to mutiny and rage,
> I should do Brutus wrong, and Cassius wrong,
> Who, you all know, are honourable men.

At this point there was a dull thud. It was Aunt Bobka falling to the floor, felled by a blow from her husband. She must have made some cutting remark about horns. The curtain had risen on the daily performance. Uncle Simon's brazen voice caulked all the cracks in the universe.

"You drag the glue out of me," cried my uncle in a voice of thunder, "drag the glue from my entrails to stuff up your dog-mouths. I've been unsouled by toil. I've nothing left to work with: no hands, no legs. A millstone you have hung around my neck, from my neck a millstone is suspended . . ."

Cursing me and Aunt Bobka with Hebrew curses, he promised us that our eyes would trickle out, that our children would rot in the womb, that we'd be unable to give each another decent burial, and that we would be dragged by the hair to a mass grave.

Little Borgman rose from his chair. He was pale, and kept looking furtively around. He couldn't understand the twists and turns of Hebrew blasphemy, but with Russian oaths he was familiar, and Uncle Simon didn't disdain them either. The bank-manager's son crumpled his little peaked cap in his hands. I saw him double as I strove to outshout all the evil in the world. My death-agony despair and the death of the already dead Caesar coalesced: I was dead, and I was shouting. A throaty croak rose from the depths of my being:

> *If you have tears, prepare to shed them now.*
> *You all do know this mantle. I remember*
> *The first time ever Caesar put it on.*
> *'Twas on a summer's evening in his tent,*
> *That day he overcame the Nervii.*
>
> *Look, in this place ran Cassius' dagger through.*
> *See what a rent the envious Casca made.*
> *Through this the well-beloved Brutus stabb'd;*
> *And as he pluck'd his cursed steel away,*
> *Mark how the blood of Caesar follow'd it. . . .*

Nothing could outshout Uncle Simon. Sitting on the floor,
Aunt Bobka was sobbing and blowing her nose. The imperturbable Leikakh was shoving the trunk around behind the
partition. And now my crazy grandfather was filled with the
desire to lend a hand. He tore himself from the clutches of
the Apelkhots, crept over to our window, and started scraping away on his fiddle, no doubt so that people passing the
house should not be able to hear Uncle Simon's bad language.
Borgman looked through the window—it was at street level
—and he started back in horror: he had beheld my poor
grandfather twisting his blue and ossified mouth. On the old
man's head was his bent top hat. He wore a long black padded
cloak with bone buttons, and his elephantine feet bulged from
the inevitable torn boots. His tobacco-stained beard hung in
tatters, swaying in the window. Mark took to his heels.

"It's quite all right," he mumbled as he made his escape.
"Quite all right, really . . ."

His little uniform and his cap with the turned-up edges
flashed across the yard.

When Mark had gone I grew calmer. I was waiting for
evening. When grandfather, having covered his square sheet
of paper with Hebrew squiggles (he was describing the Apelkhots, with whom thanks to me he had spent the day), had
lain down on his truckle bed and was asleep, I made my
way into the corridor. There the floor was earthen. I moved
through the darkness, barefooted, in my long patched shirt.
Through chinks in the boards cobblestones shot blades of
light. In the corner, as ever, stood the water barrel. Into
it I lowered myself. The water sliced me in two. I plunged my
head in, lost my breath, and surfaced again. From a shelf the
cat looked down at me sleepily. Once more I stuck it, longer
this time. The water gurgled round me, my groans were

swallowed in it. I opened my eyes and saw on the bottom of the barrel the swollen sail of my shirt and two feet pressed against one another. Again my forces failed me, again I surfaced. By the barrel stood grandfather, wearing a woman's jacket. His sole tooth shone greenly.

"Grandson," he said, pronouncing the word with scornful distinctness, "grandson, I am going to take a dose of castor oil, so as to have something to lay on your grave."

I gave a wild shriek and splooshed down into the water. Grandfather's infirm hand drew me forth again. Then for the first time that day I shed tears. And the world of tears was so huge, so beautiful, that everything save tears vanished from my eyes.

I came to myself in bed, wrapped in blankets. Grandfather was stalking about the room whistling. Fat Aunt Bobka was warming my hands on her bosom.

"How he trembles, our blessed ninny!" said Aunt Bobka. "Where can the child find the strength to tremble so?"

Grandfather tugged at his beard, gave a whistle and stalked off again. On the other side of the wall Uncle Simon snored agonizingly. Battler by day, he never woke up nights.

ALBERTO MORAVIA

Bitter Honeymoon

Alberto Moravia (1907-   ), born in Rome, achieved early fame with the publication of his novel The Age of Indifference *when he was 22. His best-known novel is* Two Women. *His many stories are realistic, psychological studies of certain recurrent types and have achieved broad reputation both in Italy and abroad. In addition to the writing of fiction, Moravia is a well-known essayist and film critic.*

THEY HAD CHOSEN Anacapri for their honeymoon because Giacomo had been there a few months before and wanted to go back, taking his bride with him. His previous visit had been in the spring, and he remembered the clear, crisp air and the flowers alive with the hum of thousands of insects in the golden glow of the sun. But this time, immediately upon their arrival, everything seemed very different. The sultry dog-days of mid-August were upon them and steaming humidity overclouded the sky. Even on the heights of Anacapri, there was no trace of the crisp air, of flowers or the violet sea whose praises Giacomo had sung. The paths winding through the fields were covered with a layer of yellow dust, accumulated in the course of four months without rain, in which even gliding lizards left traces of their passage. Long before autumn was due, the leaves had begun to turn red and brown, and occasional whole trees had withered away for lack of water. Dust particles filled the motionless air and made the nostrils quiver, and the odours of mead-

Translated by Frances Frenaye. Reprinted from BITTER HONEY-
MOON by Alberto Moravia, by permission of Farrar, Straus & Giroux,
Inc. Copyright © 1956 by Valentino Bompiani & Co.

ows and sea had given way to those of scorched stones and
dried dung. The water, which in the spring had taken its
colour from what seemed to be banks of violets floating just
below the surface, was now a grey mass reflecting the melancholy, dazzling light brought by the *scirocco* which infested
the sky.

"I don't think it's the least bit beautiful," Simona said on
the day after their arrival, as they started along the path to
the lighthouse. "I don't like it—no, not at all."

Giacomo, following several steps behind, did not answer.
She had spoken in this plaintive and discontented tone of
voice ever since they had emerged from their civil marriage
in Rome, and he suspected that her prolonged ill-humour,
mingled with an apparent physical repulsion, was not connected so much with the place as with his own person.
She was complaining about Anacapri because she was not
aware that her fundamental dissatisfaction was with her husband. Theirs was a love match to be sure, but one based
rather on the will to love than on genuine feeling. There was
good reason for his presentiment of trouble when, as he
slipped the ring on her finger, he had read a flicker of regret
and embarrassment on her face; for on their first night at
Anacapri she had begged off, on the plea of fatigue and sea-
sickness, from giving herself to him. On this, the second day
of their marriage, she was just as much of a virgin as she
had been before.

As she trudged wearily along, with a bag slung over one
shoulder, between the dusty hedges, Giacomo looked at her
with almost sorrowful intensity, hoping to take possession of
her with a single piercing glance, as he had so often done
with other women. But, as he realised right away, the piercing
quality was lacking; his eyes fell with analytical affection upon
her, but there was in them none of the transfiguring power
of real passion. Although Simona was not tall, she had childishly long legs with slender thighs, rising to an indentation,
almost a cleft at either side, visible under her shorts, where
they were joined to the body. The whiteness of her legs was
chaste, shiny and cold, she had a narrow waist and hips, and
her only womanly feature, revealed when she turned around
to speak to him, was the fullness of her low-swung breasts,
which seemed like extraneous and burdensome weights, unsuited to her delicate frame. Similarly her thick, blonde hair,
although it was cut short, hung heavily over her neck. All
of a sudden, as if she felt that she was being watched, she

wheeled around and asked: "Why do you make me walk ahead of you?"

Giacomo saw the childishly innocent expression of her big blue eyes, her small, tilted nose and equally childishly rolled-back upper lip. Her face, too, he thought to himself, was a stranger to him, untouched by love.

"I'll go ahead, if you like," he said with resignation.

And he went by her, deliberately brushing her breast with his elbow to test his own desire. Then they went on walking, he ahead and she behind. The path wound about the summit of Monte Solaro, running along a wall of mossy stones with no masonry to hold them together and rows of vines strung out above them. On the other side there was a sheer descent, through uninhabited stretches of vineyard and olive grove, to the mist-covered grey sea. Only a solitary pine tree, half-way down the mountain, with its green crest floating in the air, recalled the idyllic purity of the landscape in its better days. Simona walked very slowly, lagging farther behind at every step. Finally she came to a halt and asked: "Have we far to go?"

"We've only just started," Giacomo said lightly. "At least an hour more."

"I can't bear it," she said ill-humouredly, looking at him as if she hoped he would propose giving up the walk alto-gether. He went back to her and put his arm around her waist.

"You can't bear the exertion or you can't bear me?"

"What do you mean, silly?" she countered with unexpected feeling. "I can't bear to go on walking, of course."

"Give me a kiss."

She administered a rapid peck on his cheek.

"It's so hot . . ." she murmured. "I wish we could go home."

"We must get to the lighthouse," Giacomo answered. "What's the point of going back? . . . We'll have a swim as soon as we arrive. It's a wonderful place, and the light-house is all pink and white. . . . Don't you want to see it?"

"Yes; but I'd like to fly there instead of walking."

"Let's talk," he suggested. "That way you won't notice the distance."

"But I have nothing to say," she protested, almost with tears in her voice.

Giacomo hesitated for a moment before replying:

"You know so much poetry by heart. Recite a poem, and I'll listen; then before you know it, we'll be there."

He could see that he had hit home, for she had a truly extraordinary memory for verse.

"What shall I recite?" she asked with childish vanity.

"A canto from Dante."

"Which one?"

"The third canto of the *Inferno*," Giacomo said at random.

Somewhat consoled, Simona walked on, once more ahead of him, beginning to recite:

> *"Per me si va nella città dolente:*
> *per me si va nell'eterno dolore:*
> *per me si va tra la perduta gente . . ."*

She recited mechanically and with as little expression as a schoolgirl, breathing hard because of the double effort required of her. As she walked doggedly along, she paused at the end of every line, without paying any attention to syntax or meaning, like a schoolgirl endowed with zeal rather than intelligence. Every now and then she turned appealingly around and shot him a fleeting look, yes, exactly like a schoolgirl, with the blue-and-white cap perched on her blonde hair. After they had gone some way they reached a wall built all around a large villa. The wall was covered with ivy, and leafy oak branches grew out over it.

"*'E caddi, come l'uom, cui sonno piglia,"* Simona said, winding up the third canto; then she turned around and asked: "Whose place is this?"

"It belonged to Axel Munthe," Giacomo answered; "but he's dead now."

"And what sort of a fellow was he?"

"A very shrewd sort indeed," said Giacomo. And, in order to amuse her, he added: "He was a doctor very fashionable in Rome at the turn of the century. If you'd like to know more about him, there's a story I've been told is absolutely true. . . . Would you like to hear it?"

"Yes; do tell me."

"Once a beautiful and frivolous society woman came to him with all sorts of imaginary ailments. Munthe listened patiently, examined her, and when he saw that there was nothing wrong, said: 'I know a sure cure, but you must do exactly what I say. . . . Go and look out of that open window and lean your elbows on the sill.' She obeyed, and Munthe went after her and gave her a terrific kick in the rear. Then he escorted her to the door and said: 'Three times a week, and in a few months you'll be quite all right.'"

Simona failed to laugh, and after a moment she said bitterly, looking at the wall: "That would be the cure for me."

Giacomo was struck by her mournful tone of voice.

"Why do you say that?" he asked, coming up to her. "What's come into your head?"

"It's true. . . . I'm slightly mad, and you ought to treat me exactly that way."

"What are you talking about?"

"About what happened last night," she said with startling frankness.

"But last night you were tired and seasick."

"That wasn't it at all. I'm never seasick, and I wasn't tired, either. I was afraid, that's all."

"Afraid of me?"

"No; afraid of the whole idea."

They walked on in silence. The wall curved, following the path and hanging slightly over, as if it could hardly contain the oak trees behind it. Then it came to an end, and in front of them lay a grassy plateau, below which the mountainside fell abruptly down to the arid and lonely promontories of Rio. The plateau was covered with asphodels, whose pyramidal flowers were of a dusty rose, almost grey in colour. Giacomo picked some and handed them to his wife, saying: "Look. How beautiful. . . ."

She raised them to her nose, like a young girl on her way to the altar, inhaling the fragrance of a lily. Perhaps she was conscious of her virginal air, for she pressed close to him, in something like an embrace, and whispered into one ear: "Don't believe what I just told you. . . . I wasn't afraid. . . . I'll just have to get used to the idea. . . . To-night. . . ."

"To-night?" he repeated.

"You're so very dear to me," she murmured painfully, adding a strictly conventional phrase, which she seemed to have learned for the occasion, "To-night I'll be yours."

She said these last words hurriedly, as if she were afraid of the conventionality rather than the substance of them, and planted a hasty kiss on his cheek. It was the first time that she had ever told Giacomo that he was dear to her or anything like it, and he was tempted to take her in his arms. But she said in a loud voice: "Look! What's that down there on the sea?" And at the same time she eluded his grasp. Giacomo looked in the direction at which she was pointing and saw a solitary sail emerging from the mist that hung over the water.

"A boat," he said testily.

She started walking again, at a quickened pace, as if she were afraid that he might try once more to embrace her. And as he saw her escape him he had a recurrent feeling of impotence, because he could not take immediate possession of his beloved.

"You won't do that to me to-night," he muttered between clenched teeth as he caught up with her.

And she answered, lowering her head without looking around: "It will be different to-night. . . ."

It was really hot—there was no doubt about that—and in the heavy air all round them there seemed to Giacomo to reside the same obstacle, the same impossibility that bogged down his relationship with his wife: the impossibility of a rainfall that would clear the air, the impossibility of love. He had a sensation of something like panic, when looking at her again he felt that his will to love was purely intellectual and did not involve his senses. Her figure was outlined quite precisely before him, but there was none of the halo around it in which love usually envelops the loved one's person. Impulsively he said: "Perhaps you shouldn't have married me."

Simona seemed to accept this statement as a basis for discussion, as if she had had the same thought without daring to come out with it.

"Why?" she asked.

Giacomo wanted to answer, "Because we don't really love each other," but although this was the thought in his mind, he expressed it in an entirely different manner. Simona was a Communist and had a job at Party headquarters. Giacomo was not a Communist at all; he claimed to attach no importance to his wife's political ideas, but they had a way of cropping up at the most unexpected moments as underlying motives for disagreement. And now he was astonished to hear himself say: "Because there is too great a difference of ideas between us."

"What sort of ideas do you mean?"

"Political ideas."

He realised, then, why her standoffishness had caused him to bring politics into the picture; it was with the hope of arousing a reaction to a point on which he knew her to be sensitive. And indeed she answered immediately: "That's not so. The truth is that I have certain ideas and you have none at all."

As soon as politics came up she assumed a self-sufficient, pedantic manner, quite the opposite of childish, which always threatened to infuriate him. He asked himself in all conscience whether his irritation stemmed from some latent anti-Communist feeling within himself, but quickly set his mind at rest on this score. He had no interest in politics whatsoever, and the only thing that bothered him was the fact that his wife did have such an interest.

"Well, whether or not it's a question of ideas," he said dryly, "there is *something* between us."

"What is it, then?"

"I don't know, but I can feel it."

After a second she said in the same irritating tone of voice: "I know quite well. It *is* a question of ideas. But I hope that some day you'll see things the way I do."

"Never."

"Why never?"

"I've told you so many times before. . . . First, because I don't want to be involved in politics of any kind, and, second, because I'm too much of an individualist."

Simona made no reply, but in such cases her silence was direr than spoken disapproval. Giacomo was overcome by a wave of sudden anger. He overtook her and seized her arm.

"All this is going to have very serious consequences some day," he shouted. "For instance, if a Communist government comes to power, and I say something against it, you'll inform on me."

"Why should you say anything against it?" she retorted. "You just said that you don't want to be involved in politics of any kind."

"Anything can happen."

"And then the Communists aren't in power. . . . Why worry about a situation that doesn't exist?"

It was true then, he thought to himself, since she didn't deny it, that she would inform on him. He gripped her arm tighter, almost wishing to hurt her.

"The truth is that you don't love me," he said.

"I wouldn't have married you except for love," she said clearly, and she looked straight at him, with her lower lip trembling. Her voice filled Giacomo with tenderness, and he drew her to him and kissed her. Simona was visibly affected by the kiss; her nostrils stiffened and she breathed hard, and

although her arms hung down at her sides, she pressed her
body against his.

"My spy," he said, drawing away and stroking her face.
"My little spy."

"Why do you call me spy?" she asked, taking immediate
offence.

"I was joking."

They walked on, but as he followed her Giacomo wondered
whether he had meant the word as a joke after all. And what
about his anger? Was that a joke too? He didn't know how he
could have given way to such unreasonable anger and have
made such even more unreasonable accusations, and yet he
dimly understood that they were justified by Simona's be-
haviour. Meanwhile, they had come to the other side of the
mountain, and from the highest point of the path they looked
down at an immense expanse of air, like a bottomless well.
Five minutes later they had a view of all one side of the
island, a long, green slope covered with scattered vines and
prickly pears, and at the bottom, stretching out into the sea,
the chalky promontory on which stood the lighthouse. The
sweep of the view was tremendous, and the pink-and-white-
checked lighthouse, hung between sky and sea, seemed far
away and no larger than a man's hand. Simona clapped her
hands in delight.

"How perfectly lovely!" she exclaimed

"I told you it was beautiful, and you wouldn't believe me."

"Forgive me," she said, patting his cheek. "You always
know best, and I'm very silly."

Before he could control himself, Giacomo said: "Does that
go for politics too?"

"No; not for politics. But don't let's talk about that just
now."

He was annoyed with himself for having fallen back into
an argument, but at the same time he suffered a return of
the left-out and jealous feeling that overcame him every time
she made a dogmatic, almost religious reference to her political ideas.

"Why shouldn't we talk about it?" he said as gently as he
could. "Perhaps if we talked about it, we might understand
one another better."

Simona did not reply, and Giacomo walked on after her,
in an extremely bad humour. Now he was the one to feel
the heaviness and heat of the day, while Simona, intoxicated

by the sight of the distant sea, shouted: "Let's run down the rest of the way. I can't wait to get into the water."

With her sling bag bobbing about on her shoulder, she began to run down the path, emitting shrill cries of joy. Giacomo saw that she was throwing her legs in all directions like an untrained colt. Suddenly the thought, "To-night she'll be mine" floated through his head and quieted him. What could be the importance of belonging to a political party in comparison to that of the act of love, so ageless and so very human? Men had possessed women long before the existence of political parties or religions. And he was sure that in the moment when he possessed Simona he would drive out of her every allegiance except that of her love for him. Strengthened by this thought he ran after her, shouting in his turn: "Wait for me, Simona!"

She stopped to wait, flushed, quivering and bright-eyed. As he caught up with her he said pantingly: "Just now I began to feel very happy. I know that we're going to love one another."

"I know it too," she said, looking at him out of her innocent blue eyes.

Giacomo put one arm around her waist, catching her hand in his and compelling her to throw it over his shoulders. They walked on in this fashion, but Simona's eyes remained set on the water below. Giacomo, on the other hand, could not tear his thoughts away from the body he was holding so tightly. Simona was wearing a skimpy boy's jersey with a patch in the front. And her head was boyish in outline as well, with the unruly short hair falling over her cheeks. Yet her slender waist fitted into the curve of his arm with a womanly softness which seemed to foreshadow the complete surrender promised for the coming night. Suddenly he breathed into her ear: "You'll always be my little friend and comrade."

Simona's mind must have been on the lighthouse, and the word "comrade" came through to her alone, out of context, without the sentimental intonation that gave it Giacomo's intended meaning. For she answered with a smile: "We can't be comrades . . . at least, not until you see things the way I do. . . . But I'll be your wife."

So she was still thinking of the Party, Giacomo said to himself with excusable jealousy. The word "comrade" had for her no tender connotations, but only political significance. The Party continued to have a prior claim to her loyalty.

"I didn't mean it that way," he said disappointedly.

"I'm sorry," she said, hastening to correct herself. "That's what we call each other in the Party."

"I only meant that you'd be my lifelong companion."

"That's true," she said, lowering her head in embarrassment, as if she couldn't really accept the word except politically.

They dropped their arms and walked down the path with no link between them. As they proceeded, the lighthouse seemed to approach them, revealing its tower shape. The water beyond it had a metallic sheen, derived from the direct rays of the sun, while behind them the mountain seemed to grow higher, with a wall of red rock rising above the lower slope which they were now traversing. At the top was a summer-house with a railing around it, in which they could distinguish two tiny human figures enjoying the view.

"That vantage-point is called La Migliara," Giacomo explained. "A few years ago an Anacapri girl threw herself down the mountain from it, but first she wound her braids around her head and over her eyes so as not to see what she was doing."

Simona tossed a look over her shoulder at the top of the mountain.

"Suicide is all wrong," she said.

Giacomo felt jealousy sting him again.

"Why?" he asked. "Does the Party forbid it?"

"Never mind about the Party." She looked out over the sea and thrust her face and chest forward as if to breathe in the breeze blowing in their direction. "Suicide's all wrong because life is beautiful and it's a joy to be alive."

Again Giacomo didn't really want to get into a political argument; he wanted to make a show of the serenity and detachment which he thoroughly believed were his. But again his annoyance carried him away.

"But T——" (this was the name of a Communist friend they had in common) "committed suicide, didn't he?"

"He did wrong," she said succinctly.

"Why so? He must have had some reason. What do you know?"

"I do know, though," she said obstinately. "He did wrong. It's our duty to live."

"Our duty?"

"Yes; duty."

"Who says so?"

"Nobody. It just is."

"I might just as well say that it's our duty to take our life if we feel it's not worth living. . . . Nobody says so. It just is."

"That's not true," she answered inflexibly. "We were made to live and not to die. . . . Only someone that's sick or in a morbid state of mind can think that life's not worth living."

"So you think that T—— was either sick or in a morbid state of mind, do you?"

"At the moment when he killed himself, yes, I do."

Giacomo was tempted to ask her if this was the Party line, as seemed to him evident from that stubborn note in her voice which annoyed him so greatly, but this time he managed to restrain himself. By now they had reached the bottom of the slope and were crossing a dry, flat area, covered with woodspurge and prickly pears. Then the land turned into rock and they found themselves before the lighthouse, at the end of the path, which seemed like the end of all human habitation and the beginning of a new and lonely world of colourless chalk and stone. The lighthouse soared up above them as they plunged down among the boulders toward the sea. At a bend, they suddenly came upon a basin of green water, surrounded by rocky black cliffs, eroded by salt. Simona ran down to the cement landing and exclaimed: "Wonderful! Just what I was hoping for! Now we can swim. And we have it all to ourselves. We're quite alone."

She had no sooner spoken these words than a man's voice came out of the rocks: "Simona! What a pleasant surprise."

They turned around, and when a face followed the voice, Simona shouted: "Livio! Hello! Are you here too? What are you doing?"

The young man who emerged from the rocks was short and powerfully built, with broad shoulders. His head contrasted with this athletic body, for it was bald, with only a fringe of hair around the neck, and his flat face had a scholarly expression. The face of a ferret, Giacomo thought, taking an instant dislike to it, not exactly intelligent, but keen and treacherous. He knew the fellow by sight and was aware that he worked in Simona's office. Now Livio came into full view, pulling up his tight, faded red trunks.

"I'm doing the same thing you are, I suppose," he said by way of an answer.

Then Simona said something which gave Giacomo considerable satisfaction.

"That's not very likely. . . . Unless you've just got yourself married. . . . I'm here on my honeymoon. . . . Do you know my husband?"

"Yes; we know each other," Livio said easily, jumping down on to a big square stone and shaking Giacomo's hand so hard that the latter winced with pain as he echoed: "Yes, we've met in Rome." Livio then turned to Simona and added: "I'd heard something to the effect that you were about to marry. But you should have told the comrades. They want to share your joys."

He said all this in a colourless, businesslike voice, but one which was not necessarily devoid of feeling. Giacomo noticed that Simona was smiling and seemed to be waiting for Livio to go on, while Livio stood like a bronze statue on a stone pedestal, with his trunks pulled tightly over his voluminous pubis and all the muscles of his body standing out, and talked down to them. Giacomo felt as if he were somehow left out of their conversation, and drew away, all the while listening intently. They conversed for several minutes without moving, asking one another about various Party workers and where they had spent their vacations.

But Giacomo was struck less by what they said than by the tone in which they said it. What was this tone exactly, and why did it rub him the wrong way? There was a note of complicity in it, he concluded, a reference to some secret bond different from that of either friendship or family. For a moment he wondered if it weren't just what one would find between fellow employees in a bank or government office. But upon reflection, he realised that it was entirely different. It was . . . he searched for some time, groping for an exact definition . . . it was the tone of voice of two monks or two nuns meeting one another. And why then did it rub him the wrong way? Not because he disapproved of Livio's and Simona's political ideas; in the course of a rational discussion he might very well allow that these had some basis. No; there was nothing rational about his hostility; its cause was obscure even to himself and at times it seemed to be one with his jealousy, as if he were afraid that Simona would escape him through her Party connections. As these thoughts ran through his mind, his face grew dark and discontented, so that when Simona joined him, all smiles, a moment later, she exclaimed in surprise: "What's wrong? Why are you unhappy?"

"Nothing. . . . It's just the heat."

"Let's go in the water. . . . But first, where can we undress?"

"Just follow me. . . . This way."

He knew the place well, and now led Simona through a

narrow passage among the rocks. Behind these rocks they stepped across some other lower ones and then went around a huge mass which sealed off a tiny beach of very fine, black sand at the foot of glistening, black rocky walls around a pool of shallow water filled with black seaweed. The effect was that of a room, with the sky for a ceiling, a watery floor and walls of stone.

"No swimming-bath can match this," Giacomo observed, looking around him.

"At last I can shed my clothes," said Simona with a sigh of relief.

She put her bag down on the sand and bent over to take out her bathing-suit, while, leaning against the rocks, Giacomo stripped himself in a second of his shirt and trousers. The sight of him stark naked caused her to give a nervous laugh.

"This is the sort of place to go swimming with no suits on, isn't it?" she said.

"Unfortunately, one can never manage to be alone," Giacomo replied, thinking of Livio.

He walked, still naked, with bare feet, over the cold sand in her direction, but she did not see him coming because she was pulling her jersey over her head. Her nakedness, he reflected, made her seem more virginal than ever. Her low-swung, round breasts had large rosy nipples, and a look of purity about them, as if they had never been offered to a masculine caress. Indeed, her virginal quality was so overwhelming that Giacomo did not dare press her to him as he had intended, but stood close by while she pulled her head out of the jersey. She shook back her ruffled hair and said in surprise: "What are you doing? Why don't you put on your trunks?"

"I'd like to make love right here and now," said Giacomo.

"On these rocks? Are you mad?"

"No. I'm not mad."

They were facing each other now, he entirely naked and she naked down to the waist. She crossed her arms over her breasts as if to support and protect them and said entreatingly: "Let's wait till to-night. . . . And meanwhile let's go swimming . . . please. . . ."

"To-night you'll put me off again."

"No; it will be different to-night."

Giacomo walked silently away and proceeded to put on his trunks, while Simona, obviously relieved, hastily donned her two-piece suit. She shouted gaily: "I'm off for a swim! If you love me, you'll follow."

"Let's go in right here," Giacomo suggested.

Simona paused and stuck her white foot into the green and brown seaweed that choked the black water.

"This pool is too murky. . . . It's no more than a puddle. Let's go where we just came from."

"But we shan't be alone."

"Oh, we have plenty of time for that."

They went back to the basin, where Livio was taking a sunbath on the cement landing, lying as still as if he were dead. Somehow this increased Giacomo's dislike of him. Yes; he was the sort of fellow that goes in for purposeful tanning, and then wanders about showing it off, wearing skimpy trunks designed to exhibit his virility as well. When Livio heard them coming he leaped to his feet and said: "Come on, Simona. Let's dive in and race over to that rock."

"You'll have to give me a handicap of at least a length," she said joyfully, forgetful of her husband.

"I'll give you three lengths, if you say so."

There it was, Giacomo could not help thinking, the same intimate, conspiratorial, clubby, Party manner, that tone of voice in which, despite their marriage, she had never spoken to him, and perhaps never would speak either. Sitting on a flat rock, just above the landing, he watched his wife plunge awkwardly in and then swim like a dark shadow under the green water until she came out, with her blonde head dripping.

"That was a real belly-flop," Livio shouted, making a perfect dive to join her. He too swam underwater, but for a longer distance than Simona, so that he came out farther away. Giacomo wondered if this "Party manner" weren't all a product of his imagination, and if there hadn't been in the past some more intimate personal relationship between them. And he realised that this second hypothesis was, on the whole, less disagreeable than the first. Then he said to himself that if he were to mention any suspicion to Simona she would be outraged and brand it as utterly "bourgeois," not to say "evil-minded and filthy." The moment after he dismissed it as out of the question. No, they were comrades, as she had said, and nothing more. What still puzzled him was why he objected more to their being Party comrades than to their being lovers. With a wavering effort of good-will, he said to himself that his jealousy was absurd, and he must drive it out of his mind. . . . And all the while he watched the two of them race across the dazzling green water in the direction of a round rock which emerged at the far end of the basin. Livio got there first, and, hoisting himself up on a protruding spur, shouted back at Simona: "I win! You're all washed up!"

"Speak for yourself!" Simona retorted.

This was the sort of joking insult he and Simona should have batted back and forth between them, Giacomo reflected. If they didn't joke that way on their honeymoon, when would they ever do it? He got up decisively, ran several steps along the landing and went in after them. He landed square on his stomach and was infuriated by the pain. After swimming several strokes under water he came up and started towards the rock where Livio and Simona were sitting. They were close together, talking uninterruptedly, with their legs dangling. He didn't relish the sight; in fact, it took away all the pleasure he should have felt from plunging hot and dusty into the cool water. He swam angrily ahead, arrived at the rock breathless and said, hanging on to a ledge: "Do you know, this water's very, very cold."

"It seemed warm to me," said Simona, momentarily interrupting the conversation to shoot him a glance.

"I swam here in April," Livio put in; "it was cold then, I can tell you."

With a curiosity that seemed to Giacomo somewhat flirtatious, Simona asked him: "Were you all alone?"

"No. I came with Nella," Livio answered.

Giacomo was trying to clamber up on the rock, but the only place where he could get a solid grip was the one where Livio and Simona were sitting. They seemed to be oblivious of his struggles, and he preferred not to ask them to move over. Finally, he caught hold of a jutting piece of the rock studded with jagged points, one of which left a pain in the palm of his hand as if it had dug deep into the flesh. Just as he got himself into a sitting position, the other two, with a shout of "Let's race back!" dived into the water, showering him with spray. He looked furiously after them as they raced toward the shore. Only when he had regained his self-control did he plunge in and follow. Simona and Livio were sitting in the shelter of a cliff and Simona was opening a lunch-box that she had taken out of her bag.

"Let's have something to eat," she said to Giacomo as he approached them. "But we must share it with Livio. He says he meant to go back up the mountain, but in this heat it would be too ridiculous."

Without saying a word, Giacomo sat down in the rocks beside them. The contents of the lunch-box turned out to be scanty: some meat sandwiches, two hard-boiled eggs and a bottle of wine.

"Livio will have to be content with very little," Giacomo said gruffly.

"Don't worry," Livio answered gaily. "I'm a very abstemious fellow."

Simona seemed extremely happy as she sat with crossed legs, dividing the lunch. She gave a sandwich to each one of them, bit into her own, and asked Livio:

"Where did you get your tan?"

"On the Tiber," he replied.

"Your whole group is very river-minded, isn't it, Livio?" she asked between one bite and another.

"All except Regina. She scorns the river completely; says it isn't aristocratic enough for her."

The things they talked about were trivial and childish enough, Giacomo reflected. And yet there was a greater intimacy between them than between husband and wife.

"No matter how hard she tries, Regina will never be able to put her background behind her," Simona observed.

"Who is Regina?" asked Giacomo.

"Someone in our outfit . . . the daughter of a wealthy land-owner . . . a very fine girl, really," Livio told him. "But wiping out an old trade-mark is no easy matter."

"And in this case, what trade-mark do you mean?"

"The bourgeois trade-mark."

"If you people ever get into power," Giacomo said impulsively, "you'll have to wipe that trade-mark out of millions of people."

"That's exactly what we'll do," Livio said with complete self-confidence. "That's our job, isn't it, Simona?"

Simona's mouth was full, but she nodded assent.

"The Italian bourgeoisie will be a tough nut to crack," Livio went on, "but we'll crack it, even if we have to kill off a large proportion in the process."

"There's a chance you may be killed off yourselves," said Giacomo.

"That's the risk we have to run in our profession," Livio retorted.

Giacomo noticed that Simona did not seem to go along

with Livio's ruthlessness; at this last remark she frowned and uttered no word of approval. Livio must have been aware of this, for he brusquely changed the subject.

"Simona, you really should have told us you were getting married, you know. There are some things it's not fair to hide!"

There was a note of tenderness toward Giacomo in Simona's reply.

"We decided from one day to the next. . . . Only the legal witnesses were present. Even our own parents weren't in on it."

"You mean you didn't want them?"

"We didn't want them, and anyhow they might not have come. . . . Giacomo's father and mother didn't want him to marry me."

"Because you're too far to the left, is that it?"

"No," Giacomo interposed. "My people don't go in for politics at all. But my mother had her eye on a certain girl. . . ."

"They may not go in for politics, as you say," Livio said, after another mouthful, "but there are always political implications. How could it be otherwise? Politics gets into everything these days."

True enough, Giacomo thought to himself. Even into honeymoons and a newly-married couple's first embrace. Then, annoyed at his own train of thought, he held out the hardboiled eggs to his companions.

"You two eat them," he said. "I'm not hungry."

"Be honest now," Livio said with a look of surprise on his face.

"Why aren't you hungry?" Simona asked him.

"That damned *scirocco,* I imagine."

Livio looked up at the cloudy sky.

"There'll be a storm before night. I can promise you that," he said.

Livio's conversation was made up of commonplaces and clichés, Giacomo reflected. But Simona seemed to like them. They conveyed more to her than his own attempts to express emotions that were difficult if not impossible to put into words. Meanwhile Simona, having finished her lunch, said: "Let's lie down for a sun-bath now."

"Will you be my pillow, Simona?" Livio asked, sliding toward her with the plain intention of putting his head on her lap.

For the first time Simona took her husband's presence into account.

"It's too hot for that, and you're too heavy."

And she looked at Giacomo out of the corner of her eyes as if to say: From now on, I won't let anyone do that but you. Giacomo's spirits soared, and he once more felt that there was a possibility of love between them. He got up and said: "Shall we go for a walk among the rocks?"

"Yes," she said promptly, following his example. And she added, to Livio: "See you later. . . . We're going to explore."

"Have a good time," Livio threw after them.

Simona led the way through the passage which her husband had shown her before. She made straight for the black beach, sat down at the foot of a rock and said: "Stretch out and put your head on my legs. . . . You'll be more comfortable that way."

Overcome by joy, Giacomo threw his arms around her and drew her to him. He gave her a kiss, and Simona returned it, blowing hard through her nose, almost as if she were suffering. When they had drawn apart, she repeated: "Stretch out, and we'll snatch a bit of sleep together."

She leaned her back against the rock, and Giacomo, his heart overflowing with love, lay down and put his head on her lap. He closed his eyes, and Simona began to stroke his face. With a hesitant and timid motion, she passed her hand over his cheeks, under his chin and up to the top of his head, where she ran her fingers through his hair. When Giacomo opened his eyes for a split second he saw that she was looking at him with childish intentness and curiosity. Meeting his glance, she bent over, placed a quick kiss on each of his eyes and told him to go to sleep. Giacomo closed his eyes again and gave himself up to enjoyment of the light touch of her tireless little hand until finally he dozed off. He slept for an indefinable length of time and woke up feeling chilled. Simona was sitting in the same position, with his head on her lap. Looking up, he saw the reason for his feeling so cold. The sky was filled with heavy, black storm clouds.

"How long have I been asleep?" he asked her.

"About an hour."

"And what about you?"

"I didn't sleep. I was looking at you."

"The sun's disappeared."

"Yes."

"There's going to be quite a rainstorm."

"Livio's gone," she said by way of an answer.

"Who is that Livio, anyhow?" Giacomo asked without moving.

"A Party comrade, a friend."

"I don't care for him."

"I know that," she said with a smile. "You made it pretty plain. As he was going away he pointed to you as you lay there asleep and said: 'What's the matter? Has he got it in for me?' "

"I haven't got it in for him. . . . But he has no manners. I'm on my honeymoon, and he acts as if it were his."

"He's a good fellow."

"You used to be in love with him. Admit it!"

She came out with a peal of innocent, silvery laughter.

"You must be crazy. I couldn't possibly fall in love with him. He doesn't appeal to me in the least."

"But the way you talked to one another. . . ."

"He's a Party comrade," she repeated, "and that's the way we talk." She was silent, for a moment, and then said with unexpected bitterness: "He's unintelligent. That's why he doesn't appeal to me."

"He doesn't seem to me much more stupid than the next man."

"He said a lot of foolish things," she went on angrily. "That we'd kill people off, for instance. . . . He knows better and spoke that way just to show off. . . . But such loose talk is harmful to the Party."

"You're the one that's got it in for him now."

"No. I haven't got it in for him; but he had no business to talk that way." Then she added, more coolly, "As a matter of fact, he's of value to the Party, even if he isn't too bright. He's absolutely loyal; you could ask him to do anything."

"And what value have I?" Giacomo was bold enough to ask jokingly.

"You can't have any value, since you're not one of us."

Giacomo was displeased by this answer. He got up and looked at the lowering sky.

"We'd better get back home before it rains. What do you say?"

"Yes. I think we had better."

Giacomo hesitated for a moment, put his arm around her

waist and asked softly: "When we get there, will you be
mine . . . at last?"

She nodded, turning her head away in order not to meet
his eyes. Feeling easier in his mind, Giacomo quickly got
dressed. A few steps away, Simona pulled on her shorts and
jersey and started to adjust her bag over her shoulder. But
with a tender protectiveness such as he had not displayed
on the way down, Giacomo said: "I'll carry that for you."

They started off. First they crossed the flatland, where the
pale green branches of the prickly pears seemed to gleam
discordantly against the dark sky. As they reached the beginning of the slope they turned around to look behind them.
The pink-and-white lighthouse stood out against a majestic
mass of black storm clouds rising from the horizon to invade
that part of the sky which was still empty. These clouds,
shaped like great rampant beasts, had smoking underbellies,
and irregular fringes hung down from them over the sea,
which was spottily darkening in some places, while in others
it still shone like burnished lead in the sun. The fringes were
gusts of rain, just beginning to comb the surface of the
water. Meanwhile, a turbulent wind covered the prickly pears
with yellow dust and a blinding stroke of lightning zigzagged
diagonally across the sky from one point to another. After a
long silence they heard the thunder—no clap, but rather a
dull rumble within the clouds. Giacomo saw his wife pale
and instinctively shrink toward him.

"Lightning scares me to death," she said, looking at him.

Giacomo raised his eyes to the half-clear, half-stormy sky.

"The storm isn't here yet," he said. "It's still over the sea.
If we hurry, we may get home without a wetting."

"Let's hurry, then," she said, continuing to climb up the
path.

The clouds, apparently driven by an increasingly powerful
wind, were spreading out over the sky with startling rapidity.
Simona quickened her pace to almost a run, and Giacomo
could not help teasing her.

"Afraid of lightning? What would the comrades say to
that? A good Marxist like yourself shouldn't have any such
fear."

"It's stronger than I am," she said in a childish voice,
without turning around.

There were steps, first narrow and then wide, to facilitate
the ascent of the lower part of the path, and higher up it
rose in wide curves through groves of olive trees. Simona

was a long way ahead; Giacomo could see her striding along
fifty or sixty feet in front of him. At the top they paused to
catch their breath and look around. Anacapri, momentarily
at their backs, stood reassuringly behind a barrier of green,
looking like an Arab city, with its terraces, campanile and
grey-domed church. Giacomo pointed to the shrunken lighthouse on the promontory below, profiled against the threatening storm.

"Just think, we were right down there!" he murmured.

"I can't wait to be home," said Simona, perhaps with the
thunder and lightning in mind. Then, meeting Giacomo's eyes,
she added with hesitant coquetry: "What about you?"

"I agree," he answered in a low voice, with emotion.

The climb was over, and all they had to do now was
follow the level path to their rented house, which was well
this side of Anacapri. They walked by the wall around the
Munthe villa, along a meadow planted with oak trees, and
there, just round a bend, was the white wall of their house
and the rusty iron gate in the shade of a carob tree with
pods hanging all over it. The clouds were straight above
them now, and it was as dark as evening. Simona hurriedly
pushed open the gate and went on ahead without waiting for
her husband to follow. Giacomo walked more slowly down
the marble steps among the cactus plants. As he went, there
was another rumble of thunder, louder this time, like an over-
turned wagon-load of stones rolling down a hill. From inside
the house Simona called back: "Shut the door tight!"

The house was on a hillside, set back among the trees,
and consisted of four roughly furnished rooms. Giacomo
made his way in amid almost complete darkness. There was
no electric light, but oil lamps of various shapes and colours
were lined up on the hall table. He lifted the glass off one
of these, lit a match, touched it to the wick, put back the
glass and entered the dining-room. No one was there, but
he could hear Simona moving in the room next to it. He
did not wish to join her immediately, and, feeling thirsty,
he poured himself out a glass of white wine. Finally, he
picked up the lamp and went to the bedroom door. The
bedroom, too, was almost dark. The window giving on to
the garden was open, and through it, in what light was left
among the shadows, he could make out the terrace surrounded by lemon trees planted in big pots. Simona, in a
dressing-gown, was tidying the still unmade bed. He set the

lamp down on the bedside table and said: "Are you still afraid of the lightning?"

She was leaning over the bed, with one leg slightly raised, smoothing the sheet. Pulling herself up, she answered: "No. Now that I'm in the house I feel safer."

"And are you afraid of me?"

"I never was afraid of you."

Giacomo walked around the bed and took her into his arms. Standing beside the head of the bed, they exchanged a kiss. Giacomo undid the sash of Simona's dressing-gown and it slipped down over her shoulders and hips to the floor. But Simona did not interrupt the kiss; indeed she prolonged it with an awkward eagerness, betrayed by her characteristic way of blowing through her nose. With sudden decisiveness, Giacomo let her go.

"Lie down, will you?" he said, hurriedly taking off his clothes.

Simona hesitated and then lay down on the bed. Giacomo was aware of being impelled by strictly animal feelings, as if he were not in a house, but in a dark cave—yes, as if he were a primitive man, moved by carnal appetite alone. Yet it was with a certain tenderness that he lay down beside his wife. She was facing the wall, but brusquely she turned around and pressed herself against him, snuggling into his arms. For a few minutes they lay there, motionless, then Giacomo began chastely and gently to caress her. He wanted to possess her on her own virginal terms, without bringing any of his masculine experience into play. His light caresses and the words he whispered through her hair into one ear were intended to calm her fears and lead her almost insensibly to give herself to him. He was not in a hurry and it seemed to him that his new policy of consideration and patience would win for him what his haste of the previous evening had failed to obtain. And by degrees he had the impression that, in response to his words and caresses, she was yielding not only her body, but also that inward part of her which had resisted him heretofore. Simona did not speak, but her breathing grew gradually heavier. All of a sudden, almost involuntarily, he gave way to a natural impulse and attempted to take her. Under the impact of his body, Simona seemed at first to surrender, then brusquely she rebelled and struggled to free herself. With a mixture of anger and submission she whispered: "I can't do it! I can't!"

Giacomo refused to heed her change of heart and tried

to prevail over her by force. She defended herself with her feet and knees and hands, while he did everything to overcome her. In the combat their naked bodies were bathed in sticky perspiration. Finally Giacomo lost his patience, leaped out of bed, and went into the bathroom, saying: "I'll be back in a minute."

Guided by a furious inspiration, he groped his way to the wash basin, took the razor blade he had used for shaving that morning and plunged it into the cushion of his thumb. He felt the cold blade cut through his skin, but had no pain. Then he put the blade back on the shelf and squeezed his thumb, which gave out an abundant flow of blood. He went back to the bedroom and threw himself upon his wife, rubbing his bloody thumb on the sheet between her legs. Then he shouted angrily: "You may not realise it, but you're no longer a virgin!"

Tremblingly she asked: "How do you know?"

"Just look!"

He took the lamp from the table and threw its light upon the bed. Simona was hunched up on the pillow, with her knees against her chin and her arms crossed over breasts. She looked down at the place where Giacomo had thrown the light and saw a long streak of red blood. Batting her eyelids in disgust, she said: "Are you sure?"

"Positive!"

But just at that moment her eyes travelled to the hand in which Giacomo was holding the lamp. Blood was streaming out of the cut in the cushion of his thumb. In a plaintive voice she cried out: "It's not my blood. It's yours! . . . You cut yourself on purpose."

Giacomo put the lamp back on the table and shouted in a rage: "That's the only blood I'll see to-night or any night to come. You're still a virgin and you always will be!"

"Why do you say that? What makes you so unkind?"

"That's the way it is," he answered. "You'll never be mine. Some part of you is hostile to me, and hostile it will remain."

"What part do you mean?"

"You're closer to that fool, Livio, than you are to me," he said, coming out with his jealousy at last. "That part of you which is close to Livio is hostile to me."

"That's not true."

"Yes; it is true. And it's equally true that if your Party came to power you'd inform on me. . . ."

"Who says so?"

"You said so yourself this morning, on the way to the lighthouse."

"I said nothing at all."

"Well, what would you do, then?"

She hesitated for a moment and then said:

"Why do you bring up such things at a time like this?"

"Because they prevent you from loving me and becoming my wife."

"I wouldn't inform on you," she said at last. "I'd leave you, that's all."

"But you're supposed to inform on your enemies," he shouted, angrier than ever. "It's your duty."

Still huddled up at the head of the bed, she burst into tears.

"Giacomo, why are you so unkind? . . . I'd kill myself. That's what I'd do."

Giacomo did not have the courage to remind her that on the way to the lighthouse she had branded suicide as morbid and absolutely inadmissible. After all, this contradiction was more flattering to him than an open declaration of love. Meanwhile, still in tears, she had got down from the bed and gone over to the open window. Giacomo lay on the bed, watching. She stood straight, with her head bent to the side and one arm raised against the frame. Suddenly the room was lit up, and every object in it, her naked, white body, the garden and the potted lemon trees around the terrace. There followed a metallic crack and a violent tremor which made the window and the walls of the room tremble. Simona gave a terrified cry, left the window and threw herself sobbing into her husband's arms. Giacomo pressed her to him, and almost immediately, while still weeping, she sought his embrace, he penetrated her body without any difficulty whatsoever. He had the feeling that a hidden flower, composed of only two petals, had opened—although still remaining invisible—to something that in the dark night of the flesh played the role of the sun. Nothing was settled, he reflected later on, but for the time being it was enough to know that she would kill herself for him.

KAREL ČAPEK

The Last Judgment

Karel Čapek (1890–1938) was a Czech novelist,
playwright, and short story writer. His best known
novel,* The War with the Newts, *anticipates fascist
domination of Europe. His plays are futuristic and
often comic, as in his often-produced* R.U.R. *He is
said to have invented the word "robot." Čapek was a
prolific and highly imaginative writer in all three
genres, an unusual feat. He is supposed to have died
of a heart attack as the German army entered Prague
during World War II.*

*(chop'-ek)

THE NOTORIOUS MULTIPLE-KILLER Kugler, pursued by several warrants and a whole army of policemen and detectives,
swore that he'd never be taken. He wasn't, either—at least
not alive. The last of his nine murderous deeds was shooting
a policeman who tried to arrest him. The policeman indeed
died, but not before putting a total of seven bullets into
Kugler. Of these seven, three were fatal. Kugler's death came
so quickly that he felt no pain. And so it seemed Kugler had
escaped earthly justice.

When his soul left his body, it should have been surprised
at the sight of the next world—a world beyond space, grey,
and infinitely desolate—but it wasn't. A man who has been
jailed on two continents looks upon the next life merely as
new surroundings. Kugler expected to struggle through,
equipped only with a bit of courage, as he had in the last
world.

At length the inevitable Last Judgment got around to Kugler.

Heaven being eternally in a state of emergency, Kugler was brought before a special court of three judges and not, as his previous conduct would ordinarily merit, before a jury. The courtroom was furnished simply, almost like courtrooms on earth, with this one exception: there was no provision for swearing in witnesses. In time, however, the reason for this will become apparent.

The judges were old and worthy councillors with austere, bored faces. Kugler complied with the usual tedious formalities: Ferdinand Kugler, unemployed, born on such and such a date, died . . . at this point it was shown Kugler didn't know the date of his own death. Immediately he realized this was a damaging omission in the eyes of the judges; his spirit of helpfulness faded.

"Do you plead guilty or not guilty?" asked the presiding judge.

"Not guilty," said Kugler obdurately.

"Bring in the first witness," the judge sighed.

Opposite Kugler appeared an extraordinary gentleman, stately, bearded, and clothed in a blue robe strewn with golden stars.

At his entrance the judges arose. Even Kugler stood up, reluctant but fascinated. Only when the old gentleman took a seat did the judges again sit down.

"Witness," began the presiding judge, "Omniscient God, this court has summoned You in order to hear Your testimony in the case against Kugler, Ferdinand. As You are the Supreme Truth, You need not take the oath. In the interest of the proceedings, however, we ask You to keep to the subject at hand rather than branch out into particulars—unless they have a bearing on this case.

"And you, Kugler, don't interrupt the Witness. He knows everything, so there's no use denying anything.

"And now, Witness, if You would please begin."

That said, the presiding judge took off his spectacles and leaned comfortably on the bench before him, evidently in preparation for a long speech by the Witness. The oldest of the three judges nestled down in sleep. The recording angel opened the Book of Life.

God, the Witness, coughed lightly and began:

"Yes. Kugler, Ferdinand. Ferdinand Kugler, son of a factory worker, was a bad, unmanageable child from his earliest days. He loved his mother dearly, but was unable to show it; this made him unruly and defiant. Young man, you irked everyone! Do you remember how you bit your father on the thumb when he tried to spank you? You had stolen a rose from the notary's garden."

"The rose was for Irma, the tax collector's daughter," Kugler said.

"I know," said God. "Irma was seven years old at that time. Did you ever hear what happened to her?"

"No, I didn't."

"She married Oscar, the son of the factory owner. But she contracted a venereal disease from him and died of a miscarriage. You remember Rudy Zaruba?"

"What happened to him?"

"Why, he joined the navy and died accidentally in Bombay. You two were the worst boys in the whole town. Kugler, Ferdinand, was a thief before his tenth year and an inveterate liar. He kept bad company, too: old Gribble, for instance, a drunkard and an idler, living on handouts. Nevertheless, Kugler shared many of his own meals with Gribble."

The presiding judge motioned with his hand, as if much of this was perhaps unnecessary, but Kugler himself asked hesitantly, "And . . . what happened to his daughter?"

"Mary?" asked God. "She lowered herself considerably. In her fourteenth year she married. In her twentieth year she died, remembering you in the agony of her death. By your fourteenth year you were nearly a drunkard yourself, and you often ran away from home. Your father's death came about from grief and worry; your mother's eyes faded from crying. You brought dishonor to your home, and your sister, your pretty sister Martha, never married. No young man would come calling at the home of a thief. She's still living alone and in poverty, sewing until late each night. Scrimping has exhausted her, and patronizing customers hurt her pride."

"What's she doing right now?"

"This very minute she's buying thread at Wolfe's. Do you remember that shop? Once, when you were six years old, you bought a colored glass marble there. On that very same day you lost it and never, never found it. Do you remember how you cried with rage?"

"Whatever happened to it?" Kugler asked eagerly.

"Well, it rolled into the drain and under the gutterspout. As a matter of fact, it's still there, after thirty years. Right now it's raining on earth and your marble is shivering in the gush of cold water."

Kugler bent his head, overcome by this revelation.

But the presiding judge fitted his spectacles back on his nose and said mildly, "Witness, we are obliged to get on with the case. Has the accused committed murder?"

Here the Witness nodded his head.

"He murdered nine people. The first one he killed in a brawl, and it was during his prison term for this crime that he became completely corrupted. The second victim was his unfaithful sweetheart. For that he was sentenced to death, but he escaped. The third was an old man whom he robbed. The fourth was a night watchman."

"Then he died?" Kugler asked.

"He died after three days in terrible pain," God said. "And he left six children behind him. The fifth and sixth victims were an old married couple. He killed them with an axe and found only sixteen dollars, although they had twenty thousand hidden away."

Kugler jumped up.

"Where?"

"In the straw mattress," God said. "In a linen sack inside the mattress. That's where they hid all the money they acquired from greed and penny-pinching. The seventh man he killed in America; a countryman of his, a bewildered, friendless immigrant."

"So it was in the mattress," whispered Kugler in amazement.

"Yes," continued God. "The eighth man was merely a passerby who happened to be in Kugler's way when Kugler was trying to outrun the police. At that time Kugler had periostitis and was delirious from the pain. Young man, you were suffering terribly. The ninth and last was the policeman who killed Kugler exactly when Kugler shot him."

"And why did the accused commit murder?" asked the presiding judge.

"For the same reasons others have," answered God. "Out of anger or desire for money; both deliberately and accidentally—some with pleasure, others from necessity. However, he was generous and often helpful. He was kind to women, gentle with animals, and he kept his word. Am I to mention his good deeds?"

"Thank You," said the presiding judge, "but it isn't necessary. Does the accused have anything to say in his own defense?"

"No," Kugler replied with honest indifference.

"The judges of this court will now take this matter under advisement," declared the presiding judge, and the three of them withdrew.

Only God and Kugler remained in the courtroom.

"Who are they?" asked Kugler, indicating with his head the men who had just left.

"People like you," answered God. "They were judges on earth, so they're judges here as well."

Kugler nibbled his fingertips. "I expected . . . I mean, I never really thought about it. But I figured You would judge, since—"

"Since I'm God," finished the Stately Gentleman. "But that's just it, don't you see? Because I know everything, I can't possibly judge. That wouldn't do at all. By the way, do you know who turned you in this time?"

"No, I don't," said Kugler, surprised.

"Lucky, the waitress. She did it out of jealousy."

"Excuse me," Kugler ventured, "but You forgot about that good-for-nothing Teddy I shot in Chicago."

"Not at all," God said. "He recovered and is alive this very minute. I know he's an informer, but otherwise he's a very good man and terribly fond of children. You shouldn't think of any person as being completely worthless."

"But I still don't understand why You aren't the judge," Kugler said thoughtfully.

"Because my knowledge is infinite. If judges knew everything, absolutely everything, then they would also understand everything. Their hearts would ache. They couldn't sit in judgment—and neither can I. As it is, they know only about your crimes. I know all about you. The entire Kugler. And that's why I cannot judge."

"But why are they judging . . . the same people who were judges on earth?"

"Because man belongs to man. As you see, I'm only the witness. But the verdict is determined by man, even in heaven. Believe me, Kugler, this is the way it should be. Man isn't worthy of divine judgment. He deserves to be judged only by other men."

At that moment the three returned from their deliberation.

In heavy tones the presiding judge announced, "For repeated crimes of first degree murder, manslaughter, robbery, disrespect for the law, illegally carrying weapons, and for the theft of a rose: Kugler, Ferdinand, is sentenced to lifelong punishment in hell. The sentence is to begin immediately.

"Next case, please: Torrance, Frank.

"Is the accused present in court?"

ISAAC BASHEVIS SINGER

Gimpel the Fool

*Isaac Bashevis Singer (1904-   ), a Pole by birth,
worked as a journalist in Warsaw in the twenties and
settled in the United States in 1935. He is probably
the greatest living writer in the Yiddish tradition,
dealing often with folk material and deeply moral
themes. Among his best-known works are* The Spinoza
of Market Street, The Slave, *and more recently* The
Manor. *The winner of many prizes, he was named
Nobel Laureate for Literature in 1978.*

1

I AM GIMPEL the fool. I don't think myself a fool. On the
contrary. But that's what folks call me. They gave me the
name while I was still in school. I had seven names in all:
imbecile, donkey, flax-head, dope, glump, ninny, and fool.
The last name stuck. What did my foolishness consist of? I
was easy to take in. They said, "Gimpel, you know the rabbi's
wife has been brought to childbed?" So I skipped school.
Well, it turned out to be a lie. How was I supposed to know?
She hadn't had a big belly. But I never looked at her belly.
Was that really so foolish? The gang laughed and hee-hawed,
stomped and danced and chanted a good-night prayer. And
instead of the raisins they give when a woman's lying in, they
stuffed my hand full of goat turds. I was no weakling. If I
slapped someone he'd see all the way to Cracow. But I'm
really not a slugger by nature. I think to myself, Let it pass.
So they take advantage of me.

I was coming home from school and heard a dog barking.

I'm not afraid of dogs, but of course I never want to start up with them. One of them may be mad, and if he bites there's not a Tartar in the world who can help you. So I made tracks. Then I looked around and saw the whole market place wild with laughter. It was no dog at all but Wolf-Leib the thief. How was I supposed to know it was he? It sounded like a howling bitch.

When the pranksters and leg-pullers found that I was easy to fool, every one of them tried his luck with me. "Gimpel, the Czar is coming to Frampol; Gimpel, the moon fell down in Turbeen; Gimpel, little Hodel Furpiece found a treasure behind the bathhouse." And I like a *golem* believed everyone. In the first place, everything is possible, as it is written in the Wisdom of the Fathers, I've forgotten just how. Second, I had to believe when the whole town came down on me! If I ever dared to say, "Ah, you're kidding!" there was trouble. People got angry. "What do you mean! You want to call everyone a liar?" What was I to do? I believed them, and I hope at least that did them some good.

I was an orphan. My grandfather who brought me up was already bent toward the grave. So they turned me over to a baker, and what a time they gave me there! Every woman or girl who came to bake a pan of cookies or dry a batch of noodles had to fool me at least once. "Gimpel, there's a fair in heaven; Gimpel, the rabbi gave birth to a calf in the seventh month; Gimpel, a cow flew over the roof and laid brass eggs." A student from the yeshiva came once to buy a roll, and he said, "You, Gimpel, while you stand here scraping with your baker's shovel the Messiah has come. The dead have arisen." "What do you mean?" I said. "I heard no one blowing the ram's horn!" He said, "Are you deaf?" And all began to cry, "We heard it, we heard!" Then in came Reitze the candle-dipper and called out in her hoarse voice, "Gimpel, your father and mother have stood up from the grave. They're looking for you."

To tell the truth, I knew very well that nothing of the sort had happened, but all the same, as folks were talking, I threw on my wool vest and went out. Maybe something had happened. What did I stand to lose by looking? Well, what a cat music went up! And then I took a vow to believe nothing more. But that was no go either. They confused me so that I didn't know the big end from the small.

I went to the rabbi to get some advice. He said, "It is written, better to be a fool all your days than for one hour to be evil. You are not a fool. They are the fools. For he who causes his neighbor to feel shame loses Paradise himself." Nevertheless the rabbi's daughter took me in. As I left the rabbinical court she said, "Have you kissed the wall yet?" I said, "No; what for?" She answered, "It's a law; you've got to do it after every visit." Well, there didn't seem to be any harm in it. And she burst out laughing. It was a fine trick. She put one over on me, all right.

I wanted to go off to another town, but then everyone got busy matchmaking, and they were after me so they nearly tore my coat tails off. They talked at me and talked until I got water on the ear. She was no chaste maiden, but they told me she was virgin pure. She had a limp, and they said it was deliberate, from coyness. She had a bastard, and they told me the child was her little brother. I cried, "You're wasting your time. I'll never marry that whore." But they said indignantly, "What a way to talk! Aren't you ashamed of yourself? We can take you to the rabbi and have you fined for giving her a bad name." I saw then that I wouldn't escape them so easily and I thought, They're set on making me their butt. But when you're married the husband's the master, and if that's all right with her it's agreeable to me too. Besides, you can't pass through life unscathed, nor expect to.

I went to her clay house, which was built on the sand, and the whole gang, hollering and chorusing, came after me. They acted like bearbaiters. When we came to the well they stopped all the same. They were afraid to start anything with Elka. Her mouth would open as if it were on a hinge, and she had a fierce tongue. I entered the house. Lines were strung from wall to wall and clothes were drying. Barefoot she stood by the tub, doing the wash. She was dressed in a worn hand-me-down gown of plush. She had her hair put up in braids and pinned across her head. It took my breath away, almost, the reek of it all.

Evidently she knew who I was. She took a look at me and said, "Look who's here! He's come, the drip. Grab a seat."

I told her all; I denied nothing. "Tell me the truth," I said, "are you really a virgin, and is that mischievous Yechiel actually your little brother? Don't be deceitful with me, for I'm an orphan."

"I'm an orphan myself," she answered, "and whoever tries to twist you up, may the end of his nose take a twist. But don't let them think they can take advantage of me. I want a dowry of fifty guilders, and let them take up a collection besides. Otherwise they can kiss my you-know-what." She was very plainspoken. I said, "It's the bride and not the groom who gives a dowry." Then she said, "Don't bargain with me. Either a flat 'yes' or a flat 'no'—go back where you came from."

I thought, No bread will ever be baked from *this* dough. But ours is not a poor town. They consented to everything and proceeded with the wedding. It so happened that there was a dysentery epidemic at the time. The ceremony was held at the cemetery gates, near the little corpse-washing hut. The fellows got drunk. While the marriage contract was being drawn up I heard the most pious high rabbi ask, "Is the bride a widow or a divorced woman?" And the sexton's wife answered for her, "Both a widow and divorced." It was a black moment for me. But what was I to do, run away from under the marriage canopy?

There was singing and dancing. An old granny danced opposite me, hugging a braided white *chalah*. The master of revels made a "God 'a mercy" in memory of the bride's parents. The schoolboys threw burrs, as on *Tishe b'Av* fast day. There were a lot of gifts after the sermon: a noodle board, a kneading trough, a bucket, brooms, ladles, household articles galore. Then I took a look and saw two strapping young men carrying a crib. "What do we need this for?" I asked. So they said, "Don't rack your brains about it. It's all right, it'll come in handy." I realized I was going to be rooked. Take it another way though, what did I stand to lose? I reflected, I'll see what comes of it. A whole town can't go altogether crazy.

2.

At night I came where my wife lay, but she wouldn't let me in. "Say, look here, is this what they married us for?" I said. And she said, "My monthly has come." "But yesterday they took you to the ritual bath, and that's afterward, isn't it supposed to be?" "Today isn't yesterday," said she, "and yesterday's not today. You can beat it if you don't like it." In short, I waited.

Not four months later she was in childbed. The townsfolk hid their laughter with their knuckles. But what could I do? She suffered intolerable pains and clawed at the walls. "Gimpel," she cried, "I'm going. Forgive me!" The house filled with women. They were boiling pans of water. The screams rose to the welkin.

The thing to do was to go to the House of Prayer to repeat Psalms, and that was what I did.

The townsfolk liked that, all right. I stood in a corner saying Psalms and prayers, and they shook their heads at me. "Pray, pray!" they told me. "Prayer never made any woman pregnant." One of the congregation put a straw to my mouth and said, "Hay for the cows." There was something to that too, by God!

She gave birth to a boy. Friday at the synagogue the sexton stood up before the Ark, pounded on the reading table, and announced, "The wealthy Reb Gimpel invites the congregation to a feast in honor of the birth of a son." The whole House of Prayer rang with laughter. My face was flaming. But there was nothing I could do. After all, I *was* the one responsible for the circumcision honors and rituals.

Half the town came running. You couldn't wedge another soul in. Women brought peppered chick-peas, and there was a keg of beer from the tavern. I ate and drank as much as anyone, and they all congratulated me. Then there was a circumcision, and I named the boy after my father, may he rest in peace. When all were gone and I was left with my wife alone, she thrust her head through the bed-curtain and called me to her.

"Gimpel," said she, "why are you silent? Has your ship gone and sunk?"

"What shall I say?" I answered. "A fine thing you've done to me! If my mother had known of it she'd have died a second time."

She said, "Are you crazy, or what?"

"How can you make such a fool," I said, "of one who should be the lord and master?"

"What's the matter with you?" she said. "What have you taken it into your head to imagine?"

I saw that I must speak bluntly and openly. "Do you think this is the way to use an orphan?" I said. "You have borne a bastard."

She answered, "Drive this foolishness out of your head. The child is yours."

"How can he be mine?" I argued. "He was born seventeen weeks after the wedding."

She told me then that he was premature. I said, "Isn't he a little too premature?" She said she had had a grandmother

who carried just as short a time and she resembled this
grandmother of hers as one drop of water does another.
She swore to it with such oaths that you would have believed
a peasant at the fair if he had used them. To tell the plain
truth, I didn't believe her; but when I talked it over next day
with the schoolmaster he told me that the very same thing
had happened to Adam and Eve. Two they went up to bed,
and four they descended.

"There isn't a woman in the world who is not the grand-
daughter of Eve," he said.

That was how it was—they argued me dumb. But then,
who really knows how such things are?

I began to forget my sorrow. I loved the child madly,
and he loved me too. As soon as he saw me he'd wave his
little hands and want me to pick him up, and when he was
colicky I was the only one who could pacify him. I bought
him a little bone teething ring and a little gilded cap. He was
forever catching the evil eye from someone, and then I had
to run to get one of those abracadabras for him that would
get him out of it. I worked like an ox. You know how ex-
penses go up when there's an infant in the house. I don't
want to lie about it; I didn't dislike Elka either, for that
matter. She swore at me and cursed, and I couldn't get
enough of her. What strength she had! One of her looks
could rob you of the power of speech. And her orations! Pitch
and sulphur, that's what they were full of, and yet somehow
also full of charm. I adored her every word. She gave me
bloody wounds though.

In the evening I brought her a white loaf as well as a
dark one, and also poppyseed rolls I baked myself. I thieved
because of her and swiped everything I could lay hands on,
macaroons, raisins, almonds, cakes. I hope I may be forgiven
for stealing from the Saturday pots the women left to warm
in the baker's oven. I would take out scraps of meat, a chunk
of pudding, a chicken leg or head, a piece of tripe, whatever
I could nip quickly. She ate and became fat and handsome.

I had to sleep away from home all during the week, at
the bakery. On Friday nights when I got home she always
made an excuse of some sort. Either she had heartburn, or
a stitch in the side, or hiccups, or headaches. You know
what women's excuses are. I had a bitter time of it. It was
rough. To add to it, this little brother of hers, the bastard,
was growing bigger. He'd put lumps on me, and when I
wanted to hit back she'd open her mouth and curse so power-

fully I saw a green haze floating before my eyes. Ten times a day she threatened to divorce me. Another man in my place would have taken French leave and disappeared. But I'm the type that bears it and says nothing. What's one to do? Shoulders are from God, and burdens too.

One night there was a calamity in the bakery; the oven burst, and we almost had a fire. There was nothing to do but go home, so I went home. Let me, I thought, also taste the joy of sleeping in bed in midweek. I didn't want to wake the sleeping mite and tiptoed into the house. Coming in, it seemed to me that I heard not the snoring of one but, as it were, a double snore, one a thin enough snore and the other like the snoring of a slaughtered ox. Oh, I didn't like that! I didn't like it at all. I went up to the bed, and things suddenly turned black. Next to Elka lay a man's form. Another in my place would have made an uproar, and enough noise to rouse the whole town, but the thought occurred to me that I might wake the child. A little thing like that— why frighten a little swallow like that, I thought. All right then, I went back to the bakery and stretched out on a sack of flour, and till morning I never shut an eye. I shivered as if I had had malaria. "Enough of being a donkey," I said to myself. "Gimpel isn't going to be a sucker all his life. There's a limit even to the foolishness of a fool like Gimpel."

In the morning I went to the rabbi to get advice, and it made a great commotion in the town. They sent the beadle for Elka right away. She came, carrying the child. And what do you think she did? She denied it, denied everything, bone and stone! "He's out of his head," she said. "I know nothing of dreams or divinations." They yelled at her, warned her, hammered on the table, but she stuck to her guns: it was a false accusation, she said.

The butchers and the horse-traders took her part. One of the lads from the slaughterhouse came by and said to me, "We've got our eye on you, you're a marked man." Meanwhile the child started to bear down and soiled itself. In the rabbinical court there was an Ark of the Covenant, and they couldn't allow that, so they sent Elka away.

I said to the rabbi, "What shall I do?"

"You must divorce her at once," said he.

"And what if she refuses?" I asked.

He said, "You must serve the divorce, that's all you'll have to do."

I said, "Well, all right, Rabbi. Let me think about it."

"There's nothing to think about," said he. "You mustn't remain under the same roof with her."

"And if I want to see the child?" I asked.

"Let her go, the harlot," said he, "and her brood of bastards with her."

The verdict he gave was that I mustn't even cross her threshold—never again, as long as I should live.

During the day it didn't bother me so much. I thought, It was bound to happen, the abscess had to burst. But at night when I stretched out upon the sacks I felt it all very bitterly. A longing took me, for her and for the child. I wanted to be angry, but that's my misfortune exactly, I don't have it in me to be really angry. In the first place— this was how my thoughts went—there's bound to be a slip sometimes. You can't live without errors. Probably that lad who was with her led her on and gave her presents and what not, and women are often long on hair and short on sense, and so he got around her. And then since she denies it so, maybe I was only seeing things? Hallucinations do happen. You see a figure or a mannikin or something, but when you come up closer it's nothing, there's not a thing there. And if that's so, I'm doing her an injustice. And when I got so far in my thoughts I started to weep. I sobbed so that I wet the flour where I lay. In the morning I went to the rabbi and told him that I had made a mistake. The rabbi wrote on with his quill, and he said that if that were so he would have to reconsider the whole case. Until he had finished I wasn't to go near my wife, but I might send her bread and money by messenger.

3.

Nine months passed before all the rabbis could come to an agreement. Letters went back and forth. I hadn't realized that there could be so much erudition about a matter like this.

Meantime Elka gave birth to still another child, a girl this time. On the Sabbath I went to the synagogue and invoked a blessing on her. They called me up to the Torah, and I named the child for my mother-in-law, may she rest in peace. The louts and loudmouths of the town who came into the bakery gave me a going over. All Frampol refreshed its spirits because of my trouble and grief. However, I resolved that I would always believe what I was told. What's the good of *not* believing? Today it's your wife you don't believe; tomorrow it's God Himself you won't take stock in.

By an apprentice who was her neighbor I sent her daily a corn or a wheat loaf, or a piece of pastry, rolls or bagels, or, when I got the chance, a slab of pudding, a slice of honeycake, or wedding strudel—whatever came my way. The apprentice was a goodhearted lad, and more than once he added something on his own. He had formerly annoyed me a lot, plucking my nose and digging me in the ribs, but when he started to be a visitor to my house he became kind and friendly. "Hey, you, Gimpel," he said to me, "you have a very decent little wife and two fine kids. You don't deserve them."

"But the things people say about her," I said.

"Well, they have long tongues," he said, "and nothing to do with them but babble. Ignore it as you ignore the cold of last winter."

One day the rabbi sent for me and said, "Are you certain, Gimpel, that you were wrong about your wife?"

I said, "I'm certain."

"Why, but look here! You yourself saw it."

"It must have been a shadow," I said.

"The shadow of what?"

"Just of one of the beams, I think."

"You can go home then. You owe thanks to the Yanover rabbi. He found an obscure reference in Maimonides that favored you."

I seized the rabbi's hand and kissed it.

I wanted to run home immediately. It's no small thing to be separated for so long a time from wife and child. Then I reflected, I'd better go back to work now, and go home in the evening. I said nothing to anyone, although as far as my heart was concerned it was like one of the Holy Days. The women teased and twitted me as they did every day, but my thought was, Go on, with your loose talk. The truth is out, like the oil upon the water. Maimonides says it's right, and therefore it is right!

At night, when I had covered the dough to let it rise, I took my share of bread and a little sack of flour and started homeward. The moon was full and the stars were glistening, something to terrify the soul. I hurried onward, and before me darted a long shadow. It was winter, and a fresh snow had fallen. I had a mind to sing, but it was growing late and I didn't want to wake the householders. Then I felt like whistling, but remembered that you don't whistle at night because it brings the demons out. So I was silent and walked as fast as I could.

Dogs in the Christian yards barked at me when I passed, but I thought, Bark your teeth out! What are you but mere dogs? Whereas I am a man, the husband of a fine wife, the father of promising children.

As I approached the house my heart started to pound as though it were the heart of a criminal. I felt no fear, but my heart went thump! thump! Well, no drawing back. I quietly lifted the latch and went in. Elka was asleep. I looked at the infant's cradle. The shutter was closed, but the moon forced its way through the cracks. I saw the newborn child's face and loved it as soon as I saw it—immediately—each tiny bone.

Then I came nearer to the bed. And what did I see but the apprentice lying there beside Elka. The moon went out all at once. It was utterly black, and I trembled. My teeth chattered. The bread fell from my hands and my wife waked and said, "Who is that, ah?"

I muttered, "It's me."

"Gimpel?" she asked. "How come you're here? I thought it was forbidden."

"The rabbi said," I answered and shook as with a fever.

"Listen to me, Gimpel," she said, "go out to the shed and see if the goat's all right. It seems she's been sick." I have forgotten to say that we had a goat. When I heard she was unwell I went into the yard. The nannygoat was a good little creature. I had a nearly human feeling for her.

With hesitant steps I went up to the shed and opened the door. The goat stood there on her four feet. I felt her everywhere, drew her by the horns, examined her udders, and found nothing wrong. She had probably eaten too much bark. "Good night, little goat," I said. "Keep well." And the little beast answered with a "Maa" as though to thank me for the good will.

I went back. The apprentice had vanished.

"Where," I asked, "is the lad?"

"What lad?" my wife answered.

"What do you mean?" I said. "The apprentice. You were sleeping with him."

"The things I have dreamed this night and the night before," she said, "may they come true and lay you low, body and soul! An evil spirit has taken root in you and dazzles your sight." She screamed out, "You hateful creature! You moon calf! You spook! You uncouth mane! Get out, or I'll scream all Frampol out of bed!"

Before I could move, her brother sprang out from behind the oven and struck me a blow on the back of the head. I thought he had broken my neck. I felt that something about me was deeply wrong, and I said, "Don't make a scandal. All that's needed now is that people should accuse me of raising spooks and *dybbuks*." For that was what she had meant. "No one will touch bread of my baking."

In short, I somehow calmed her.

"Well," she said, "that's enough. Lie down, and be shattered by wheels."

Next morning I called the apprentice aside. "Listen here, brother!" I said. And so on and so forth. "What do you say?" He stared at me as though I had dropped from the roof or something.

"I swear," he said, "you'd better go to an herb doctor or some healer. I'm afraid you have a screw loose, but I'll hush it up for you." And that's how the thing stood.

To make a long story short, I lived twenty years with my wife. She bore me six children, four daughters and two sons. All kinds of things happened, but I neither saw nor heard. I believed, and that's all. The rabbi recently said to me, "Belief in itself is beneficial. It is written that a good man lives by his faith."

Suddenly my wife took sick. It began with a trifle, a little growth upon the breast. But she evidently was not destined to live long; she had no years. I spent a fortune on her. I have forgotten to say that by this time I had a bakery of my own and in Frampol was considered to be something of a rich man. Daily the healer came, and every witch doctor in the neighborhood was brought. They decided to use leeches, and after that to try cupping. They even called a doctor from Lublin, but it was too late. Before she died she called me to her bed and said, "Forgive me, Gimpel."

I said, "What is there to forgive? You have been a good and faithful wife."

"Woe, Gimpel!" she said. "It was ugly how I deceived you all these years. I want to go clean to my Maker, and so I have to tell you that the children are not yours."

If I had been clouted on the head with a piece of wood it couldn't have bewildered me more.

"Whose are they?" I asked.

"I don't know," she said, "there were a lot. . . . But they're not yours." And as she spoke she tossed her head to the side, her eyes turned glassy, and it was all up with Elka. On her whitened lips there remained a smile.

I imagined that, dead as she was, she was saying, "I deceived Gimpel. That was the meaning of my brief life."

4.

One night, when the period of mourning was done, as I lay dreaming on the flour sacks, there came the Spirit of Evil himself and said to me, "Gimpel, why do you sleep?"

I said, "What should I be doing? Eating *kreplach?*"

"The whole world deceives you," he said, "and you ought to deceive the world in your turn."

"How can I deceive all the world?" I asked him.

He answered, "You might accumulate a bucket of urine every day and at night pour it into the dough. Let the sages of Frampol eat filth."

"What about judgment in the world to come?" I said.

"There is no world to come," he said. "They've sold you a bill of goods and talked you into believing you carried a cat in your belly. What nonsense!"

"Well then," I said, "and is there a God?"

He answered, "There is no God either."

"What," I said, "*is* there, then?"

"A thick mire."

He stood before my eyes with a goatish beard and horns, longtoothed, and with a tail. Hearing such words, I wanted to snatch him by the tail, but I tumbled from the flour sacks and nearly broke a rib. Then it happened that I had to answer the call of nature, and, passing, I saw the risen dough, which seemed to say to me, "Do it!" In brief, I let myself be persuaded.

At dawn the apprentice came. We kneaded the bread, scattered caraway seeds on it, and set it to bake. Then the apprentice went away, and I was left sitting in the little trench by the oven, on a pile of rags. Well, Gimpel, I thought, you've revenged yourself on them for all the shame they've put on you. Outside the frost glittered, but it was warm beside the oven. The flames heated my face. I bent my head and fell into a doze.

I saw in a dream, at once, Elka in her shroud. She called to me, "What have you done, Gimpel?"

I said to her, "It's all your fault," and started to cry.

"You fool!" she said. "You fool! Because I was false is everything false too? I never deceived anyone but myself. I'm paying for it all, Gimpel. They spare you nothing here."

I looked at her face. It was black. I was startled and waked, and remained sitting dumb. I sensed that everything hung in the balance. A false step now and I'd lose Eternal Life. But God gave me His help. I seized the long shovel and took out the loaves, carried them into the yard, and started to dig a hole in the frozen earth.

My apprentice came back as I was doing it. "What are you doing, boss?" he said, and grew pale as a corpse.

"I know what I'm doing," I said, and I buried it all before his very eyes.

Then I went home, took my hoard from its hiding place, and divided it among the children. "I saw your mother tonight," I said. "She's turning black, poor thing."

They were so astounded they couldn't speak a word.

"Be well," I said, "and forget that such a one as Gimpel ever existed." I put on my short coat, a pair of boots, took the bag that held my prayer shawl in one hand, my stick in the other, and kissed the *mezzuzah*. When people saw me in the street they were greatly surprised.

"Where are you going?" they said.

I answered, "Into the world." And so I departed from Frampol.

I wandered over the land, and good people did not neglect me. After many years I became old and white; I heard a great deal, many lies and falsehoods, but the longer I lived the more I understood that there were really no lies. Whatever doesn't really happen is dreamed at night. It happens to one if it doesn't happen to another, tomorrow if not today, or a century hence if not next year. What difference can it make? Often I heard tales of which I said, "Now this is a thing that cannot happen." But before a year had elapsed I heard that it actually had come to pass somewhere.

Going from place to place, eating at strange tables, it often happens that I spin yarns—improbable things that could never have happened—about devils, magicians, windmills, and the like. The children run after me, calling, "Grandfather, tell us a story." Sometimes they ask for particular stories, and I try to please them. A fat young boy once said to

me, "Grandfather, it's the same story you told us before."
The little rogue, he was right.

So it is with dreams too. It is many years since I left
Frampol, but as soon as I shut my eyes I am there again.
And whom do you think I see? Elka. She is standing by
the washtub, as at our first encounter, but her face is shining
and her eyes are as radiant as the eyes of a saint, and she
speaks outlandish words to me, strange things. When I wake
I have forgotten it all. But while the dream lasts I am
comforted. She answers all my queries, and what comes out
is that all is right. I weep and implore, "Let me be with
you." And she consoles me and tells me to be patient. The
time is nearer than it is far. Sometimes she strokes and kisses
me and weeps upon my face. When I awaken I feel her
lips and taste the salt of her tears.

No doubt the world is entirely an imaginary world, but
it is only once removed from the true world. At the door
of the hovel where I lie, there stands the plank on which
the dead are taken away. The gravedigger Jew has his spade
ready. The grave waits and the worms are hungry; the
shrouds are prepared—I carry them in my beggar's sack.
Another *shnorrer* is waiting to inherit my bed of straw.
When the time comes I will go joyfully. Whatever may be
there, it will be real, without complication, without ridicule,
without deception. God be praised: there even Gimpel cannot
be deceived.

LUIGI PIRANDELLO

War

> *Luigi Pirandello (1867-1936) was born in Girgenti,
> Sicily, and educated first in Rome and then at the
> University of Bonn in Germany. He is best known
> as a dramatist, having written about fifty plays and
> received the Nobel Prize for literature in 1934. His
> play* Six Characters in Search of an Author *(1921)
> is his best known in the United States, where it is
> still frequently performed. Pirandello's short stories
> are intensely poetic and often more metaphysical in
> nature than those of American writers. The economy
> and power with which he is able to convey deeply
> emotional crises are beautifully evident in "War."*

THE PASSENGERS WHO had left Rome by the night express
had had to stop until dawn at the small station of Fabriano
in order to continue their journey by the small old-fashioned
"local" joining the main line with Sulmona.

At dawn, in a stuffy and smoky second-class carriage in
which five people had already spent the night, a bulky woman,
in deep mourning, was hoisted in—almost like a shapeless
bundle. Behind her—puffing and moaning, followed her husband—a tiny man, thin and weakly, his face death-white,
his eyes small and bright and looking shy and uneasy.

Having at last taken a seat he politely thanked the passengers who had helped his wife and who had made room for
her; then he turned round to the woman trying to pull
down the collar of her coat and politely enquired:

"Are you all right, dear?"

The wife, instead of answering, pulled up her collar again to her eyes, so as to hide her face.

"Nasty world," muttered the husband with a sad smile.

And he felt it his duty to explain to his travelling companions that the poor woman was to be pitied for the war was taking away from her her only son, a boy of twenty to whom both had devoted their entire life, even breaking up their home at Sulmona to follow him to Rome where he had to go as a student, then allowing him to volunteer for war with an assurance, however, that at least for six months he would not be sent to the front and now, all of a sudden, receiving a wire saying that he was due to leave in three days' time and asking them to go and see him off.

The woman under the big coat was twisting and wriggling, at times growling like a wild animal, feeling certain that all those explanations would not have aroused even a shadow of sympathy from those people who—most likely—were in the same plight as herself. One of them, who had been listening with particular attention, said:

"You should thank God that your son is only leaving now for the front. Mine has been sent there the first day of the war. He has already come back twice wounded and been sent back again to the front."

"What about me? I have two sons and three nephews at the front," said another passenger.

"Maybe, but in our case it is our *only* son," ventured the husband.

"What difference can it make? You may spoil your only son with excessive attentions, but you cannot love him more than you would all your other children if you had any. Paternal love is not like bread that can be broken into pieces and split amongst the children in equal shares. A father gives all his love to each one of his children without discrimination, whether it be one or ten, and if I am suffering now for my two sons, I am not suffering half for each of them but double. . . ."

"True . . . true . . ." sighed the embarrassed husband, "but suppose (of course we all hope it will never be your case) a father has two sons at the front and he loses one of them, there is still one left to console him . . . while . . ."

"Yes," answered the other, getting cross, "a son left to console him but also a son left for whom he must survive, while in the case of the father of an only son if the son

dies the father can die too and put an end to his distress.
Which of the two positions is the worse? Don't you see how
my case would be worse than yours?"

"Nonsense," interrupted another traveller, a fat, red-faced
man with bloodshot eyes of the palest grey.

He was panting. From his bulging eyes seemed to spurt
inner violence of an uncontrolled vitality which his weakened
body could hardly contain.

"Nonsense," he repeated, trying to cover his mouth with
his hand so as to hide the two missing front teeth. "Nonsense.
Do we give life to our children for our own benefit?"

The other travellers stared at him in distress. The one
who had had his son at the front since the first day of the
war sighed: "You are right. Our children do not belong to
us, they belong to the Country. . . ."

"Bosh," retorted the fat traveller. "Do we think of the
Country when we give life to our children? Our sons are
born because . . . well, because they must be born and when
they come to life they take our own life with them. This
is the truth. We belong to them but they never belong to
us. And when they reach twenty they are exactly what we
were at their age. We too had a father and mother, but
there were so many other things as well . . . girls, cigarettes,
illusions, new ties . . . and the Country, of course, whose
call we would have answered—when we were twenty—even
if father and mother had said no. Now, at our age, the love
of our Country is still great, of course, but stronger than it
is the love for our children. Is there any one of us here
who wouldn't gladly take his son's place at the front if he
could?"

There was a silence all round, everybody nodding as to
approve.

"Why then," continued the fat man, "shouldn't we consider the feelings of our children when they are twenty?
Isn't it natural that at their age they should consider the
love for their Country (I am speaking of decent boys, of
course) even greater than the love for us? Isn't it natural
that it should be so, as after all they must look upon us as
upon old boys who cannot move any more and must stay
at home? If Country exists, if Country is a natural necessity
like bread, of which each of us must eat in order not to
die of hunger, somebody must go to defend it. And our sons
go, when they are twenty, and they don't want tears, because
if they die, they die inflamed and happy (I am speaking,

of course, of decent boys). Now, if one dies young and
happy, without having the ugly sides of life, the boredom of
it, the pettiness, the bitterness of disillusion . . . what more
can we ask for him? Everyone should stop crying: everyone
should laugh, as I do . . . or at least thank God—as I do—
because my son, before dying, sent me a message saying
that he was dying satisfied at having ended his life in the
best way he could have wished. That is why, as you see,
I do not even wear mourning. . . ."

He shook his light fawn coat as to show it; his livid
lip over his missing teeth was trembling, his eyes were watery
and motionless and soon after he ended with a shrill laugh
which might well have been a sob.

"Quite so . . . quite so . . ." agreed the others.

The woman who, bundled in a corner under her coat,
had been sitting and listening had—for the last three months
—tried to find in the words of her husband and her friends
something to console her in her deep sorrow, something that
might show her how a mother should resign herself to send
her son not even to death but to a probable danger of life.
Yet not a word had she found amongst the many which had
been said . . : and her grief had been greater in seeing
that nobody—as she thought—could share her feelings.

But now the words of the traveller amazed and almost
stunned her. She suddenly realized that it wasn't the others
who were wrong and could not understand her but herself
who could not rise up to the same height of those fathers
and mothers willing to resign themselves, without crying,
not only to the departure of their sons but even to their
death.

She lifted her head, she bent over from her corner trying
to listen with great attention to the details which the fat
man was giving to his companions about the way his son
had fallen as a hero, for his King and his Country, happy
and without regrets. It seemed to her that she had stumbled
into a world she had never dreamt of, a world so far unknown to her and she was so pleased to hear everyone
joining in congratulating that brave father who could so
stoically speak of his child's death.

Then suddenly, just as if she had heard nothing of what
had been said and almost as if waking up from a dream, she
turned to the old man, asking him:

"Then . . . is your son really dead?"

Everybody stared at her. The old man, too, turned to

look at her, fixing his great, bulging, horribly watery light grey eyes, deep in her face. For some little time he tried to answer, but words failed him. He looked and looked at her, almost as if only then—at that silly, incongruous question —he had suddenly realized at last that his son was really dead . . . gone for ever . . . for ever. His face contracted, became horribly distorted, then he snatched in haste a handkerchief from his pocket and, to the amazement of everyone, broke into harrowing, heart-rending, uncontrollable sobs.

WOLFGANG HILDESHEIMER

A World Ends

Wolfgang Hildesheimer (1916-   ) is one of a group of writers who began producing remarkable short stories after World War II. A native of Hamburg, he went to Palestine in 1933 and from there to England, where he studied art and worked as a stage designer. In 1939 he returned to Palestine to edit a magazine of art criticism. It has only been in recent years that he has given up art for a writing career, winning the Buchner Prize in 1966. His work explores the schism between the harsh realities of modern life and the metaphysical fable upon which so much earlier German writing is based.

THE MARCHESA MONTETRISTO'S last evening party has impressed itself indelibly on my memory. This is partly due, of course, to its extraordinary conclusion but in other ways as well the evening was unforgettable.

My acquaintance with the Marchesa—a Waterman by birth, of Little Gidding, Ohio—came about by a coincidence. I had sold her, through the intermediary of my friend, Herr von Perlhuhn (I mean of course the Abraham-a-Santa Clara expert, not the neo-mystic), the bathtub in which Marat was murdered. It is perhaps not generally known that it had been until then in my possession. Gambling debts obliged me to offer it for sale. So it was that I came to the Marchesa who had long wanted this appliance for her collection of eighteenth-century washing utensils. This was the occasion of my

Translated by Christopher Holme. Reprinted by permission of Suhrkamp Verlag. Copyright © Suhrkamp Verlag, Frankfurt am Main, 1962. American agent, Joan Daves.

getting to know her. From the bathtub our conversation soon passed to more general esthetic topics. I noticed that the possession of this collector's piece had given me a certain prestige in her eyes. And I was not surprised when one day I was invited to one of her famous parties in her palazzo on the artificial island of San Amerigo. The Marchesa had had the island thrown up a few miles southeast of Murano on a sudden whim, for she detested the mainland—she said it was hurtful to her spiritual equilibrium, and she could find nothing to suit her in the existing stock of islands. So here she resided, devoting her life to the cult of the antique and forgotten, or, as she liked to put it, of the "true and eternal."

The invitation card gave the time of the party as eight o'clock, which meant that the guests were expected at ten. So custom ordered it. Further it ordered that the guests should come in gondolas. In this fashion, it is true, the crossing lasted nearly two hours and was moreover uncomfortable when the sea was rough, but these were unwritten rules of behavior at which no one but a barbarian would cavil—and barbarians were not invited. Besides, many of the younger guests, not yet fully sensible of the dignity of the occasion, would hire a *vaporetto* to take them within a hundred yards of the island whence they were ferried over one by one in a gondola which had been brought in tow.

The splendor of the building needs no description from me. For outside it was an exact replica of the Palazzo Vendramin, and inside every period, from the Gothic onward, was represented. But of course they were not intermingled. Each one had its own room. The Marchesa could really not be accused of breaches of style. Nor need the opulence of the catering be referred to here. Anyone who has ever attended a state banquet in a monarchy—and it is to such that I principally address myself—knows what it was like. Moreover it would hardly be true to the spirit of the Marchesa and her circle to mention the pleasures of the table, especially here, where I have to describe the last hours on earth of some of the most eminent figures of the age, which I as sole survivor had the privilege to witness.

After exchanging a few civilities with my hostess and stroking the long-haired Pekinese which never stirred from her side, I was introduced to the Dombrowska, a woman doubly famous, first for her contributions to the rhythmic-expressionist dance, a vanishing art form, and secondly as

the author of the book *Back to Youth,* which, as the title
indicates, argued in favor of a return to youthfulness of
style and which, I need hardly remind the reader, has won
adherents far and wide. While we were chatting together,
an elderly gentleman of upright bearing came up to us. It
was Golch. The Golch. (Unnecessary to give further particulars of a man whose share in the enrichment of our intellectual life is so widely known.) The Dombrowska
introduced me: "Herr Sebald, the late owner of Marat's
bathtub." My fame had spread.

"Aha," said Golch. I inferred, from the inflection he gave
to these syllables, that he was weighing my potentialities
as a candidate for the cultural élite. I asked him how he had
liked the exhibition of contemporary painting in Luxemburg.
For one might, indeed one must, assume that those here
assembled had seen, read, and heard everything of any real
importance. That was why they were here. Golch raised his
eyes as if looking for a word in space and said, "Passé."
(He used the English accentuation of the word which was
then in fashion. The words "cliché" and "pastiche" too were
pronounced *à l'anglaise.* I don't know what the current usage
is. I am now too much taken up with everyday affairs to
concern myself with such matters.) I noticed in any case
that I had blundered in thus mentioning the contemporary.
I had gone down a step, but I had learnt my lesson.

A move was made to the buffet. Here I encountered Si-
gnora Sgambati, the astrologer, who had recently made a
considerable stir by her theory that not only the fate of individuals but whole trends in the history of ideas could be
read in the stars. She was no ordinary phenomenon, this
Sgambati, as was at once clear from her appearance. Yet
I find it incomprehensible in the circumstances that she did
not see in the constellation of the heavens the imminent
engulfment of so many substantial members of the intellectual
world. She was deep in conversation with Professor Kuntz-
Sartori, the politician and royalist, who had been trying for
decades to introduce a monarchy in Switzerland. Another
notable figure.

After taking some refreshment the company moved to the
Silver Room for what was to be the climax of the evening's
entertainment, a performance of a special kind—the world
première of two flute sonatas by Antonio Giambattista Bloch,
a contemporary and friend of Rameau, who had been discovered by the musicologist Weltli. He too of course was

there. They were played by the flautist Beranger (yes, a descendant) and accompanied by the Marchesa herself, on the self-same harpsichord on which Celestine Rameau had initiated her son into the fundamental principles of counterpoint, and which had been sent for from Paris. The flute too had a history, but I have forgotten it. The two performers had put on rococo costume for the occasion, and the little ensemble looked—they had purposely so arranged themselves —like a picture by Watteau. The performance of course took place by the dimmest of candlelight. There was not a person there who would have found electric light for such an occasion anything but intolerable. By a further sensitive whim of the Marchesa the guests were required after the first sonata (D major) to move over from the Silver Room (Baroque) to the Golden Room (early Rococo), there to enjoy the second sonata. For the Silver Room had a major resonance, the Golden, it could not be disputed, a minor.

At this point I must remark that the tedious elegance which clings to the flute sonatas of second-rank, and more particularly of newly discovered, masters of this period, was in the present case to be explained by the fact that no such person as Giambattista Bloch had ever lived. The works here performed had in reality been composed by the musicologist Weltli. Although this circumstance did not become known till later, I cannot, in retrospect, help feeling it a humiliation for the Marchesa that she should have employed her last moments in the interpretation, however masterly, of a forgery.

During the second movement of the F minor sonata I saw a rat creeping along the wall. I was astonished. At first I thought it might have been lured from its hole by the sound of the flute—such things do happen, they say—but it was creeping in the opposite direction. It was followed by another rat. I looked at the guests. They had not noticed anything, and indeed most of them were keeping their eyes closed in order to be able to abandon themselves to the harmonies of Weltli's forgery. I now heard a dull reverberation, like very distant thunder. The floor began to vibrate. Again I looked at the guests. If they had heard anything— and something they must be hearing—it was at any rate not discernible from their hunched-up postures. I however was made uneasy by these strange symptoms.

A manservant entered. This is barely the place to remark that in the unusual costume worn by the Marchesa's domes-

tic staff he looked like a character out of *Tosca*. He went
up to the performers and whispered something in the Marchesa's ear. I saw her turn pale. How well it suited her in
the dim candlelight! But she controlled herself and without
interruption played the *andante* calmly to the end. Then she
nodded to the flautist, stood up, and addressed the company.

"Ladies and gentlemen," she said, "I have just learnt that
the foundations of the island and those of the palace with
them are breaking up. The Office of Submarine Works has
been informed. The right thing, I think we shall all agree,
is to go on with the music."

She sat down again, gave the sign to Monsieur Beranger,
and they played the *allegro con brio,* the last movement,
which did seem to me at the time, though I had yet no
inkling that it was a forgery, little suited to the uniqueness
of the situation.

On the polished floor small puddles were forming. The
reverberation had grown louder and sounded nearer. Most
of the guests were now sitting upright, their faces ashen in
the candlelight, and looking as if they were long dead already. I stood up and said, "I'm going," not so loud as to
give offense to the musicians, but loud enough to intimate
to the other guests that I had the courage to admit my fear.
The floor was now almost evenly covered with water. Although
I walked on tiptoe, I could not help splashing an evening
dress or two as I passed. But, in view of what was soon
to come, the damage I did must be reckoned inconsider-
able. Few of the guests thought me worthy of a glance,
but I did not care. As I opened the door to the passage a
wave of water poured into the room and caused Lady Fitz-
jones (the preserver of Celtic customs) to draw her fur
wrap more closely about her—no doubt a reflex movement,
for it could not be of any use. Before shutting the door behind me I saw Herr von Perlhuln (the neo-mystic, not the
Abraham-a-Santa Clara expert) casting a half-contemptuous,
half-melancholy glance in my direction. He too was now
sitting in water almost to his knees. So was the Marchesa,
who could no longer use the pedals. I do not as a matter
of fact know how essential they are on the harpsichord. I
remember thinking that if the piece had been a cello sonata,
they would perforce have had to break it off here since the
instrument would not sound in water. Strange what irrelevant
thoughts occur to one in such moments.

In the entrance hall it was suddenly as quiet as in a grotto, only in the distance a sound of rushing water was to be heard. I divested myself of my tail coat and was soon swimming through the sinking palace toward the portals. My splashes echoed mysteriously from the walls and columns. Not a soul was to be seen. Evidently the servants had all fled. And why should they not? They had no obligation to the true and eternal culture, and those assembled here had no further need of their services.

Outside the moon shone as if nothing were amiss, and yet a world, no less, was here sinking beneath the ocean. As if at a great distance I could still hear the high notes of Monsieur Beranger's flute. He had a wonderful *embouchure*, that one must allow him.

I unhitched the last gondola which the escaping servants had left behind and pushed out to sea. Through the windows past which I paddled the water was now flooding into the palace. I saw that the guests had risen from their seats. The sonata must be at an end, for they were clapping, their hands held high over their heads, since the water was now up to their chins. With dignity the Marchesa and Monsieur Beranger were acknowledging the applause, though in the circumstances they could not bow.

The water had now reached the candles. Slowly they were extinguished, and as the darkness grew, it became quiet; the applause was silenced. Suddenly I heard the crash and roar of a building in collapse. The Palazzo was falling. I steered the gondola seaward so as not to be hit by plaster fragments.

After paddling some hundreds of yards across the lagoon in the direction of the island of San Giorgio, I turned round once more. The sea lay dead calm in the moonlight as if no island had ever stood there. A pity about the bathtub, I thought, for that was a loss which could never be made good. The thought was perhaps rather heartless but experience teaches us that we need a certain distance from such events in order to appreciate their full scope.

JAKOV LIND

Journey through the Night

Jakov Lind, born in Vienna in 1927, fled as a boy to Holland when the Germans annexed Austria, surviving there with forged papers. After various jobs as construction worker, fisherman, photographer, and orange picker, he settled in England, where he now lives with his wife and two children. His first volume of short stories, Soul of Wood, brought him an international reputation. Savage and surrealistic, his stories often picture a world so emotionally dislocated that only the madman is sane. The cannibal in "Journey through the Night" comes to seem more reasonable than the victim, who can find no more reason for living than to take a walk in the city.

WHAT DO YOU see when you look back? Not a thing. And when you look ahead? Even less. That's right. That's how it is.

It was three o'clock in the morning and raining. The train didn't stop anywhere. There were lights somewhere in the countryside, but you couldn't be sure if they were windows or stars.

The tracks were tracks—but why shouldn't there be tracks in the clouds?

Paris was somewhere at the end of the trip. Which Paris? The earthly Paris—with cafés, green buses, fountains, and grimy whitewashed walls? Or the heavenly Paris? Carpeted bathrooms with a view of the Bois de Boulogne?

From SOUL OF WOOD AND OTHER STORIES. Translated by Ralph Manheim. Reprinted by permission of Grove Press, Inc. Copyright © 1964 by Jonathan Cape Ltd., London.

The fellow-passenger looked still paler in the bluish light
His nose was straight, his lips thin, his teeth uncommonly small
He had slick hair like a seal. A moustache, that's what he needs
He could do a balancing act on his nose. Under his clothes he i
wet. Why doesn't he show his tusks?

After 'that's how it is' he said nothing. That settled every
thing. Now he is smoking.

His skin is grey, that's obvious—it's taut, too. If he scratche
himself it will tear. What else is there to look at? He has only
one face and his suitcase. What has he got in the suitcase
Tools? Saw, hammer and chisel? Maybe a drill? What does h
need a drill for? To bore holes in skulls? Some people drink bee
that way. When empty, they can be painted. Will he paint m
face? What colours? Watercolour or oil? And what for? Children
at Eastertime play with empty eggshells. His play with skulls.

Well, he said non-committally, putting out his cigarette. H
crushed it against the aluminum, making a scratching sound
Well, how about it?

I don't know, I said. I can't make up my mind. Doesn't th
fellow understand a joke?

Maybe you need a little more spunk, he said. Now's the tim
to make up your mind; in half an hour you'll be asleep anyway
then I'll do what I want with you.

I won't sleep tonight, I said. You've given me fair warning.

Warning won't do you any good, he said. Between three an
four everybody falls into a dead sleep. You're educated, yo
should know that.

Yes, I know. But I got self-control.

Between three and four, said the man, rubbing the moustach
that was yet to grow, all of us get locked away in our littl
cubicles, don't hear nothing, don't see nothing. We die, every
last one of us. Dying restores us, after four we wake up and lif
goes on. Without that people couldn't stick it out so long.

I don't believe a word of it. You can't saw me up.

I can't eat you as you are, he said. Sawing's the only way
First the legs, then the arms, then the head. Everything in it
proper order.

What do you do with the eyes?

Suck 'em.

Can the ears be digested or have they got bones in them?

No bones, but they're tough. Anyway, I don't eat everything
do you think I'm a pig?

A seal is what I thought.

That's more like it. So he admitted it. A seal, I knew it. How come he speaks German? Seals speak Danish and nobody can understand them.

How is it you don't speak Danish?

I was born in Sankt Pölten, he said. We didn't speak Danish in our family. He's being evasive. What would you expect? But maybe he is from Sankt Pölten; I've heard there are such people in the region.

And you live in France?

What's it to you? In half an hour you'll be gone. It's useful to know things when you've a future ahead of you, but in your situation . . .

Of course he's insane, but what can I do? He has locked the compartment (where did he get the keys?), Paris will never come. He's picked the right kind of weather. You can't see a thing and it's raining; of course he can kill me. When you're scared you've got to talk fast. Would you kindly describe it again. Kindly will flatter his vanity. Murderers are sick. Sick people are vain. The kindly is getting results.

Well, first comes the wooden mallet, he said, exactly like a schoolteacher . . . you always have to explain everything twice to stupid pupils; stupidity is a kind of fear, teachers give out cuffs or marks.

. . . then after the mallet comes the razor, you've got to let the blood out, most of it at least, even so you always mess up your chin on the liver; well, and then, as we were saying, comes the saw.

Do you take off the leg at the hip or the knee?

Usually at the hip, sometimes the knee. At the knee when I have time.

And the arms?

The arms? Never at the elbow, always at the shoulder. Why?

Maybe it's just a habit, don't ask me. There isn't much meat on the forearm, in your case there's none at all, but when it's attached, it looks like something. How do you eat the leg of a roast chicken?

He was right.

If you want pointers about eating people, ask a cannibal. Do you use spices?

Only salt. Human flesh is sweet, you know that yourself. Who likes sweet meat?

He opened the suitcase. No, I screamed, I'm not asleep yet.

Don't be afraid, you scarecat, I just wanted to show you I wasn't kidding. He fished about among the tools. There were only five implements in the suitcase, but they were lying around loose. It was a small suitcase, rather like a doctor's bag. But a doctor's instruments are strapped to the velvet lid. Here they were lying around loose. Hammer, saw, drill, chisel and pliers. Ordinary carpenter's tools. There was also a rag. Wrapped in the rag was the salt-cellar. A common glass salt-cellar such as you find on the tables in cheap restaurants. He's stolen it somewhere, I said to myself. He's a thief.

He held the salt-cellar under my nose. There was salt in it. He shook some out on my hand. Taste it, he said, first-class salt. He saw the rage in my face, I was speechless. He laughed. Those little teeth revolted me.

Yes, he said and laughed again, I bet you'd rather be salted alive than eaten dead.

He shut the suitcase and lit another cigarette. It was half past three. The train was flying over the rails, but there won't be any Paris at the end. Neither earthly nor heavenly. I was in a trap. Death comes to every man. Does it really matter how you die? You can get run over, you can get shot by accident, at a certain age your heart is likely to give out, or you can die of lung cancer, which is very common nowadays. One way or another you kick the bucket. Why not be eaten by a madman in the Nice-Paris express?

All is vanity, what else. You've got to die, only you don't want to. You don't have to live, but you want to. Only necessary things are important. Big fish eat little ones, the lark eats the worm and yet how sweetly he sings, cats eat mice and no one ever killed a cat for it—every animal eats every other just to stay alive, men eat men, what's unnatural about that? Is it more natural to eat pigs or calves? Does it hurt more when you can say 'it hurts'? Animals don't cry, human beings cry when a relative dies, but how can anybody cry over his own death? Am I so fond of myself? So it must be vanity. Nobody's heart breaks over his own death. That's the way it is.

A feeling of warmth and well-being came over me. Here is a madman, he wants to eat me. But at least he wants something. What do I want? Not to eat anybody. Is that so noble? What's left when you don't want to do what you certainly ought to do?

If you don't do that which disgusts you, what becomes of your disgust? It sticks in your throat. Nothing sticks in the throat of the man from Sankt Pölten. He swallows all.

A voice spoke very softly, it sounded almost affectionate: There, you see you're getting sleepy, that comes from thinking. What have you got to look forward to in Paris? Paris is only a city. Whom do you need anyway, and who needs you? You're going to Paris. Well, what of it? Sex and drinking won't make you any happier. And certainly working won't. Money won't do you a particle of good. What are you getting out of life? Just go to sleep. You won't wake up, I can promise you.

But I don't want to die, I whispered. Not yet. I want . . . to go for a walk in Paris.

Go for a walk in Paris? Big deal. It will only make you tired. There are enough people taking walks and looking at the shop windows. The restaurants are overcrowded. So are the whore-houses. Nobody needs you in Paris. Just do me a favour, go to sleep. The night won't go on for ever; I'll have to gobble everything down so fast you'll give me a belly-ache.

I've got to eat you. In the first place I'm hungry, and in the second place I like you. I told you right off that I liked you and you thought, the guy is a queer. But now you know. I'm a simple cannibal. It's not a profession, it's a need. Good Lord, man, try to understand: now you've got an aim in life. Your life has purpose, thanks to me. You think it was by accident you came into my compartment? There's no such thing as an accident. I watched you all along the platform in Nice. And then you came into my compartment. Why mine and not someone else's? Because I'm so good-looking? Don't make me laugh. Is a seal good-looking? You came in here because you knew there'd be something doing.

Very slowly he opened the little suitcase. He took out the mallet and closed the suitcase. He held the mallet in his hand.

Well, how about it? he said.

Just a minute, I said. Just a minute. And suddenly I stood up. God only knows how I did it, but I stood up on my two feet and stretched out my hand. The little wire snapped, the lead seal fell, the train hissed and screeched. Screams came from next door. Then the train stopped. The man from

Sankt Pölten stowed the mallet quickly in his suitcase and took his coat; he was at the door in a flash. He opened the door and looked around: I pity you, he said. This bit of foolishness is going to cost you a ten-thousand-franc fine, you nitwit, now you'll have to take your walk in Paris.

People crowded into the compartment, a conductor and a policeman appeared. Two soldiers and a pregnant woman shook their fists at me.

Already the seal from Sankt Pölten was outside, right under my window. He shouted something. I opened the window: See, he shouted, you've made an ass of yourself for life. Look who wants to live. He spat and shrugged his shoulders. Carrying his suitcase in his right hand, he stepped cautiously down the embankment and vanished in the dark. Like a country doctor on his way to deliver a baby.

HEINZ HUBER

The New Apartment

Heinz Huber (1922–   ) is a native of Württemberg and grew up in a village in the Black Forest. His study of applied graphics in Stuttgart was interrupted by military service and a period as a prisoner of war. Upon his release in 1947, he found work as a window decorator for a chain grocery store, and it was at this time that he began his first writing attempts. Through a fortunate contact, he was able to get a hearing for his work on radio, and had several radio plays and features successfully produced.

Since 1953 Huber has been a TV director for documentary features in Stuttgart. In 1963 he published The Third Reich, *a two-volume work containing his written documentaries and including several of his short stories. His somewhat surrealistic and satirical style is well illustrated in "The New Apartment."*

THE OTHER EVENING we were invited round to the Messemers. Marx Messemer is a colleague of mine at the works, and a most gratifying friendship has grown up in course of time between our two families. Without wishing to overestimate our importance, I do believe that the function we fulfill through modest social gatherings like this is of some significance. It is the development of a form of society, of a social type even, which is adapted to our changed environment. When we began, there was no social intercourse and no society. Our grandparents were dead, our parents had

Translated by Christopher Holme. Reprinted by permission of Diogenes Verlag and the translator.

made a mess of things, and those who had made rather less
of a mess were not our parents. A zero-point situation,
as the literary periodicals called it. I think I can say that
we coped with this situation rather well. We read the literary
periodicals and we looked for a profession and found one.
We began to earn money and began also to invite one another out, and today we constitute a kind of new social
grouping, one which is beginning to develop a style of its
own, and which once more commands every respect.

To return to the Messemers, it is not long since they
moved into a new apartment. Our place, too, is new but
we have been in it rather longer. The Messemers have had
theirs done up completely new, and we were keen to see
how it would look.

The fact is that I think a lot of Marx Messemer. Or let's
say that I admire him, at least up to a certain point. What
I admire above all is the reliability of his judgment, his
taste, his modernity. With him everything is exactly right,
while with me there's always something just short of per-
fection. In our home the new tea service always has two
cups broken and the tea table is still one of the old kidney-
shaped kind. Somehow we just don't manage to replace it
with a more modern piece, though we know perfectly well
what we want—long and narrow, in reddish-brown wood. It
would go so well with our sand-colored chair covers. And
then a pigeon-blue carpet—but we'll never achieve them.
At least not for the present.

The Messemers on the other hand—as we walked in at
their door, from our feet to the horizon of the far-distant
baseboard there stretched a fine pile surface in graphite gray.
At the vanishing point of the perspective lines, in front of
a bare wall, a strange-looking branch projected from a large
glass vase, standing on the ground. Echoes of surrealism, I
thought to myself, early Chirico. Perhaps Messemer himself
was unconscious of them. He says he understands nothing
about art, says he's a rationalist, a technician, a man of
his hands (no doubt, so are we all) but he quite simply has
it, that unerring sense of style, that infallible modernity.

A well-marked characteristic of our particular circle is
that we have no feelings of mutual rivalry. Everyone is
conscious of his own worth, even as I am, and so I have
no reason to envy Marx Messemer. Yet when I saw his work
table I was seized by a spasm of envy. There stood not, as
might have been expected, a breathtakingly lovely, elegantly

simple, wickedly expensive writing desk, Scandinavian of course and made by hand (he could have afforded it after all, just as I could) but no, not a bit of it. There stood a slab of raw deal, massive, of unusual size, in its natural whiteness, not polished but planed, and on it his typewriter. That's Marx Messemer all over. He's an expert in cool jazz, and that's what his whole flat is like—cool jazz converted into armchairs, carpets, lamps (or rather light-fittings), and pictures.

For a long time we were all devotees of the theory that pictures had played out their part as adornments to a room, and our craze was all for empty walls. That was of course an extreme fad, and we soon moved away from it. Nothing could be more foreign to our outlook than snobbery. We aim to have principles, but we try also to modify them. So the Messemers once more had a picture on the wall, placed asymmetrically on a very daring wallpaper, one picture only, but that an original. I stood in front of it and was annoyed with myself. I too have pictures on the wall, but prints, fastened to it with drawing pins. To this day I have somehow just not managed at least to have them framed, though I'm always meaning to.

For Messemer such things are no problem and that's what impresses me so much about him. Exact improvisation, cool jazz, precision of living style.

We stood about informally, informally chatting on the graphite-gray carpet, holding beautifully shaped glasses in our hands—brandy and soda. Whisky and soda, that's high society, at our social level it would be snobbery, and snobbish is the one thing we're not. We have a well-defined sense of what is appropriate. We're middle-class (I don't mean bourgeois, of course) and we know what's fitting for us. Brandy and soda.

Besides on social occasions like these we're generally moderate with the drink—hence the soda. The only one who drank neat brandy on this particular evening was Fräulein Kliesing who'd also been asked, and is anyhow for my taste a little bit eccentric, yes, decidedly eccentric. It's something I'm not so keen on, and I have trained myself little by little to a certain tolerance, till now I really rather like Fräulein Kliesing. We all have our faults.

There was a slight *contretemps* as we were all arranging ourselves up at the sitting end. Fräulein Kliesing lowered herself into the Messemers' new armchair but immediately shot up again as if she had sat on a pin; her salmon-pink dress, she said, clashed horribly with the raspberry pink of the chair cover, and she was right, too. What made it worse was that this "shocking" pink of the cover was chosen with great finesse to contrast with the equally shocking emerald green of the wallpaper behind it. I should never have dared anything like that, but Messemer does dare and, you see, he brings it off.

In any case harmony was restored when Fräulein Kliesing transferred her salmon-colored dress to the clear gray of the couch while my wife's sky-blue contrasted correctly with the raspberry pink chair. We're not esthetes, let this be clearly stated, but technicians, men of our hands. Yet just for that very reason it disturbs us if something of this kind, or indeed anything at all, is not quite in key.

In my home it is the sofa cushions which are wrong. Not that they're actually in bad taste, but they have come together rather by chance, not so carefully matched with one another and with their surroundings as at the Messemers'. But that can easily be changed.

We take such a matter no more seriously than it deserves and the color problem of Fräulein Kliesing and the armchair did not occupy us for long. We were now talking about the Messemers' new apartment in general.

"How did you find this place to begin with?" "Well, we really did have rather a stroke of luck," said Kay, Messemer's delicious wife. "We hunted for ages, but there was always something. Extra conversion costs, and so on. You know the story. Then finally someone we knew, who had some connection with this property, told us there might be a possibility here. Only we should have to do it up ourselves. I didn't want to at first, but Marx thought . . ."

"I was for it straight away," said Marx. "But you can't imagine what it looked like in here when I first came to see the place. I could never have dreamed that anything like it existed nowadays."

Messemer took his time, lit his pipe, poured himself another brandy and soda, and then told the story of the apartment, and we sat in the new armchairs on the graphite-gray carpet, drank brandy and soda, and listened—although, to be candid, we were not all that interested. But what should one talk about? We neither can nor do we want to make fashionable conversation, and our common professional affairs, well, there's a tacit agreement that on such social occasions they

are not discussed. Or should we have talked about Marcel
Proust? One doesn't talk about Proust, with us you might say
Proust is taken for granted, just like our love for our wives.
To speak about the one would be sentimentality, about the
other snobbery, betraying in either case a faulty sense of
style. Rather the Messemers' new apartment than that. Besides which, he tells a good story, even though he does overdo
it a bit at times.

"When I first saw this room," he began, "it wasn't being
lived in any longer, but the furniture was still here. I couldn't
imagine how any human creature could have found room
to exist here among all the furniture. I could see nothing
but furniture. That's to say, at first I didn't even see that,
the windows were curtained, the room dark. It was only
when the woman with the keys turned on the light that
solid ground began to be distinguishable in the darkness. The
source of the gloomy light was a low-hanging lampshade,
above shot silk and dust, below long, rectangular plate-glass
pendants and cobwebs. All this close down over a broad
table-top, stains and dust here too, losing themselves in the
half-darkness behind. At the sides, chair backs reared themselves, and over the nearest of them there hung an old-fashioned woman's hat. Behind it serried ranks of bookshelves,
cupboards, whatnots, a sofa in the darkness, deeper still in
the darkness an endless vista of grand piano, piles of books
on the piano, dust on the books, scarcely room to move
between them, not so much a living room as a second-hand
furniture dealer's warehouse. Or a stage set for 'The Mad-
woman of Chaillot'—if it had been written by Ionesco."

In descriptions like these Messemer is unbeatable. When
he's up to his style, his descriptions range themselves one
on another like the colored flags which a conjuror pulls out
of his mouth on a never-ending string, gay and effortless.
Fräulein Kliesing stared at Messemer in open-mouthed admiration. Moreover her admiration was so to speak sexless,
for on the one hand Messemer had his delicious wife, and
on the other Fräulein Kliesing had a man friend of her own.
So nothing of that sort. We don't much go in for erotic
disturbance, any more than we go in for illness.

Messemer was in full swing. "A nineteenth-century lumber
room. The sloughed-off body-case of an old-fashioned insect.
The flat had belonged to a professor's widow. I think he
was a painter or something of the sort, but nothing distinguished. Later I found in the cellar a few rolls of painted

canvas, landscape sketches and portrait studies. They were
so stiff and brittle that the paint came off in layers when I
unrolled them. I can even say the painting was not at all
bad, for my taste."

"A bid academic surely," said Fräulein Kliesing.

"I wouldn't say that, not altogether. At any rate, the
life led by the professor's widow was no longer very academic. Between ourselves, the woman in charge of the flat
told me that the old lady, having no more room among all
this furniture and old lumber, had moved into the cubby-
hole next door. . . ."

"Where we now have our built-in wardrobe and shoe
closet," Kay put in.

". . . and there behind a cupboard arranged herself a
sort of berth on which most of her last days were spent.
Once, she said, the old lady did not appear for four days,
so that in the house it was thought something must have
happened to her and the police were sent for to break open
the door. But the old lady had only been lying behind her
cupboard and staring at the wall. There was nothing else the
matter with her. She was in fact very old, an old lady
with whalebone and crumbling lace about her neck, contemplating in the gloom the professor's half-finished oil paintings on the wall, perhaps thinking of her honeymoon journey
to Florence or perhaps of nothing at all, just fading away,
slowly dying. . . ."

Messemer left his story in the air as if, having served
him for a felicitous piece of description, he no longer had
any further use for it. Now it was his wife's turn.

"And the dirt in the rooms, after all the old rags had
been removed, you can't imagine. The wallpaper hung in
tatters, covered with dust, or had been fastened back with
drawing pins; the ceiling was black with soot and cobwebs,
with huge cracks in it—we had to strip all the plaster off,
right to the laths—and the whole floor had to be replaned
it was so dirty. At first we thought of varnishing it. . . ."

"Matte or glossy?" asked my wife.

"Matte of course, I imagine?" said Fräulein Kliesing.

"Probably glossy," answered Kay, "But then we liked this
velour carpeting so much that we decided to closecarpet the
whole room instead, although that worked out a good deal
more expensive."

"In the long run it's worth it, though," said Fräulein
Kliesing. "When you have a floor varnished, you still have to

have it waxed after a time, and then after two or three years
the varnish must be renewed, while a good carpet lasts for
years." Fräulein Kliesing, who had a charming little flat of
her own, was quite an expert in such matters.

The nice thing about our circle is that we never work a
subject to death; we're interested in everything, so that our
talk never gets boring. Without meaning to, we have developed a very pleasant style of social intercourse; neither
stiff conventionality nor amorphous bohemianism, but a free
and open, sober modernity. We keep clear of fashionable and
tepid conversation just as carefully as we do those night-
long discussions which go round and round in circles. One
must avoid exaggeration at all costs.

We turned again to the previous history of the Messemers' apartment.

"It wasn't altogether easy to get hold of this apartment,"
said Messemer. "In this room here as I've said lived the
professor's widow, and she had finally died. But that was
far from making it possible for us to move in, for in the
second room, where our dining recess now is, there lived a
second old lady who didn't die and who obstinately refused
to go into an old people's home, although it was really more
necessary for her than for her companion. The two women
had been friends when years before they had taken this
apartment. It was then new of course. But time—day after
day so cramped together, ill, poor, a bit odd, the two of
them—time dissipated their friendship. In the end they had
the connecting door between the two rooms nailed up, and
the great tiled stove which heated both rooms was no longer
kept going. Instead each one put a small iron stove in her
room. Up there behind the new wallpaper you can still see
the hole which had to be made for the stovepipes."

"Really!" said Fräulein Kliesing. "Let's hope we don't all
get like that one day."

"The professor's widow died simply of old age, but as for
the one in the other room, she was certainly a bit dotty,"
Messemer said.

"About birdseed," his wife added. "Yes, birdseed. There
can be no other explanation. Who would like another drink?"

We allowed our glasses to be refilled with brandy and
soda, and Messemer continued, although his story, interesting as it was, for my taste was already going on rather
too long.

"This one, in contrast to the other, had almost no furniture. Her walls, doors, and windowframes were stuck all over with nails and hooks of all shapes and sizes—for clothes, for towels, for bits of string with nothing attached to them any more, for key labels, dishcloths, oven rakes, and spotted photographs of babies long since grown up. A great deal of this stuff we later found, when we were able to get into the room, under the great heap of birdseed. The woman must have lived the whole time with a regular mountain of birdseed in the room—it took up a quarter of the floor space. Just simply poured out on the floor knee high. The house people told us how she had the window practically always open and the birds flew in and out the whole time, summer and winter. The birds come hopping around the room even now, though it's quite a while since the mountain of birdseed was removed. And we found the oddest things under the birdseed: medicine bottles, bits of stuff, old illustrated papers, prospectuses of bathing resorts, a glove, and a whole collection of varicolored powders each carefully folded up in paper—all buried under the birdseed."

"How ghastly!" said Fräulein Kliesing.

"Well," said Messemer, "the whole thing could almost have been called tragic. So far as can be discovered, the husband of the birdseed crone got lost in the Third Reich. And he wasn't even politically active. They said he had passed on something or other to someone else, or that sort of thing. Probably the whole thing was a mistake. In any case the husband never came back. It was his wife, then, who later on had this room and the heap of birdseed. The place was really not fit for human habitation, but she simply refused to move into the old people's home. What was more, she couldn't pay the rent any longer."

I had a feeling that Messemer now had really gone a bit too far, for an ordinary party.

Kay threw him a glance and told the rest of the story herself. "After the death of the professor's widow the birdseed woman became the principal tenant of the apartment. So first of all we had ourselves put down as nominal subtenants of the room that was now free, so that we should have a prior claim on the whole apartment if the birdseed woman should go. And besides that we paid the landlord the arrears of rent of the two old women. Then we had a word with the tenants of the other flats in the building, and wrote to the relations of the birdseed woman and got a place for her in an old people's home. And then we organized the removal for her and undertook the sale of those things she couldn't take with her into the home—it wasn't much in any case. Finally, after we had so taken her in hand and arranged everything for her, she presumably could see no further reason for holding out and moved to the old people's home where she has since settled down quite contentedly. We had the whole apartment transferred to us as principal tenants and could now begin to do it up. What we made of it you can see for yourselves. You wouldn't believe it was the same place if you'd seen the rooms before, when the two old women still lived here."

"It's really a delightful apartment," said Fräulein Kliesing. "I'm quite enthusiastic over the way you've done it. You couldn't possibly tell it was an old one."

"No, you hardly could," said Kay smiling, "only in the one room we simply cannot altogether get rid of the bird-seed. Every so often I find myself sweeping a handful of it out of cracks in the floor. I thought it would be better once we had a vacuum cleaner, but we have got one now and it's just as bad. Perhaps we shall simply have to cover the floor with linoleum."

"I shouldn't have linoleum," said my wife. "It shows every footmark."

"No, I'm against linoleum, too," said Fräulein Kliesing. "I find that linoleum has more or less had its day."

Of course we didn't spend the whole evening talking about carpets and built-in cupboards. After Messemer had once more proved his power to hold an audience, for which I so envy him, he played us his newest cool jazz records. Then we discussed the question whether illnesses have physical or mental causes, and finally Messemer gave an account of the World Exhibition in Brussels. Again he was very entertaining, on top of his subject, sparkling like the outer skin of the Atomium itself with metallic phrases. All in all, the evening, as always at the Messemers', was most enjoyable.

At about one o'clock we took our leave and went home. We had to take a taxi because we have no car. The Messemers of course have a car, but we for some reason or other haven't achieved one yet. But I'm quite confident we shall have one next year or the year after—provided that nothing comes in between, which I think rather improbable.

We've got plenty of time yet to get ourselves properly fixed up.

HEINRICH BÖLL

Murke's Collected Silences

*Heinrich Böll (1917-   ). A Catholic, an artist,
and a sharp critic of contemporary life, Böll is one
of the important voices in modern Germany. His
stories and his novels speak strongly against the
stupidity of war and express his fears for the sterility he sees in much of modern society. His novel*
The Clown *has been widely acclaimed, as has the
1974 novel,* The Lost Honor of Katherina Blum. *He
won the Nobel Prize in 1972, and his many short
stories have impressively widened his American audience. Much of his work is still untranslated. Essentially a moralist and a humanist, Böll seeks out
authentic values in a society he sees given over to
materialism and hypocrisy.*

EVERY MORNING, AFTER entering Broadcasting House, Murke
performed an existential exercise. Here in this building the
elevator was the kind known as a paternoster—open cages
carried on a conveyor belt, like beads on a rosary, moving
slowly and continuously from bottom to top, across the top
of the elevator shaft, down to the bottom again, so that
passengers could step on and off at any floor. Murke would
jump onto the paternoster but, instead of getting off at
the second floor, where his office was, he would let himself
be carried on up, past the third, fourth, fifth floors, and he
was seized with panic every time the cage rose above the
level of the fifth floor and ground its way up into the empty
space where oily chains, greasy rods and groaning machinery
pulled and pushed the elevator from an upward into a down-

ward direction, and Murke would stare in terror at the bare brick walls, and sigh with relief as the elevator passed through the lock, dropped into place, and began its slow descent, past the fifth, fourth, third floors. Murke knew his fears were unfounded: obviously nothing would ever happen, nothing could ever happen, and even if it did it could be nothing worse than finding himself up there at the top when the elevator stopped moving and being shut in for an hour or two at the most. He was never without a book in his pocket, and cigarettes; yet as long as the building had been standing, for three years, the elevator had never once failed. On certain days it was inspected, days when Murke had to forego those four and a half seconds of panic, and on these days he was irritable and restless, like people who had gone without breakfast. He needed this panic, the way other people need their coffee, their oatmeal or their fruit juice.

So when he stepped off the elevator at the second floor, the home of the Cultural Department, he felt light-hearted and relaxed, as light-hearted and relaxed as anyone who loves and understands his work. He would unlock the door to his office, walk slowly over to his armchair, sit down and light a cigarette. He was always first on the job. He was young, intelligent, and had a pleasant manner, and even his arrogance, which occasionally flashed out for a moment— even that was forgiven him since it was known he had majored in psychology and graduated *cum laude.*

For two days now, Murke had been obliged to go without his panic-breakfast: unusual circumstances had required him to get to Broadcasting House at eight a.m., dash off to a studio and begin work right away, for he had been told by the Director of Broadcasting to go over the two talks on The Nature of Art which the great Bur-Malottke had taped and to cut them according to Bur-Malottke's instructions. Bur-Malottke, who had converted to Catholicism during the religious fervor of 1945, had suddenly, "overnight," as he put it, "felt religious qualms," he had "suddenly felt he might be blamed for contributing to the religious overtones in radio," and he had decided to omit God, Who occurred frequently in both his half-hour talks on The Nature of Art, and replaced Him with a formula more in keeping with the mental outlook which he had professed before 1945. Bur-Malottke had suggested to the producer that the word God be replaced by the formula "that higher Being Whom we revere," but he had refused to retape the talks, requesting instead that God be cut out of the tapes and replaced by "that higher Being Whom we revere." Bur-Malottke was a friend of the Director, but this friendship was not the reason for the Director's willingness to oblige him: Bur-Malottke was a man one simply did not contradict. He was the author of numerous books of a belletristic-philosophical-religious and art-historical nature, he was on the editorial staff of three periodicals and two newspapers, and closely connected with the largest publishing house. He had agreed to come to Broadcasting House for fifteen minutes on Wednesday and tape the words "that higher Being Whom we revere" as often as God was mentioned in his talks: the rest was up to the technical experts.

It had not been easy for the Director to find someone whom he could ask to do the job; he thought of Murke, but the suddenness with which he thought of Murke made him suspicious—he was a dynamic, robust individual—so he spent five minutes going over the problem in his mind, considered Schwendling, Humkoke, Miss Broldin, but he ended up with Murke. The Director did not like Murke; he had, of course, taken him on as soon as his name had been put forward, the way a zoo director, whose real love is the rabbits and the deer, naturally accepts wild animals too for the simple reason that a zoo must contain wild animals—but what the Director really loved was rabbits and deer, and for him Murke was an intellectual wild animal. In the end his dynamic personality triumphed, and he instructed Murke to cut Bur-Malottke's talks. The talks were to be given on Thursday and Friday, and Bur-Malottke's misgivings had come to him on Sunday night—one might just as well commit suicide as contradict Bur-Malottke, and the Director was much too dynamic to think of suicide.

So Murke spent Monday afternoon and Tuesday morning listening three times to the two half-hour talks on The Nature of Art; he had cut out God, and in the short breaks which he took, during which he silently smoked a cigarette with the technician, reflected on the dynamic personality of the Director and the inferior Being Whom Bur-Malottke revered. He had never read a line of Bur-Malottke, never heard one of his talks before. Monday night he had dreamed of a staircase as tall and steep as the Eiffel Tower, and he had climbed it but soon noticed that the stairs were slippery with soap, and the Director stood down below and called out: "Go on, Murke, go on . . . show us what you can do—go on!" Tuesday night the dream had been similar: he had been at a fairground, strolled casually over to the roller coaster, paid his thirty pfennigs to a man whose face seemed familiar, and as he got on the roller coaster he saw that it was at least ten miles long, he knew there was no going back, and realized that the man who had taken his thirty pfennings had been the Director. Both mornings after these dreams he had not needed the harmless panic-breakfast up there in the empty space above the paternoster.

Now it was Wednesday. He was smiling as he entered the building, got into the paternoster, let himself be carried up as far as the sixth floor—four and a half seconds of panic, the grinding of the chains, the bare brick walls—he rode down as far as the fourth floor, got out and walked toward the studio where he had an appointment with Bur-Malottke. It was two minutes to ten as he sat down in his green chair, waved to the technician and lit his cigarette. His breathing was quiet, he took a piece of paper out of his breast pocket and glanced at the clock: Bur-Malottke was always on time, at least he had a reputation for being punctual; and as the second hand completed the sixtieth minute of the tenth hour, the minute hand slipped onto the twelve, the hour hand onto the ten, the door opened, and in walked Bur-Malottke. Murke got up, and with a pleasant smile walked over to Bur-Malottke and introduced himself. Bur-Malottke shook hands, smiled and said: "Well, let's get started!" Murke picked up the sheet of paper from the table, put his cigarette between his lips, and, reading from the list, said to Bur-Malottke:

"In the two talks, God occurs precisely twenty-seven times —so I must ask you to repeat twenty-seven times the words we are to splice. We would appreciate it if we might ask you to repeat them thirty-five times, so as to have a certain reserve when it comes to splicing."

"Granted," said Bur-Malottke with a smile, and sat down.

"There is one difficulty, however," said Murke: "where God occurs in the genitive, such as 'God's will,' 'God's love,' 'God's purpose,' He must be replaced by the noun in question followed by the words 'of that higher Being Whom we revere.' I must ask you, therefore, to repeat the words 'the will' twice, 'the love' twice, and 'the purpose' three times, followed each time by 'of that higher Being Whom we revere,' giving us a total of seven genitives. Then there is one spot where you use the vocative and say 'O God'— here I suggest you substitute 'O Thou higher Being Whom we revere.' Everywhere else only the nominative case applies."

It was clear that Bur-Malottke had not thought of these complications; he began to sweat, the grammatical transposition bothered him. Murke went on: "In all," he said, in his pleasant, friendly manner, "the twenty-seven sentences will require one minute and twenty seconds radio time, whereas the twenty-seven times 'God' occurs require only twenty seconds. In other words, in order to take care of your alterations we shall have to cut half a minute from each talk."

Bur-Malottke sweated more heavily than ever; inwardly he cursed his sudden misgivings and asked: "I suppose you've already done the cutting, have you?"

"Yes, I have," said Murke, pulling a flat metal box out of his pocket; he opened it and held it out to Bur-Malottke: it contained some darkish sound-tape scraps, and Murke said softly: "God twenty-seven times, spoken by you. Would you care to have them?"

"No I would not," said Bur-Malottke, furious. "I'll speak to the Director about the two half-minutes. What comes after my talks in the program?"

"Tomorrow," said Murke, "your talk is followed by the regular program Neighborly News, edited by Grehm."

"Damn," said Bur-Malottke, "it's no use asking Grehm for a favor."

"And the day after tomorrow," said Murke, "your talk is followed by Let's Go Dancing."

"Oh God, that's Huglieme," groaned Bur-Malottke, "never yet has Light Entertainment given way to Culture by as much as a fifth of a minute."

"No," said Murke, "it never has, at least—" and his youthful face took on an expression of irreproachable modesty— "at least not since I've been working here."

"Very well," said Bur-Malottke and glanced at the clock, "we'll be through here in ten minutes, I take it, and then I'll have a word with the Director about that minute. Let's go. Can you leave me your list?"

"Of course," said Murke, "I know the figures by heart."

The technician put down his newspaper as Murke entered the little glass booth. The technician was smiling. On Monday and Tuesday, during the six hours they listened to Bur-

Malottke's talks and did their cutting, Murke and the technician had not exchanged a single personal word; now and again they exchanged glances, and when they stopped for a breather the technician had passed his cigarettes to Murke and the next day Murke passed his to the technician, and now when Murke saw the technician smiling he thought: If there is such a thing as friendship in this world, then this man is my friend. He laid the metal box with the snippets from Bur-Malottke's talk on the table and said quietly: "Here we go." He plugged into the studio and said into the microphone: "I'm sure we can dispense with the run-through, Professor. We might as well start right away—would you please begin with the nominatives?"

Bur-Malottke nodded, Murke switched off his own microphone, pressed the button which turned on the green light in the studio and heard Bur-Malottke's solemn, carefully articulated voice intoning: "That higher Being Whom we revere—that higher Being . . ."

Bur-Malottke pursed his lips toward the muzzle of the mike as if he wanted to kiss it, sweat ran down his face, and through the glass Murke observed with cold detachment the agony that Bur-Malottke was going through; then he suddenly switched Bur-Malottke off, stopped the moving tape that was recording Bur-Malottke's words, and feasted his eyes on the spectacle of Bur-Malottke behind the glass, soundless, like a fat, handsome fish. He switched on his microphone and his voice came quietly into the studio: "I'm sorry, but our tape was defective, and I must ask you to begin again at the beginning with the nominatives." Bur-Malottke swore, but his curses were silent ones which only he could hear, for Murke had disconnected him and did not switch him on again until he had begun to say "that higher Being . . ." Murke was too young, considered himself too civilized, to approve of the word hate. But here, behind the glass pane, while Bur-Malottke repeated his genitives, he suddenly knew the meaning of hatred: he hated this great fat, handsome creature, whose books—two million three hundred and fifty thousand copies of them—lay around in libraries, bookstores, bookshelves and bookcases, and not for one second did he dream of suppressing this hatred. When Bur-Malottke had repeated two genitives, Murke switched on his own mike and said quietly: "Excuse me for interrupting you: the nominatives were excellent, so was the first genitive, but would you mind doing the second genitive again? Rather gentler in tone,

rather more relaxed—I'll play it back to you." And although
Bur-Malottke shook his head violently he signaled to the
technician to play back the tape in the studio. They saw
Bur-Malottke give a start, sweat more profusely than ever,
then hold his hands over his ears until the tape came to an
end. He said something, swore, but Murke and the technician
could not hear him; they had disconnected him. Coldly Murke
waited until he could read from Bur-Malottke's lips that he
had begun again with the higher Being, he turned on the
mike and the tape, and Bur-Malottke continued with the genitives.

When he was through, he screwed up Murke's list into a
ball, rose from his chair, drenched in sweat and fuming, and
made for the door; but Murke's quiet, pleasant young voice
called him back. Murke said: "But Professor, you've forgotten
the vocative." Bur-Malottke looked at him, his eyes blazing
with hate, and said into the mike: "O Thou higher Being
Whom we revere!"

As he turned to leave, Murke's voice called him back once
more. Murke said: "I'm sorry, Professor, but, spoken like
that, the words are useless."

"For God's sake," whispered the technician, "watch it!"
Bur-Malottke was standing stock-still by the door, his back
to the glass booth, as if transfixed by Murke's voice.

Something had happened to him which had never happened
to him before: he was helpless, and this young voice, so
pleasant, so remarkably intelligent, tortured him as nothing
had ever tortured him before. Murke went on:

"I can, of course, paste it into the talk the way it is, but
I must point out to you, Professor, that it will have the
wrong effect."

Bur-Malottke turned, walked back to the microphone, and
said in low and solemn tones:

"O Thou higher Being Whom we revere."

Without turning to look at Murke, he left the studio. It
was exactly quarter past ten, and in the doorway he collided
with a young, pretty woman carrying some sheet music. The
girl, a vivacious redhead, walked briskly to the microphone,
adjusted it, and moved the table to one side so she could stand
directly in front of the mike.

In the booth Murke chatted for half a minute with Huglieme, who was in charge of Light Entertainment. Pointing to
the metal container, Huglieme said: "Do you still need that?"
And Murke said, "Yes, I do." In the studio the redhead was

singing, "Take my lips, just as they are, they're so lovely."
Huglieme switched on his microphone and said quietly: "D'you
mind keeping your trap shut for another twenty seconds, I'm
not quite ready." The girl laughed, made a face, and said:
"O.K., pansy dear." Murke said to the technician: "I'll be
back at eleven; we can cut it up then and splice it all together."

"Will we have to hear it through again after that?" asked
the technician. "No," said Murke, "I wouldn't listen to it
again for a million marks."

The technician nodded, inserted the tape for the red-haired
singer, and Murke left.

He put a cigarette between his lips, did not light it, and
walked along the rear corridor toward the second paternoster,
the one on the south side leading down to the coffee shop.
The rugs, the corridors, the furniture and the pictures, everything irritated him. The rugs were impressive, the corridors
were impressive, the furniture was impressive, and the pictures
were in excellent taste, but he suddenly felt a desire to take
the sentimental picture of the Sacred Heart which his mother
had sent him and see it somewhere here on the wall. He
stopped, looked round, listened, took the picture from his
pocket and stuck it between the wallpaper and the frame of
the door to the Assistant Drama Producer's office. The taw-
dry little print was highly colored, and beneath the picture
of the Sacred Heart were the words: *I prayed for you at St.
James' Church.*

Murke continued along the corridor, got into the paternoster, and was carried down. On this side of the building
the Schrumsnot ashtrays, which had won a Good Design
Award, had already been installed. They hung next to the
illuminated red figures indicating the floor: a red four, a
Schrumsnot ashtray, a red three, a Schrumsnot ashtray, a red
two, a Schrumsnot ashtray. They were handsome ashtrays,
scallop-shaped, made of beaten copper, the beaten copper
base an exotic marine plant, nodular seaweed—and each ashtray had cost two hundred and fifty-eight marks and seventy-
seven pfennigs. They were so handsome that Murke could
never bring himself to soil them with cigarette ash, let alone
anything as sordid as a butt. Other smokers all seemed to
have had the same feeling—empty packs, butts and ash littered the floor under the handsome ashtrays: apparently no
one had the courage to use them as ashtrays; they were
copper, burnished, forever empty.

Murke saw the fifth ashtray next to the illuminated red zero rising toward him, the air was getting warmer, there was a smell of food. Murke jumped off and stumbled into the coffee shop. Three free-lance colleagues were sitting at a table in the corner. The table was covered with used plates, cups, and saucers.

The three men were the joint authors of a radio series, *The Lung, A Human Organ*; they had collected their fee together, breakfasted together, were having a drink together, and were now throwing dice for the expense voucher. One of them, Wendrich, Murke knew well, but just then Wendrich shouted: "Art!"—"art," he shouted again, "art, art!" and Murke felt a spasm, like the frog when Galvani discovered electricity. The last two days Murke had heard the word *art* too often, from Bur-Malottke's lips; it occurred exactly one hundred and thirty-four times in the two talks; and he had heard the talks three times, which meant he had heard the word *art* four hundred and two times, too often to feel any desire to discuss it. He squeezed past the counter toward a booth in the far corner and was relieved to find it empty. He sat down, lit his cigarette, and when Wulla, the waitress, came, he said: "Apple juice, please," and was glad when Wulla went off again at once. He closed his eyes tight, but found himself listening willy-nilly to the conversation of the free-lance writers over in the corner, who seemed to be having a heated argument about art; each time one of them shouted "art" Murke winced. It's like being whipped, he thought.

As she brought him the apple juice Wulla looked at him in concern. She was tall and strongly built, but not fat, she had a healthy, cheerful face, and as she poured the apple juice from the jug into the glass she said: "You ought to take a vacation, sir, and quit smoking."

She used to call herself Wilfriede-Ulla, but later, for the sake of simplicity, she combined the names into Wulla. She especially admired the people from the Cultural Department.

"Lay off, will you?" said Murke, "please!"

"And you ought to take some nice ordinary girl to the movies one night," said Wulla.

"I'll do that this evening," said Murke, "I promise you."

"It doesn't have to be one of those dolls," said Wulla, "Just some nice, quiet, ordinary girl, with a kind heart. There are still some of those around."

"Yes," said Murke, "I know they're still around, as a matter of fact I know one." Well, that's fine then, thought Wulla, and went over to the free lances, one of whom had ordered three drinks and three coffees. Poor fellows, thought Wulla, art will be the death of them yet. She had a soft spot for the free lances and was always trying to persuade them to economize. The minute they have any money, she thought, they blow it; she went up to the counter and, shaking her head, passed on the order for the three drinks and the three coffees.

Murke drank some of the apple juice, stubbed out his cigarette in the ashtray, and thought with apprehension of the hours from eleven to one when he had to cut up Bur-Malottke's sentences and paste them into the right places in the talks. At two o'clock the Director wanted both talks played back to him in his studio. Murke thought about soap, about staircases, steep stairs and roller coasters, he thought about the dynamic personality of the Director, he thought about Bur-Malottke, and was startled by the sight of Schwendling coming into the coffee shop.

Schwendling had on a shirt of large red and black checks and made a beeline for the booth where Murke was hiding. Schwendling was humming the tune which was very popular just then: "Take my lips, just as they are, they're so lovely. . . ." He stopped short when he saw Murke, and said: "Hullo, you here? I thought you were busy carving up that crap of Bur-Malottke's."

"I'm going back at eleven," said Murke.

"Wulla, let's have some beer," shouted Schwendling over to the counter, "a pint. Well," he said to Murke, "you deserve extra time off for that, it must be a filthy job. The old man told me all about it."

Murke said nothing, and Schwendling went on:

"Have you heard the latest about Muckwitz?"

Murke, not interested, first shook his head, then for politeness' sake asked: "What's he been up to?"

Wulla brought the beer, Schwendling swallowed some, paused for effect, and announced: "Muckwitz is doing a feature about the Steppes."

Murke laughed and said: "What's Fenn doing?"

"Fenn," said Schwendling, "Fenn's doing a feature about the Tundra."

"And Weggucht?"

"Weggucht is doing a feature about me, and after that I'm going to do a feature about him, you know the old saying: You feature me, I'll feature you. . . ."

Just then one of the free lances jumped up and shouted across the room: "Art—art—that's the only thing that matters!"

Murke ducked, like a soldier when he hears the mortars being fired from the enemy trenches. He swallowed another mouthful of apple juice and winced again when a voice over the loudspeaker said: "Mr. Murke is wanted in Studio Thirteen—Mr. Murke is wanted in Studio Thirteen." He looked at his watch, it was only half-past ten, but the voice went on relentlessly: "Mr. Murke is wanted in Studio Thirteen—Mr. Murke is wanted in Studio Thirteen." The loudspeaker hung above the counter, immediately below the motto the Director had had painted on the wall: *Discipline Above All.*

"Well," said Schwendling, "that's it, you'd better go."

"Yes," said Murke, "that's it."

He got up, put money for the apple juice on the table, pressed past the free lances' table, got into the paternoster outside and was carried up once more past the five Schrumsnot ashtrays. He saw his Sacred Heart picture still sticking in the Assistant Producer's doorframe and thought:

"Thank God, now there's at least one corny picture in this place."

He opened the door of the studio booth, saw the technician sitting alone and relaxed in front of three cardboard boxes, and asked wearily: "What's up?"

"They were ready sooner than expected, and we've got an extra half hour in hand," said the technician. "I thought you'd be glad of the extra time."

"I certainly am," said Murke, "I've got an appointment at one. Let's get on with it then. What's the idea of the boxes?"

"Well," said the technician, "for each grammatical case I've got one box—the nominatives in the first, the genitives in the second, and in that one—" he pointed to the little box on the right with the words "Pure Chocolate" on it, and said: "In that one I have the two vocatives, the good one in the right-hand corner, the bad one in the left."

"That's terrific," said Murke, "so you've already cut up the crap."

"That's right," said the technician, "and if you've made a note of the order in which the cases have to be spliced it won't take us more than an hour. Did you write it down?"

"Yes, I did," said Murke. He pulled a piece of paper from

his pocket with the numbers 1 to 27; each number was followed by a grammatical case.

Murke sat down, held out his cigarette pack to the technician; they both smoked while the technician laid the cut tapes with Bur-Malottke's talks on the roll.

"In the first cut," said Murke, "we have to stick in a nominative."

The technician put his hand into the first box, picked up one of the snippets and stuck it into the space.

"Next comes a genitive," said Murke.

They worked swiftly, and Murke was relieved that it all went so fast.

"Now," he said, "comes the vocative; we'll take the bad one, of course."

The technician laughed and stuck Bur-Malottke's bad vocative into the tape.

"Next," he said, "next!" "Genitive," said Murke.

The Director conscientiously read every listener's letter. The one he was reading at this particular moment went as follows:

Dear Radio,

I am sure you can have no more faithful listener than myself. I am an old woman, a little old lady of seventy-seven, and I have been listening to you every day for thirty years. I have never been sparing with my praise. Perhaps you remember my letter about the program: "The Seven Souls of Kaweida the Cow." It was a lovely program —but now I have to be angry with you! The way the canine soul is being neglected in radio is gradually becoming a disgrace. And you call that humanism. I am sure Hitler had his bad points: if one is to believe all one hears, he was a dreadful man, but one thing he did have: a real affection for dogs, and he did a lot for them. When are dogs going to come into their own again in German radio? The way you tried to do it in the program "Like Cat and Dog" is certainly not the right one: it was an insult to every canine soul. If my little Lohengrin could only talk, he'd tell you! And the way he barked, poor darling, all through your terrible program, it almost made me die of shame. I pay my two marks a month like any other listener and stand on my rights and demand to know: When are dogs going to come into their own again in German radio?

With kind regards—in spite of my being so cross with you,

Sincerely yours,
Jadwiga Herchen (retired)

P.S. In case none of those cynics of yours who run your programs should be capable of doing justice to the canine soul, I suggest you make use of my modest attempts, which are enclosed herewith. I do not wish to accept any fee. You may send it direct to the S.P.C.A. Enclosed: 35 manuscripts.

Yours,
J.H.

The Director sighed. He looked for the scripts, but his secretary had evidently filed them away. The Director filled his pipe, lit it, ran his tongue over his dynamic lips, lifted the receiver and asked to be put through to Krochy. Krochy had a tiny office with a tiny desk, although in the best of taste, upstairs in Culture and was in charge of a section as narrow as his desk: Animals in the World of Culture.

"Krochy speaking," he said diffidently into the telephone.

"Say, Krochy," said the Director, "when was the last time we had a program about dogs?"

"Dogs, sir?" said Krochy. "I don't believe we ever have, at least not since I've been here."

"And how long have you been here, Krochy?" And upstairs in his office Krochy trembled, because the Director's voice was so gentle; he knew it boded no good when that voice became gentle.

"I've been here ten years now, sir," said Krochy.

"It's a disgrace," said the Director, "that you've never had a program about dogs; after all, that's your department. What was the title of your last program?"

"The title of my last program was—" stammered Krochy.

"You don't have to repeat every sentence," said the Director, "we're not in the army."

"Owls in the Ruins," said Krochy timidly.

"Within the next three weeks," said the Director, gentle again now, "I would like to hear a program about the canine soul."

"Certainly, sir," said Krochy; he heard the click as the

Director put down the receiver, sighed deeply and said: "Oh God!"

The Director picked up the next listener's letter.

At this moment Bur-Malottke entered the room. He was always at liberty to enter unannounced, and he made frequent use of this liberty. He was still sweating as he sank wearily into a chair opposite the Director and said:

"Well, good morning."

"Good morning," said the Director, pushing the listener's letter aside. "What can I do for you?"

"Could you give me one minute?"

"Bur-Malottke," said the Director, with a generous, dynamic gesture, "does not have to ask me for one minute; hours, days, are at your disposal."

"No," said Bur-Malottke, "I don't mean an ordinary minute, I mean one minute of radio time. Due to the changes my talk has become one minute longer."

The Director grew serious, like a satrap distributing provinces. "I hope," he said, sourly, "it's not a political minute."

"No," said Bur-Malottke, "It's half a minute of Neighborly News and half a minute of Light Entertainment."

"Thank God for that," said the Director. "I've got a credit of seventy-nine seconds with Light Entertainment and eighty-three seconds with Neighborly News. I'll be glad to let someone like Bur-Malottke have one minute."

"I am overcome," said Bur-Malottke.

"Is there anything else I can do for you?" asked the Director.

"I would appreciate it," said Bur-Malottke, "if we could gradually start correcting all the tapes I have made since 1945. One day," he said—he passed his hand over his forehead and gazed wistfully at the genuine Kokoschka above the Director's desk—"one day I shall—" he faltered, for the news he was about to break to the Director was too painful for posterity "—one day I shall—die," and he paused again, giving the Director a chance to look gravely shocked and raise his hand in protest, "and I cannot bear the thought that after my death tapes may be run off on which I say things I no longer believe in. Particularly in some of my political utterances, during the fervor of 1945, I let myself be persuaded to make statements which today fill me with serious misgivings and which I can only account for on the basis of that spirit of youthfulness which has always distinguished my work. My written works are already in process of being corrected, and

I would like to ask you to give me the opportunity of correcting my spoken works as well."

The Director was silent, he cleared his throat slightly, and little shining beads of sweat appeared on his forehead: it occurred to him that Bur-Malottke had spoken for at least an hour every month since 1945, and he made a swift calculation while Bur-Malottke went on talking: twelve times ten hours meant one hundred and twenty hours of spoken Bur-Malottke.

"Pedantry," Bur-Malottke was saying, "is something that only impure spirits regard as unworthy of genius; we know, of course"—and the Director felt flattered to be ranked by the We among the pure spirits—'that the true geniuses, the great geniuses, were pedants. Himmelsheim once had a whole printed edition of his *Seelon* rebound at his own expense because he felt that three or four sentences in the central portion of the work were no longer appropriate. The idea that some of my talks might be broadcast which no longer correspond to my convictions when I depart this earthly life—I find such an idea intolerable. How do you propose we go about it?"

The beads of sweat on the Director's forehead had become larger. "First of all," he said in a subdued voice, "an exact list would have to be made of all your broadcast talks, and then we would have to check in the archives to see if all the tapes were still there."

"I should hope," said Bur-Malottke, "that none of the tapes has been erased without notifying me. I have not been notified, therefore no tapes have been erased."

"I will see to everything," said the Director.

"Please do," said Bur-Malottke curtly, and rose from his chair. "Good-by."

"Good-by," said the Director, as he accompanied Bur-Malottke to the door.

The free lances in the coffee shop had decided to order lunch. They had had some more drinks, they were still talking about art, their conversation was quieter now but no less intense. They all jumped to their feet when Wanderburn suddenly came in. Wanderburn was a tall, despondent-looking writer with dark hair, an attractive face somewhat etched by the stigma of fame. On this particular morning he had not shaved, which made him look even more attractive. He walked over to the table where the three free lances were sitting, sank exhausted into a chair and said: "For God's sake, give me a drink. I always have the feeling in this building that I'm dying of thirst."

They passed him a drink, a glass that was still standing on the table, and the remains of a bottle of soda water. Wanderburn swallowed the drink, put down his glass, looked at each of the three men in turn, and said: "I must warn you about the radio business, about this pile of junk—this immaculate, shiny, slippery pile of junk. I'm warning you. It'll destroy us all." His warning was sincere and impressed the three young men very much; but the three young men did not know that Wanderburn had just come from the accounting department where he had picked up a nice fat fee for a quick job of editing the Book of Job.

"They cut us," said Wanderburn, "they consume our substance, splice us together again, and it'll be more than any of us can stand."

He finished the soda water, put the glass down on the table and, his coat flapping despondently about him, strode to the door.

On the dot of noon Murke finished the splicing. They had just stuck in the last snippet, a genitive, when Murke got up. He already had his hand on the doorknob when the technician said: "I wish I could afford a sensitive and expensive conscience like that. What'll we do with the box?" He pointed to the flat tin lying on the shelf next to the cardboard boxes containing the new tapes.

"Just leave it there," said Murke.

"What for?"

"We might need it again."

"D'you think he might get pangs of conscience all over again?"

"He might," said Murke, "we'd better wait and see. So long." He walked to the front paternoster, rode down to the second floor, and for the first time that day entered his office. His secretary had gone to lunch; Murke's boss, Humkoke, was sitting by the phone reading a book. He smiled at Murke, got up and said: "Well, I see you survived. Is this your book? Did you put it on the desk?" He held it out for Murke to read the title, and Murke said: "Yes, that's mine." The book had a jacket of green, gray and orange and was called "Batley's Lyrics of the Gutter"; it was about a young English writer a hundred years ago who had drawn up a catalogue of London slang.

"It's a marvelous book," said Murke.

"Yes," said Humkoke, "it is marvelous, but you never learn."

Murke eyed him questioningly.

"You never learn that one doesn't leave marvelous books lying around when Wanderburn is liable to turn up, and Wanderburn is always liable to turn up. He saw it at once, of course, opened it, read it for five minutes, and what's the result?"

Murke said nothing.

"The result," said Humkoke, "is two hour-long broadcasts by Wanderburn on 'Lyrics of the Gutter.' One day this fellow will do a feature about his own grandmother, and the worst of it is that one of his grandmothers was one of mine too. Please, Murke, try and remember: never leave marvelous books around when Wanderburn is liable to turn up, and, I repeat, he's always liable to turn up. That's all, you can go now, you've got the afternoon off, and I'm sure you've earned it. Is the stuff ready? Did you hear it through again?"

"It's all done," said Murke, "but I can't hear the talks through again, I simply can't."

" 'I simply can't' is a very childish thing to say," said Humkoke.

"If I have to hear the word Art one more time today I shall become hysterical," said Murke.

"You already are," said Humkoke, "and I must say you've every reason to be. Three hours of Bur-Malottke, that's too much for anybody, even the toughest of us, and you're not even tough." He threw the book on the table, took a step toward Murke and said: "When I was your age I once had to cut three minutes out of a four-hour speech of Hitler's, and I had to listen to the speech three times before I was considered worthy of suggesting which three minutes should be cut. When I began listening to the tape for the first time I was still a Nazi, but by the time I had heard the speech for the third time I wasn't a Nazi any more; it was a drastic cure, a terrible one, but very effective."

"You forget," said Murke quietly, "that I had already been cured of Bur-Malottke before I had to listen to his tapes."

"You really are a vicious beast!" said Humkoke with a

laugh. "That'll do for now, the Director is going to hear it through again at two. Just see that you're available in case anything goes wrong."

"I'll be at home from two to three," said Murke.

"One more thing," said Humkoke, pulling out a yellow biscuit tin from a shelf next to Murke's desk, "what's this scrap you've got here?"

Murke colored. "It's—" he stammered, "I collect a certain kind of left-overs."

"What kind of left-overs?" asked Humkoke.

"Silences," said Murke, "I collect silences."

Humkoke raised his eyebrows, and Murke went on: "When I have to cut tapes, in the places where the speakers sometimes pause for a moment—or sigh, or take a breath, or there is absolute silence—I don't throw that away, I collect it. Incidentally, there wasn't a single second of silence in Bur-Malottke's tapes."

Humkoke laughed: "Of course not, he would never be silent. And what do you do with the scrap?"

"I splice it together and play back the tape when I'm at home in the evening. There's not much yet, I only have three minutes so far—but then people aren't silent very often."

"You know, don't you, that it's against regulations to take home sections of tape?"

"Even silences?" asked Murke.

Humkoke laughed and said: "For God's sake, get out!" And Murke left.

When the Director entered his studio a few minutes after two, the Bur-Malottke tape had just been turned on:

> . . . and wherever, however, why ever, and whenever we begin to discuss the Nature of Art, we must first look to that higher Being Whom we revere, we must bow in awe before that higher Being Whom we revere, and we must accept Art as a gift from that higher Being Whom we revere. Art. . . .

No, thought the Director, I really can't ask anyone to listen to Bur-Malottke for a hundred and twenty hours. No, he thought, there are some things one simply cannot do, things I wouldn't want to wish even on Murke. He returned to his office and switched on the loudspeaker just in time to hear Bur-Malottke say: "O Thou higher Being Whom we revere. . . ." No, thought the Director, no, no.

Murke lay on his chesterfield at home smoking. Next to him on a chair was a cup of tea, and Murke was gazing at the white ceiling of the room. Sitting at his desk was a very pretty blonde who was staring out of the window at the street. Between Murke and the girl, on a low coffee table, stood a tape recorder, recording. Not a word was spoken, not a sound was made. The girl was pretty and silent enough for a photographer's model.

"I can't stand it," said the girl suddenly, "I can't stand it, it's inhuman, what you want me to do. There are some men who expect a girl to do immoral things, but it seems to me that what you are asking me to do is even more immoral than the things other men expect a girl to do."

Murke sighed. "Oh hell," he said, "Rina dear, now I've got to cut all that out; do be sensible, be a good girl and put just five more minutes' silence on the tape."

"Put silence," said the girl, with what thirty years ago would have been called a pout. "Put silence, that's another of your inventions. I wouldn't mind putting words onto a tape—but putting silence. . . ."

Murke had got up and switched off the tape recorder. "Oh Rina," he said, "if you only knew how precious your silence is to me. In the evening, when I'm tired, when I'm sitting here alone, I play back your silence. Do be a dear and put just three more minutes' silence on the tape for me and save me the cutting; you know how I feel about cutting." "Oh all right," said the girl, "but give me a cigarette at least."

Murke smiled, gave her a cigarette and said: "This way I have your silence in the original and on tape, that's terrific." He switched the tape on again, and they sat facing one another in silence till the telephone rang. Murke got up, shrugged helplessly, and lifted the receiver.

"Well," said Humkoke, "the tapes ran off smoothly, the boss couldn't find a thing wrong with them. . . . You can go to the movies now. And think about snow."

"What snow?" asked Murke, looking out onto the street, which lay basking in brilliant summer sunshine.

"Come on now," said Humkoke, "you know we have to start thinking about the winter programs. I need songs about snow, stories about snow—we can't fool around for the rest of our lives with Schubert and Stifter. No one seems to have any idea how badly we need snow songs and snow stories. Just imagine if we have a long hard winter with lots of snow and freezing temperatures: where are we going to get our snow programs from? Try and think of something snowy."

"All right," said Murke, "I'll try and think of something." Humkoke had hung up.

"Come along," he said to the girl, "we can go to the movies."

"May I speak again now?" said the girl.

"Yes," said Murke, "speak!"

It was just at this time that the Assistant Drama Producer had finished listening again to the one-act play scheduled for that evening. He liked it, only the ending did not satisfy him. He was sitting in the glass booth in Studio Thirteen next to the technician, chewing a match and studying the script.

(*Sound-effects of a large empty church*)
ATHEIST: (*in a loud clear voice*) Who will remember me when I have become the prey of worms?
(*Silence*)
ATHEIST: (*his voice a shade louder*) Who will wait for me when I have turned into dust?
(*Silence*)
ATHEIST: (*louder still*) And who will remember me when I have turned into leaves?
(*Silence*)

There were twelve such questions called out by the atheist into the church, and each question was followed by—? Silence.

The Assistant Producer removed the chewed match from his lips, replaced it with a fresh one and looked at the technician, a question in his eyes.

"Yes," said the technician, "if you ask me: I think there's a bit too much silence in it."

"That's what I thought," said the Assistant Producer; "the author thinks so too and he's given me leave to change it. There should just be a voice saying: "God"—but it ought to be a voice without church sound-effects, it would have to be spoken somehow in a different acoustical environment. Have you any idea where I can get hold of a voice like that at this hour?"

The technician smiled, picked up the metal container which was still lying on the shelf. "Here you are," he said, "here's a voice saying 'God' without any sound-effects."

The Assistant Producer was so surprised he almost swallowed the match, choked a little and got it up into the front of his mouth again. "It's quite all right," the technician said with a smile, "we had to cut it out of a talk, twenty-seven times."

"I don't need it that often, just twelve times," said the Assistant Producer.

"It's a simple matter, of course," said the technician, "to cut out the silence and stick in God twelve times—if you'll take the responsibility."

"You're a godsend," said the Assistant Producer, "and I'll be responsible. Come on, let's get started." He gazed happily at the tiny, lusterless tape snippets in Murke's tin box. "You really are a godsend," he said, "come on, let's go!"

The technician smiled, for he was looking forward to being able to present Murke with the snippets of silence: it was a lot of silence, altogether nearly a minute; it was more silence than he had ever been able to give Murke, and he liked the young man.

"O.K.," he said with a smile, "here we go."

The Assistant Producer put his hand in his jacket pocket, took out a pack of cigarettes; in doing so he touched a crumpled piece of paper, he smoothed it out and passed it to the technician: "Funny, isn't it, the corny stuff you can come across in this place? I found this stuck in my door."

The technician took the picture, looked at it, and said: "Yes, it's funny," and he read out the words under the picture:

I prayed for you at St. James' Church.

TOMMASO LANDOLFI

Gogol's Wife

*Tommaso Landolfi (1908-   ) is an Italian writer
and translator whose fame has increased steadily
since his first volume of short stories,* Dialogue on
the Greater Harmonies, *appeared in 1937. A grad-
uate of the University of Florence, he took a degree
in Russian Literature. His published work now in-
cludes many volumes of stories, novels, and transla-
tions. His stories are surrealistic in nature, sometimes
presenting a conversation or a situation that seems
trivial but is actually quite pointed, sometimes, as in
"Gogol's Wife," exploring an unreal or absurd situation that has profoundly symbolic echoes, reminiscent
of Kafka.*

At this point, confronted with the whole complicated
affair of Nikolai Vassilevitch's wife, I am overcome by hesitation. Have I any right to disclose something which is unknown
to the whole world, which my unforgettable friend himself
kept hidden from the world (and he had his reasons), and
which I am sure will give rise to all sorts of malicious and
stupid misunderstandings? Something, moreover, which will
very probably offend the sensibilities of all sorts of base, hypocritical people, and possibly of some honest people too, if
there are any left? And finally, have I any right to disclose
something before which my own spirit recoils, and even tends
toward a more or less open disapproval?

But the fact remains that, as a biographer, I have certain
firm obligations. Believing as I do that every bit of information
about so lofty a genius will turn out to be of value to us and to
future generations, I cannot conceal something which in any
case has no hope of being judged fairly and wisely until the
end of time. Moreover, what right have we to condemn? Is
it given to us to know, not only what intimate needs, but even
what higher and wider ends may have been served by those
very deeds of a lofty genius which perchance may appear to
us vile? No indeed, for we understand so little of these privileged natures. "It is true," a great man once said, "that I also
have to pee, but for quite different reasons."

But without more ado I will come to what I know beyond
doubt, and can prove beyond question, about this controversial matter, which will now—I dare to hope—no longer be so.
I will not trouble to recapitulate what is already known of it,
since I do not think this should be necessary at the present
stage of development of Gogol studies.

Let me say it at once: Nikolai Vassilevitch's wife was not a
woman. Nor was she any sort of human being, nor any sort of
living creature at all, whether animal or vegetable (although
something of the sort has sometimes been hinted). She was
quite simply a balloon. Yes, a balloon; and this will explain
the perplexity, or even indignation, of certain biographers who
were also the personal friends of the Master, and who com-
plained that, although they often went to his house, they never
saw her and "never even heard her voice." From this they
deduced all sorts of dark and disgraceful complications—yes,
and criminal ones too. No, gentlemen, everything is always
simpler than it appears. You did not hear her voice simply
because she could not speak, or to be more exact, she could
only speak in certain conditions, as we shall see. And it was
always, except once, in tête-à-tête with Nikolai Vassilevitch.
So let us not waste time with any cheap or empty refutations
but come at once to as exact and complete a description as
possible of the being or object in question.

Gogol's so-called wife was an ordinary dummy made of
thick rubber, naked at all seasons, buff in tint, or as is more
commonly said, flesh-colored. But since women's skins are not
all of the same color, I should specify that hers was a light-
colored, polished skin, like that of certain brunettes. It, or
she, was, it is hardly necessary to add, of feminine sex. Perhaps
I should say at once that she was capable of very wide
alterations of her attributes without, of course, being able to

alter her sex itself. She could sometimes appear to be thin, with hardly any breasts and with narrow hips more like a young lad than a woman, and at other times to be excessively well-endowed or—let us not mince matters—fat. And she often changed the color of her hair, both on her head and elsewhere on her body, though not necessarily at the same time. She could also seem to change in all sorts of other tiny particulars, such as the position of moles, the vitality of the mucous membranes and so forth. She could even to a certain extent change the very color of her skin. One is faced with the necessity of asking oneself who she really was, or whether it would be proper to speak of a single "person"—and in fact we shall see that it would be imprudent to press this point.

The cause of these changes, as my readers will already have understood, was nothing else but the will of Nikolai Vassile-vitch himself. He would inflate her to a greater or lesser degree, would change her wig and her other tufts of hair, would grease her with ointments and touch her up in various ways so as to obtain more or less the type of woman which suited him at that moment. Following the natural inclinations of his fancy, he even amused himself sometimes by producing gro-tesque or monstrous forms; as will be readily understood, she became deformed when inflated beyond a certain point or if she remained below a certain pressure.

But Gogol soon tired of these experiments, which he held to be "after all, not very respectful" to his wife, whom he loved in his own way—however inscrutable it may remain to us. He loved her, but which of these incarnations, we may ask our-selves, did he love? Alas, I have already indicated that the end of the present account will furnish some sort of an answer. And how can I have stated above that it was Nikolai Vassile-vitch's will which ruled that woman? In a certain sense, yes, it is true; but it is equally certain that she soon became no longer his slave but his tyrant. And here yawns the abyss, or if you prefer it, the Jaws of Tartarus. But let us not anticipate.

I have said that Gogol obtained with his manipulations *more or less* the type of woman which he needed from time to time. I should add that when, in rare cases, the form he ob-tained perfectly incarnated his desire, Nikolai Vassilevitch fell in love with it "exclusively," as he said in his own words, and that this was enough to render "her" stable for a certain time —until he fell out of love with "her." I counted no more than three or four of these violent passions—or, as I suppose they would be called today, infatuations—in the life (dare I say in

the conjugal life?) of the great writer. It will be convenient
to add here that a few years after what one may call his
marriage, Gogol had even given a name to his wife. It was
Caracas, which is, unless I am mistaken, the capital of Vene-
zuela. I have never been able to discover the reason for this
choice: great minds are so capricious!

Speaking only of her normal appearance, Caracas was what
is called a fine woman—well built and proportioned in every
part. She had every smallest attribute of her sex properly
disposed in the proper location. Particularly worthy of attention were her genital organs (if the adjective is permissible in
such a context). They were formed by means of ingenious
folds in the rubber. Nothing was forgotten, and their operation was rendered easy by various devices, as well as by the
internal pressure of the air.

Caracas also had a skeleton, even though a rudimentary one.
Perhaps it was made of whalebone. Special care had been devoted to the construction of the thoracic cage, of the pelvic
basin and of the cranium. The first two systems were more or
less visible in accordance with the thickness of the fatty layer,
if I may so describe it, which covered them. It is a great pity
that Gogol never let me know the name of the creator of
such a fine piece of work. There was an obstinacy in his refusal which was never quite clear to me.

Nikolai Vassilevitch blew his wife up through the anal
sphincter with a pump of his own invention, rather like those
which you hold down with your two feet and which are used
today in all sorts of mechanical workshops. Situated in the
anus was a little one-way valve, or whatever the correct technical description would be, like the mitral valve of the heart,
which, once the body was inflated, allowed more air to come
in but none to go out. To deflate, one unscrewed a stopper
in the mouth, at the back of the throat.

And that, I think, exhausts the description of the most note-
worthy peculiarities of this being. Unless perhaps I should
mention the splendid rows of white teeth which adorned her
mouth and the dark eyes which, in spite of their immobility,
perfectly simulated life. Did I say simulate? Good heavens,
simulate is not the word! Nothing seems to be the word, when
one is speaking of Caracas! Even these eyes could undergo
a change of color, by means of a special process to which,
since it was long and tiresome, Gogol seldom had recourse.
Finally, I should speak of her voice, which it was only once
given to me to hear. But I cannot do that without going more

fully into the relationship between husband and wife, and in this I shall no longer be able to answer to the truth of everything with absolute certitude. On my conscience I could not—so confused, both in itself and in my memory, is that which I now have to tell.

Here, then, as they occur to me, are some of my memories.

The first and, as I said, the last time I ever heard Caracas speak to Nikolai Vassilevitch was one evening when we were absolutely alone. We were in the room where the woman, if I may be allowed the expression, lived. Entrance to this room was strictly forbidden to everybody. It was furnished more or less in the Oriental manner, had no windows and was situated in the most inaccessible part of the house. I did know that she could talk, but Gogol had never explained to me the circumstances under which this happened. There were only the two of us, or three, in there. Nikolai Vassilevitch and I were drinking vodka and discussing Butkov's novel. I remember that we left this topic, and he was maintaining the necessity for radical reforms in the laws of inheritance. We had almost forgotten her. It was then that, with a husky and submissive voice, like Venus on the nuptial couch, she said point-blank: "I want to go poo poo."

I jumped, thinking I had misheard, and looked across at her. She was sitting on a pile of cushions against the wall; that evening she was a soft, blonde beauty, rather well-covered. Her expression seemed commingled of shrewdness and slyness, childishness and irresponsibility. As for Gogol, he blushed violently and, leaping on her, stuck two fingers down her throat. She immediately began to shrink and to turn pale; she took on once again that lost and astonished air which was especially hers, and was in the end reduced to no more than a flabby skin on a perfunctory bony armature. Since, for practical reasons which will readily be divined, she had an extraordinarily flexible backbone, she folded up almost in two, and for the rest of the evening she looked up at us from where she had slithered to the floor, in utter abjection.

All Gogol said was: "She only does it for a joke, or to annoy me, because as a matter of fact she does not have such needs." In the presence of other people, that is to say of me, he generally made a point of treating her with a certain disdain.

We went on drinking and talking, but Nikolai Vassilevitch seemed very much disturbed and absent in spirit. Once he suddenly interrupted what he was saying, seized my hand in his and burst into tears. "What can I do now?" he exclaimed. "You understand, Foma Paskalovitch, that I loved her?"

It is necessary to point out that it was impossible, except by a miracle, ever to repeat any of Caracas' forms. She was a fresh creation every time, and it would have been wasted effort to seek to find again the exact proportions, the exact pressure, and so forth, of a former Caracas. Therefore the plumpish blonde of that evening was lost to Gogol from that time forth forever; this was in fact the tragic end of one of those few loves of Nikolai Vassilevitch, which I described above. He gave me no explanation; he sadly rejected my proffered comfort, and that evening we parted early. But his heart had been laid bare to me in that outburst. He was no longer so reticent with me, and soon had hardly any secrets left. And this, I may say in parenthesis, caused me very great pride.

It seems that things had gone well for the "couple" at the beginning of their life together. Nikolai Vassilevitch had been content with Caracas and slept regularly with her in the same bed. He continued to observe this custom till the end, saying with a timid smile that no companion could be quieter or less importunate than she. But I soon began to doubt this, especially judging by the state he was sometimes in when he woke up. Then, after several years, their relationship began strangely to deteriorate.

All this, let it be said once and for all, is no more than a schematic attempt at an explanation. About that time the woman actually began to show signs of independence or, as one might say, of autonomy. Nikolai Vassilevitch had the extraordinary impression that she was acquiring a personality of her own, indecipherable perhaps, but still distinct from his, and one which slipped through his fingers. It is certain that some sort of continuity was established between each of her appearances—between all those brunettes, those blondes, those redheads and auburn-headed girls, between those plump, those slim, those dusky or snowy or golden beauties, there was a certain something in common. At the beginning of this chapter I cast some doubt on the propriety of considering Caracas as a unitary personality; nevertheless I myself could not quite, whenever I saw her, free myself of the impression that, however unheard of it may seem, this was fundamentally the same woman. And it may be that this was why Gogol felt he had to give her a name.

An attempt to establish in what precisely subsisted the common attributes of the different forms would be quite another thing. Perhaps it was no more and no less than the creative afflatus of Nikolai Vassilevitch himself. But no, it would have been too singular and strange if he had been so much divided off from himself, so much averse to himself. Because whoever she was, Caracas was a disturbing presence and even—it is better to be quite clear—a hostile one. Yet neither Gogol nor I ever succeeded in formulating a remotely tenable hypothesis as to her true nature; when I say formulate, I mean in terms which would be at once rational and accessible to all. But I cannot pass over an extraordinary event which took place at this time.

Caracas fell ill of a shameful disease—or rather Gogol did—though he was not then having, nor had he ever had, any contact with other women. I will not even try to describe how this happened, or where the filthy complaint came from; all I know is that it happened. And that my great, unhappy friend would say to me: "So, Foma Paskalovitch, you see what lay at the heart of Caracas; it was the spirit of syphilis."

Sometimes he would even blame himself in a quite absurd manner; he was always prone to self-accusation. This incident was a real catastrophe as far as the already obscure relationship between husband and wife, and the hostile feelings of Nikolai Vassilevitch himself, were concerned. He was compelled to undergo long-drawn-out and painful treatment—the treatment of those days—and the situation was aggravated by the fact that the disease in the woman did not seem to be easily curable. Gogol deluded himself for some time that, by blowing his wife up and down and furnishing her with the most widely divergent aspects, he could obtain a woman immune from the contagion, but he was forced to desist when no results were forthcoming.

I shall be brief, seeking not to tire my readers, and also because what I remember seems to become more and more confused. I shall therefore hasten to the tragic conclusion. As to this last, however, let there be no mistake. I must once again make it clear that I am very sure of my ground. I was an eyewitness. Would that I had not been!

The years went by. Nikolai Vassilevitch's distaste for his wife became stronger, though his love for her did not show any signs of diminishing. Toward the end, aversion and attachment struggled so fiercely with each other in his heart that he became quite stricken, almost broken up. His restless eyes, which habitually assumed so many different expressions and sometimes spoke so sweetly to the heart of his interlocutor, now almost always shone with a fevered light, as if he were under the effect of a drug. The strangest impulses arose in him, accompanied by the most senseless fears. He spoke to me of Caracas more and more often, accusing her of unthinkable and amazing things. In these regions I could not follow him, since I had put a sketchy acquaintance with his wife, and hardly any intimacy—and above all since my sensibility was so limited compared with his. I shall accordingly restrict myself to reporting some of his accusations, without reference to my personal impressions.

"Believe it or not, Foma Paskalovitch," he would, for example, often say to me: "Believe it or not, *she's aging!*" Then, unspeakably moved, he would, as was his way, take my hands in his. He also accused Caracas of giving herself up to solitary pleasures, which he had expressly forbidden. He even went so far as to charge her with betraying him, but the things he said became so extremely obscure that I must excuse myself from any further account of them.

One thing that appears certain is that toward the end Caracas, whether aged or not, had turned into a bitter creature, querulous, hypocritical and subject to religious excess. I do not exclude the possibility that she may have had an influence on Gogol's moral position during the last period of his life, a position which is sufficiently well known. The tragic climax came one night quite unexpectedly when Nikolai Vassilevitch and I were celebrating his silver wedding—one of the last evenings we were to spend together. I neither can nor should attempt to set down what it was that led to his decision, at a time when to all appearances he was resigned to tolerating his consort. I know not what new events had taken place that day. I shall confine myself to the facts; my readers must make what they can of them.

That evening Nikolai Vassilevitch was unusually agitated. His distaste for Caracas seemed to have reached an unprecedented intensity. The famous "pyre of vanities"—the burning of his manuscripts—had already taken place; I should not like to say whether or not at the instigation of his wife. His state of mind had been further inflamed by other causes. As to his physical condition, this was ever more pitiful, and strengthened my impression that he took drugs. All the same, he began to talk in a more or less normal way about Belinsky, who was giving him some trouble with his attacks on the *Selected Correspondence*. Then suddenly, tears rising to his eyes, he interrupted himself and cried out: "No. No. It's too much, too much. I can't go on any longer," as well as other obscure and disconnected phrases which he would not clarify. He seemed to be talking to himself. He wrung his hands, shook his head, got up and sat down again after having taken four or five anxious steps round the room. When Caracas appeared, or rather when we went in to her later in the evening in her Oriental chamber, he controlled himself no longer and began to behave like an old man, if I may so express myself, in his second childhood, quite giving way to his absurd impulses. For instance, he kept nudging me and winking and senselessly repeating: "There she is, Foma Paskalovitch; there she is!" Meanwhile she seemed to look up at us with a disdainful attention. But behind these "mannerisms" one could feel in him a real repugnance, a repugnance which had, I suppose, now reached the limits of the endurable. Indeed . . .

After a certain time Nikolai Vassilevitch seemed to pluck up courage. He burst into tears, but somehow they were more manly tears. He wrung his hands again, seized mine in his, and walked up and down, muttering: "That's enough! We can't have any more of this. This is an unheard of thing. How can such a thing be happening to me? How can a man be expected to put up with *this?*"

He then leapt furiously upon the pump, the existence of which he seemed just to have remembered, and, with it in his hand, dashed like a whirlwind to Caracas. He inserted the tube in her anus and began to inflate her. . . . Weeping the while, he shouted like one possessed: "Oh, how I love her, how I love her, my poor, poor darling! . . . But she's going to burst! Unhappy Caracas, most pitiable of God's creatures! But die she must!"

Caracas was swelling up. Nikolai Vassilevitch sweated, wept and pumped. I wished to stop him but, I know not why, I had not the courage. She began to become deformed and shortly assumed the most monstrous aspect; and yet she had not given any signs of alarm—she was used to these jokes. But when she began to feel unbearably full, or perhaps when Nikolai Vassilevitch's intentions became plain to her, she took on an expression of bestial amazement, even a little beseeching, but still without losing that disdainful look. She was afraid, she was even committing herself to his mercy, but still she could not believe in the immediate approach of her fate; she could not believe in the frightful audacity of her husband. He could

not see her face because he was behind her. But I looked at
her with fascination, and did not move a finger.

At last the internal pressure came through the fragile bones
at the base of her skull, and printed on her face an inde-
scribable rictus. Her belly, her thighs, her lips, her breasts and
what I could see of her buttocks had swollen to incredible proportions. All of a sudden she belched, and gave a long hissing
groan; both these phenomena one could explain by the increase in pressure, which had suddenly forced a way out
through the valve in her throat. Then her eyes bulged franti-
cally, threatening to jump out of their sockets. Her ribs flared
wide apart and were no longer attached to the sternum, and
she resembled a python digesting a donkey. A donkey, did
I say? An ox! An elephant! At this point I believed her already
dead, but Nikolai Vassilevitch, sweating, weeping and repeating: "My dearest! My beloved! My best!" continued to pump.

She went off unexpectedly and, as it were, all of a piece.
It was not one part of her skin which gave way and the rest
which followed, but her whole surface at the same instant. She
scattered in the air. The pieces fell more or less slowly, according to their size, which was in no case above a very restricted
one. I distinctly remember a piece of her cheek, with some
lip attached, hanging on the corner of the mantelpiece. Nikolai
Vassilevitch stared at me like a madman. Then he pulled himself together and, once more with furious determination, he
began carefully to collect those poor rags which once had
been the shining skin of Caracas, and all of her.

"Good-by, Caracas," I thought I heard him murmur, "Good-
by! You were too pitiable!" And then suddenly and quite
audibly: "The fire! The fire! She too must end up in the fire."
He crossed himself—with his left hand, of course. Then,
when he had picked up all those shriveled rags, even climbing
on the furniture so as not to miss any, he threw them straight
on the fire in the hearth, where they began to burn slowly
and with an excessively unpleasant smell! Nikolai Vassilevitch, like all Russians, had a passion for throwing important
things in the fire.

Red in the face, with an inexpressible look of despair, and
yet of sinister triumph too, he gazed on the pyre of those
miserable remains. He had seized my arm and was squeezing
it convulsively. But those traces of what had once been a
being were hardly well alight when he seemed yet again to
pull himself together, as if he were suddenly remembering

something or taking a painful decision. In one bound he was
out of the room.

A few seconds later I heard him speaking to me through
the door in a broken, plaintive voice: "Foma Paskalovitch, I
want you to promise not to look. *Golubchik*, promise not to
look at me when I come in."

I don't know what I answered, or whether I tried to re-
assure him in any way. But he insisted, and I had to promise
him, as if he were a child, to hide my face against the wall
and only turn round when he said I might. The door then
opened violently and Nikolai Vassilevitch burst into the room
and ran to the fireplace.

And here I must confess my weakness, though I consider
it justified by the extraordinary circumstances. I looked round
before Nikolai Vassilevitch told me I could; it was stronger
than me. I was just in time to see him carrying something
in his arms, something which he threw on the fire with all the
rest, so that it suddenly flared up. At that, since the desire
to see had entirely mastered every other thought in me, I
dashed to the fireplace. But Nikolai Vassilevitch placed himself between me and it and pushed me back with a strength
of which I had not believed him capable. Meanwhile the object was burning and giving off clouds of smoke. And before
he showed any sign of calming down there was nothing left
but a heap of silent ashes.

The true reason why I wished to see was because I had
already glimpsed. But it was only a glimpse, and perhaps I
should not allow myself to introduce even the slightest element
of uncertainty into this true story. And yet, an eyewitness
account is not complete without a mention of that which the
witness knows with less than complete certainty. To cut a long
story short, that something was a baby. Not a flesh and blood
baby, of course, but more something in the line of a rubber
doll or a model. Something, which, to judge by its appearance,
could have been called *Caracas'* son.

Was I mad too? That I do not know, but I do know that
this was what I saw, not clearly, but with my own eyes.
And I wonder why it was that when I was writing this just
now I didn't mention that when Nikolai Vassilevitch came
back into the room he was muttering between his clenched
teeth: "Him too! Him too!"

And that is the sum of my knowledge of Nikolai Vassilevitch's wife. In the next chapter I shall tell what happened
to him afterwards, and that will be the last chapter of his

life. But to give an interpretation of his feelings for his wife, or indeed for anything, is quite another and more difficult matter, though I have attempted it elsewhere in this volume, and refer the reader to that modest effort. I hope I have thrown sufficient light on a most controversial question and that I have unveiled the mystery, if not of Gogol, then at least of his wife. In the course of this I have implicitly given the lie to the insensate accusation that he ill-treated or even beat his wife, as well as other like absurdities. And what else can be the goal of a humble biographer such as the present writer but to serve the memory of that lofty genius who is the object of his study?

YURI KAZAKOV

Autumn in the Oak Woods

*Yuri Kazakov (1927–   ) is one of the younger
generation of Soviet writers. Born in Moscow, he
was educated at the Gorki Institute, and published
his first book, Smoke, in 1953. Although a native of
Moscow who has lived all his life in the Soviet
world, he has not escaped political criticism of his
work, which often portrays the hard realities of life
in modern Russia. His realism, however, is softened
by a strain of poetry and a strong feeling for nature,
both important characteristics of earlier generations
of Russian writers.*

I TOOK THE pail to get some water from the spring. I was
happy that night because she was arriving on the night boat.
But I knew about that kind of happiness and how unreliable
it can be, so I took the pail purposely, in the pretense that
I was simply going for water, and not thinking about her
arrival at all. Something too good had been taking form inside me all that autumn.

It was a blue-black night in late autumn, and I didn't feel
like going out, but I went anyway. It took me a long time
to get my lantern lit, and when it finally caught, the glass
fogged over and the feeble patch of light flickered and flickered. But it stayed lit and finally the glass dried and cleared.

I purposely left a light on at home, so I could see the
lighted window as I went down the leaf-covered path to Oka.
My lantern cast a flickering light ahead of me and to the
sides and I probably resembled a watchman in a railroad

From GOING TO TOWN AND OTHER STORIES. Reprinted by
permission of Houghton Mifflin Company.

yard, except that under my feet piles of maple leaves rustled wetly, and even in the dim light of the lantern the larch needles looked golden and the barberries glowed on the naked branches.

It's terrible walking alone at night with a lantern. Your boots make the only noise, you are the only thing exposed by light; everything else is hiding and contemplating you in silence.

The light in my house vanished as soon as the path dipped sharply over the bank and lost itself in a disorderly jumble of fir and oak branches. The last tall camomile flowers, the tips of fir branches, and various naked twigs brushed against my pail, some noiselessly, some with a clear boom! boom!

The path became steeper, more twisted, more lined with birch trees, their white trunks stepping momentarily out of the gloom. Then there were no more birch trees, the path became stony, there was a fresh wind, and though I could see nothing beyond the patch of lantern light, I had the feeling of broad expanse ahead of me. I had reached the river.

I could already see the buoy far out to my right. Its red light had a twin in the reflection in the water. Then I saw the nearer buoy bobbing on my side and I could make out the outline of the whole river.

I walked down to the river through the wet grass and willow branches, to the place where the boat usually stopped if anyone was getting off in our remote neck of the woods. The spring was murmuring and gurgling monotonously in the darkness. I set the lantern down, went to the spring, scooped some water into the pail, had a drink, and wiped my face on my sleeve. Then I set the dripping pail next to the lantern, and began to watch the landing pier far down the river.

The boat was at the pier already, its green and red deck lights just barely visible. I sat down and lit a cigarette. My hands were cold and shaking. I suddenly thought if she's not on board and they see my lantern they'll stop, thinking I want to get on. I put out the lantern.

And it was dark suddenly, the river pinpricked by the buoy lights. The silence was resonant. At that hour I was probably the only one around for miles. Up on the hill, behind the oak woods, the little village was dark; everyone there had long been asleep. Only in my house, at the edge of the woods, was there a light burning.

I thought about the distance she had had to come, just to

see me, sleeping or sitting by the train window talking to
someone, all the way from Archangelsk. About how she'd
been thinking all that time, just as I had, about our meeting.
About how she'd see the shores of Oka that I'd described
when I'd asked her to come. About her coming out on deck,
the wind blowing in her face, bringing the scent of the wet
oak woods. About her conversations en route, sitting down
in the warm cabins, next to sweating windows, listening to explanations about where to get off and where to spend the night
if no one was there to meet her.

Then I remembered my own wanderings in the north country, how I'd lived in a fishery and how during the white nights
she and I had gone harpooning while the fishermen were
snoring away in their beds. We would wait for low tide and
then take the boat out to sea. She used to row without a
sound while I searched the depths, looking through the seaweed for the outline of a fish. I'd let the harpoon down silently, jab the sharp white prongs into the fish's back and then
I'd lean over and bring it out of the water. Flailing and
splashing water into our faces, its terrible jaws agape, it would
tie itself into a knot and straighten itself out again like a
triton. Then it would writhe in the bottom of the boat for a
long time, trembling in the grip of death.

And I thought about the year just passed, how happy it
had been for me, how many stories I'd been able to write,
and how many more, probably, in what was left of the quiet
solitary days on the river, surrounded by nature as it faded
slowly into winter.

The night was all around me. When I inhaled, the bright
spark of my cigarette lit up my face and hands and boots
but I could still see the stars. There were so many and they
were so brilliant this fall that the river, the trees, the white
stones along the shore, the dark rectangular fields on the hills
were all illuminated in their smoky light. In the ravines it was
much darker and more fragrant.

And I thought that the most important thing was not whether you lived thirty or fifty or eighty years, because whatever
the number it wouldn't be much, and dying would still be
horrible. The most important thing was how many nights you
had in life like this one.

The boat had already moved away from the pier. It was
still so far away that it was impossible to detect its movement.
It seemed to be standing still, but the distance was growing
between it and the pier. That meant it was moving upriver

toward me. Pretty soon I heard the high roar of the diesel, and I was suddenly afraid that she wasn't coming, that she wasn't on the boat, and that I was waiting in vain. I thought of all the time and distance that had to be overcome in order for her to get to me, and I realized how fragile all my plans for a happy life here together were.

"What am I doing?" I said aloud, and stood up. I couldn't sit still any longer and I began to pace the shore. "What am I doing?" I kept repeating hopelessly as I watched the boat, thinking how odd I'd feel climbing back up with my water all by myself, thinking how empty my house would seem, wondering finally if we were really so unlucky that, after all this time, after all our failures, we weren't going to meet again, and thus turn everything to dust.

I remembered how three months ago I had left the north for home, and she had come unexpectedly from the fishery to see me off. As I got into the motorboat that would take me to the ship, she'd stood on the pier saying over and over, "Where are you going? You don't understand anything. You don't understand anything. Where are you going?" And sitting in the boat, amid the farewells, women's tears, the shouts of boys, and all kinds of noise, I had understood that I was doing something childish by leaving and I hoped, vaguely, to make it all right in the future.

I recalled a month after that in Moscow and what had happened to us there, but recalled it hurriedly, fleetingly, because it had been a bad time, and had just about finished everything between us.

The boat was now quite near and I stopped pacing. I stood at the very edge of the bank over the black water, unable to take my eyes off the boat, squinting and breathing hard in excitement and anticipation.

The sound of the motor suddenly dropped, the searchlight went on in the wheelhouse and a smoky beam of light played along the shore, jumping from tree to tree. They were looking for a place to land. The boat turned to the right and the intense light of the searchlight hit me in the face. I turned away and then looked back. On the upper deck a sailor was standing ready to let the ladder down over the side to shore. And next to him, dressed in a light-colored dress, she was standing.

The prow of the boat dug softly, deep into the sand. The sailor let the ladder down and helped her off. I took her suitcase, carried it back and set it down next to the pail, and then I slowly turned around. The searchlight blinded me. I couldn't see her at all. Then she was coming toward me, throwing an enormous flickering shadow on the wooded slope above. I wanted to kiss her, but changed my mind. Not standing in the light of the searchlight. We just stood there, shielding our eyes from the light, smiling tensely, watching the boat. The boat went into reverse, the searchlight swung around and went out; down below the diesel rang out and the boat moved quickly upriver, the entire length of its lower deck alight. We were left alone.

"Well hello!" I said in confusion. She got up on tiptoes, took a painful grip on my shoulders and kissed my eyes.

I coughed. "Let's go," I said. "God, it's dark. Wait, I'll light the lantern."

I lit it and again it fogged over and we had to wait for the flame to take hold and for the glass to dry and clear. Then we started off: I went ahead with the lantern and suitcase, and she came behind with the pail.

"That's not too heavy for you?" I asked after a moment.

"Go on, go on," she said huskily.

She'd always had a low, husky voice. She was tough and husky in general, and for a long time I hadn't liked it in her. Because I like sweetness in women. But now on the river-bank at night, as we followed each other up to the house, after all the days of anger and separation, letters, of strange and ominous dreams, her voice, her strong body, her rough hands, her northern accent, were like the song of a strange bird, left behind after the autumn migration.

We turned right, into the ravine where there was a narrow road up the hill, which someone had cobbled once, but overgrown now with nut trees and pines and ashberry. We started up, our lantern barely lighting the way in the dark, and a river of stars floated over us, strewn with black pine branches, alternately obscuring and revealing the stars.

Scarcely breathing, we reached the leafy path and started walking side by side.

I suddenly had the urge to tell her all about the place, about its wild life, about various minor incidents. "Take a whiff," I said, "doesn't it smell good?"

"Like wine," she said, breathing fast, trying to keep up. "I smelled it back on the ship."

"That's leaves. Now, come over here."

We left our things on the path and taking the lantern, jumped across the ditch into the underbrush.

"Should be here someplace," I muttered.

"Mushrooms!" she marveled. "Mushrooms!"

Finally I found what I was looking for. A place where the grass and needles and yellow leaves were scattered with white chicken feathers.

"Look," I said, shining the light. "We have a chicken farm in the village. When the chickens grow up, they let them go free. And every day a fox comes here, hides in the bushes and gets one as they wander past. And eats it right on the spot."

I pictured the gray-snouted fox to myself, licking and snorting, trying to get the feathers out of his nose.

"He should be killed," she said.

"I have a gun; you and I can go into the woods and maybe we'll be lucky."

We returned to the path and went on. The lighted window in my house appeared and I began to think about how it would be when we got there. Suddenly I wanted a drink. I had some berry wine that I'd made myself. I enjoy making wine: picking the berries in the woods, bringing them home, putting them through a sieve until they run out in an amber stream, and then pouring the juice in a bottle with some vodka.

"And at home it's winter now!" she said as if it were an amazing thought. "Dvina is frozen over except for a passage broken by the icebreakers. Everything is white but the passage, which is black and steamy. When a boat comes through the dogs run along the ice beside it. For some reason they run in threes."

She said "threes" with a northern accent, and I could see Dvina, the ships, Archangelsk, her village on the White Sea. The empty two-story buildings, the black walls, the silence and the solitude.

"Is there any ice in the sea yet?" I asked.

"There will be soon," she said, and thought for a minute, trying to remember something perhaps. "I'll have to go back by reindeer, if . . ."

She stopped. I waited, listening to her footsteps and her breathing. Then "If what?" I asked.

"Nothing," she said, in a slow husky voice. "If the sea freezes over, that's what!"

We stamped across the porch and went in.

"Ooooo!" she said, looking around, taking off her scarf.

Whenever she was surprised and happy, she made that low, drawn-out "ooo."

It was a little old house I'd rented from a Muscovite who lived in it only during the summer. There was almost no furniture, only some old beds, a table, and some chairs. The walls were rough hewn, and powdered white. There was electricity, a radio, a stove, and some fat old books I loved to read in the evenings.

"Take off your coat," I said. "We'll get the stove going."

I went outside to get some kindling for the stove. I was so happy I was beside myself; my head was ringing, my hands were shaking, I felt weak all over and needed to sit down. The stars twinkled, small and bright. There'll be frost tonight, I thought. That means the leaves will be gone by morning. Winter will be here soon.

Three slow hoots rose up and hung over Oka, echoing in the hills. A tugboat was passing down below, one of the few old steam tugs left. The new cutters and barges have high, short, nasal whistles. Awakened by the noise, several roosters at the chicken farm screeched out in a falsetto.

I cut some kindling, picked up some logs, and went back in. She'd taken off her coat and was standing with her back to me, rustling some newspapers around, getting something out of her suitcase. She had on a colored dress that was too tight for her. If I had taken her out somewhere in Moscow, to see friends or to a club, everyone would have laughed at her, although it was probably her best dress. I remembered that she usually wore tights tucked into her boots, with an old faded skirt on top, and it looked very good.

I put on the kettle and began to kindle the stove. Pretty soon it started humming and snapping, sending off the smell of smoke and firewood.

"This is for you," she said, standing behind me.

I turned and saw a salmon lying on the table. A splendid, pale silver salmon, with a wide dark body, and a jutting lower jaw. The house smelled of fish and the sea. And I had a yearning for wide open spaces again.

She was from the White Sea. She was even born at sea, in a motorboat, one white-gold night in summer. But white nights meant nothing to her; it's only the stranger who looks at them and goes crazy with the loneliness and the silence. It's only when you're visiting, torn away from everyone, forgotten by everyone, that you lie awake at night thinking, thinking, saying to yourself, Now, now, it's all right, it's just the white nights, you won't be here forever. What's it to you that the sun has stolen a slice of the sea, go to sleep, go to sleep . . .

But she? She slept soundly in her curtained-off room at the fishery, because she knew she'd have to get up in the morning, row out to the nets with the fishermen, bring in the fish, cook the fish soup, wash the dishes. And that was her life, every summer, until I came.

And here we were at Oka, drinking berry wine, eating salmon, talking and reminiscing. About how we used to go harpooning in the white nights; how we used to help the fishermen bring in the nets before a storm, gulping the salty water in our excitement; going to the lighthouse for bread; sitting with our shoes and coats off at night in the village library, reading all the newspapers and magazines that had come in our absence.

We reminisced about everything, but not about Moscow which was just a month afterwards, because that was our worst time.

I threw my coat on the floor, fur side up, and putting down the teakettle and some candy, we took our cups and lay down, by turns looking at each other, the coals, and the sparks skittering around in the fire. In order to make it last longer, I'd get up from time to time and throw more wood into the stove and when it caught and snapped, we had to turn away from the heat.

At about two o'clock I got up in the darkness, because I couldn't sleep. It seemed to me that if I fell asleep she'd go off somewhere, and I wouldn't have her next to me. I wanted to know she was with me all the time. Take me into your dream, so I can be with you always, I wanted to say, because we can't be separated for long. Then I thought about people who go away and whom we never see again—that they are as good as dead to us. And we to them. It's strange, the thoughts that come into your head at night when you can't sleep for joy or pain.

"Are you asleep?" I asked quietly.

"No," she answered from bed. "I'm fine. Don't look and I'll get dressed."

I went to the corner where the radio was and turned it on. I was looking for music but all I could find was static and muttered announcements. I knew there must be some, and I found it. A velvety male voice said something in En-

glish, and then there was a pause, and I realized they were
going to play music.

I jumped when I heard the melody because I recognized
it. Whenever I'm feeling especially good, or especially bad,
I remember this particular jazz melody. It's not my kind of
music, but there's an idea hidden in it. I don't know whether
it's an idea of joy or of sorrow. It often comes back to me
when I'm traveling somewhere, or when something has made
me happy or depressed. I remembered that night in Moscow
when we'd ridden and ridden and walked and walked, lonely
and unhappy, and though I didn't hear one word of reproach
from her, I felt ashamed.

She was leaving for Archangelsk after five horrible days
in Moscow. Everything was as usual in a Moscow railway
station: the porters were wheeling around on their baggage
carts, bumping into each other, everyone was in a hurry,
everyone saying goodbye, precious minutes flying. She was
leaving, although she didn't have to, she still had time, several
more free days. I was disappointed, bitter, angry with myself
and with her. I thought how empty I'd be without her, drinking again, trying to cope somehow with unhappiness.

"Don't go," I said.

She just smiled and looked up at me, her eyes flickering.
Her eyes are dark with green lights in them and it's impossible
to tell if they are green or black. But at the moment she
looked at me, they were black, that I remember distinctly.

"This is stupid!" I said. "First I leave the north, with nothing understood between us, and now you. How stupid. Don't
go!"

"What more is there to say?" she muttered fiercely.

"You shouldn't have stayed with those relatives of yours,
they were always at home."

"Who with then? At your place maybe? It would have
been the same," she persisted. "What more is there to say?"

"Let's go to a hotel, you'll stay a few more days."

"The train's coming," she said, turning.

"No, stay, think for a minute. After everything we said in
those letters, we can be alone together, just think!"

She didn't say anything for a long time, biting her lips,
her eyes moving across my face. Finally, hurt and wistful,
she asked, "And you'll be glad if I stay?"

I found it hard to breathe, and there was a lump in my
throat. I turned quickly and entered her car, bumping and
elbowing my way, and found her compartment, grabbed her

bag and left. I still remember how the conductors standing by the train stared at us.

"Let's go," I said.

"What about my ticket?" she asked, her eyes shimmering, her mouth trembling.

"To hell with it!" I said and took her hand. We went out to the square and found a taxi.

"To the hotel," I said.

"Which?" the driver asked.

"I don't care which!"

The car started, and moved toward the glow of the city's lights, past railway stations, apartment buildings, crowds of people.

"Stop here, old man," I told the driver at a store, and got out to buy a bottle of wine.

I came back, tucking it into my pocket. I pictured us drinking it, sitting alone with raised glasses, looking into each other's eyes. I could actually taste it when we came to a hotel and I went in to the desk.

"We haven't any rooms," he calmly informed me.

"Any room will do, you understand, any at all. The worst or the best you have."

"We haven't any rooms," he repeated sharply, and grabbed in irritation for the incessantly ringing telephone.

She was waiting for me in the lobby, looking in awe at the tremendous columns and mirrors. And she looked awed by me too, as if I were lord and master of it all! We went back to the taxi.

"Take us to another," I said irritably.

She got in without a murmur, and we began driving around Moscow. I dropped in on a friend to borrow some money and nearly asked him to put us up, but his sister had guests. I looked at them, the wine on the table, down at the cassock supporting all those feet in narrow moccasins, and I didn't ask him. But I took some more money.

"Have a drink," he said suddenly, intercepting my glance.

"No thanks, they're waiting for me."

An hour, two hours passed and we were still driving, driving and always the same thing, "no room." Coming out on the street, I looked up at the tall hotel and apartment buildings, story upon story, row upon row of windows, so many still lighted, and I thought of everyone sitting or lounging peacefully at this hour, listening to the radio, reading them-

selves to sleep, holding their wives in their arms, and there
was a stab in my heart.

Worn out finally, we took her bag to the station, checked
it, and walked off slowly to Sokolniki. It was twelve o'clock
midnight.

"What are we going to do?" I asked with a laugh.

"I don't know," she said wearily. "Maybe we could go to
a restaurant? I'd like something to eat."

"The restaurants are all closed," I said with another stupid
laugh, looking at my watch. "Let's go downtown, and walk
around."

We strode along, the way we used to walk the seashore
in the north, when we didn't want to be late for the movie
in the club which was six miles away. All lights were out
except for one on the other side of the street. There were
almost no people on the streets. Finally we got to Tverskii
Boulevard and sat down on a bench.

"And your place is impossible?" she asked hopefully.

"Idiot! Why else have we had to walk all over town? And
just where would you have my mother and father go?"

"All right, all right," she said. "Don't get nasty. I'm leaving
tomorrow, there's a train in the morning. Then . . ." she
sighed, "then you can come see us again sometime."

I took her in my arms. She pressed close and closed her
eyes.

"We can just sit like this, can't we?" she murmured, shifting into a more comfortable position on the bench. "You're
sweet, I love you, you dope, I was in love with you up
north, you just didn't know it."

Sitting up for a minute, she slipped off her shoes, drew
up her legs, and pulled her skirt down over them.

"My feet hurt," she murmured sleepily. "Shoes . . . I'm not
used to them. Why don't people in Moscow go barefoot?"

Two policemen emerged from a back alley. Seeing us, one
of them stepped into the light and came toward us.

"Move along, friend." For some reason he spoke only to
me. "That's not allowed."

"What isn't allowed?" I asked as she fumbled in embarrassment, getting her shoes back on her swollen feet.

"No back talk! You heard me, move along!"

We got up and left. I began looking at the apartment house
windows again, and kept seeing a room with a cassock. There
was nothing else in that room but a soft pink light and a
cassock.

"Listen, shall we duck into a doorway somewhere?" I asked uncertainly.

"Yes let's," she agreed, with a faint smile. "We can sit on the steps and I'll take off my shoes."

We entered a dark courtyard, went back to the farthest doorway in the corner, went in, closed the door behind us, and sat on the steps. She took off her shoes immediately and began wiping off the step.

"You tired?" I asked and lit a cigarette. "Poor thing, we haven't had much luck in Moscow."

"True." She rubbed her cheek on my shoulder. "It's a very big city."

We heard footsteps. The door opened and the janitress came in and saw us.

"You get out of here!" she shrieked. "Curses on the both of you devils, alley cats! Get out or I'll start blowing!"

And she pulled a shiny whistle out of her apron pocket. She had a mean, high cheekboned face. We went back into the courtyard, followed by the janitress swearing at us all the while. Back on the street, we looked at each other and burst out laughing.

"It's not much like your White Sea," I said.

"Never mind," she said soothingly, "let's just walk. Or shall we go to the station and sleep on the benches?"

"All right," I agreed, then suddenly something struck me. "Listen, I'm a dope, let's go for a drive. We can take a taxi, I've the money, and we can go fifteen miles or so, that's what we'll do!"

A taxi was cruising down the street. Coming home late at night, I always love to watch the taxis. They weave a charmed circle through the sleeping city, their vacant lights blinking. Those green lights always make you want to take off for somewhere far away.

We hailed a taxi.

"Out of town?" the driver repeated. "I'll take you for," visibly jacking his price up, "seven and a half."

"All right," I said. I didn't care.

The drive made me sleepy. The road was deserted. It was dark in the west, but the east was growing light, the sun beginning to come up. A steady wind was blowing outside, and the cab reeked of gasoline.

"Anywhere here?" asked the driver, slowing down near a grove of trees.

"This is as far as we're going. The outskirts all right with you?" he asked, looking at her.

We got out and shivered in the predawn cold.

"Half hour enough?" he asked, looking at me appraisingly. "I'm going to sleep. Wake me when you get back. Got a cigarette? Let me have it . . ."

He turned off to the side of the road and we went through the tall grass toward the woods. I was feeling damp and cold, nothing more. My suit grew stiff and heavy, my shoes were wet, and my pants lost their crease. I watched the dusky light in the woods, wondering what to do. She looked tired and sleepy and there were rings under her eyes. Suddenly she gave a great yawn and looked around blankly, as if she were wondering what we had come for.

"Back to the woods," she half muttered, and gave me a sudden hostile look.

Then I yawned too, feeling bored and irritable about not being home in bed, but out here in the damp and cold.

"I'm fed up," she said, in the midst of a yawn, huskily pronouncing "fed" "fad." "Oh God, what's the point, I don't want this, let's go back."

"All right with me," I said listlessly, and yawned again. "But let's drink this, or it'll go to waste."

I got out the bottle and tried to uncork it, but the cork was in very tight. So I shoved it inside.

"Drink," I said, handing her the warm bottle.

"I don't want any," she murmured, but took the bottle and with a sigh began to drink.

Two streams ran down her chin like blood. She coughed and gave the bottle back to me. I finished it and threw it away.

"Let's go," I said, feeling better.

We made our way back through the wet woods, through the ferns, across the rolling meadow, and all the way she held her dress up so as not to stain the hem.

"Why so early?" the driver sneered, looking at me. "You didn't suit each other?"

"Let's roll," I said furiously, barely able to refrain from hitting him.

We dozed on the way back, falling against each other on the curves, and I remember finding those contacts with her body unpleasant, and she probably did too. It was five in the morning and we had three more hours to kill before train time. I felt bad, the wine had gone to my head, leaving it heavy and foggy.

Those three hours were a torture, mainly because I couldn't go away, but had to stay with her to the end. We lasted it out somehow and then once more I was putting her on the train without knowing what to say. My head was splitting.

"All right then, write me," she said, taking the handrail. I found the strength to put my arms around her.

"Don't be angry," I muttered, kissed her forehead, and made for the exit. I remember feeling surprised at how relieved I was when I left her, but somewhere deep inside it was sad somehow, my soul smarted with a hurt of some kind, and I was ashamed.

I dragged the coat over to the radio and we sat on it, leaning against each other. All these months I'd had the feeling of loss, and now what I had found was even better than what I had imagined.

The bass murmured elegiacally, searching in the darkness for its counterpoint, losing its way in uncertainty, rising and falling, its slow pace reminiscent of the movement of the stars. The saxophone listened compassionately, but the trumpet rose up angrily again and again, the piano chords coming between them like the Revelation. And underneath, like a metronome, like time, the soft, hollow, syncopating beat of the drum.

"Let's not turn on the light, all right?" she said, looking at the little blinking eye on the green dial of the radio.

"All right," I agreed, and thought that I might never have a night like this again. I was sad that three hours of it had already passed. I wanted it to be starting from the beginning, so I could go down to wait with the lantern again, so we could reminisce again, and then be afraid again of letting each other go in the darkness.

She got up to get something, and looked out the window. "It's snowing," she said huskily.

I got up too and looked out into the darkness. Silently, the snow was falling. The first real snow of the year. I pictured the mousetracks that would be around the pile of brushwood in the woods tomorrow, and the rabbit tracks around the locust tree where rabbits like to nibble at night. I thought of my gun and I felt so good a quiver of joy ran through me. God, how good! How glorious that the snow was falling, that we were alone with music, with our past and with a future that might be better than our past, that tomorrow I'd be taking her to all my favorite spots, Oka, the fields, the hills, the woods and ravines. The night was passing, but

we couldn't sleep. We went on talking in whispers, holding
each other, afraid of losing each other. We rekindled the
stove and stared into its fiery jaws, watching the red light
reflected in each other's faces. At seven, when the windows
were already growing light, we fell asleep. We slept a long
time because there was no one in our house to wake us.

The sun came up while we were asleep, and everything
melted, only to freeze again. After tea I took my gun and we
went out. The winter light in our eyes was so white and
the clean air so sharp that at first they were painful. The
snow had stopped, but there was an icy, thin, almost trans-
parent crust over everything. The cowbarn was steaming
fragrantly and some calves were huddled near it, their hoofs
clattering as if they were on a wooden bridge. This was because the wash water from the barn was running just underneath the upper crust of snow. Several of them, their curly
gray flanks spread wide apart, were urinating over and over
again, wagging their tails in enthusiasm, producing emerald patches of young wet rye in the snow.

We took the road. The ruts were smoothly frosted over
but when our boots broke through the crust, there was a
brown splash of muddy water. In the woods the last pale
yellow dandelions poked through the ice. Needles, leaves, and
the last of the mushrooms could all be seen frozen into the
ice and when we kicked at the mushrooms, they broke off
and skittered around. The snow under our feet turned gray
and crunched loudly all around us, in front, in back, and to
the sides.

From a distance the fields on the hillsides were a smoky
green and looked as if they had been sprinkled with flour.
The haystacks looked black, and the woods, naked and pen-
etrable and dark, were sharply accentuated by an occasional
white birch trunk. The aspen trunks were covered with a shiny
velvet green, and yes, there was still some color on the wooded
hill, the last unfallen leaves red-capping the trees. Through
the woods the river could be seen and looked, at that distance,
deserted and cold. We went down into the snowy ravine,
leaving deep dirty prints at first, then clean ones. We had a
drink from a spring near a chopped-down ash tree. Oak and
maple leaves were settling thickly to the bottom of the spring
box, and the tree stump, which had turned an amber color,
smelled bitter and cold.

"Nice?" I asked and looked at her. I was amazed: her eyes were green!

"Nice!" she said, licking her lips as she looked around.

"Better than the White Sea?" I asked.

She looked at the river again and up the slope. Her eyes turned even greener.

"Well the White Sea . . ." she said vaguely. "We have, ah . . . But you have oak trees here!" she interrupted herself. "How did you find this place?"

I was happy, but I felt strange and fearful. This autumn had turned out very well. I lit a cigarette, trying to relax, exhaling smoke and steam. A tug coming from Aleksin appeared, cresting a wave swiftly as we watched. Steam poured up from its engines and jets of water spewed from the sides into the river.

When the tug finally disappeared around the bend, we climbed up through the woods, holding hands, so we could get another look at Oka from above. We walked in silence, in a dream that had brought us together at last.

ALAN SILLITOE

Isaac Starbuck

Alan Sillitoe (1928-   ) is the son of a tannery laborer in Nottingham, England, a background that accounts for his powerful and clear-eyed view of English working-class life. He left school at 14, worked at various jobs as a laborer, joined the R.A.F., and worked for some time as a radio operator in Malaya.

He is probably the strongest of the young English writers who rebel against the institutionalized life they see as the typical lot of the working man. In his most famous stories, Saturday Night and Sunday Morning *and* The Loneliness of the Long Distance Runner, *the aimlessness and narrowness of life come through with graphic power, but there is also humor and warmth. Isaac Starbuck is an angry young man who seeks escape from the routinized trap he feels life to be. He is far two human and three dimensional, however, to be merely the abstraction "the angry young man." He is a prolific novelist, playwright and story writer whose best-known recent works are* The Widower's Son *(1976) and* The Story Teller *(1979).*

"WHY DON'T YOU go out?" was something Beatty never thought she'd need to say to anyone she married, especially Isaac Starbuck. The kids were in bed, the house quiet. The odd car cracked by, the shout of a youth calling some girl. Fire rattled its flames, a knife and fork eating up coal. "You do nothing but stay in night after night."

"I know. I want to read, and there's no other time to do it."

"Ah, cowboy books. War books." She'd taken to knitting again. "Let's see if this pullover's too long." He stood like

some robust animal ready for the slaughter, full of weight
and dignity with which to incriminate the unthinking actions
of the world. "Sit down then, ox."

"There's nowhere to go," he said, "in any case."

"That's only because you're content to sit here. You won't
bother yourself. Why don't you go and see Tom?"

"And play Monopoly? He switches off the TV because he
thinks it's bad manners to have it on when anybody calls,
then gets out his bloody Monopoly set after he's asked how
you and the kids are; I want to talk—about the world, about
politics, but all Tom's interested in is selling houses and hotels! It's kids' stuff."

"I just thought you wanted to go out."

"When I do, you want me to stay in. Make up your mind.
I come back from a union meeting and you look at me as
if I've been knocking on with some fancy woman."

"Only because it's so late. Don't think I'd care though if
you did go with somebody else. I might even be glad to get
rid of you."

"I'll bet you would. You'd run down to a lawyer to get a
maintenance order even before charging off with the kids
to Tom's and Mary's."

She held herself back: "I might surprise you by doing something you never thought I'd do. Like having another chap
of my own, ready to go off with."

"And the kids?"

"Yes. With three kids. I know somebody who'd have them
this minute. He'd run if I was as much as to snap my fingers."

"Snap, then," he said curtly, "and see if I care."

"I don't want to. I'm just telling you."

"Well don't. I don't want to know." Not that he was afraid
for her, but he was scared for himself, any minute ready
to go out on the wild. Such open talk made it seem as if
they'd already done it on each other.

"You brought it up," she said, "talking about fancy women.
I can see the way your mind's running."

"Why don't you let it drop? I might have brought it up,
but you're worrying it to death."

"Still, don't let me hear of you with any woman."

"You won't," he said, shaken that they should talk about
what had been on his mind for months.

"Not that I wouldn't know," she taunted. "You'd never
be able to hide anything like that from me. I'd know in a
flash."

"There'll never be anything to know," he said. "Don't think I wouldn't be able to keep it from you though if there was. I wasn't born yesterday. Nor the day before yesterday, either."

"You seem bloody sure of yourself."

"You wouldn't think I was up to much if I wasn't, would you?"

"Not in that way, you deceitful rat. Don't think I don't keep an eye on you. We've got three kids, and they aren't going to suffer."

He laughed. "You've been reading too much of that *Women's Realm* tripe. Nothing's happened, you know."

"Maybe not, but watch as it don't."

"Are you trying to tell me what to do and what not to do? Because if you are, you can pack it in. All you're doing is putting ideas into my head."

"I can't put anything in as wasn't there before."

"Don't be too sure. I'm as innocent as driven snow. I'm not guilty. All I've got suspicious is a few blackheads on my face, and that ain't through V. D. either. If you can tell me when I might have time to carry on with other women I'd be grateful, because I can't think of any."

After supper, she said: "So you want to go on the loose? As if I didn't know. Men are all alike. They get married, make sure their wives have a house full of kids, then get out and enjoy themselves."

"I think you want me to go on the loose," he said, feeling lighter in mood with food inside him, "the way you're talking."

"I'm just trying to find out which way your mind lies."

"Now you know."

"Yes, now I know."

"I'd rather do that than play Monopoly with that pop-eyed brother of yours, and that's a fact."

"He's not pop-eyed. He's got more intelligence and go in him than you'll ever have. At least he went out to Canada."

"He came back as well. It didn't get him very far."

"Why don't you try it and see how far it gets you? You've got a few hundred in the bank."

"That's to buy a car with. I've got my work here. When I've got no work, that's the time to get out. I don't like snow, so if I go anywhere it'll be Australia. Plenty of sun would suit me better."

He bought a car the following spring. While lukewarm sun

still lay over water and fields, he'd take them at weekends and after work on long excursions up Trent valley, beyond Bleasby and Thurgarton, Farndon and Newark. Nothing more was said about him staying late at union meetings. Now it was: "Why don't you ever take me out? You never take me."

"That's a lie."

"Calling me a liar now. I'm not a liar. I wish I was. As good a liar as you are, anyway."

"I often take you out in the car, you know I do."

"Always with the kids. A quick run ten miles out to Matlock or Southwell, a quick pint and then back. I mean out."

"You want to go to Buckingham Palace and have tea? I'll get queenie on the blower. We go out on Saturday night. I could get you to union meetings, but you aren't interested. You've met my pals and you don't like them because we talk about work and politics. What more can I do?"

"I want some life," she said.

"Why don't you go out on your own, then? Or with Mary, or some pals? I won't mind."

"I know you wouldn't. You'd just use it as an excuse to go off gallivanting."

"You said you weren't jealous. Make up your mind."

"I'm not jealous. It's just that I don't want you going all over the place."

"I've got my own life. I'm not tied to your apron strings."

"And I've got my life as well."

"Use it, then."

"I will. I'm not tied to your bootlaces, either."

"I wouldn't want you to be."

"That's the trouble. You don't want me around at all. I think you'd feel fine if me and the kids vanished off the face of the earth. Then you'd be as free as you've always wanted to be." The words stung, because she was dead right. But if he didn't swear blind she was dead wrong the marriage would collapse like dust and ashes.

2

Before he knew what was happening he'd fetched her a drink, and under the foggy noise of the pub was saying how much he loved her. She was slim, though well-figured, with a round face and short dark hair. Plump pale cheeks and a small mouth indicated a lascivious discontent. "You've only just met me," she said, "so how can you know?"

"Because I could pick you up and carry you upstairs," he said, "if I was to try."

"I don't weigh all that much, so it wouldn't make you a Samson."

He drank: "I never take a woman to bed I can't pick up. Golden rule. Have another."

"No, thanks. What's wrong with women you can't lift up?"

"Too fat. Half a pound of meat before you get to it. Your sort's more passionate."

"I save my passion for my husband."

"All married women should be like you."

"Isn't your wife like me—like that?"

"I'm not married. Made up my mind at ten to stay with my mother all my life."

"You've got too many answers. I don't trust you. I never trust a man who won't go to bed with a woman he can't pick up."

In her bedroom she asked: "Shall I take all my clothes off?"

"Of course," he answered. "You think I'm a pervert?" He was surprised at himself, one minute because he should have done it sooner, and the next because he'd done it already. Five years faithful to one wife must be a record. He was half drunk, but that was no excuse. "Where's your husband?"

"Away till tomorrow night."

"Suits me"—and he was in.

"Don't spill your cocoa"—and he wondered how common you could get.

His large grey car rumbled down the cobblestoned street, feathers of blue smoke spinning from its exhaust. Hanging between the rear fender and the last rib of the luggage rack a man outside was fisting with all his might at the roof.

Isaac lifted his foot from the gas pedal, hoping his passenger would drop off without a twisted ankle or a blue-black face. Noise at work had been robbing him of sleep, the rattling brainkill of assembling tractors. Friday gave way to human noise, but now the insane drumming above his hungover tongue persisted all down the street. He slid his vehicle neatly to the kerb and, hating fuss and violence, got out and walked leisurely towards the back.

They collided with a shout, like two shields, but without damage. A morning paperboy heard the elder man say: "I caught you red-handed, you foul rotter."

Isaac denied nothing: "Are you going to stop climbing on my car?"

"You filthy beast, with my wife."

"Yes, or no?"

"I want your name and address. This'll come up in court."

"I know. But don't hit the roof of my car again like that, because I can't stand it. My whole system rebels against it at this time of the morning." There was no answer. Face and hard words matched. A combined smack-and-knuckle snapped along the street.

He left the man dazed and muttering. Taking a corner with one hand, he flung out his broken unlit cigarette. The car glistened in week-end sunshine, metal and gentle heat mutually caressing, a well-polished wonderbug going between factory and railway yards. His left cheek was emery-papered from the scuffle. How was he to know the husband would be back so soon? But his wife should have, unless she liked seeing him get knocked about every week. Maybe he'll come around the pubs and pick me out when Beatty's there. I'll get that luggage rack tightened in case he pulled it loose.

He didn't want to go home to his wife on this Saturday morning, nor kids—those brass-fisted tow-headed devil's anchors. Terry had fallen arse over backwards out of the bedroom window, somersaulting on to up-and-coming fungus while Beatty was in the kitchen frying his meat-slab for tea. A voice wailed above sizzling fat, and Terry was back on his feet before she could get to him, knees grazed into purple patches, yelling at the shock of seeing soil one minute and speeding along the plumbline of his own stare the next. Meanwhile the pan was flaring and Isaac's burnt offering was too black to offer.

Alert and alive, he levelled the car-snout at Lenton steeple, wheeled right over the bridge, half-whistled music for the thinking stage spreading behind his brain—before which the audience of himself would laugh or jeer, so that a red-haired cyclist in shorts thought he was mocking her, and a pink tongue flashed in his mirror.

He turned north into the patchwork country. A rabbit-hutch bungalow stood for sale in a rabbit-food field. He imagined it worth three thousand pounds. Could get it for a couple of quid after the four-minute warning. Five bob, perhaps, as the owner runs terrified for the woods, hair greying at every step—if I wanted to own property and get a better deal in heaven.

Needle shivering at cold eighty, he felt something like love for the machine under him, the smooth engine swilled and kissed by oil, purring with fuel, cooled by the best water. Out of the rut of family, the trough of drink and the sud-skies of low-roofed factories, he flicked on his yellow winkers, pipped his hooter, and swung to overtake a vast lorry laden with castings and grinding Newarkwards—lips in a half-whistle and mind emptiest at greatest speeds.

Sweat ran down his face, and he put up his hand as if to brush off a fly. The needle seemed pinned at ninety, his eyes looking too hard at the road-belt unwinding under his wheels, flagged by signposts and a corridor of upright trees snowing off leaves in early sun-lit autumn, everything fresh as a kid's crayon-drawing he might have done at school when jolted by the shock of something new. He couldn't look at his dial, but the odour of tarmac burning his tyres acted like smelling salts and drew his well-shod foot back from the pedal. Within a minute the speed was down to an anchor-dragging sixty and back on the right side of death, so that he could light a cigarette.

The pickings of freedom felt good, gave him a weight not known since before getting married, dream-years ago. He'd had enough, had realised it for a long time but somehow had been frozen, stiff with indecision. Last night he'd broken free, but for how long? He was surprised that guilt had vanished so soon, in which case maybe he could have a fling every so often, his marriage and Beatty none the worse for it— though telling her where he'd been would need a few choice lies she'd never believe. What the eye doesn't see the heart doesn't grieve. That, anyway, would be better than a bloody rupture with tears and shrapnel spitting far and wide, and him in the middle burning to hell for something he couldn't now wear the credit for. Yet even that wasn't real trouble, could be solved and smoothed over if he wanted it to be.

Drawing down the window, he felt cold air swording through the car as if frontier soldiers were stabbing haybales for escaping citizens. In spite of the blue sky, he shut it again.

3

"If you don't stop it," she shouted at Chris and Terry fighting in their room across the landing, "I'll come in and bang your heads together." She sat at the dressing-table in her pyjamas, wondering where the hell Isaac was: "Beatty Stathern, he'll never be any good to you," my mother always said. But my mother was wrong, or had been until last night, for what else could you do but think the worst when Isaac-rotten-Starbuck was involved? Yet if anything was wrong with being out all night why wasn't she sobbing in some police station and pushing aside a mug of sweet tea some fatherly copper handed her?

He might be flattened under that fast car she'd tried all her might to stop him buying. He'd had no time for her since then, saved up year by year and after weeks of dogfight had settled for the car instead of a downpayment on some bungalow at Cossal or Bramcote. As it was, he preferred to go on living in this hundred-year slum, and they would have been in two rooms still if mam hadn't let us take it over when she died.

Luckily he never knew mam's real opinion of him, otherwise he'd have called her blind. She was wrong though, because as far as I know, and I know it to be the truth, he ain't yet done it on me with a living soul, not in all the five years we've been married, and there's not many as hold out so long in this neighbourhood. I love him, and he loves me, but all the same, I'd love to know what he was up to last night.

Went to see one of his mates, I suppose, and his car broke down. He could have walked, or come home in a taxi. Perhaps he went to his sister's, took her for a drink and got too blindoe to drive back. I hate him boozing like that, tell him to do what it says on TV and stay sober at the wheel: "There's two things I don't like doing when I'm kay-lied, and one is driving a car," he said, a maddening smile all over his clock.

The bedroom suite was shabbier than when they bought it, plywood and paint-knocked, no gloss left on its hundred-pound exterior. But there wasn't much hope of getting a new one with that car costing the earth to run. The mirror signalled her face, hazel eyes of a cat in springtime, more magical (and in colour) than any television set, but disappointing because it cost less. Beatty's skin was clear and firm of a morning, matching her eyes and setting off the falling bands of auburn hair. Her head was delicately shaped, a fine forehead, ears with almost no lobes, lips sardonic and lively. Her unsupported breasts, round and firm under her top, were clamped a little higher when she stood to dress. He doesn't know what he's missing, she thought. They say men wear better than women, but she had all her teeth still, whereas Isaac already had two false ones.

The kids were bumping the telly to bring on pictures—though she'd often told them it was too early in the day. Isaac once joked that the best time was at four in the morning, when they had an hour of blue movies. Hardly anyone knew of this, but he'd discovered it by accident on staying up all night when she was having Chris. He'd told her about it in such detail that she'd come even before they fell on to the settee.

She forced them to the table. "Stay there and get your breakfast." The first cup of tea was broached, drunk scalding to the odour of toasted bread. A heaped-up plate was brought in, and Chris snatched one before touchdown. She smacked his hand: "Hold back, or you'll get my fist." He pretended to cry, then splayed into laughter at the mock-docility of his brother. "If you don't behave I'll tell your dad."

She might, but where was he? They're the last bloody kids I'll have, I know that much, up to my neck in breakfast and house while he's running around with some woman for all I know, unless he's in hospital covered in plaster of paris or laid out smashed to bits in a deadhouse. That would be the end of it right enough. A widow at twenty-six, though I've no fear that plenty would have me still.

The thought frightened her, a slice of toast going cold while dwelling on it. Dead houses and television sets, cars rumbling through outside sunshine, people calling to each other before Saturday shopping, didn't connect till such moments as this—as they had for tragic certainty when her mother died and Isaac was the one to soften it and do everything. My God! Whatever would I do if he's gone the same way? If he stepped through that door I'd throw this pot of scalding tea in his face, frightening me like this.

She went out of the back gate and turned towards the main road. At least the sun's out, though it'll still be cloudy for him when he gets back. Not that I care whether he does or not, since no excuse will satisfy me, because I've had my fill of him this last year or two. If he hadn't given me the housekeeping money before sliding off last night I'd have told Mary to put me up till I found a place of my own. And if I don't do that, it's only because there's no need and not because I don't want to.

At the butcher's she bought a fine-looking piece of lamb she knew he'd get stuck into after his walk and couple of pints on Sunday. He was healthy and in the spice of life, while some of those he'd gone to school with looked worn and balding in a way he never would, even at ninety.

By the bus stop she met her brother-in-law—thin, pale, longjawed Tom. Nine-tenths of the time his eyes were rabbit-dead, as if he'd lost his job while others got a raise, buried his mother on August Bank-holiday, or just found his correct treble-chance unposted while reading of someone else getting the two hundred thousand. But at Sunday tea he'd have the salad shaking with the rest of them by acting out those three conditions of his lost and gloomy face recalled by Beatty as they greeted each other by the fishmonger's.

With Mary and three kids he'd set off once for a new life in Canada. "They need skilled carpenters like me," he'd said. Eighteen months later he was back, docked at Liverpool one wet midsummer day. Isaac and Beatty met him, and coming over the pungent rainsoaked Pennines heard him preferring death to idleness, dishonour to destitution. Enveloped in the lugubrious sad pride of a man with no guts, he understood a lack of work in winter, but unemployment had for some reason lasted into the summer, and Mary's confinement used up his savings.

A smart wind flicked the supermarket doors. "What's wrong?"

She laughed: "I'm worried about whether I'll make ends meet. I'm worried about whether my kids are all right in the house. I'm worried about whether Isaac will go on short time next week."

"That's not worry, duck. That's life. What is it?"

"Isaac went out last night and isn't back yet. I'm wondering if anything's happened."

He lit two cigarettes, gave her one. She recalled his words: If I hadn't met your sister I'd have married you, Beatty. I'll never forgive Isaac for meeting you first. "I shouldn't worry about him. He can drive that machine like a pair of skates. And Isaac's not the sort to go on the tiles."

"There's always the first time," she said.

Maybe it isn't even the first time, he thought, though there'd never have been anything like that with me. "Not with him. He'll be back. Perhaps the car broke down. Or he fell in with a crowd of pals from work. You know what they are. They wouldn't want to haul him back to you on a shutter, flat-out and groaning. They're considerate that way. Probably slept in somebody's parlour with a Co-op rug over him."

"It's not funny. I'm worried to death. It's the first time he's done anything like this. Still, I expect he'll be back by dinnertime."

"If he ain't," he said, picking up her bags, "I'll go and scout for him. I know a few of his haunts."

4

Ignition off, he surveyed the outside world, for the first time feeling unreal in his car, as if its walls barred him from the way of all true senses. He'd looked on it as his friend, horse, brother-in-arms, cockpit in which to speed through streets that deadened around him.

He walked fifty yards, then turned back because he'd left his lighter—unwilling to see anyone sent to jail or borstal for helping themselves to it. A policeman stood by: "Excuse me, is this car yours?"

Isaac took his time locking the door. "It is—if you want to know."

"Well, I was asking you."

"Well, I'm telling you."

"What's your name?"

"Isaac Starbuck."

"Oh?"

"That's right." Isaac saw through him, a pool of water, frog-spawn and dead leaves, back to schooldays when some new bully had pushed him against a wall, demanding to know who had killed Jesus Christ, because his name was Isaac. "I did," Isaac said, a savage bash into the middle of next week.

"Do you mind showing me your papers?" He was of similar build, more blue-eyed and less clean-shaven, a smile flickering further behind his eyes than in the ironic gaze Isaac turned on him. He lit a cigarette: "What are you booking me on?"

"Don't get funny. I'm not booking you. I'm asking you for your means of identity."

"You think this car isn't mine? Or that I've been nicking things from it?"

"I'd like to see your papers, or I'll have you down at the station." What a story: phone Beatty, when they turned me loose from the cop-shop hoping to see the last of me before they burst into tears at the certainty of my suing them, and say look where I've been while you and Tom sat calling me blind for knocking-on with all the squidge tarts in Sneinton.

"Let's go then. My car will be safe enough for an hour or two now I've locked it."

"I'm here to protect it," the policeman said. "I've watched you going to and from this car, and I haven't seen proof that it's yours yet. My job is to make sure nobody takes things from cars."

"You should come and see my job," Isaac said, also affable. "There's no comparison." If I'd had that worried-about-money look between my brows he wouldn't have bothered me. They stood like two brothers, one in plain clothes come to see what the other one wanted for his supper that night. "People slip me dough in my job," Isaac said, "and I don't worry 'em. Hear all, see all, and say nowt. The world couldn't get on without a bit of grease on the old palm. A town like this would fall to pieces. No transport, telephones, newspapers, shops, factories—everything dead. People on the streets rioting. All because of no bribes, no tips. How do you think I got my car? Honest work? Don't kid yourself. A commissionaire at our place died the other week, been on the gate twenty-eight years. You know what he left in his will? It was in the paper. Eight thousand pounds. Eight thousand. On eleven pounds a week and five kids to keep? Tell me another one! My barber has an Austin Healey, and he didn't get that at three bob a nob either. Does a roaring trade in little girls and has a lezzie brothel in his bungalow at Wollaton. He said to me, 'Isaac, you don't blame me, do you? I see all these nice cars floating about so I want to have one. That's natural, ain't it? I want twenty-two carat gold-tipped shoe-laces, not to mention plutonium spec-frames. Everybody's got these things nowadays. I take my fancy-friends to Formentor instead of Blackpool.' The world's got to go around"—tapping his car—"and if I could think of a better way I'd cut my throat for being a dirty Red. Every man for himself in this marvellous world, because nobody can deny it's a terrific place, the way the money changes hands and blokes like us get jack-all for it."

The policeman was amused: "I was trying to see that your car was O.K."

"I appreciate it," Isaac said. "I'm off for a drink with my mates, so if you'd keep your eyes on it, I shan't forget you when I get back."

"That's all right," the copper said.

He'll expect a couple of quid, Isaac thought, but I'll steal my own car back from under his snooping nose.

5

Pushing into the midday beerstink he spotted Freddy and
Larry about to draw on their first full pints of the day. He
felt himself again, back in an all-enclosing world that he
seemed to have been born and brought up in. Outside he'd
not noticed the sun, but seeing it pour through the top
windows made him feel more exalted than if he'd been in
one of those churches he'd heard about. "You're looking black
today," Freddy said. "Have your kidneys burst or something?"

"I was out all night," Isaac told them, unbuttoning his
coat. "My sister's husband's brother-in-law just got married,
and I was heaved into his slosh-up after a joke at the registry
office. I only meant to have a cup of beef-tea at my sister's,
and was all set to leave at eleven but somebody said: 'One
for the road, just a small one,' and then I woke up on the
road, dogends and horseshit all around me and a double-
decker Trent Valley traction bus burning my headache off
with its headlights and about to grind over me. So somebody
carried me into his house, and I woke up this morning to
the smell of frying bacon, and while this bloke was setting out
the Pinnochio cornflake dishes I went into the next room,
jumped his wife before she could say 'Hey what the bloody
hell do you think you're on with?' then staggered downstairs
to borrow her husband's razor for a shave. So you can imagine
how I feel."

"What a life," Freddy said, "it's full of sin. If I was out
all night, even innocently, my wife would finish with me."

"So would mine," Isaac said. "I want to ask you a favour.
Will it be all right if I tell Beatty that I got too drunk to
drive home, and that I made for your place? She'll believe
you if you say I kipped there. You can back it up when you
call for me next week on your way to the meeting. O.K.?"

One of the men at work said that Freddy was such a quiet
sort that bibles wouldn't melt in his mouth. Middling in
height, he had high cheekbones, and was dark in colour as
opposed to Isaac's yellowish robustness, and Larry's texture
of salmon-pink. He was the oldest of the three, a studious-
looking Jamaican who had been an air-gunner in the war
and flown over Germany sixty times to see that his plane
kept clear of fighters while flobbing down its four-tonners,
belligerence which he now devoutly regretted. "I've never told

a lie in my life before," he said with sincerity. "You're the best pal I have, but I don't think I can do it."

"Forget it, then," Isaac said. "Come on, let me get you another, you boozing Baptist. I've had such a run-around since last night that I'm ready to pour a barrel into myself. When I left that house this morning the husband was hanging on the luggage rack of my car, so I had to stop and punch him off it. He just wouldn't let go."

Freddy shook his head. "You always seemed so steady to me."

"Maybe. But I fell for that bint like a ton of bricks and I wasn't even drunk. It was marvellous while it lasted. Let's drink to it."

"I'm sorry it happened though," Freddy said, drinking.

"The first time since I was married. And the last. I'm going home after this one. Not that I want to go home. I don't want to go at all. I'm knackered and brain-bashed, heartsore and full of stones. I want to walk across Africa, America, Russia. I've got more strength than I've ever had—but it's as much as I can do to lift this pint to my gob."

"If you feel like walking," Freddy said, "walk. Can't you do what you feel like?"

Isaac lit a fag: "It's got to come over you like a storm, so that you don't think at all, but before you know what's happening you're doing it."

"You work enough. Do you want a war, or something?"

"If I knew what I wanted I wouldn't be chinning over a pint at Saturday dinnertime. And you stand need to talk about war, after your record. I'm glad you did it though, Freddy. If you hadn't they'd have had us in them death camps before we could pick up bricks to smash their heads in. I'm a Red, and not only are you a Red, but you're coloured as well. Fancy being born the way we are."

"I'm not a Red," Freddy corrected him. "I'm a Baptist. I go to church, pray and study my Bible."

"I don't know why I bother to talk to you," Isaac said. "If I was a Baptist I wouldn't know where to put my face."

"If I was a Red," Freddy answered, "I'd get on my knees and pray."

"Reds don't pray," Isaac said. "That's why I'm a Red."

"Nothing's sacred to you," Freddy told him.

"I know," Isaac said. "But don't worry: I shan't bring up your criminal past again. I don't see why you should be ashamed of bombing Germany, even though you was only bombing fellow workers like us. You weren't to know. You was young in those days, immature. Don't get upset, Freddy. It was a tragedy, that's all."

"Isaac, you're a bastard. Why don't you drop dead?"

"I can't. There's still some ale left in my jar. Come on, drink up. It wasn't true about bombing the Reds. I just made that up to get your goat. I'm the guilty one, because I was on to my mate the other day in the air force. He's an air vice marshal. I got him on the phone: " 'Hello? RAF? Put me through to Jack. Jack? Isaac here. Look, do you think you could manage a thousand for tomorrow night? Sure. Yes. Germany. Nazis keep on coming up. Make a start at Düsseldorf, O.K.? Thousand off at seven. Settled. And Jack, just a minute, what about the night after? You can? You'd do anything for an old pal? Ah, I know you would, you dirty old man. Fine. Make it Munich. I'll treat you to a pint when I see you. Sure. Anytime. Missis? She's fine, thanks. How's yours? That makes eight, don't it? You'll have a football team in a year or two! Yes. Play each other. So long then.' I know I'm a murderer, Freddy, for thinking things like that. My mind's full of evil thoughts, but so's everybody's. They're the right sort of evil thoughts, that's all I can say."

"I'll pray for you," Freddy said.

"That won't do me any good. You remember that Pole at work, Ted his name was, who got ten years for burying an axe in his mate's skull when they were pally and drunk? He told me one tea break how he saw Germans in Poland making Jews dig their own graves. Then the Germans shot them all. I asked: 'What did you do about it?' 'Nothing,' he said, 'I just stood around.' 'I would have done something,' I told him. Then a week later he kills his mate, full of friendship. What a world. That's why I got old Jack on the blower."

"All I can do is pray for you."

"You think I'm a sinner," Isaac said, "but you should have seen me before I was married. I didn't stand in pubs and talk. I used to get hold of all the women I could. A homewrecker, I was."

"It's terrible. But why did you get married then, and expose yourself to similar dangers?"

"I walked into a trap. All the time I was scattering my load some sly little bastard hiding in my liver kept saying: 'Where's that trap? I've to find that trap. I'll die if I don't find that trap, even if it is the marrying trap.' There was nothing else to do but go for the low-down kicks of that trap. It's all finished now. The teeth are rusty and the chain has snapped. I'm an old man of ninety-nine and can't get into a hundred."

"Wait till you're a hundred and can't get back to being twenty-seven," Freddy smiled. "You'll like that even less."

"We'll get bombed before then."

"Don't bank on it." Larry came back, carrying his wide shoulders and freshly shaved face, black hair plastered down. "Pass me that box of hubs, Blackclock," a new man at work once shouted. Larry put down his brush and strolled over: "What did you say?" The man was just out of the army, tall, spruce and bronzed: "Give me that box of hubs. I can't waste time. I'm on piece work." Larry, a foot shorter, looked up at him: "You called me Blackclock," he said, deceptively tearful. "You said: 'Pass me that box of hubs, Blackclock.' I heard you." "Well," the man said, "I had to refer to you as something. Come on, be a good chap and pass them hubs." Isaac stood beside him: "What's up?" "This streak of withered piss called me Blackclock. He's a scab"—up to his face that grew more astonished with each insult—"a screw-gut, a gett-face, a rat-eyed dog who thinks he's still in Kenya or Cyprus. 'Blackclock,' he shouted, and even the women on viewing heard it."

He greeted them soberly. "Still slinging 'em down?"

Freddy called for more: "Jawing, you mean. Isaac was saying we're as likely to get blown up by American atom bombs as by Russian."

"It's all the same to me," Larry said. "I don't mind the Russians coming, to tell you the truth. As long as they don't send them Mongolian hordes. I wouldn't like them Mongolians raping my wife. I wouldn't fancy that at all." Isaac sputtered in his beer, a stitch in his stomach as if his appendix had turned into a dum-dum bullet. He had seen Larry's wife once, outside the factory, and though he imagined the Mongolians might not be over-particular regarding their women, he failed to see her as anything but safe when they swarmed one fine day over the Trent.

The man's blow pushed Larry against the machine, thickset brawn saving him among levers and spindles. He was geared for the spring-back: "Hold off," Isaac said. The foreman had seen it: hadn't the army trained him in team spirit and comradeship? Or were such qualities overridden by a desire to disregard life among dangerous machinery? He told Larry and Isaac not to bother the man, just because he didn't like the idea of joining a union. Isaac swore: as far as he knew the man was in a union already. He'd only stood by to make sure nobody came to harm. The ex-soldier was moved to the packing department.

A fortnight later Larry walked in with a black eye and a graze down the side of his face. "I punched that bloke up last night."

"Trust him to make that crack about getting him to join the union," Isaac said, still brooding on it.

"They've got their hooks into you," Larry said. They certainly had, thought Isaac. In this life of profit and loss, fighting to keep your wages up, and battling against the ever-increasing threat of the double stint, existence was getting harder. They'd drive you into the ground with that velvet glove if you didn't play the flick knife now and again. They shoved out the message that you were having it good, all the time making sure you had it worse and worse. Agitation, the lightning strike, the big shout and the black look were always in use, for if one small advantage crept against you the whole line collapsed. People would get laid off for no reason, and the next reduction of hours and increase of the flat rate would be impossible to achieve. The only spiritual unity left to those in the factory was the fight for material conditions. That's what religion had come to, with never an amen among the steel-wool clouds.

"Join the communists, then," Larry said, as Isaac talked on about it. "Like me."

"I go around on my own. When the balloon goes up, I'll know what do do."

"I'll just sing," Larry said.

"I'm too Red to join any party," Isaac said. "They'd throw me out if they heard my ideas. I think factories should have M.P.'s, not districts. Only people with insurance cards should vote. That'd be fair."

"Maybe only those with ration cards," Freddy said.

Isaac caught his irony. "Same thing. I could run our factory, though. I've worked in every department and seen the whole process going for years. If I could keep some of the chargehands I'd send that production sky-high, and people wouldn't drop dead from fatigue either. As for those bastards trying to run it now, I'm always on the lookout for a wall that's long enough to mow them down against. I don't want social justice anymore; I want revenge."

Larry scoffed: "Why cut your own throat though?"

"The only time that might be possible," Freddy said, "is when that four-minute warning goes and the bombs start dropping. And there'll be no four-minute warning given to the public, only to Civil Defence, police and army so that they can be ready for us, man."

"I was round at Wally Jones's place on the worst night last time," Isaac said, "and he's got a German mauser and a couple of shot-guns. We were making plans in case there was trouble. I'm going to get a gun. I'm taking no chances. I'll get a few Tory bastards before I go. I shan't die like a cat."

"The best thing is to make your peace with God."

"That's what they play on, and expect you not to care." He was hungry and bought three meat pies, but they were old and stale as if, he said, pushing his aside, they'd been made from pensioned-off pit ponies. Larry wolfed his down. Freddy ate half: "It's a sin to waste food. It's feeding the devil."

"That's what my mother says when anyone slings grub on the fire," Isaac told him, taking the stomach out of his pint.

"The trouble is," Larry said, "you've got no ambition, Isaac. You should have taken that chargehand's job that was offered you. Me, I'll never get anywhere. I know that. But you, you've got it in you. You're just the age for a few steps up in factory life. If you was just a little bit on their side the gaffers would pull you in with a golden handshake and fart all over you with pleasure."

"He's right," Freddy put in. "Who sharpens tools when the chargehand's gone for a walk? Isaac. Who fixed my machine in two minutes when it broke down, latched on my belt when it snapped? You think the foreman didn't notice? You'd have been the gaffer's golden-haired boy years ago if you hadn't been such a troublemaker, taking home twenty every week just for things you've been able to do for years."

Isaac felt, behind his stony face, as if yet unborn, though his nerves were jumping and ready to eat him up. Maybe I'm getting a cold, or a bilious bout. Freddy put an arm over his shoulder: "When I drop in on Thursday I'll let Beatty know where you were last night. My wife took you a cup of cocoa and an extra blanket before you dropped off, pure as driven coal-gas."

"Maybe I won't need an alibi. Thanks, though." He stood up and fastened his coat: "See you on Monday."

Fresh air knocking out of a blue sky doused him as if after a cold tap-wash. Each footstep took him further from the

unrealistic comfort of his friends. He felt raw-hearted in
these streets, with no ally but his own self to protect or destroy him. He felt rotten for what happened last night. That
way of existence was awful and putrid because it drained life
away and gave nothing back. To blame it was useless perhaps, only dodging from the real wound bleeding deep in his
purple innards. His life seemed a black deadend darkness when
he looked at things closer than most people cared to. There
was no one to blame for this, yet if some new system of
social life came to involve him deeply then this piece of
stupid personal confusion might bother him less than it did.
Such logic seemed incontrovertible—a steamroller decked
with trimmings that would set him handclapping if ever he
saw it in motion.

6

Saturday was tin-dinner day at Tom and Mary's: tinned
peas and tinned steak, followed by tinned rhubarb or rice
pudding, with tinned beer to see it through if you felt so
inclined—as if for one day a week they acquired the status
of explorers lost on some spiritual ice-cap of the world.

Though it seemed a tasty enough meal to Mary, Beatty couldn't get through half of it.

Thumbs were down on Isaac, the grating lifted, the lions
out. Tom jumped his motorbike to cruise innumerable districts of the city in which he might be found—a hopeless
job, but he went just the same, withdrawing his long hymnal
of a head from every smoky pub, as if a dart player might
swing a fine-feathered missile in his direction. The recon-
naissance was as much to quieten Beatty as to find Isaac.
After all—sliding a crash helmet from the kitchen shelf—
he's capable of coming back when and if he feels like it.

Beatty had given him up, could tell it was finished by the
hard-as-crystal air, cool and passive. She wanted a long sit
down, with cups of tea and fags. He'd gone, and it didn't
bother her a bit, there being worse things than a broken
home. It was less than a day, yet seemed like weeks because
the solid bedwarming hump had been absent last night, logged
up no doubt with some other woman. But how could that be
true when they'd been happy for so long? The wild passion
had gone out of it, yet love was still there. He had no reason
to run away and hide, to do it on her, die.

"Don't worry, love, he'll be back—worse luck. Maybe men

and women would be better off without marriage and all this facing-things-together stuff." Beatty didn't think much of Mary for spouting this bit of comfort, felt insulted at Mary thinking she needed it. It wasn't meant anyway, just said casually because Mary couldn't bear to see anyone upset, often being more upset than the actual victim. Mary was her sister, ten years more buxom, and born from a different father, so maybe they didn't see things as real sisters should.

"I'm not worrying," Beatty said, spent fag thrown to the fire. "I've got so used to feeling safe with him that I can't think anything's wrong. Yet that car worries me."

"You'd have heard by now if it was that."

"There's no telling how far he's gone in that thing. If I knew he hadn't got in an accident I'd know how to take it. I've finished with him though."

"Wait and see what's happened," Mary cautioned. "He's only gone since last night."

She shook her head. What was the use? You just stop living until you know. "Don't tell me to wait and see again, because what else do you think I'm doing?"

Mary was annoyed, at the sympathy that wasn't easy being slung back in her face. Hadn't she said many a time that there was no saying when he'd go off the rails? It might be lack of opportunity or will but the certainty was always there, waiting to do it on her without warning when the shock would be hardest to bear. "I've got to say something, haven't I?"

"No," Beatty said, "you haven't." She wanted peace, to be left alone. Even the sound of her kids playing in the street with Mary's travestied the pure burning openness of her mind that did not know what to think and kept her on a perch of hope and misery unable even to light another cigarette that she so much wanted. She dreaded the kids bursting in to unruffle this calm death weaving around her, hoped that Tom would come back, that Isaac would kick his way into the room and demand to know why she wasn't at home getting his tea ready, thirsty and famished after spilling a genuine list of misadventures.

She regretted bringing her troubles to Tom and Mary. A lot of good they were when the only comfort possible could be from Isaac. He was a rotter, leaving her like this, and to keep saying it soothed her, as if such words were a magic bait to draw the wandering fish back to her net.

She laughed: sarcasm, bitterness, lack of hope. Mary was startled from her newspaper, angry at her sister's easy surrender to the hard ways of the world. They fastened their claws into everyone's heart and soul, but you couldn't admit that they got you down or made you suffer, since other miseries existed that could make your present state seem a bit of a joke. "There's worse things at sea," she said.

"But we aren't at bloody sea," Beatty snapped. "You wouldn't be so cheerful if Tom walked out on you."

"I wouldn't make such a fuss about it. And don't say I don't love him, either. I'd grin and bear it if he lit off."

"You sound as if you want him to go," Beatty said, lifted from her troubles by the fascinating snap of conviction in her sister's voice.

Mary's face flushed. "Trust you to think that. You take everything the wrong way."

"Except my own troubles," Beatty said, subdued again. "I wonder where he's got to? And Tom's been gone hours."

7

Rifle Street, Gatling Street, Bastion Street, Redoubt Street, Citadel Street—fighting monickers made up by some fat and comfortable swine who'd never heard a bomb or had a fist in his face. A smart young girl went into a shop with a basket of bottles: Miss Joggletits of nineteen-umpity-jump, such smart-knockers as he'd never seen. I'd name them Love Street, Vagina Row, Womb Lane—paint the houses, pave the road-way, disinfect the gutters, change that smashed drainpipe and give the woman there five bob for some glass and putty to mend her window. Where it says Vote for Sludgebump get a famous artist to paint a bare woman. Tart the place up a bit.

The afternoon was half over, walking among the cobbled streets and inhaling smells of moss, backyards and fevergrates. The rhythmic tread of still-gleaming shoes, the warm lug of his overcoat, and the continual faglight not too far from his chin, brought back last night's prowl and unexpected adventure. Maybe I come from a family of fornicators, and that's all there is to it. He remembered a story of his long-dead grandfather who at sixty was discovered standing in with the same woman as his married son—such a depth charge upsetting the placid water of three generations.

If I'm heading for the knackers' yard I'll go there sober, feel jack-all when the pole-axe drops and sends me slithering into the dream-chute of blood and guts. Fits and fevers, miseries and screams—something's got to give and it won't

be me. I'm twenty-seven, and eighteen was too old to change
my habits. When I was thirteen I'd never forget a grudge,
and at seventeen I'd always look people in the eye. At twenty-
two I got the key of the door but there's been no deep-down
happening in my lowest coal galleries since then. Marriage
and kids is nothing to get God on the blower about.

He walked, turning three corners to come in half a minute
to the copper's slab back and broach his own car unseen.
The weight of his legs, sinews, bootlaces and lungs seemed
to hold him from real speed, every footlift needing a steam-
hammering piston to generate power in the back of each heel
—though he looked smart and full of purpose walking towards
himself in a plate glass window.

Sunlight threw a line of bars along the polished flank of
his car. He observed it, as if inside a special prison that he
was not able to enter. The copper stood at the end of the
street, a clear, dark, indisputable toy shape guarding hard-
earned glamour from the claws of its rightful owner. He
grinned, not so much at the funny situation, as at the sense
of waiting for the copper to continue his beat so that he could
step along the pavement and steal his roadster without committing a crime, and without showing his papers as proof
that it belonged to him.

But the copper only went as far as the corner. Isaac braked
and drew back—to another stalemate. The copper turned,
as if his gimlet-eyes were looking straight at him. A couple
of years ago, beaten well into the trough of married blight,
he might have been willing to show his licence and laugh off
the forceput of it, but nowadays his back was up, obstinacy
permeating every last bay and fibre of his emerging world.
Maybe he'd never again see each tenth of a mile registered
in orange figurines whose wheelspins, strictly accounted for,
were marked off against his credit.

To see this mileage meant he could either go up directly,
and show his papers if necessary, or saunter by and glimpse
it from the pavement, risk being recognised. He preferred
the policeman to vanish, leave him in freedom to take control
of his car, but that wasn't how things worked. God, chance,
or fate was an old believer of the hard way, the grinding
jewel clipping at the brain until you acted, and took a gamble
on whether it worked or not.

A few right-hand turns, and the copper still stood at his
accustomed spot. Isaac switched back, en route for what must
become his. He took out black, large, hornrimmed spectacles

for driving on rainy nights: distant objects such as dogs and
architectural decrepitudes appeared slightly clearer, but the
weight was really compensated for by their power of disguise.
He drew a thin mustard-coloured cap jauntily over his head,
so that from a rough-faced factory worker in his week-end
best he became a whippet-featured anglo-intellectual adman
trying to look like a sensitive artisan, who knew of a short
cut across the slums from one area of good houses to another.

He even felt different but, adding a final touch of incongruous realism, pulled a sawn-off briar from his back pocket
and latched it between his teeth. Over a few rows of slate-
roofed houses lay a captive car that he hoped to release by
the use of outlandish guile. Through a reflecting window he
saw the vicious, driving, debonair creation he'd become if he
stopped being himself.

The policeman walked by without a glance. Isaac gloated,
not even bothering to read the milometer on his car, turned at
the end of the street to see the policeman strolling away as
if at last to give other property a fairer share of his protection.

Game successful, tricks finished, he took off cap, pipe and
glasses. The click of car keys going into the lock like Christmas
sleighbells was drowned by a motorbike throttling along the
street. Isaac saw him first, knelt as if having trouble with the
handle and hoping that tinpot push-button peoples' bike would
pass on the far side and carry his search-party brother-in-law
to another zone of fruitlessness. The roar increased, stopped,
and Isaac stood slowly, as if under a ceiling only high enough
for a dwarf: "What are you doing around this way?"

He lit a cigarette, as if to say nothing more, knowing
Tom had been sent out to bring him back dead or alive,
drunk or sober. "I was just passing," Tom said, parking his
bike by the kerb, "and saw your car." He took off his crash
helmet (as advertised on TV) and strode over as if for a
long chat, his face like a miner's safety lamp: solid, shining,
aware of all dangers, indestructable. "Beatty happened to mention you hadn't been in all night."

They faced each other across the bonnet. "I was with some
of my mates," Isaac said, bending to get in his car. "We got
a bit drunk."

Tom took his arm. "Just a bit. You can't go like that."

He had never liked Beatty's sister, mother, or brother-in-law,
saw them as too dull and solid in their sloth, looking on pale
normality as blood-curdling life, contemptible dummies trying

to drag him down. He pushed Tom away: "Keep your hands off me or I'll put you in the gutter."

"You ought to come back to your wife and kids," Tom said, white-faced at such violence. "You know how Beatty worries. Why don't you just come and let her see you're all right?"

"Then I can come out again and play? Listen, jam-face, don't act big brother with me." The wind rattled them. Isaac saw the situation so clearly that the result was confusing. Pictures proliferated like poison-ivy in the brain, gave him a pain in the head.

Tom went on spouting. Rockets of deadly advice sloped towards heaven in threatening colours, and cracker mottoes came down by parachute. He was sorry Isaac wasn't sorry for all the trouble he might be going to cause, and Isaac smiled at this, noticed how he put a hand in his pocket out of nervousness and rattled at his money like a sex-maniac. Tom spoke of how tragic it was that a good marriage should crash for no reason, especially with three beautiful kiddies asking since last night when their dad was coming home. Isaac wanted to laugh, at Tom with glowing eyes and dull conviction saying what crimes Isaac ought not to commit—because Tom had always wanted to get stuck into them but hadn't the guts. "What shall I tell her?"

"I'll tell her myself."

"Will you come back now, though?" Tom wanted everything neat, a piece of wedding cake tied up with blue ribbon, all the happy suffering locked inside. Isaac thought him too hasty, a careful saver out of his element. Tom had always been tidy in mind and dress, even carried it off with a dry sort of humour. You not only had to laugh at his jokes, you had to understand them as well—which often cut the heart out of the laugh. He was the kind of person who would iron his own bootlaces. He wouldn't even let his wife do it.

"You shouldn't let her suffer so," he said, still anxious.

"I'll be back."

"I know you like to do things your own way, but come and talk to her yourself."

"I can't. Tell her not to worry."

"It ain't that she thinks you've left her. She just wonders where you've got to."

Isaac saw it beginning all over again, the same words in different order, putting him in the wrong like the lowest worm. "Get off my back," he threatened. "I'll settle things my own way when I'm ready."

A feline explosion burst from Tom: "Who do you think you are?"

"If you don't get away from me," Isaac bellowed, "I'll wrap that motorbike round your neck and throttle you with it."

Maybe the policeman was drawn to the street by their quarrel, or perhaps he'd merely returned to it after a natural lapse of his beat. Isaac had Tom by the strings of his windjammer: "Get back to your rabbit hutch, you sanctimonious bastard."

"What's all the argument?" the policeman wanted to know.

Isaac was opening his own car door: "Having a talk. But it's finished now."

"I'll say it is," Tom agreed, his lampface dimming out.

"It sounded a bit more than that to me," the copper said. "Is that car yours? You're the chap as was here a couple of hours ago, aren't you?"

"Yes, it is my car," Isaac told him. "Ask my brother-in-law."

Tom was astride his motorbike, crash-helmet and chin-straps proving ownership. "I don't know what he's talking about. I just stopped to light a fag." His foot stamped on the pedal and the engine crowed, hosannahed from one end of the street to the other.

"You'd better show me your papers."

"Tell him it's mine," Isaac called.

With a gliding motion Tom was propelled to the middle of the road, showed a straight self-righteous back as he turned the corner.

"I'd like to see them papers," the copper said.

Even his monument to sweat and thrift was disputed, which at last proved fatally, yet to his satisfaction, that you had no right to have property at all. Property blacked out your teeth, ploughed lanes of baldness through your hair, turned down your mouth, lopped off your ears, gave you a blinding squint, splayed your nose flat. He owned a car but it compromised his dignity. Even the licence and insurance weren't enough: "It says the car belongs to Isaac Starbuck, but I'm not to know you're not somebody else, am I? If you've got no more proof than this you can come with me. Maybe we'll help you to find it."

Half drunk from the shuttling racket of life since last night, Isaac took out his brand-new dark-blue stiff-backed passport.

Though not as yet travel-worn, it was an impressive certificate to respectability and intentions.

"That's all right," the policeman said, handing it back. "We have to keep on our toes, you know. There's been a lot of car thieving lately around this area, even in daytime."

Isaac got into the car, feeling as if the lights were on him. A black volcanic bile boiling up, he wanted to leave the scene of his defeat quickly, before he spewed over the well-kept upholstery. He spun his car on to the main road. Not yet, not yet, not yet. The bomb had exploded and the smoke goes up. It may drift for weeks. But you can't in any case crawl away until the debris has cleared. I can hold myself in now until the time comes. Then I can fill this emptiness with something real.

FRANK O'CONNOR

First Confession

Frank O'Connor (1903-1966) was born in Cork, Ireland. Too poor to attend a university, he supported himself as a librarian. He began to write early and soon became known for his sensitive and delightful stories. He attracted the attention and friendship of Yeats and George Russell, and became an important literary figure himself in contemporary Ireland. He was a critic and a poet, but his reputation is primarily based on his short stories, which show warmth, humor, and a poignant sensitivity to emotional nuances.

ALL THE TROUBLE began when my grandfather died and my grandmother—my father's mother—came to live with us. Relations in the one house are a strain at the best of times, but, to make matters worse, my grandmother was a real old countrywoman and quite unsuited to the life in town. She had a fat, wrinkled old face, and, to Mother's great indignation, went round the house in bare feet—the boots had her crippled, she said. For dinner she had a jug of porter and a pot of potatoes with—sometimes—a bit of salt fish, and she poured out the potatoes on the table and ate them slowly, with great relish, using her fingers by way of a fork.

Now, girls are supposed to be fastidious, but I was the one who suffered most from this. Nora, my sister, just sucked up to the old woman for the penny she got every Friday out of the old-age pension, a thing I could not do. I was too honest, that was my trouble; and when I was playing with Bill

Connell, the sergeant-major's son, and saw my grandmother steering up the path with the jug of porter sticking out from beneath her shawl I was mortified. I made excuses not to let him come into the house, because I could never be sure what she would be up to when we went in.

When Mother was at work and my grandmother made the dinner I wouldn't touch it. Nora once tried to make me, but I hid under the table from her and took the bread-knife with me for protection. Nora let on to be very indignant (she wasn't, of course, but she knew Mother saw through her, so she sided with Gran) and came after me. I lashed out at her with the bread-knife, and after that she left me alone. I stayed there till Mother came in from work and made my dinner, but when Father came in later Nora said in a shocked voice: "Oh, Dadda, do you know what Jackie did at dinnertime?" Then, of course, it all came out; Father gave me a flaking; Mother interfered, and for days after that he didn't speak to me and Mother barely spoke to Nora. And all because of that old woman! God knows, I was heart-scalded.

Then, to crown my misfortunes, I had to make my first confession and communion. It was an old woman called Ryan who prepared us for these. She was about the one age with Gran; she was well-to-do, lived in a big house on Montenotte, wore a black cloak and bonnet, and came every day to school at three o'clock when we should have been going home, and talked to us of hell. She may have mentioned the other place as well, but that could only have been by accident, for hell had the first place in her heart.

She lit a candle, took out a new half-crown, and offered it to the first boy who would hold one finger—only one finger! —in the flame for five minutes by the school clock. Being always very ambitious I was tempted to volunteer, but I thought it might look greedy. Then she asked were we afraid of holding one finger—only one finger!—in a little candle flame for five minutes and not afraid of burning all over in roasting hot furnaces for all eternity. "All eternity! Just think of that! A whole lifetime goes by and it's nothing, not even a drop in the ocean of your sufferings." The woman was really interesting about hell, but my attention was all fixed on the half-crown. At the end of the lesson she put it back in her purse. It was a great disappointment; a religious woman like that, you wouldn't think she'd bother about a thing like a half-crown.

Another day she said she knew a priest who woke one night

to find a fellow he didn't recognize leaning over the end of his bed. The priest was a bit frightened—naturally enough—but he asked the fellow what he wanted, and the fellow said in a deep, husky voice that he wanted to go to confession. The priest said it was an awkward time and wouldn't it do in the morning, but the fellow said that last time he went to confession, there was one sin he kept back, being ashamed to mention it, and now it was always on his mind. Then the priest knew it was a bad case, because the fellow was after making a bad confession and committing a mortal sin. He got up to dress, and just then the cock crew in the yard outside, and —lo and behold!—when the priest looked round there was no sign of the fellow, only a smell of burning timber, and when the priest looked at his bed didn't he see the print of two hands burned in it? That was because the fellow had made a bad confession. This story made a shocking impression on me.

But the worst of all was when she showed us how to examine our conscience. Did we take the name of the Lord, our God, in vain? Did we honour our father and our mother? (I asked her did this include grandmothers and she said it did.) Did we love our neighbours as ourselves? Did we covet our neighbour's goods? (I thought of the way I felt about the penny that Nora got every Friday.) I decided that, between one thing and another, I must have broken the whole ten commandments, all on account of that old woman, and so far as I could see, so long as she remained in the house I had no hope of ever doing anything else.

I was scared to death of confession. The day the whole class went I let on to have a toothache, hoping my absence wouldn't be noticed; but at three o'clock, just as I was feeling safe, along comes a chap with a message from Mrs. Ryan that I was to go to confession myself on Saturday and be at the chapel for communion with the rest. To make it worse, Mother couldn't come with me and sent Nora instead.

Now, that girl had ways of tormenting me that Mother never knew of. She held my hand as we went down the hill, smiling sadly and saying how sorry she was for me, as if she were bringing me to the hospital for an operation.

"Oh, God help us!" she moaned. "Isn't it a terrible pity you weren't a good boy? Oh, Jackie, my heart bleeds for you! How will you ever think of all your sins? Don't forget you have to tell him about the time you kicked Gran on the shin."

"Lemme go!" I said, trying to drag myself free of her. "I don't want to go to confession at all."

"But sure, you'll have to go to confession, Jackie," she replied in the same regretful tone. "Sure, if you didn't, the parish priest would be up to the house, looking for you. 'Tisn't, God knows, that I'm not sorry for you. Do you remember the time you tried to kill me with the bread-knife under the table? And the language you used to me? I don't know what he'll do with you at all, Jackie. He might have to send you up to the bishop."

I remember thinking bitterly that she didn't know the half of what I had to tell—if I told it. I knew I couldn't tell it, and understood perfectly why the fellow in Mrs. Ryan's story made a bad confession; it seemed to me a great shame that people wouldn't stop criticizing him. I remember that steep hill down to the church, and the sunlit hillsides beyond the valley of the river, which I saw in the gaps between the houses like Adam's last glimpse of Paradise.

Then, when she had manœuvred me down the long flight of steps to the chapel yard, Nora suddenly changed her tone. She became the raging malicious devil she really was.

"There you are!" she said with a yelp of triumph, hurling me through the church door. "And I hope he'll give you the penitential psalms, you dirty little caffler."

I knew then I was lost, given up to eternal justice. The door with the coloured-glass panels swung shut behind me, the sunlight went out and gave place to deep shadow, and the wind whistled outside so that the silence within seemed to crackle like ice under my feet. Nora sat in front of me by the confession box. There were a couple of old women ahead of her, and then a miserable-looking poor devil came and wedged me in at the other side, so that I couldn't escape even if I had the courage. He joined his hands and rolled his eyes in the direction of the roof, muttering aspirations in an anguished tone, and I wondered had he a grandmother too. Only a grandmother could account for a fellow behaving in that heartbroken way, but he was better off than I, for he at least could go and confess his sins; while I would make a bad confession and then die in the night and be continually coming back and burning people's furniture.

Nora's turn came, and I heard the sound of something slamming, and then her voice as if butter wouldn't melt in her mouth, and then another slam, and out she came. God, the hypocrisy of women! Her eyes were lowered, her head was bowed, and her hands were joined very low down on her stomach, and she walked up the aisle to the side altar looking like a saint. You never saw such an exhibition of devotion; and I remembered the devilish malice with which she had tormented me all the way from our door, and wondered were all religious people like that, really. It was my turn now. With the fear of damnation in my soul I went in, and the confessional door closed of itself behind me.

It was pitch-dark and I couldn't see priest or anything else. Then I really began to be frightened. In the darkness it was a matter between God and me, and He had all the odds. He knew what my intentions were before I even started; I had no chance. All I had ever been told about confession got mixed up in my mind, and I knelt to one wall and said: "Bless me, father, for I have sinned; this is my first confession." I waited for a few minutes, but nothing happened, so I tried it on the other wall. Nothing happened there either. He had me spotted all right.

It must have been then that I noticed the shelf at about one height with my head. It was really a place for grown-up people to rest their elbows, but in my distracted state I thought it was probably the place you were supposed to kneel. Of course, it was on the high side and not very deep, but I was always good at climbing and managed to get up all right. Staying up was the trouble. There was room only for my knees, and nothing you could get a grip on but a sort of wooden moulding a bit above it. I held on to the moulding and repeated the words a little louder, and this time something happened all right. A slide was slammed back; a little light entered the box, and a man's voice said: "Who's there?"

" 'Tis me, father," I said for fear he mightn't see me and go away again. I couldn't see him at all. The place the voice came from was under the moulding, about level with my knees, so I took a good grip of the moulding and swung myself down till I saw the astonished face of a young priest looking up at me. He had to put his head on one side to see me, and I had to put mine on one side to see him, so we were more or less talking to one another upside-down. It struck me as a queer way of hearing confessions, but I didn't feel it my place to criticize.

"Bless me, father, for I have sinned; this is my first confession," I rattled off all in one breath, and swung myself down the least shade more to make it easier for him.

"What are you doing up there?" he shouted in an angry voice, and the strain the politeness was putting on my hold of the moulding, and the shock of being addressed in such an uncivil tone, were too much for me. I lost my grip, tumbled, and hit the door an unmerciful wallop before I found myself flat on my back in the middle of the aisle. The people who had been waiting stood up with their mouths open. The priest opened the door of the middle box and came out, pushing his biretta back from his forehead; he looked something terrible. Then Nora came scampering down the aisle.

"Oh, you dirty little caffler!" she said. "I might have known you'd do it. I might have known you'd disgrace me. I can't leave you out of my sight for one minute."

Before I could even get to my feet to defend myself she bent down and gave me a clip across the ear. This reminded me that I was so stunned I had even forgotten to cry, so that people might think I wasn't hurt at all, when in fact I was probably maimed for life. I gave a roar out of me.

"What's all this about?" the priest hissed, getting angrier than ever and pushing Nora off me. "How dare you hit the child like that, you little vixen?"

"But I can't do my penance with him, father," Nora cried, cocking an outraged eye up at him.

"Well, go and do it, or I'll give you some more to do," he said, giving me a hand up. "Was it coming to confession you were, my poor man?" he asked me.

" 'Twas, father," said I with a sob.

"Oh," he said respectfully, "a big hefty fellow like you must have terrible sins. Is this your first?"

" 'Tis, father," said I.

"Worse and worse," he said gloomily. "The crimes of a lifetime. I don't know will I get rid of you at all today. You'd better wait now till I'm finished with these old ones. You can see by the looks of them they haven't much to tell."

"I will, father," I said with something approaching joy.

The relief of it was really enormous. Nora stuck out her tongue at me from behind his back, but I couldn't even be bothered retorting. I knew from the very moment that man opened his mouth that he was intelligent above the ordinary. When I had time to think, I saw how right I was. It only stood to reason that a fellow confessing after seven years would have more to tell than people that went every week. The crimes of a lifetime, exactly as he said. It was only what he expected, and the rest was the cackle of old women and girls with their talk of hell, the bishop, and the penitential psalms. That was all they knew. I started to make my examination of conscience, and barring the one bad business of my grandmother it didn't seem so bad.

The next time, the priest steered me into the confession box himself and left the shutter back the way I could see him get in and sit down at the further side of the grille from me.

"Well, now," he said, "what do they call you?"

"Jackie, father," said I.

"And what's a-trouble to you, Jackie?"

"Father," I said, feeling I might as well get it over while I had him in good humour, "I had it all arranged to kill my grandmother."

He seemed a bit shaken by that, all right, because he said nothing for quite a while.

"My goodness," he said at last, "that'd be a shocking thing to do. What put that into your head?"

"Father," I said, feeling very sorry for myself, "she's an awful woman."

"Is she?" he asked. "What way is she awful?"

"She takes porter, father," I said, knowing well from the way Mother talked of it that this was a mortal sin, and hoping it would make the priest take a more favourable view of my case.

"Oh, my!" he said, and I could see he was impressed.

"And snuff, father," said I.

"That's a bad case, sure enough, Jackie," he said.

"And she goes round in her bare feet, father," I went on in a rush of self-pity, "and she knows I don't like her, and she gives pennies to Nora and none to me, and my da sides with her and flakes me, and one night I was so heart-scalded I made up my mind I'd have to kill her."

"And what would you do with the body?" he asked with great interest.

"I was thinking I could chop that up and carry it away in a barrow I have," I said.

"Begor, Jackie," he said, "do you know you're a terrible child?"

"I know, father," I said, for I was just thinking the same thing myself. "I tried to kill Nora too with a bread-knife under the table, only I missed her."

"Is that the little girl that was beating you just now?" he asked.

" 'Tis, father."

"Someone will go for her with a bread-knife one day, and he won't miss her," he said rather cryptically. "You must have great courage. Between ourselves, there's a lot of people I'd like to do the same to but I'd never have the nerve. Hanging is an awful death."

"Is it, father?" I asked with the deepest interest—I was always very keen on hanging. "Did you ever see a fellow hanged?"

"Dozens of them," he said solemnly. "And they all died roaring."

"Jay!" I said.

"Oh, a horrible death!" he said with great satisfaction. "Lots of the fellows I saw killed their grandmothers too, but they all said 'twas never worth it."

He had me there for a full ten minutes talking, and then walked out the chapel yard with me. I was genuinely sorry to part with him, because he was the most entertaining character I'd ever met in the religious line. Outside, after the shadow of the church, the sunlight was like the roaring of waves on a beach; it dazzled me; and when the frozen silence melted and I heard the screech of trams on the road my heart soared. I knew now I wouldn't die in the night and come back, leaving marks on my mother's furniture. It would be a great worry to her, and the poor soul had enough.

Nora was sitting on the railing, waiting for me, and she put on a very sour puss when she saw the priest with me. She was mad jealous because a priest had never come out of the church with her.

"Well," she asked coldly, after he left me, "what did he give you?"

"Three Hail Marys," I said.

"Three Hail Marys," she repeated incredulously. "You mustn't have told him anything."

"I told him everything," I said confidently.

"About Gran and all?"

"About Gran and all."

(All she wanted was to be able to go home and say I'd made a bad confession.)

"Did you tell him you went for me with the bread-knife?" she asked with a frown.

"I did to be sure."

"And he only gave you three Hail Marys?"

"That's all."

She slowly got down from the railing with a baffled air. Clearly, this was beyond her. As we mounted the steps back to the main road she looked at me suspiciously.

"What are you sucking?" she asked.

"Bullseyes."

"Was it the priest gave them to you?"

" 'Twas."

"Lord God," she wailed bitterly, "some people have all the luck! 'Tis no advantage to anybody trying to be good. I might just as well be a sinner like you."

MARY LAVIN

The Great Wave

*Mary Lavin (1912-   ) was born in Massachusetts
but has lived most of her life in Ireland. Educated
at Loreto College in Dublin and at the National University, she is the wife of a Dublin attorney and the
mother of three daughters. Her first collection of
short stories,* Tales from Bective Bridge, *won the
James Tait Black Memorial Prize for 1942, and her
novels have won wide critical acclaim.*

*Mary Lavin's work has been compared to that of
the Russians. Her greatest fame, however, is as a
prolific short story writer, many volumes of whose
collected stories are now available. Her range is wide,
and she moves with ease from the airily witty to the
almost biblical tragedy of the strange and moving
story included here, "The Great Wave."*

THE BISHOP WAS sitting in the stern of the boat. He was
in his robes, with his black overcoat thrown across his shoulders for warmth, and over his arm he carried his vestments,
turned inside out to protect them from the salt spray. The
reason he was already robed was because the distance across
to the island was only a few miles, and the island priest was
spared the embarrassment of a long delay in his small damp
sacristy.

The islanders had a visit from their Bishop only every four
years at most, when he crossed over, as now, for the Con-
firmation ceremony, and so to have His Grace arrive thus in
his robes was only their due share: a proper prolongation of

Originally appeared in *The New Yorker*, June 13, 1959. Reprinted by
permission; © 1959 The New Yorker Magazine, Inc.

episcopal pomp. In his albe and amice he would easily be picked out by the small knot of islanders who would gather on the pier the moment the boat was sighted on the tops of the waves. Yes: it was right and proper for all that the Bishop be thus attired. His Grace approved. The Bishop had a reason of his own too, as it happened, but it was a small reason, and he was hardly aware of it anywhere but in his heart.

Now, as he sat in the boat, he wrapped his white skirts tighter around him, and looked to see that the cope and chasuble were well doubled over, so that the coloured silks would not be exposed when they got away from the lee of the land and the waves broke on the sides of the currach. The cope above all must not be tarnished. That was why he stubbornly carried it across his arm: the beautiful cope that came all the way from Stansstad, in Switzerland, and was so overworked with gilt thread that it shone like cloth of gold. The orphreys, depicting the birth and childhood of Christ, displayed the most elaborate work that His Grace had ever seen come from the Paramentenwerkstätte, and yet he was far from unfamiliar with the work of the Sisters there, in St. Klara. Ever since he attained the bishopric he had commissioned many beautiful vestments and altar cloths for use throughout the diocese. He had once, at their instigation, broken a journey to Rome to visit them. And when he was there, he asked those brilliant women to explain to him the marvel, not of their skill, but of his discernment of it, telling them of his birth and early life as a simple boy, on this island towards which he was now faced.

"Mind out!" he said, sharply, as one of the men from the mainland who was pushing them out with the end of an oar, threw the oar into the boat, scattering the air with drops of water from its glossy blade. "Could nothing be done about this?" he asked, seeing water under the bottom boards of the boat. It was only a small sup, but it rippled up and down with a little tide of its own, in time with the tide outside that was already carrying them swiftly out into the bay.

"Tch, tch, tch," said the Bishop, for some of this water had saturated the hem of the albe, and he set about tucking it under him upon the seat. And then, to make doubly sure of it, he opened the knot of his cincture and re-tied it as tight about his middle as if it were long ago and he was tying up a sack of spuds at the neck. "Tch, tch," he repeated, but no one was unduly bothered by his ejaculations because of his soft and mild eyes, and, didn't they know him? They knew that in his complicated, episcopal life he had to contend with a lot, and it was known that he hated to give his old housekeeper undue thumping with her flat iron. But there was a thing would need to be kept dry—the crozier!

"You'd want to keep that yoke there from getting wet though, Your Grace," said one of the men, indicating the crozier that had fallen on the boards. For all that they mightn't heed his little old-womanish ways, they had a proper sense of what was fitting for an episcopal appearance.

"I could hold the crozier perhaps," said Father Kane, the Bishop's secretary, who was farther up the boat. "I still think it would be more suitable for the children to be brought over to you on the mainland, than for you to be traipsing over here like this, and in those foreign vestments at that!"

He is thinking of the price that was paid for them, thought the Bishop, and not of their beauty or their workmanship. And yet, he reflected, Father Kane was supposed to be a highly-educated man, who would have gone on for a profession if he hadn't gone for the priesthood, and who would not have had to depend on the seminary to put the only bit of gloss on him he'd ever get—Like me—he thought! And he looked down at his beautiful vestments again. A marvel, no less, he thought, savouring again the miracle of his power to appreciate such things.

"It isn't as if *they*'ll appreciate them over there," said Father Kane, with sudden venom, looking towards the island, a thin line of green on the horizon.

"Ah, you can never say that for certain," said the Bishop mildly, even indifferently. "Take me, how did I come to appreciate such things?"

But he saw the answer in the secretary's hard eyes. He thinks it was parish funds that paid for my knowledge, and diocesan funds for putting it into practice! And maybe he's right! The Bishop smiled to himself. Who knows anything at all about how we're shaped, or where we're led, or how in the end we are ever brought to our rightful haven?

"How long more till we get there?" he asked, because the island was no longer a vague green mass. Its familiar shapes were coming into focus; the great high promontory throwing its purple shade over the shallow fields by the shore, the sparse white cottages, the cheap cement pier, constantly in need of repairs. And, higher up, on a ledge of the promontory itself there was the plain cement church, its spire only standing out against the sky, bleak as a crane's neck and head.

To think the full height of the promontory was four times the height of the steeple.

The Bishop gave a great shudder. One of the rowers was talking to him.

"Sure, Your Grace ought to know all about this bay. Ah, but I suppose you forget them days altogether now!"

"Not quite, not quite," said the Bishop, quickly. He slipped his hand inside his robes and rubbed his stomach that had begun already to roll after only a few minutes of the swell.

When he was a little lad, over there on the island, he used to think he'd run away, some day, and join the crew of one of the French fishing trawlers that were always moving backwards and forwards on the rim of the sky. He used to go to a quiet place in the shade of the Point, and settling into a crevice in the rocks, out of reach of the wind, he'd spend the day long staring at the horizon; now in the direction of Liverpool, now in the direction of the Norwegian fjords.

Yet, although he knew the trawlers went from one great port to another, and up even as far as Iceland, he did not really associate them with the sea. He never thought of them as at the mercy of it in the way the little currachs were that had made his mother a widow, and that were jostled by every wave. The trawlers used to seem out of reach of the waves, away out on the black rim of the horizon.

He had in those days a penny jotter in which he put down the day and hour a trawler passed, waiting precisely to mark it down until it passed level with the pier. He put down also other facts about it which he deduced from the small vague outline discernible at that distance. And he smiled to remember the sense of satisfaction and achievement he used to get from that old jotter, which his childish imagination allowed him to believe was a full and exhaustive report. He never thought of the long nights and the early dawns, the hours when he was in the schoolroom, or the many times he was kept in the cottage by his mother, who didn't hold with his hobby.

"Ah son, aren't you all I've got! Why wouldn't I fret about you?" she'd say to him, when he chafed under the yoke of her care.

That was the worst of being an only child, and the child of a sea widow into the bargain. God be good to her! He used to have to sneak off to his cranny in the rocks when he got her gone to the shop of a morning, or up to the chapel of an afternoon to say her beads. She was in sore dread of

his even looking out to sea, it seemed! And as for going out
in a currach! Hadn't she every currach-crew on the island
warned against taking him out?

"Your mammy would be against me, son," they'd say, when
he'd plead with them, one after another on the shore, and
they getting ready to shove their boats down the shingle
and float them out on the tide.

"How will I ever get out to the trawlers if I'm not let out
in the currachs?" he used to think. That was when he was a
little fellow, of course, because when he got a bit older he
stopped pestering them, and didn't go down near the shore
at all when they were pulling out. They'd got sharp with him
by then.

"We can't take any babbies out with us—a storm might
come up. What would a babby like you do then?" And he
couldn't blame them for their attitude because by this time
he knew they could often have found a use for him out in
the boats when there was a heavy catch.

"You'll never make a man of him hiding him in your
petticoats," they'd say to his mother, when they'd see him with
her in the shop. And there was a special edge on the remark,
because men were scarce, as could be seen anywhere on the
island by the way the black frieze jackets of the men made
only small patches in the big knots of women, with their
flaming red petticoats.

His mother had a ready answer for them.

"And why are they scarce?" she'd cry.

"Ah, don't be bitter, Mary."

"Well, leave me alone then. Won't he be time enough taking
his life in his hands when there's more to be got for a netful
of ling than there is this year!"

For the shop was always full of dried ling. When you
thought to lean on the counter, it was on a long board of
ling you lent. When you went to sit down on a box or a
barrel it was on top of a bit of dried ling you'd be sitting.
And right by the door, a greyhound bitch had dragged down a
bit of ling from a hook on the wall and was chewing at
it, not furtively, but to the unconcern of all, growling when
it found it tough to chew, and attacking it with her back teeth
and her head to one side, as she'd chew an old rind of hoof
parings in the forge. The juice of it, and her own saliva mixed,
was trickling out of her mouth on to the floor.

"There'll be a good price for the first mackerel," said poor
Maurya Keely, their near neighbour, whose husband was ail-

ing, and whose son Seoineen was away in a seminary on the mainland studying to be a priest. "The seed herring will be coming in any day now."

"You'll have to let Jimeen out on that day if it looks to be a good catch," she said, turning to his mother. "We're having our currach tarred, so's to be all ready against the day."

Everyone had sympathy with Maurya, knowing her man was nearly done, and that she was in great dread that he wouldn't be fit to go out and get their share of the new season's catch, and she counting on the money to pay for Seoineen's last year in the seminary. Seoineen wasn't only her pride, but the pride of the whole island as well, for, with the scarcity of men folk, the island hadn't given a priest to the diocese in a decade.

"And how is Seoineen? When is he coming home at all?" another woman asked, as they crowded around Maurya. "He'll soon be facing into the straight," they said, meaning his ordination, and thinking, as they used the expression, of the way, when Seoineen was a young fellow, he used to be the wildest lad on the island, always winning the ass-race on the shore, the first to be seen flashing into sight around the Point, and he coming up the straight, keeping the lead easily to finish at the pierhead.

"He'll be home for a last leave before the end," said his mother, and everyone understood the apprehension she tried to keep out of her voice, but which steals into the heart of every priest's mother thinking of the staying power a man needs to reach that end. "I'm expecting him the week after next," she said, then suddenly her joy in the thought of having him in the home again took place over everything else.

"Ah, let's hope the mackerel will be in before then!" said several of the women at the one time, meaning there would be a jingle in everyone's pocket then, for Seoineen would have to call to every single cottage on the island, and every single cottage would want to have plenty of lemonade and shop-biscuits too, to put down before him.

Jimeen listened to this with interest and pleased anticipation. Seoineen always took him around with him, and he got a share in all that was set down for the seminarian.

But that very evening Seoineen stepped onto the pier. There was an epidemic in the college and the seminarists that were in the last year like him were let home a whole week before their time.

"Sure, it's not for what I get to eat that I come home,

Mother!" he cried, when Maurya began bewailing having no
feasting for him. "If there's anything astray with the life I've
chosen it's not shortage of grub! And anyway, we won't
have long to wait!" He went to the door and glanced up at
the sky. "The seed will be swimming inward tomorrow on the
first tide!"

"Oh God forbid!" said Maurya. "We don't want it that
soon either, son, for our currach was only tarred this day!"
and her face was torn with two worries now instead of one.

Jimeen had seen the twinkle in Seoineen's eye, and he
thought he was only letting-on to know about such things,
for how would he have any such knowledge at all, and he
away at schools and colleges the best part of his life.

The seed was in on the first tide, though, the next day.

"Oh, they have curious ways of knowing things that you'd
never expect them to know," said Jimeen's own mother. It
was taken all over the island to be a kind of prophesy.

"Ah, he was only letting-on, Mother," said Jimeen, but
he got a knock of her elbow over the ear.

"It's time you had more respect for him, son," she said,
as he ran out the door for the shore.

Already most of the island boats were pulling hard out into
the bay. And the others were being pushed out as fast as
they could be dragged down the shingle.

But the Keely boat was still upscutted in the dune grass
under the promontory, and the tar wetly gleaming on it. The
other women were clustered around Maurya, giving her con-
solation.

"Ah sure, maybe it's God's will," she said. "Wasn't himself
doubled up with pain the early hours, and it's in a heavy sleep
he is this minute—I wouldn't wake him up whether or no!—He
didn't get much sleep last night. It was late when he got to his
bed. Him and Seoineen stayed up talking by the fire. Seoineen was explaining to him all about the ordination, about the
fasting they have to do beforehand, and the holy oils and
the chrism and the laying-on of hands. It beat all to hear him!
The creatureen, he didn't get much sleep himself either, but
he's young and able, thank God. But I'll have to be going
back now to call him for Mass."

"You'll find you won't need to call Seoineen," said one of
the women. "Hasn't him, and the like of him, got God's
voice in their hearts all day and they ever and always listening
to it. He'll wake of himself, you'll see. He'll need no calling!"

And sure enough, as they were speaking, who came running down the shingle but Seoineen.

"My father's not gone out without me, is he?" he cried, not seeing their own boat, or any sign of it on the shore, a cloud coming over his face that was all smiles and laughter when he was running down to them. He began to scan the bay that was blackened with boats by this time.

"He's not then," said Maurya. "He's above in his bed still, but leave him be, Seoineen—leave him be—" she nodded her head back towards the shade of the promontory. "He tarred the boat yesterday, not knowing the seed 'ud be in so soon, and it would scald the heart out of him to be here and not able to take it out. But as I was saying to these good people it's maybe God's will the way it's happened, because he's not fit to go out this day!"

"That's true for you, Mother," said Seoineen, quietly. "The poor man is nearly beat, I'm fearing." But the next minute he threw back his head and looked around the shore. "Maybe I'd get an oar in one of the other boats. There's surely a scarcity of men these days?"

"Is it you?" cried his mother, because it mortally offended her notion of the dignity due to him that he'd be seen with his coat off maybe—in his shirt sleeves maybe—red in the face maybe along with that and—God forbid—sweat maybe breaking out of him!

"To hear you, Mother, anyone would think I was a priest already. I wish you could get a look into the seminary and you'd see there's a big difference made there between the two sides of the fence!" It was clear from the light in his eyes as they swept the sea at that moment that it would take more than a suit of black clothes to stop him from having a bit of fun with an oar. He gave a sudden big laugh, but it fell away as sudden when he saw that all the boats had pulled out from the shore and he was alone with the women on the sand.

Then his face hardened.

"Tell me, Mother," he cried. "Is it the boat or my father that's the unfittest? For if it's only the boat then I'll make it fit! It would be going against God's plenitude to stay idle with the sea teeming like that—Look at it!"

For even from where they stood when the waves wheeled inward they could see the silver herring seed glistening in the curving wheels of water, and when those slow wheels broke on the shore they left behind them a spate of seed sticking to everything, even to people's shoes.

"And for that matter, wasn't Christ Himself a fisherman! Come, Mother—tell me the truth! Is the tar still wet or is it not?"

Maurya looked at him for a minute. She was no match for arguing with him in matters of theology, but she knew all about tarring a currach. "Wasn't it only done yesterday, son," she said. "How could it be dry today?"

"We'll soon know that," said Seoineen, and he ran over to the currach. Looking after him they saw him lay the palm of his hand flat on the upturned bottom of the boat, and then they heard him give a shout of exultation.

"It's not dry surely?" someone exclaimed, and you could tell by the faces that all were remembering the way he prophesied about the catch. Had the tar dried at the touch of his hands maybe?

But Seoineen was dragging the currach down the shingle.

"Why wouldn't it be dry?" he cried. "Wasn't it a fine dry night. I remember going to the door after talking to my father into the small hours, and the sky was a mass of stars, and there was a fine, sharp wind blowing that you'd be in dread it would dry up the sea itself! Stand back there, Mother," he cried, for her face was beseeching something of him, and he didn't want to be looking at it. But without looking he knew what it was trying to say. "Isn't it towards my ordination the money is going? Isn't that argument enough for you?"

He had the boat nearly down to the water's edge. "No, keep back there, young Jimeen," he said. "I'm able to manage it on my own, but let you get the nets and put them in and then be ready to skip in before I push out, because I'll need someone to help haul in the nets."

"Is it Jimeen?" said one of the women, and she laughed, and then all the women laughed. "Sure, he's more precious again nor you!" they said.

But they turned to his mother all the same.

"If you're ever going to let him go out at all, this is your one chance, surely? Isn't it like as if it was into the Hands of God Himself you were putting him, woman?"

"Will you let me, Ma?" It was the biggest moment in his life. He couldn't look at her for fear of a refusal.

"Come on, didn't you hear her saying yes—what are you waiting for?" cried Seoineen, giving him a push, and the next minute he was in the currach, and Seoineen had given it a great shove and he running out into the water in his fine shoes and all. He vaulted in across the keel. "I'm destroyed already at the very start!" he cried, laughing down at his feet and trouser legs, and that itself seemed part of the sport for him. "I'll take them off," he cried, kicking the shoes off him, and pulling off his socks, till he was in his bare white feet. "Give me the oars," he cried, but as he gripped them he laughed again, and loosed his fingers for a minute, as one after the other, he rubbed his hands on a bit of sacking on the seat beside him. For, like the marks left by the trawler men on the white bollard at the pier, the two bleached oars were marked with the track of his hands, palms, and fingers, in pitch black tar.

"The tar was wet!"

"And what of it?" cried Seoineen. "Isn't it easy give it another lick of a brush?"

But he wasn't looking at Jimeen and he saying it, his eyes were leaping along the tops of the waves to see if they were pulling near the other currachs.

The other currachs were far out in the bay already: the sea was running strong. For all that, there was a strange still look about the water, unbroken by any spray. Jimeen sat still, exulting in his luck. The waves did not slap against the sides of the currach like he'd have thought they would do, and they didn't even break into spray where the oars split their surface. Instead, they seemed to go lolloping under the currach and lollop up again the far side, till it might have been on great glass rollers they were slipping along.

"God! Isn't it good to be out on the water!" cried Seoineen, and he stood up in the currach, nearly toppling them over in his exuberance, drawing in deep breaths, first with his nose, and then as if he were drinking it with his mouth, and his eyes at the same time taking big draughts of the coast-line that was getting farther and farther away. "Ah, this is the life: this is the real life," he cried again, but they had to look to the oars and look to the nets, then, for a while, and for a while they couldn't look up at sea or sky.

When Jimeen looked up at last, the shore was only a narrow line of green.

"There's a bit of a change, I think," said Seoineen, and it was true.

The waves were no longer round and soft, like the little cnoceens in the fields back of the shore, but they had small sharp points on them now, like the rocks around the Point, that would rip the bottom out of a boat with one tip, the way a tip of a knife would slit the belly of a fish.

That was a venomous comparison though and for all their appearance, when they hit against the flank of the boat, it was only the waves themselves that broke and patterned the water with splotches of spray.

It was while he was looking down at these white splotches that Jimeen saw the fish.

"Oh look, Seoineen, look!" he cried, because never had he seen the like.

They were not swimming free, or separate, like you'd think they'd be, but a great mass of them together, till you'd think it was at the floor of the sea you were looking, only it nearer and shallower.

There must have been a million fish; a million, million, Jimeen reckoned wildly, and they pressed as close as the pebbles on the shore. And they might well have been motionless and only seeming to move like on a windy day you'd think the grass on the top of the promontory was running free like the waves, with the way it rippled and ran along a little with each breeze.

"Holy God, such a sight!" cried Seoineen. "Look at them!"

But Jimeen was puzzled.

"How will we get them into the net?" he asked, because it didn't seem that there was any place for the net to slip down between them, but that it must lie on the top of that solid mass of fish, like on a floor.

"The nets: begod, I nearly forgot what we came out here for!" cried Seoineen, and at the same time they became aware of the activity in the other boats, which had drawn near without their knowing. He yelled at Jimeen. "Catch hold of the nets there, you lazy good-for-nothing. What did I bring you with me for if it wasn't to put you to some use!" and he himself caught at a length of the brown mesh, thrown in the bottom of the boat, and began to haul it up with one hand, and with the other to feed it out over the side.

Jimeen, too, began to pull and haul, so that for a few minutes there was only a sound of the net swishing over the wood, and every now and then a bit of a curse, under his breath, from Seoineen as one of the cork floats caught in the thole pins.

At first it shocked Jimeen to hear Seoineen curse, but he reflected that Seoineen wasn't ordained yet, and that, even if he were, it must be a hard thing for a man to go against his nature.

"Come on, get it over the side, damn you," cried Seoineen again, as Jimeen had slowed up a bit owing to thinking about the cursing. "It isn't one net-full but thirty could be filled this day! Sure you could fill the boat in fistfuls," he cried, suddenly leaning down over the side, delving his bare hand into the water. With a shout, he brought up his hand with two fish, held one against the other in the same grip, so that they were as rigid as if they were dead. "They're overlaying each other a foot deep," he cried, and then he opened his fist and freed them. Immediately they writhed apart to either side of his hand in two bright arcs and then fell, both of them, into the bottom of the boat. But next moment they writhed into the air again, and flashed over the side of the currach.

"Ah begorras, you'll get less elbow-room there than here, my boys," cried Seoineen, and he roared laughing, as he and Jimeen leant over the side, and saw that sure enough, the two mackerel were floundering for a place in the glut of fishes.

But a shout in one of the other currachs made them look up.

It was the same story all over the bay. The currachs were tossing tipsily in the water with the antics of the crews, that were standing up and shouting and feeding the nets ravenously over the sides. In some of the boats that had got away early, they were still more ravenously hauling them up, strained and swollen with the biggest catch they had ever held.

There was not time for Seoineen or Jimeen to look around either, for just then the keel of their own currach began to dip into the water.

"Look out! Pull it up—! Catch a better grip than that, damn you. Do you want to be pulled into the sea. Pull, damn you, pull!" cried Seoineen.

Now every other word that broke from his throat was a curse, or what you'd call a curse if you heard them from another man, or in another place, but in this place, from this man, hearing them issue wild and free, Jimeen understood that they were a kind of psalm. They rang out over the sea in a kind of praise to God for all his plenitude.

"Up! Pull hard—up, now, up!" he cried, and he was pulling at his end like a madman.

Jimeen pulled too, till he thought his heart would crack, and then suddenly the big white belly of the loaded net came in sight over the water.

Jimeen gave a groan, though, when he saw it.

"Is it dead they are?" he cried, and there was anguish in his voice.

Up to this, the only live fish he had ever seen were the few fish tangled in the roomy nets, let down by the old men over the end of the pier, and *they* were always full of life, needling back and forth insanely in the spacious mesh till he used to swallow hard, and press his lips close together fearing one of them would dart down his gullet, and he'd have it ever after needling this way and that inside him! But there was no stir at all in the great white mass that had been hauled up now in the nets.

"Is it dead they are?" he cried again.

"Aahh, why would they be dead? It's suffocating they are, even below in the water, with the welter of them is in it," cried Seoineen.

He dragged the net over the side where it emptied and spilled itself into the bottom of the boat. They came alive then all right! Flipping and floundering, and some of them flashing back into the sea. But it was only a few on the top that got away, the rest were kept down by the very weight and mass of them that was in it. And when, after a minute, Seoineen had freed the end of the net, he flailed them right and left till most of them fell back flat. Then, suddenly, he straightened up and swiped a hand across his face to clear it of the sweat that was pouring out of him.

"Ah sure, what harm if an odd one leps for it," he cried. "We'll deaden them under another netful! Throw out your end," he cried.

As Jimeen rose up to his full height to throw the net wide out, there was a sudden terrible sound in the sky over him, and the next minute a bolt of thunder went volleying overhead, and with it, in the same instant it seemed, the sky was knifed from end to end with a lightning flash.

Were they blinded by the flash? Or had it suddenly gone as black as night over the whole sea?

"Oh God's Cross!" cried Seoineen. "What is coming? Why didn't someone give us a shout? Where are the others? Can you see them? Hoy there! Marteen! Seumas? Can you hear—?"

For they could see nothing. And it was as if they were all alone in the whole world. Then, suddenly, they made out

Marteen's currach near to them, so near that, but for Seoineen
flinging himself forward and grabbing the oars, the two currachs would have knocked together. Yet no sooner had they
been saved from knocking together than they suddenly seemed
so far sundered again they could hardly hear each other
when they called out.

"What's happening, in Christ's name?" bawled Seoineen, but
he had to put up his hands to trumpet his voice, for the
waves were now so steep and high that even one was enough
to blot out the sight of Marteen. Angry white spume dashed
in their faces.

"It's maybe the end of the world," said Jimeen, terror-
stricken.

"Shut up and let me hear Marteen!" said Seoineen, for
Marteen was bawling at them again.

"Let go the nets," Marteen was bawling—"let go the nets
or they'll drag you out of the boat."

Under them then they could feel the big pull of the net
that was filled up again in an instant with its dead weight
of suffocating fish.

"Let it go, I tell you," bawled Marteen.

"Did you hear? He's telling us to let it go," piped Jimeen
in terror, and he tried to free his own fingers of the brown
mesh that had closed tight upon them with the increasing
weight. "I can't let go," he cried, looking to Seoineen, but
he shrank back from the strange wild look in Seoineen's eyes.
"Take care would you do anything of the kind!"

"It's cutting off my fingers!" he screamed.

Seoineen glared at him.

"A pity about them!" he cried, but when he darted a look
at them, and saw them swelling and reddening, he cursed.
"Here—wait till I take it from you," he cried, and he went
to free his own right hand, but first he laced the laden
fingers of his left hand into the mesh above the right hand,
and even then, the blood spurted out in the air when he
finally dragged it free of the mesh.

For a minute Seoineen shoved his bleeding fingers into
his mouth and sucked them, then he reached out and caught
the net below where Jimeen gripped it. As the weight slack-
ened, the pain of the searing strings lessened, but next minute
as the pull below got stronger, the pain tore into Jimeen's
flesh again.

"Let go now, if you like, now I have a bit of a hold of

it anyway—now I'm taking the weight of it off you," said
Seoineen.

Jimeen tried to drag free.

"I can't," he screamed in terror, "—the strings are eating
into my bones!"

Seoineen altered his balance and took more weight off the
net at that place.

"Now!"

"I can't! I can't!" screamed Jimeen.

From far over the waves the voice of Marteen came to
them again, faint, unreal, like the voices you'd hear in a
shell if you held it to your ear.

"Cut free—cut free," it cried, "or else you'll be destroyed
altogether."

"Have they cut free themselves? That's what I'd like to
know?" cried Seoineen.

"Oh, do as he says, Seoineen. Do as he says," screamed
Jimeen.

And then, as he saw a bit of ragged net, and then another
and another rush past like the briery patches of foam on
the water that was now almost level with the rowlocks, he
knew that they had indeed all done what Marteen said; cut
free.

"For the love of God, Seoineen," he cried.

Seoineen hesitated for another instant. Then suddenly made
up his mind and, reaching along the seat, he felt without
looking for the knife that was kept there for slashing dog-
fish.

"Here goes," he cried, and with one true cut of the knife
he freed Jimeen's hands the two together at the same time,
but, letting the knife drop into the water, he reached out
wildly to catch the ends of the net before they slid into it,
or shed any of their precious freight.

Not a single silver fish was lost.

"What a fool I'd be," he gasped, "to let go. They think
because of the collar I haven't a man's strength about me
any more. Then I'll show them. I'll not let go this net, not
if it pull me down to hell." And he gave another wild laugh.
"And you along with me!" he cried. "Murder?" he asked then,
as if he had picked up the word from a voice in the wind.
"Is it murder? Ah sure, I often think it's all one to God
what a man's sin is, as long as it's sin at all. Isn't sin poison
—any sin at all, even the smallest drop of it? Isn't it death
to the soul that it touches at any time? Ah then! I'll not

let go!" And even when, just then, the whole sea seemed littered with tattered threads of net, he still held tight to his hold. "Is that the way? They've all let go! Well then, I'll show them one man will not be so easy beat! Can you hear me?" he cried, because it was hard to hear him with the crazy noise of the wind and the waves.

"Oh cut free, Seoineen," Jimeen implored, although he remembered the knife was gone now to the bottom of the sea, and although the terrible swollen fingers were beyond help in the mangling ropes of the net.

"Cut free is it? Faith now! I'll show them all," cried Seoineen. "We'll be the only boat'll bring back a catch this night, and the sea seething with fish." He gave a laugh. "Sure that was the only thing that was spoiling my pleasure in the plenty! Thinking that when the boats got back the whole island would be fuller of fish than the sea itself, and it all of no more value than if it was washed of its own accord on to the dirty counters of the shop! Sure it wouldn't be worth a farthing a barrel! But it will be a different story now, I'm thinking. Oh, but I'll have the laugh on them with their hollow boats, and their nets cut to flitters! I'll show them a man is a man, no matter what vows he takes, or what way he's called to deny his manhood! I'll show them! Where are they, anyway? Can you—see them—at all?" he cried, but he had begun to gasp worse than the fishes in the bottom of the boat. "Can you—see them—at all? Damn you, don't sit there like that! Stand up—there—and tell me—can—you —see—them!"

It wasn't the others Jimeen saw though, when he raised his eyes from the torn hands in the meshes. All he saw was a great wall, a great green wall of water. No currachs anywhere. It was as if the whole sea had been stood up on its edge, like a plate on a dresser. And down that wall of water there slid a multitude of dead fish.

And then, down the same terrible wall, sliding like the dead fish, came an oar; a solitary oar. And a moment afterwards, but inside the glass wall, imprisoned, like under a glass dome, he saw—oh God!—a face, looking out at him, staring out at him through a foot of clear green water. And he saw it was the face of Marteen. For a minute the eyes of the dead man stared into his eyes.

With a scream he threw himself against Seoineen, and clung to him tight as iron.

How many years ago was that? The Bishop opened his

eyes. They were so near the shore he could pick out the people by name that stood on the pier-head. His stomach had stopped rolling. It was mostly psychological; that feeling of nausea. But he knew it would come back in an instant if he looked leftward from the shore, leftwards and upwards, where, over the little cement pier and over the crane-bill steeple of the church, the promontory that they called the Point rose up black with its own shadow.

For it was on that promontory—four times the height of the steeple—they had found themselves, he and Seoineen, in the white dawn of the day after the Wave, lying in a litter of dead fish, with the netful of fish like an anchor sunk into the green grass.

When he came to himself in that terrible dawn, and felt the slippy bellies of the fish all about him, he thought he was still in the boat, lying in the bottom among the mackerel, but when he opened his eyes and saw a darkness as of night, over his head, he thought it was still the darkness of the storm and he closed them again in terror.

Just before he closed them, though, he thought he saw a star, and he ventured to open them again, and then he saw that the dark sky over him was a sky of skin, stretched taut over timber laths, and the star was only a glint of light—and the blue light of day at that—coming through a split in the bottom of the currach. For the currach was on top of him!—Not he in the bottom of it.

Why then was he not falling down and down and down through the green waters? His hands rushed out to feel around him. But even then, the most miraculous thing he thought to grasp was a fistful of sand, the most miraculous thing he thought to have to believe was that they were cast up safe upon the shore.

Under his hands though, that groped through the fishes, he came, not on sand, but on grass, and not upon the coarse dune grass that grew back from the shore at the foot of the Point. It was soft, sweet little grass, that was like the grass he saw once when Seoineen and he had climbed up the face of the Point, and stood up there, in the sun, looking down at all below, the sea and the pier, and the shore and the fields, and the thatch of their own houses, and on a level with them, the grey spire of the chapel itself!

It was, when opening his eyes wide at last, he saw, out from him a bit, the black grey tip of that same chapel-spire that he knew where he was.

Throwing the fish to left and right he struggled to get to his feet.

It was a miracle! And it must have been granted because Seoineen was in the boat. He remembered how he prophesied the seed would be on the tide, and in his mind he pictured their currach being lifted up in the air and flown, like a bird, to this grassy point.

But where was Seoineen?

"Oh Seoineen, Seoineen!" he cried, when he saw him standing on the edge of the Point looking downward, like they looked, that day, on all below. "Oh Seoineen, was it a miracle?" he cried, and he didn't wait for an answer, but he began to shout and jump in the air.

"Quit, will you!" said Seoineen, and for a minute he thought it must be modesty on Seoineen's part, it being through him the miracle was granted, and then he thought it must be the pain in his hands that was at him, not letting him enjoy the miracle, because he had his two hands pressed under his armpits.

Then suddenly he remembered the face of Marteen he had seen under the wall of water, and his eyes flew out over the sea that was as flat and even now, as the field of grass under their feet. Was Marteen's currach lost? And what of the others?

Craning over the edge of the promontory he tried to see what currachs were back in their places, under the little wall, dividing the sand from the dune, turned upside down and leaning a little to one side, so you could crawl under them if you were caught in a sudden shower.

There were no currachs under the wall: none at all.

There were no currachs on the sea.

Once, when he was still wearing a red petticoat like a girsha, there had been a terrible storm and half a score of currachs were lost. He remembered the night with all the women on the island down on the shore with storm lamps, swinging them and calling out over the noise of the waves. And the next day they were still there, only kneeling on the pier, praying and keening.

"Why aren't they praying and keening?" he cried then, for he knew at last the other currachs, all but theirs, were lost.

"God help them," said Seoineen, "at least they were spared that."

And he pointed to where, stuck in the latticed shutters on

the side of the steeple, there were bits of seaweed, and—yes
—a bit of the brown mesh of a net.

"God help you," he said then, "how can your child's mind
take in what a grown man's mind can hardly hold—but you'll
have to know some time—we're all alone—the two of us—on
the whole island. All that was spared by that wall of
water——"

"All that was on the sea, you mean?" he cried.

"And on the land too," said Seoineen.

"Not my mother——?" he whimpered.

"Yes, and my poor mother," said Seoineen. "My poor mother that tried to stop us from going out with the rest."

But it was a grief too great to grasp, and yet, yet even in
face of it, Jimeen's mind was enslaved to the thought of
their miraculous salvation.

"Was it a miracle, Seoineen?" he whispered. "Was it a
miracle we were spared?"

But Seoineen closed his eyes, and pushed his crossed arms
deeper under his arm-pits. The grimace of pain he made
was—even without words—a rebuke to Jimeen's exaltation.
Then he opened his eyes again.

"It was my greed that was the cause of all," he said,
and there was such a terrible sorrow in his face that Jimeen,
only then, began to cry. "It has cost me my two living hands,"
said Seoineen, and there was a terrible anguish in his voice.

"But it saved your life, Seoineen," he cried, wanting to
comfort him.

Never did he forget the face Seoineen turned to him.

"For what?" he asked. "For what?"

And there was, in his voice, such despair, that Jimeen knew
it wasn't a question but an answer; so he said no more for a
few minutes. Then he raised his voice again, timidly.

"You saved my life too, Seoineen."

Seoineen turned dully and looked at him.

"For what?"

But as he uttered them, those same words took on a change,
and a change came over his face, too, and when he repeated
them, the change was violent.

"For what?" he demanded. "For what?"

Just then, on the flat sea below, Jimeen saw the boats,
coming across from the mainland, not currachs like they had
on the island, but boats of wood made inland, in Athlone,
and brought down on lorries.

"Look at the boats," he called out, four, five, six, any amount of them; they came rowing for the island.

Less than an hour later Seoineen was on his way to the hospital on the mainland, where he was to spend long months before he saw the island again. Jimeen was taken across a few hours later, but when he went it was to be for good. He was going to an aunt, far in from the sea, of whom he had never heard tell till that day.

Nor was he to see Seoineen again, in all the years that followed. On the three occasions that he was over on the island, he had not seen him. He had made enquiries, but all he could ever get out of people was that he was a bit odd.

"And why wouldn't he be?" they added.

But although he never came down to the pier to greet the Bishop like the rest of the islanders, it was said he used to slip into the church after it had filled up and he'd think he was unnoticed. And afterwards, although he never once would go down to the pier to see the boat off, he never went back into his little house until it was gone clear across to the other side of the bay. From some part of the island it was certain he'd be the last to take leave of the sight.

It had been the same on each visit the Bishop made, and it would be the same on this one.

When he would be leaving the island, there would be the same solicitous entreaties with him to put on his overcoat. Certainly he was always colder going back in the late day. But he'd never give in to do more than throw it over his shoulders, from which it would soon slip down on to the seat behind him.

"You'd do right to put it on like they told you," said the secretary, buttoning up his own thick coat.

But there was no use trying to make him do a thing he was set against. He was a man had deep reasons for the least of his actions.

SHORT FICTION
that does not fall short of
EXCELLENCE